The Phantom of Barker Mill

Blue Moon Investigations

Book 2

Steve Higgs

For Gemma.

Guys this is my singular piece of relationship advice: If you find yourself a princess, treat her like one. Don't try to turn her into Cinderella.

Table of Contents

Barker Steel Mill. Friday, July 5th, 1954

Two weeks into the job and Samuel was beginning to feel that he fitted in. The initial jokes about being the new boy had died off by the end of the first week and he had learned his way around the place. Well, pretty much anyway. The steel mill was a warren of corridors and passageways. He had really caught it from Mr. Miller, the shift supervisor on his third day when they sent him for a tool and he had got lost for forty minutes. He had found the tool shack but had come back into the Mill by a different door and had got turned about. His absence had held up production and he had been fined a day's wages.

Expecting and prepared for a degree of banter there had been relatively little of it as if the older workers just couldn't be bothered with him. His grandad had told him about some of the tricks they might play on him, like sending him for a long wait or asking him to find some sky hooks. None of that came to pass though. At least not yet anyway. He followed everyone to the local working men's club on the first Friday night after work. Mill employment meant automatic membership and not only was the beer cheap but there were lots of girls that went there. He had been hearing about it from his mate Barry for more than a year. At the pub, the tall tales started.

The old fellas were doing their best to convince him that the Mill had a genuine phantom haunting it. Even Barry was playing along.

'Oh yes, lad,' said Roger. One of the middle-aged chaps from his shift. 'You mark my words. You work there long enough, and you will see it for yourself.'

Samuel had heard about the phantom plenty of times before. It was a local legend, but he put no credence to the tales he heard. It didn't seem like a good idea to voice his opinion though, so he drank his beer and smiled without comment while surreptitiously eyeing up Margaret Miller who was sitting at the bar. Margaret was the shift manager's daughter and was one hot number. She was perched on a bar stool sipping a Babycham and being chatted up by half a dozen guys simultaneously. Samuel bet she never had to buy a drink.

Just then she laughed at something Barry said, then excused herself and hopped off her stool. The rumour was that Barry was already having his way with her, but Barry had admitted that he hadn't got there yet. He clearly fancied his chances though. Samuel thought it might not be worth the risk as all the lads were under threat of sack by Mr. Miller should they so much as look at his daughter. Fortunately, Mr. Miller never mingled with the lowly workers, so would not enter the working men's club and see what was going on.

That was last Friday and now it was the end of the second week and Samuel was looking forward to another night in the bar. Barry had recently bought a Ford Cortina, so the big plan was to head up to London tomorrow night. The car wasn't much, but none of the other lads had one and all the girls wanted to go to the big town for a night out. Samuel was only too happy to be included. Barry was going to invite Margaret tonight, so Samuel had to find a date as well.

Distracted by his thoughts, he missed the accident entirely. It was noisy in the Mill so he didn't hear it either. It was only when Roger whacked him on the arm that he realised anything was amiss.

'It's the Phantom,' yelled Roger, an annoyingly pedantic man in his fifties who Samuel seemed to keep getting stuck with. 'You stay here and manage the degassing. Otherwise, the whole casting will be scrap. Okay?'

Samuel nodded, although he did not understand what was going on. Chaps were rushing past, all heading in the same direction. This seemed like a lot of effort just to play a trick on him. He was glad though that they were finally getting it over with.

'Are you sure you know what to do?' asked Roger. 'Don't mess this up.'

'Come on,' shouted another man on his way past. Samuel thought the man's name was Arthur but could not be certain. He had grabbed Roger in passing and Samuel was left alone. It was the first time he had been left unsupervised. He started to feel a bit nervous. He thought he knew what to do, but he had never been allowed to touch the controls before. He watched the pressure gauge on the degassing rig. The rig supplied a mix of soluble gasses to bubble through the steel. The purpose of the process

2

was to purge any hydrogen. Beyond that, he didn't really understand what it did. Hydrogen in the steel was bad. Apparently, his education on the subject did not need to extend beyond that.

He could hear a kerfuffle of some kind around the corner. He stayed at his station watching the pressure gauge but after a minute curiosity got the better of him, he took a couple of paces to see if he could peer around the corner. He expected to see them all hiding just out of sight, but they were not. Maybe they were not playing a joke on him after all. He glanced back at the gauge, it all seemed fine - the needle was firmly in the safe zone. He took another few paces and leaned around a steel column to see what was going on.

An entire raised walkway had collapsed!

One hundred feet away, in the middle of the mill, a steel walkway was hanging down from one end. Some of the floor plates from it had come loose and fallen to the ground thirty feet below. Men were all around the accident. Through a gap, he could see prone figures. Samuel wanted desperately to see what was happening but knew he should not leave his post. They might sack him if the cast ruined.

Then he spotted movement away from everyone else. Off to the left, high up in the rafters where the walkway had fallen from, something had moved. He looked around, no one else had seen it. He stared up, squinting. There it was again. Something black moving in a shadowed background. Light from the foundry furnace? Was it just light playing tricks? Then he saw it again, silhouetted as it moved along a walkway. It was man size and proportions, only also somehow not.

He shouted to the men clustered around the accident. If they heard him they did not react. He shouted again, this time the loudest bellow he could muster. Still nothing. Cursing the noise-absorbing machinery of the mill, he checked the gauge once more. The gauge seemed disinclined to do anything exciting. Right next to him was a cat ladder leading upwards. Should he go?

He glanced up again just as the shadow passed overhead. He could not discern what it was, but something was moving. He grabbed a rung and started climbing.

Thirty feet up he emerged onto a steel walkway. The floor was a grid of steel that you could see through all the way back down to the ground below. It unsettled his stomach. Ahead of him, the grating stretched out in both directions until it met the mill wall and became a solid floor. He had been up here, or somewhere that looked a lot like here, last week when he got lost. Near the mill wall, the shape passed under a lamp and he got a good look at it for the first time.

It was a cloaked figure, head to foot in shabby black cloth, a cowl over its head. The shape made no noise on the steel grating. As Samuel watched, it turned the corner and vanished from view.

He ran after it. Any thought of danger had simply not occurred to him. Curiosity demanded that he discover what he was looking at. He reached the corner and found ahead of him a short corridor with a door to the left. By the door, just fading to black was a burnt handprint in the brick. Of the figure, there was no sign.

He touched the handprint and snatched his fingers away swearing. He stuck his fingers in his mouth to cool them. They were all blistered. Angry, he kicked the door open and went through.

There, down a short flight of stairs, the cloaked figure was just about to go through another door.

'Hey!' Samuel shouted.

The cloaked figure spun around instinctively and looked up. Light from above illuminated the inside of the hood for a brief second. Then it spun away and shot through the door. Samuel heard the door lock and knew there was no point in following.

He had seen its face.

His mind whirling, he moved on autopilot back along the corridor, along the steel walkway and back down the cat ladder, taking care not to grip the rungs with the ends of his burned fingers. He was still focused upon the face he had seen when he got to the bottom and was rudely yanked from the ladder.

'Where the blazes have you been?' roared Roger. 'The whole cast is ruined.'

'What happened?' Samuel asked, dazed by all that had occurred.

'What happened? I'll tell you what happened. You wandered off, the soluble gas pressure dropped and because you were not here to switch the rig over to the auxiliary tank the last three hours work was for nothing. You idiot.'

'No, I mean, what happened with the walkway? Was anyone hurt?'

'It was the Phantom,' came a voice from behind him. Samuel turned. It was Arthur, or whatever his name was if it was not Arthur. 'You mark my words, lad. This will be his work. I bet when we search there will be a fresh handprint burnt into the mill somewhere. He always leaves his mark.'

'Was anyone hurt?' Samuel repeated his question.

'Aye, lad. Three lads were on the walkway when it collapsed. Colin Higgins, Denis Lawson, and Barry Dunford. They are all in pretty bad shape. Broken bones and the like. Lucky to be alive I reckon.'

'Barry,' Samuel repeated as a murmur. He wandered away then. He needed to check something. Behind him, Roger was still shouting at him for ruining the cast and threatening hell when Mr. Miller found out.

In My Bed. Thursday, 7th October 0503hrs

I slowly opened my eyes as I came awake. It was early still and dark outside. I stayed where I was, warm and comfortable under the covers. I glanced across at the clock to see that it was 0503hrs. This was about the time I usually came awake. My name is Tempest Michaels. I used to be a soldier in the British Army, but I left when I felt it was time to do so and decided to set myself up as a private investigator. My first advert got misread by a copy girl at the local newspaper and I was presented to the world as a Paranormal Investigator. At the time, I was incensed but before I could do anything about it the enquiries started coming and they have not stopped yet. That was a little over six months ago now and life since has been interesting, to say the least.

I receive at least one hundred emails every day, of which probably a dozen or more are genuinely interesting enquiries for my services. In pretty much every one of those cases, the person turning to me for help has come across a problem or a situation that they either cannot explain or can only find a supernatural explanation for. Mostly, in fact, they have found an explanation and have convinced themselves, or allowed someone else to convince them that they are being haunted or that their teenage daughter has been possessed or that their dentist is a ghoul practising dark magic with the teeth they extract. My clients approach me with utter conviction, knowing in their hearts that the supernatural is completely real and I charge them money to prove how daft they are. I have worried at times that I could be considered a con man or charlatan, but it is not I that has created the ruse, I am the one exposing it.

The paranormal, supernatural world of spirits, fairies, werewolves and other wonderful and horrific creatures is pure fantasy. Knowing this means that I can approach each case looking for an explanation that makes more sense than *my mother-in-law is a witch* and has cursed me with impotence. The answer to that particular case was that your mother-in-law is not a witch, she is just ugly, and you have impotence because you drink too much and watch porn constantly. It took me less than two hours to investigate and solve that case and I charged him at an hourly rate because he seemed too stupid to take advantage of.

6

The life of a paranormal investigator is not all fun and silly games though. I have encountered some people who could definitely be classed as dangerous, including, quite recently, a serial killer pretending to be a vampire. I have sustained injuries, had my life and the lives of family members and friends threatened and genuinely thought I was going to be killed by the serial killing vampire-wannabe just a few days ago. Good timing and luck had saved me in the end.

As I lay in bed thinking idle thoughts, I sensed movement behind me on the other side of the bed. Someone was coming awake. I rolled to my left to look at the face on the pillow next to me. Deep chocolate brown eyes were looking back at me sleepily. There was real affection in those eyes.

'Good morning,' I said, stifling a yawn as I did so.

In return, the face leaned forward a little and licked me on the nose.

I scratched my head and yawned. The face belonged to Dozer, one of my miniature Dachshunds. His brother Bull would be somewhere close by. The pair of them usually climbed into the bed uninvited at night. In the summer, when it is warm they will sleep on top of the duvet, but in the winter, they tunnel under the covers. Is it hygienic that I allow two dogs to share my bed? Probably not, but I find it comforting and no one else has been kind enough to share it since I moved into the house, so it seemed the practice was unlikely to cause offence. I rolled out of bed and sat on the edge for a moment while I scratched my head again and argued with the lazy version of myself who thought going back to sleep was a great idea. Forcing myself, somewhat reluctantly, to get moving, I found my gym clothes and bag, left the dogs where they were and headed for a workout.

Still the favourable side of forty, I was very conscious that I was beginning to feel the years, that my testosterone levels were undoubtedly falling and that to stay in shape I was going to have to work at it.

My time in the Army had been dominated by fitness training. I had been relatively athletic, so found myself selected to participate in numerous sporting events. The training for such events had been on top

7

of the usual fitness training that all service personnel undergo weekly and going to the gym had become a routine and very regular part of my life. Now that I was no longer in the Army and could avoid such activities if I chose to, I found that I wanted to go more than ever.

I had read many years ago that the between the age of eighteen and sixty the human body loses fifty percent of its muscle mass. It just wastes away through lack of use, which is why older persons struggle to get off the sofa. It was entirely tenable though to combat the loss by building replacement muscle. How accurate the article was I could not say, but it sounded plausible and I liked the idea of maintaining worthwhile functional muscle purely from a vanity perspective.

I probably spent between three and five hours in the gym each week and did not feel that I was overdoing it. At this early hour, the gym I frequented was mostly empty but there were some usual faces I saw quite often at this time of the day. I suppose they were mostly people that liked to get their work out done before work. I had never bothered to learn their names despite seeing them most weeks. This was born of the belief that most people want to be left alone in the gym to get on with what they are there for. Having got up early, I thought it unlikely they were there for conversation or social interaction. I offered to spot for people occasionally because it was the polite thing to do but actively avoided talking to the ladies in the gym as I so often saw sweaty guys hitting on them as they rested between sets.

A little more than an hour later I was walking back through my front door, content in the knowledge that, whatever else the day had in store for me, I had a workout under my belt. The cool autumn air had reduced my body temperature, so I was no longer sweating by the time I got home. At the sound of my return, the dogs had finally hauled themselves out of bed and were now standing at the top of the stairs staring down at me and wagging their tails.

I went halfway up, leaned and scooped them, plopped them on the ground by my feet at the bottom of the stairs and let them into the garden where they promptly disappeared to chase the neighbour's cat.

Whether the neighbour's cat was in our garden never seemed to enter their equation.

I showered and dressed in office casual work clothes, headed back downstairs to feed the dogs and set the kettle to boil because there are few things in life as refreshing as the day's first cup of tea.

I was hungry having been out of bed for nearly two hours and had probably burned a thousand calories already. I allowed myself a filling breakfast of pancakes made with chocolate protein powder and topped them with bananas, pecans, blueberries, natural yoghurt and maple syrup. It was a breakfast of champions.

Suitably satisfied, I clipped leads to the two dogs and took them for a pleasing walk around the village. I live in Finchampstead, which is little more than a collection of houses a few miles outside of Maidstone. It is not far from where my parents settled after dad left the Royal Navy and ticked enough of my boxes for me to justify paying the price for the country cottage I had bought. Within a two-minute walk, I could find myself in either woodland or vineyards depending on which direction I elected to head. The village had a pub, which I made a point of going to at least once a week since so many village taverns were shutting down due to lack of custom, and a village store which sold everything you could imagine. The village was very green and very quiet, and I liked living there. During my walk, I amused myself by considering my options with Amanda. Amanda was a police officer I had met just a few weeks ago. She was also a goddess that I had been instantly enamoured by.

As I walked, I found myself thinking back to Friday night. Soon after I had returned from the pub that night, there had been a knock at my door. I had wondered at the time if it might be remnants of the Brotherhood of the Dead vampire LARP club, a Live Action Role Play club for people who thought it would be fun to be a vampire. They had become embroiled in *The Vampire* serial killer case, had their clubhouse burnt to the ground and had since disbanded. I had been responsible for getting several of them arrested and incarcerated, but I dismissed the notion that it might be them at my door as it seemed unlikely that anyone coming to exact retribution would bother knocking first.

9

So, I had answered the door and found Amanda there smiling at me. She had on a pair of tall heels, expensive looking to my untrained eye and a long, but elegant coat undone to reveal a cocktail dress inside. She was wearing her hair up which exposed the skin of her delicate neck wonderfully. It was late on a Friday night, we had just solved a case together and stopped a serial killer, so naturally, I assumed she had come to have sex with me. Perhaps the word assumed is wrong, perhaps the term should be hoped, prayed and clung desperately to the belief that she might have come to have sex with me. Amanda Harper is beautiful. Real world beautiful if that makes sense. Her figure is graceful, yet athletic, she is tall and lithe with wonderful flowing blonde hair that I expect many women would kill for. Her teeth are perfect, she has high cheekbones and sparkling blue eyes. I had no idea why she was at my door late on a Friday night, but I was utterly infatuated by her and the alcohol inside me was making me think thoughts I might otherwise quash.

A moment ticked by and I realised I was just staring at her. A voice from just below my belt yelled, *"Battle stations!"* Then, thankfully, a dog barked from the kitchen just behind me and I managed to get my thoughts in order.

'Are you going to invite me in?' she asked smiling.

'Of course, Amanda. Come in, please.' She did, stepping lightly over the door frame and into the house. I closed the door behind her.

'To what do I owe this pleasure?' I asked. Was I slurring? Had I drunk that much? I decided that it was just my paranoia making me worry.

'Are you slurring?' she asked.

Bugger.

'I have been at the pub with Ben, licking our wounds.' Best to come clean.

'Oh. If this is an inconvenient time I can come back tomorrow. Or visit you at the office next week.' she said.

All hope of naked entwinement evaporated immediately as she was clearly not here to take a ride on Mr. Wriggly. Disappointed, but trying not to show it, I invited her through to the kitchen. 'Watch the dogs do not claw your legs,' I advised as I opened the kitchen door and they tumbled out. 'They can get a little over excited.'

'It is so nice to see both together again,' Amanda said from her crouched position where she was petting them. 'Dozer seems none the worse for his adventure.' My dopier dog had ended up in the river while I was battling the serial killing vampire wannabe and had been missing for several days. I had presumed that he was dead until he joyously turned up a few miles downriver and was found by a little old lady.

'His waist is still a little thinner than it was, but the vet assured me that he is in good health and will not suffer any long-term problems for his temporary starvation in the wild,' I replied.

Amanda stood up and followed me into the kitchen. 'Can I offer you a drink?' I asked. I was keen to hear why she was on my doorstep after dark on a Friday night if it was not a social call, yet manners dictated that I play the host before I pressed her for an answer.

'Just a tea please,' her reply.

I nodded and set out two mugs while the kettle boiled. I selected an Ironman mug for myself, I felt it set the right tone and dug to the back of the cupboard where the guest mugs were kept finding one with a pink unicorn on it.

The silence felt like it was stretching out while I was waiting for the tea to brew. 'To what do I owe the pleasure of your company tonight?' I asked again while stirring the tea bags around. Amanda had been fiddling with her phone but put it away in her tiny clutch handbag now. She smiled at me as I crossed the room to get milk from the fridge and had to take a short step back to allow me access. Her perfume hit my nose and went directly to my groin as always.

'I have a proposition for you,' she said while looking directly into my eyes. That got my attention and instantly I could hear Mr. Wriggly

11

humming Barry White tunes to himself. The she said, 'I am looking for a job. I wondered if you wanted a partner?'

'Oh,' I said a little dumbly.

Not here for rampant sex then.

I rallied my disappointment in case it was glaringly obvious that I was and fixed her with a quizzical expression. I hoped it was quizzical anyway. The alcohol was making me a little woozy, so there was a chance my face just looked intellectually challenged. 'I thought you had a job and wanted to progress in it?'

'I thought so too. However, the last couple of weeks has shown me that there are other opportunities. I think, in fact, that I am fed up being a police officer and would much rather be a private investigator. Like you.' She left that hanging for a moment.

When it dawned on me that I was holding both cups of tea and not doing anything with them, I managed to engage my brain and pass her one.

She said, 'Thank you.' As she took it from me. She sipped it a little, her eyes focused on the cup or perhaps the floor. Then she looked back up and spoke again. 'So, what do you think?'

'You have caught me a little off guard I'm afraid.' I wanted to open up and tell her that I was really attracted to her and that I had hoped for her as a different kind of partner. The more sensible part of my brain was arguing with the horny part though and was trying to convince it that if she wanted sex we would already be in bed and that therefore I should stay quiet. Sensible won the day. 'Have you already quit your job?' I asked, somewhat deflecting her question.

'No, but I spoke with my career councillor yesterday about my options for advancement and they are less promising than I had hoped. I think I will be quitting no matter what you say.'

I was trying to work out all the variables. I needed a partner, I had acknowledged that to myself already and here was a trained and experienced police officer applying for the job. Okay, I was a little bit in love with the job applicant, but otherwise, she was ideal for the post. The tussle I was having then was whether I could work with her and forget my attraction or whether having her work with me would, in fact, result in the attraction developing into something mutual.

Why is being a man so difficult? Or is it just me making hard work of it?

'Tempest?' Amanda spoke to break my train of thought.

'Sorry?' I answered, making eye contact with her.

'Err, you haven't spoken for about five minutes and your lips were moving like you were having a conversation with yourself.' She sipped her tea again. 'Do you need some time to think?'

'No. Err, sorry. Just having a little internal debate. I guess my answer must be, yes. Yes, please in fact. I need the help. My caseload keeps increasing and I will not be surprised if the recent exposure from *The Vampire* case results in even more calls for my services.'

Amanda blew out a breath as if she had been holding it. 'Well, that's a relief. We need to have a serious discussion about it all, but I feel that now is not the right time.' Amanda put her cup down and stood up straight. 'I ought to go home. I'm sorry for just dropping by like this, I have been wanting to speak to you about this for days and knew I would not sleep tonight if I didn't get it over with.'

'That's okay,' I said slowly. My fantasy woman was leaving, the chance of playing humpy-bumpy tonight now non-existent. 'I would like the weekend to consider how we proceed, please. I have never run my own business before, never had to consider payroll or expenses or tax for employees and need to do some research. Can we meet on Monday?'

'Of course,' Amanda replied. She scooped up her little clutch purse, tucked it under her left arm and extended her right hand to shake mine. I didn't want to shake her hand. I wanted to grab it and pull her into a kiss - to tell her how I felt. The voice from my pants was convinced it was what she was waiting for and that I just needed to show her my dominant manly side for her to succumb and be my woman.

I bet she isn't wearing any knickers. The voice said.

Like a chump, I ignored it, shook her hand and watched her walk towards my front door. 'Why the fancy outfit?' I asked. She looked like she was going to or coming from a cocktail party or event of some kind.

'Oh, I was on a date,' she replied casually as if the answer would not cut me to the bone.

She was out the door and I was closing it behind her, bidding her a good night as she went. Of course, she had been on a date. She was an attractive woman and ought to be out on dates. Come to think of it, the world would be a topsy-turvy place if women that looked like Amanda were in doing the ironing on a Friday night.

Since I needed a partner to share the caseload she was an obvious choice. Amanda knew police procedure and was trained for conflict management among other things. She was strong, confident and brave and she did not believe in the paranormal any more than the next sane person. That notwithstanding, I worried that working with her would be a continuous loop of me pretending not to dribble in her direction every time she bent over to pick something up. It was a conundrum, but one I could not currently see a way to avoid. Besides, it seemed abundantly clear that she was not interested in me. I never fooled myself that I was that much of a catch anyway. I looked after my figure as best as I could, but at six feet I was neither short nor tall, my face was as unremarkable as many others and being a great guy does not win first place in the here's-the-key-to-my-knickers contest. Ever.

By the time I had finished walking the dogs and reflecting on last Friday night, I was wandering back down the path to my house. I had subjected myself to twenty minutes of chastisement over my feelings for Amanda and felt I was ready to employ her and make the best of it.

An hour later, it was 0906hrs and I was in my office, fresh macchiato from the coffee house across the street cooling on my desk and local paper The Weald Word spread out in front of me. The Weald Word was so called because the area it reported on was known as the Kent Weald. Technically, or perhaps that should be geographically, I believe that Maidstone and in fact Rochester, where I was now reading the paper fell outside of the Weald, but the paper was popular enough to be sold throughout most of Kent. Amanda would be with me shortly, so I had too little time to kill to get on with anything worthwhile and reading the local paper seemed as good a pursuit as any other.

The paper was the one in which my business advert ran and the one that had managed to misspell it in the first place. I had never thanked them for doing so and often wondered what kind of success I would have enjoyed as an ordinary, vanilla private investigator. I doubted I could do that now. I had found my niche, or perhaps it had found me, and I was too well known and being too successful to risk changing tack.

I sipped at my macchiato and turned to the next page. So far, I had found nothing in the local news to pique my interest but at the top of page three was a photograph of a sinister looking clown. I had never been one for clowns, something about the painted-on smile that seemed suspicious I guess, but this clown did not have a painted-on smile, instead its facial expression said: "I am going to gut you like a fish and wear your liver as a hat." The story below was not really about anything. The picture of the clown had been taken late at night by a woman on her way home. She had spotted the clown when she got off the bus but thought nothing of it. The text claimed that she had dismissed it as someone on their way home from a fancy-dress party. However, as she walked home she spotted it again and then again, which had freaked her out. She had called out to ask him what he wanted and snapped his picture before running the last one hundred yards to her house. The clown had not spoken to her, had not been threatening and had made no attempt to chase her she said. Despite that I could see why she had run - the clown's face was terrifying. The photograph was black and white, so I could not tell what colour its outfit was, but it wore a long-sleeved top with horizontal stripes of at least three colours and large waisted pants held up by braces over his shoulders. The feet were out of shot but I suspected I would not see over-length clown shoes if they had been visible.

Something about the story bothered me, something about the eyes was familiar. I read on but there was not much more to ingest. The lady that took the picture had not revealed her name and although she gave a description of the height, weight etcetera of the man inside the suit, I was not convinced it would be all that reliable.

I turned a few more pages but found adverts for local services, local forthcoming events, and a centre spread on the Birling harvest festival that had taken place over the weekend. I sucked down the last of the coffee, dropped the cup into the trash bin next to my desk and before I could consider what to do next, I heard the door at the bottom of the stairs open and someone coming up.

My office sits above an aging travel agent's office in Rochester. It is only about twenty-five yards from the cathedral and I picked it up for a song as the chap had never thought to rent it before. The travel agent business had been far busier a few years back before computers and online holiday agents had made it far harder for independent high street firms. My office had once been storage space for the many thousands of brochures he needed to keep, but as the business had dwindled, he needed the space less and less and then needed extra income more and more. I had got lucky and was looking for an office precisely when he was talking to a real estate firm about renting it. I had helped him empty all the old junk out of it and had decorated it myself to encourage the low monthly rental price.

'Good morning, Tempest,' Amanda called out from halfway up the stairs. I had expected that it would be her as visitors at this time would be unusual and it was now 0928hrs, bang on punctual for her 0930hrs appointment.

I got up and moved around the desk, so I could meet her at the top of the stairs rather than sitting imperiously behind the desk. As I got to the office door Amanda was just getting to the top of the stairs. She smiled at me and shook my hand as we went back inside to sit in the two seats by the window that overlooks Rochester High Street.

'Would you like a tea?' I asked, being polite.

'No, thank you. I just had one,' she replied. 'Shall we get down to business?'

'Of course.' I leaned across to my desk and grabbed a notebook and pen which I keep there. I had made some notes to make sure I went through everything I thought necessary. 'This isn't an interview thankfully, so we need not bother with any daft questions. I do feel it pertinent though to point out that I have never run a business before, never had to consider employing anyone before and largely have no idea what I am doing.'

'Yes, I got most of that from speaking to you. Lack of experience does not seem to be holding you back though, Tempest.'

'That's very kind of you, but I wanted to make it clear that you are looking for a job at a business that has not been long established, is reliant largely upon idiots as its customers and may not have longevity. Forewarned and all that.' I crossed *warn her what she is getting into* off the list.

'Understood. I do not believe there is all that much to worry about. I believe that you will continue to get clients and will be able to build and expand this business if you choose to. I am throwing my lot in early based on that belief.' I wondered if she was right. There did seem to be no end of people trying to engage my services.

Amanda and I talked for well over an hour and she left just before 1100hrs. By that time, we had established wages and expenses, what could and could not be charged to the firm's account, how we would share the workload, sift clients and how we would respond to those we elected not to represent. I took her through my business plan so that she understood the overhead and what she added to it, where our breakeven point was, where we started making profit, and how we could maximise profit by tackling the right cases. Amanda had asked whether I had considered getting an admin assistant to deal with sifting emails, responding to clients and dealing with invoices and expenses etcetera. I had, and when I had considered taking someone extra on it had been for precisely those tasks. Now that there were two investigators instead of one, I still needed the admin assistant but the added overhead it created, which was holding me back before, was now even greater on the concerns list. Despite that, I suspected she was entirely right and that our time was best spent solving cases and billing hours than it was sifting emails and shuffling paperwork. I had promised to give it some thought.

With everything seemingly settled, Amanda had gone to work, she was not actually on duty today but needed to see HR and officially quit. I guess she wanted it done. Before she left, I had brought her up to speed on my latest cases - there were none. My next task was to look for more work I had told her. She was due to officially start at the business full time in four weeks but was going to tag along on anything I was doing from now on, provided she was not still working one of her final shifts for Kent police.

With the office empty once more, I turned to my computer and read my emails. Client enquiries came via email or phone and occasionally by regular mail. I preferred email simply because I could sort and dismiss the truly crazy ones, not so easy to do once they are on the phone unless one is prepared to be rude. The email app claimed I had one hundred and thirteen unread emails. I performed a very basic sift to get rid of the spam, then started at the oldest unread email and went through them one by one.

The first email was from herbert27@googlemail.co.uk. Herbert believed his supervisor at work was a ghoul and wanted me to provide him with a safe method of ensuring that once he had killed him he would stay dead. I filed that under *probably need to inform the police* and moved on. The next email was from prettyprincessy@aol.com. She (I assumed a she, but it could easily be a three-hundred-pound sweaty man in a tutu and a tiara sending the email) needed to engage my services because she had been cursed with a fat spell. I was unsure what to do about this case. There would be no fat spell, just cupboards full of inappropriate foods and a bin filled with takeaway cartons. I felt inclined to help but was certain there was nothing I could do that I could justify being paid for.

There were several enquiries that held merit, but from a business perspective, almost all the enquiries were asking me to bill them money to find the perfectly ordinary explanation for the problem they faced. With an admin assistant to sift these, I suspected that the ninety minutes I had just spent on it could have been used to solve several without even the need to leave the office.

One case though stood out as both immediately solvable and directly associated with my line of work. The client, Paul Blake had fairies in his garden. In his email, he explained that he had told everyone, called the papers and TV but no one would listen to him or take him seriously. Whenever he was able to get a person to come to his house the fairies would not show themselves. He was begging me to bring whatever specialist paranormal equipment I might have to record them and prove their existence.

I called the number he had given in his email.

He answered with, 'Hello.'

'Mr. Blake, this is Tempest Michaels of the Blue Moon Investigation Agency. You emailed me about fairies in your garden.'

'Oh, thank God. They are out there right now. I am going nuts that no one believes me. How soon can you get here?'

'Mr. Blake before we go any further, I think I must explain that I do not believe you have fairies in your garden. I am a paranormal investigator, but nothing I have yet seen has proven to be even slightly paranormal.'

'Well, you are about to be shocked to your very core, Mr. Michaels.' I could almost hear his knowing smile. I was certainly curious.

'Okay, Mr. Blake. If you are quite sure you wish to engage my services, this is what it is going to cost.' I outlined my appearance fee with the aim of putting him off. He was however convinced that he was on the cusp of making the scientific discovery of the century and that I was the key to it. Furthermore, he was happy to pay whatever I asked. I took his address and left the office.

Paul Blake lived in Seal, a small town not far from the very nice town of Sevenoaks. Getting there was simple enough as I would take the A25 out of Maidstone. It linked a whole series of towns and villages going from East to West across the south of England. I could not afford to live in Seal, so felt a little happier about taking his money. My journey took twenty-four minutes and the satnav delivered me right to his door. I say door, but what I mean is his lengthy driveway. There were small terraced houses in Seal, I had passed a few of them on the way. Paul Blake, however, lived in an Oast House on the outskirts of town. His house was fantastic.

I pulled up at the front of the house, the gravel driveway crunching magnificently beneath my tyres. Before I could get out of my car, Mr. Blake was already bounding out of his front door.

'Mr. Michaels? Thank goodness you got here so quickly. The fairies are in the garden now.' He was perhaps in his early sixties and had a shock of hair sticking out madly from his head at every angle. It was turning from grey to white and matched his overgrown mustache. Much the same effect could be achieved by sticking one's finger into an electrical socket or perhaps simply ignoring one's appearance for a decade or so. He was wearing faded denim dungarees but there was no evidence of any other attire. He may have been wearing some form of underwear but socks, shoes, and a shirt were absent. The dungarees, and to a lesser extent Mr. Blake himself, were covered in spatters of paint in myriad different colours. I passed no judgement, but he was certainly an individual that could be considered eccentric or flamboyant or some other descriptive that would never be applied to me.

I shook his hand as I exited my car. 'Please show me,' I asked. I might as well indulge him.

He turned and scurried back into the house, his bare feet seemingly oblivious to the cool air and painful bite of the gravel beneath them. As I followed him, I noted that I had already dismissed one of my explanations for the fairies: He wore glasses, but they were devoid of spots on the lenses.

His house was filled, and I mean filled, with canvasses on which all manner of objects were painted. Some I could discern as a pot or a vase of flowers or in one what appeared to be a cat humping another cat. Mostly though, they looked like globs of paint thrown erratically at a white background. I acknowledged to myself that I knew nothing about art. It was a knowledge gap I felt no need to bridge, but it meant my opinion, should I feel it necessary to air it, was worthless. For all I knew, Mr. Blake was a famous and respected artist and had paid for his lavish house by selling his work.

He threaded his way through the house between canvasses stacked against walls, against furniture and on top of furniture and came to his kitchen. The kitchen was boldly inconsistent with the rest of the house and was not only tidy but also minimalist, modern and devoid of any clutter.

He stopped by the window in his kitchen where it overlooked his well-tended garden. He smiled broadly and pointed. I stared where he was indicating.

'Can you see them?' he asked in a tone that suggested I was blind if I could not.

I continued staring. I thought to myself, not for the first time, that I should have refused the case. The poor man was clearly seeing things and taking his money felt wrong. Then my heart stopped.

I squinted my eyes and continued to stare. I had seen something. A few seconds passed. Then a sparkly pink light zipped in front of a clipped privet hedge.

'I knew it!' exclaimed Mr. Blake loudly, making me jump. He had been watching my face and had clearly seen my expression change. He began to perform a jig next to me. Disbelievingly, I continued to stare at the same spot in his garden. Once again, a tiny streak of light zipped in front of the hedge. This time it had an orange hue. Then two lights simultaneously moving in different directions, one pink and one blue.

'The pink one I call Delila. The blue one is Bartholomew.' Mr. Blake told me. He was utterly serious. 'I have identified seven different fairies so far. Each has their own colour. Those doubters. Fairies I told them. No one believed me. No one. Oh, I cannot wait to see all their faces when I am on TV and can publicly say that I told them so. I cannot wait.'

'Sorry to interrupt, dear fellow. I need to get a closer look.' I said, moving to his back door.

'Yes, Yes. Of course,' he replied; an enormous smug grin still stuck to his face.

I needed to get a better look because I wanted to find the cause of the dancing lights. Since it could not be fairies it had to be something else. Right? I certainly hoped it was something else because finding fairies would mess with my sense of reality in a major way. The little whizzing balls of light were thus far defying explanation to the extent that calling them fairies made sense.

Mr. Blake had a neat garden path for me to walk down but I stepped off it and onto his neatly manicured lawn as I neared the place where I had seen the lights.

'Are they still there?' whispered Mr. Blake from behind my right shoulder making me jump once again. In his bare feet, he had made no sound at all.

As I paused and looked, a little light did in fact zip across the same spot. Behind me, Mr. Blake let out a barely suppressed noise of excitement. A shadow then fell across the garden as a cloud moved to block the sun and the lights instantly winked out. I took a few steps to my right and scanned around in the trees nearby. It took only a few seconds to spot what I had expected to find.

I went back to the spot I had been standing in next to Mr. Blake and waited for the cloud to continue its path and once more reveal the sun.

'I can bring you your fairies, Mr. Blake.'

'Can you?' his voice full of awe and so excited I worried that he might faint.

'In just a moment, yes. It may not be what you have expected or hoped for though.'

He gave me a quizzical look.

The shadow cast by the cloud moved across the garden, bathing us in sunlight once more. A second or so later the fairies reappeared, dancing in front of the privet hedge just a few metres away.

Mr. Blake squeaked with excitement again when I took a step forward. I only took two paces though then stopped under a silver birch tree. I reached up into its lower branches and after a few seconds of fiddling, I withdrew a broken and tangled coloured-glass windchime. It had been snagged in the tree and had not been visible until I stepped beyond the tree and looked for it.

'Here are your fairies,' I said handing the windchime over. 'Light was refracting through the glass and causing the moving lights you have been seeing.'

His reluctant hands took the windchime from me. His mouth was opening and closing as if he was supposed to be talking but could find no words inside his head. When he looked up at me again his eyes were filled with tears.

'You were supposed to prove that I have fairies,' he wailed.

I genuinely felt sorry for him. 'I'm sorry, Mr. Blake. I did state during our first phone call that I did not believe you had fairies. I'm afraid there is no such thing.'

He looked miserable.

'Can you put it back where it was?' he asked meekly. His voice barely more than a whisper and threatening to break into sobs. 'I think I would prefer to continue seeing them and pretend to myself. I will miss Delila otherwise.'

I nodded, took the windchime from his unresisting grasp and did my best to fix it back where it had been, tangled and forgotten in an old silver birch tree.

As I stood back, the lights appeared once more, dancing across the privet hedge. Mr. Blake smiled as a single tear ran down his left cheek.

I was very glad to collect my fee and get back into my car. Despite doing exactly what I said I would do, I felt as though I had just told a child that Father Christmas was not real while simultaneously setting fire to their presents.

I pointed the car in the direction of my office and left Mr. Blake and his fairies behind me.

My Office. Thursday, 7th October 1511hrs

The clock on the wall told me it was 1511hrs. I had done nothing much constructive for the last hour so decided it was time to knock off. It was sunny out if a little cool, but the smell of autumn was ripe, promising conker battles for the kids, sweet chestnut stuffing freshly made for my Sunday roast and the glorious changing colours of the countryside. I got up to leave, grabbed my bag from the desk to pop a few pieces of paperwork in it and just as I was leaving, the phone rang. I sat on the corner of my desk to answer it.

'Blue Moon Investigations. Tempest Michaels speaking. How may I help you?'

'Mr. Michaels, jolly good. My name is Margaret Barker. I believe I need to engage your services.' The lady's voice told me lots. She was educated or well bred, probably had money and was used to having people do as she asked. The accent I could not place though. Distinctly English but it just came across as posh to my untrained ear rather than giving me a region of the country.

'I can make myself available at your convenience.'

'Today would be convenient, Mr. Michaels. Can you meet with me this afternoon?' she asked.

'I can, but I think it prudent to establish what it is you wish to engage my services for before I commit to anything further. Can you outline the nature of your enquiry please?' I had no other cases to distract me, but without a little more detail I could easily be suckered into investigating a ghostly goldfish. Plus, she had not yet told me where I would be going.

'Well, Mr. Michaels,' she started and then paused as if gathering her thoughts or taking a moment to determine what she wanted to tell me. 'My Husband was killed three days ago. The police are claiming natural causes because he had a heart condition, but he is,' she paused again, 'was the owner of the Barker Steel Mill in Dartford. The Barker Mill has long been plagued by a phantom, a phantom that causes accidents and breaks equipment and has been responsible for deaths in the past. Now, I wish to be clear that I do not believe there is an actual phantom involved here, but I do believe that the recent sightings reported by the staff are real and that my husband was murdered. In essence, there is a murderer dressing as a phantom and I want you to catch him.' There was some distress to her voice, which given that her husband had died very recently, seemed perfectly normal. I was going to take the case, there was no doubt about that.

'Thank you, Mrs. Barker. I can be in Dartford within the hour, does that suit you?' My interest was definitely piqued. A murder, a phantom, a history of acts blamed on an apparition. Honestly, I could not wait to get started.

I could hear Mrs. Barker making hmming noises. 'Very good, Mr. Michaels,' she replied after a few seconds. Her voice was breaking, she was struggling to get the words out without crying. 'I will meet you at my private residence.' She gave me the address and disconnected. I had promised to be there by 1630hrs.

I swung myself off the desk and back into my seat behind it. I grabbed the mouse and clicked it a couple of times while moving it to make the computer wake up. I did not need to set off yet, it was only about a half hour drive to the address she had given me, so I was going to spend a few minutes researching the Barker Steel Mill and in particular the phantom.

The search did not take long, in fact, all I had to do was type *Barker Mill Phantom* into the search engine and it pinged back images, newspaper report extracts, and a Wikipedia page. The phantom had first been reported in 1912 when two deaths had occurred. There was a grainy black and white photograph that showed what appeared to be a cloaked figure on a walkway above the mill equipment.

Barker Mill was a steel mill that created several steel products for the construction industry a new search revealed. The firm's website showed various pictures of the mill itself, both inside and outside and on a separate page, pictures of their products. I did not know much about steel, but I recognised beams and flat bars and had seen them being used in the erection of steel framed buildings. I guessed there were other uses for them, but it seemed unimportant to the case in hand. The Barker Mill was opened by Mr. Tristan Barker in 1907 and had stayed in the hands of the Barker family ever since. Passing from father to son, the recently deceased Mr. George Barker was the fourth Barker to run the Mill. It would now pass to his son I assumed. Was there some motive there? Too early to tell.

The phantom I read, had struck terror into the mill's employees and brought destruction to mill property over several generations. It had never been caught. In 1912 there had been a series of accidents where equipment had been tampered with or sabotaged. The two deaths occurred when an overhead crane broke free from its moorings and poured molten steel onto the hapless workers below. Since then there had been phantom sightings reported in the forties, fifties and seventies but nothing from then until this year when a new series of accidents had led to an investigation and an employee had been fired after safety lockouts from a crane had been found in his car.

There had been investigations in the past, most notably in 1912 when they had hired Archibald Quibly. The article I was reading went on to describe that Quibly was a special investigator often hired by the police of that era to assist them with unexplained crimes. Quibly had been a police detective originally but had moved to the private sector after the death of his wife in unusual circumstances. It did not elaborate on what the circumstances were.

I felt that the further back in time I looked, the more superstitious and ready to believe in unnatural explanations people were. I could well believe that in 1912 the workers at the Mill and the general populace would buy into the idea of a phantom.

I had scribbled a few notes on a pad I kept on the desk while I had been reading. I looked through these again now.

- Mr. Barker was dead, probably of natural causes
- Mrs. Barker was convinced he had been murdered

27

- The phantom had been blamed for the recent spate of accidents
- Someone had been blamed and fired
- The phantom seemed to be the first cause considered whenever anything occurred at the Mill

It was an intriguing case. I considered whether I should call Amanda. If she was to be my partner from here on I would need to include her. It felt like the right thing to do, so I picked up my phone once more and placed the call.

The caller ID on the phone screen read PC Hotstuff, I would need to change that before she saw it.

Amanda answered almost immediately, 'Tempest.'

'Amanda, we have a case. I will be off to interview a lady shortly. Are you available?'

She swore. 'I have an interview with HR in thirty minutes. Thank you for including me but my proper start at the firm will have to wait I guess.'

'Understood. Well, I don't suppose I will solve this one this afternoon.' I outlined the case to her. She asked a couple of questions I did not yet have an answer to and we disconnected with a promise that I would fill her in on the case tomorrow morning when she had more time off.

It was time to go. I placed my notebook and pen in my shoulder bag, along with a camera and a few other items, and headed out to my car. Traffic could be quite iffy at this time of the day on the run to Dartford. It is close to London and the motorway bridge over the Thames where altogether too many cars try to funnel through a small gap. At peak times all movement appears to cease. I had allowed fifty percent longer than the journey ought to take and hoped that it would be enough.

Mrs. Barker. Thursday, 7th October 1630hrs

On the way to Dartford, the phone in my car rang. Caller ID claimed it was my mother. I groaned a little internally and debated not answering. My mother probably caused me no more grief than other people suffered from theirs, but for me, our conversations were a continuous loop of what so and so's son is doing now, how many children he and his wife have produced etcetera. Each time the theme would culminate in the eternal question of when I planned to settle down and provide her with Grandchildren. *You are the only male in the family, Tempest. You must continue the family name.* Her voice echoed in my head.

In the end, I hit the answer button because I knew she would just keep calling if I didn't. 'Hello, mother.'

'Where are you, Tempest?'

'Working mother and currently on my way to Dartford on the M2.'

'Dartford?'

'Yes, mother. Dartford.'

'What is in Dartford?'

'A client, mother.'

'A client?' Goodness this conversation was becoming a struggle already. I elected to move it along at a pace that might be slightly less than glacial.

'How can I help you, mother? I will arrive where I am going soon, so you do not have long.'

'I need you to organise your sister's baby shower.' I have a twin sister, she is fifteen minutes older than me and never lets me forget it. Rachael already has two children, a fact that I had expected would alleviate my mother's pressure on me to produce a grandchild for her but apparently, I simply failed to grasp the requirement of the male heir. I let the demand sink in for a few seconds while I considered what I was being asked to do.

29

'Am I not missing a vital piece of equipment required to take that task on, mother?'

'What do you mean?' she asked.

'I don't have a vagina, mother. Organising and running a baby shower is principally the remit of the female relatives and friends of the expectant mother, mother. I do not have any children, my friends do not have any children, I don't know anything about babies or childbirth and have never been to a baby shower to have gained any experience from which I could plan a baby shower.'

'That is a little sexist, Tempest,' chided my mother.

My right eye was starting to twitch. I indicated to leave the motorway and cruised down the offramp. The satnav claimed that I had less than one mile and only one minute to go to my destination.

'Are you there, Tempest? You have stopped speaking.'

'I am here, mother. But I am arriving at my meeting, so I need to go. I would like to know though how you come to be asking me to organise a baby shower for Rachael? Surely she has friends lining up to do this.'

'Actually, she asked me,' Mother replied, and I understood how it came to land at my door. 'I thought that since you are so good at organisation you would be happy to help me.'

Resignedly I admitted defeat. If I left it to mother, the event would be in the church hall with all the pensionable age ladies from the church in attendance, and the gifts would all be hand knitted clothes and toys.

'I have to go mum, but I will call later to discuss it with you.'

'Thank you, Tempest.' She disconnected.

The satnav took me around a final corner and instructed me that I was now at my destination. Unfortunately, as so often happens when following a satnav, there was nothing actually there. To my right was a brick wall stretching as far as the eye could see and a good two metres high. Behind it was a forest of coniferous trees stretching toward the sky. The general message appeared to be to *keep out*. I drove on for a minute or so and spied ahead a gap in the wall which turned out to be a double gate entrance. The gates were huge and ornate and very much closed. Beyond them, a driveway stretched between oak trees for what must have been a quarter of a mile. Where it terminated, stood a house that could probably be called a stately home.

There was no question about whether I was at the right place or not, as set within the gates, arranged symmetrically on each side was the name Barker in huge wrought iron letters. The entrance had an intercom which I pulled up to.

I pressed the button and waited for a voice. 'How may I help?' it asked politely.

'Tempest Michaels to see Mrs. Barker,' I answered.

'You are expected. Please park at the front of the house where you will be met.' The intercom fell silent again as the person took their finger off the button at their end. Moments later the gates began to open, the soundless motion a statement of quality.

It was an impressive, imposing place to visit. To either side of the driveway were fields of grass with trees and bushes as if a naturally occurring piece of the countryside had been captured and brought here. I spotted zebras to my right, silhouetted against the trees in the distance. The enormous house loomed as I neared it. It was a giant box of a structure, all brick, and ornately carved stone. The roof was either flat, or the front fascia extended upwards to hide it and there were fourteen windows I could count each side of the massive front doors going up three floors. I wondered how many people lived there. The driveway was almost wide enough for two cars to pass without either needing to move over. I discovered though that it was only almost wide enough, when just before I got to the end of the long line of trees, a yellow Nissan Skyline swung into view and belted down the driveway towards me. My brain told me it was not going to stop or even slow down. In fact, it was picking up speed, probably doing fifty and accelerating towards me. I had very little time to react, it had appeared so suddenly. I twitched my steering wheel to the right to get out of its way.

At the wheel was a young man. A young member of the Barker family I assumed since he drove like he owned the place and had not spared so much as a glance in my direction despite forcing me off the road.

Unfazed, I pulled back onto the driveway and continued towards the house.

As promised I was met by my car. It was a young chap in a suit that came out to meet me and escort me inside. He said very little, but I did get, 'Please come with me.' And when we arrived in a small anteroom a minute later, 'Please wait here.'

I pulled my notepad from the bag slung over my shoulder and scribbled a few questions:

- Circumstances of the death.
  - Where was he?
  - What time was he found?
  - By whom?
  - How long after he died was he found
- Details of what killed him if the natural causes report is correct?
- Why does Mrs. Barker think he was murdered?
- Who does she believe is to blame?

The list went on for a bit and I was still pondering questions I might want to ask when a lady entered the room. The lady was short at perhaps five feet and two inches but wearing heels that elevated her by at least three inches. She was slim, and her clothes fit her very well. I estimated her age at a shade over fifty, which made her a good two and a half decades younger than her late husband, whose particulars I had researched before I left the office. Mrs. Barker was wearing a simple, yet very elegant fitted navy-blue dress and sheer, nude stockings over matching blue heels. She was a very attractive middle-aged woman.

I took three paces in her direction as she came towards me and extended my hand. 'Mrs. Barker?' I enquired.

'Yes, Mr. Michaels. Thank you for coming on such short notice.' I nodded rather than make more of it than was necessary. 'Will you walk with me?' she asked indicating toward the door back out of the room.

'Lead on, please.' Mrs. Barker turned elegantly and went back out the door she had just come through. I followed her down a short corridor and into a great entrance hall leading away from the massive front doors. I had been escorted in through a side door, probably a tradesman's entrance once upon a time.

'I see you looking around at the opulence of the Barker residence, Mr. Michaels. I find myself doing that still and I have lived here for twenty-three years now.' I was listening to her voice and watching her body language. Mrs. Barker seemed sad. Whether it was sadness for the loss of her husband or for another reason I could not tell, but what I saw was a woman trying to pretend she was not weighed down by a terrible burden. I had a built-in need to rescue women. It did me few favours, but right now I wanted to solve this case for her.

'It is an impressive place,' I conceded.

'The gentleman that opened the steel mill, my husband's Great-Grandfather, had it built at the turn of the last century using money his Grandfather had made. The Barker fortune has passed from eldest son to eldest son for generations and the last four generations have lived in this house. It is surprisingly uncomfortable to live in.' I raised an eyebrow, which she saw, and she smiled before continuing. 'I realise that must sound ridiculous. The house is so large that it is impossible to heat in the winter. One can heat small portions of it and try to shut them off, so that the heat does not escape. The windows though cannot be replaced by modern heat retaining versions because the house is listed. They shed warmth all winter long and when one gets to one's car and discovers one has left an item in the bedroom it is a fifteen-minute trip to go back for it.' She was silent for a moment as if considering something. 'I am describing first-world problems I realise. Perhaps we should get to the matter in hand.'

We had arrived in an office of sorts. The double height ceiling and enormous expanse of the room made it the biggest office I had ever been in. Mrs. Barker strolled across the room to a window and took a seat on one of four sofas arranged around a knee-high coffee table.

'To business,' Mrs. Barker said. 'I am sure you must have lots of questions for me but let me begin by framing the case I want you to investigate.'

'Very good, Mrs. Barker.' I sat back on the sofa, adjacent to her and with my back to the windows. The notebook and pen were in my hands ready for taking notes should I feel anything noteworthy.

'My husband, George had been ill for several years. He had a triple-bypass in 2012 and was taking medication to prevent further heart failure. The drug was Captopril.' She paused so I could write that down. 'He was very good about taking the medication, but the coroner stated in his report that there was no trace of the drug in his system and that he must have stopped taking it weeks, if not months ago. Despite the heart issues, George had lived a full life and worked every day. He loved the Mill, which he inherited when his father died in 1988, but worked there from the day he left university. He had grown up with the Mill as a focal point in his life and everything he did was for the good of the Mill and the people that work there. You are probably wanting to ask why I think he was murdered, so let me pre-empt the question. It seems likely that the coroner was right and that the drug had indeed left his system, but I think he was still taking the medicine, so I can only believe that someone had switched the pills. Worse yet I think the person that switched the drug was his grandson, Brett.'

I wrote that snippet down and circled it, then wrote *grandson is not hers with a question mark* and drew a line between the two.

'I am sure you can expand on that.' She really needed to.

'Brett has been vocally opposed to everything my husband has been doing for years. The Mill does not make enough money in his opinion, the staff are too old and not productive enough and he wants to tear it all down and sell it off. Brett, like all the Barker men before him, has worked at the Mill all his life, he is thirty-two now and seems to have had enough of it. He and I do not communicate very well I'm afraid, which is adding an additional level of difficulty to the current situation as I am the Financial Director for the business and he is the new owner. I believe Brett wants to sell the Mill, realise an instant fortune and leave. My husband, his grandfather, stood in the way of that but most damningly my husband suspected Brett's plans and was looking to hand the Mill on to someone else.' She paused for a moment while I was writing.

'Continue please,' I prompted.

As I looked up from my notebook, she began speaking again, 'Well, there are other Barkers of course. The eldest son has always inherited the Mill, but the younger siblings are out there so George reached out to the eldest son of his brother. Thomas Barker made a career as a lawyer and has an MBA. My Husband felt he would make a worthy successor. Brett found out that my husband was considering naming him as heir and they had a big fight. That was two weeks ago. Now my husband is dead, and Brett is the new owner.'

I had a question, 'What happened to his father? There is a generation missing.'

'Brett's father died in a skiing accident fifteen years ago. I do not think there was anything untoward about it, he was an adventurous sort and broke his neck going too far off piste.'

'Understood.' I said, making another note. 'So, please tell me, how does the Phantom fit into all this?'

Mrs. Barker sighed at the question, looked down at her dress, brushed some imaginary crumbs from her lap and looked back up again. 'The Phantom is a fairy tale perpetuated by the workers at the Mill. Some of the men are past retirement age and remember the attacks and accidents in the nineteen seventies and many of them had fathers and grandfathers that worked there who would regale them with tales of the Phantom from even earlier incidents. There is an infamous photograph someone took a hundred years ago which shows a cloaked figure in the rafters above what is now B furnace. I expect it was faked at the time, just some chaps having a bit of a jape. The Phantom is supposed to leave a mark whenever there is an attack, a burnt handprint can always be found somewhere near the scene of the accident or event. A burnt handprint was found on the doorframe of my husband's office the night he was found dead.' Mrs. Barker was fighting to control her voice. It threatened to crack and hinted of sobbing episodes already endured.

'I will need to see that handprint Mrs. Barker and any other handprints that remain in the Mill anywhere from previous incidents. You said accidents and events, can you elaborate on what specifically happened at any point? More recent events would be more pertinent.'

Mrs. Barker uncrossed her legs and sat forward. 'I think it best you go to the Mill, Mr. Michaels. I will have you met by Ronald Drake. Ronald is one of the senior shop floor shift managers and has been at the Mill for over forty years. He will show you what you want to see.' I wrote down the name while she was retrieving her phone from her handbag. 'Are you able to go directly there?'

I checked my watch: 1707hrs. There was nothing I needed to do other than feed the dogs and they would probably just sleep until I returned anyway. 'Yes, I can.' I replied. Mrs. Barker nodded and dialled a number. I listened to one half of a conversation in which she relayed instructions to the person at the other end. The person was to find Mr. Drake and have him meet me in reception at half past five.

Mrs. Barker disconnected. 'Ronald will finish at six o'clock, so you will need to get there soon.' she told me.

I still had some questions for her though, 'Your grandson...'

'My husband's grandson,' she corrected me. 'I am my late husband's third wife and I have no children, Mr. Michaels.' I wrote that down in case it was important later.

I started again, 'Your husband's grandson, Brett. You accuse him of murder, do you have any evidence?'

'No, Mr. Michaels. That is why I have engaged your services.' A fair point. 'I have had my personal assistant prepare a pack containing Brett's financial statements as they pertain to the firm, plus a copy of his personnel file, his old school reports and anything else she was able to obtain.' This would provide me with some riveting reading this evening. It was good to have some of the research done for me though, so I was not complaining.

'Did your husband have any enemies? Rivals that had fallen foul of him at any point? Disgruntled former employees? Anyone that might have wished ill of him?' I liked the idea that it was the grandson because it was nice and neat and solving a case is always easier if you already know the solution and need only to find the evidence. However, I did not want to waste time blindly following a lead at the expense of all other options only to discover it to be false later.

'Only one that I can think of. My husband was well liked and respected. To my knowledge, he did not incur enemies, but two weeks ago he fired a young executive. Brett went mad, the man was his right hand, but we had suffered several accidents at the Mill in the preceding weeks, there was a tip-off and they found safety lockouts from an overhead crane in the boot of his car. He was blamed for sabotage and summarily dismissed.' Mrs. Barker paused to allow me to scribble on my pad and continued when I looked up. 'His name is Owen Larkin. He threatened to sue, get an employment tribunal etcetera, but Brett paid him off with company money.'

I wrote motivation next to his name and underlined it and drew a line to Brett's name to join the two. Something screwy was going on, that was for certain.

'Mrs. Barker, I will have more questions for you but for now, I think I have enough to get on with my investigation. We need to discuss my fees.' I outlined what I charged by way of billing hours and expenses and made sure she understood where my responsibility ended as all too many of my clients seemed to think I had some special powers of arrest. I would gather evidence, identify a killer if there was one, find the Phantom and if her husband was murdered I would hand that person over to the police. Mrs. Barker seemed utterly unconcerned about my fees, but given the house I was sitting in, I guessed she was not short of money.

I bid her good day, shook her hand once more and headed back to my car. She had given me the address for the Mill. It was only a five-minute drive away, so I was going there next.

Barker Mill. Thursday, 7th October 1747hrs

The drive to Barker Mill somehow avoided all traffic until the last five hundred metres, whereupon I ceased forward motion and remained stationary for several minutes. I began slowly moving again after a short, but boring interlude and crept along the road to the Mill entrance. I knew where the Mill was because I had passed it many times on my way to other places. I had never really looked at it before though and did not know its name until now. It sat on the south bank of the Thames in the shadow of the Queen Elizabeth the Second bridge that had been built in the nineties. It was a huge brick building with two tall thin chimneys escaping it to grasp at the sky. As I turned into the wide entrance, the plant stretched out in front of me and went on for as far as I could see. A forty-foot-long articulated truck rolled out of the front gate past me loaded with steel to deliver. Emblazoned on the side was *Barker Steel* in big blue letters against the snow-white background of the vehicle's body. A billboard-sized map of the plant was on my left, I slowed the car, so I could get a good look at it.

Just ahead of me the map claimed, was the reception. It would be the shiny, new glass-fronted building I could see dead centre of my windscreen. I had already passed a sign instructing visitors to report to reception upon arrival. That was where Ronald Drake would be waiting for me.

I parked the car in the first space I came to, which was also about as far away from reception as I could get, while still parking in the designated area for visitors. I looked across to reception to see if I had been observed but no one inside was paying attention. I wanted to have a look around for myself without being guided or controlled. I had a few minutes before I was expected, plus I was sure that Ronald would wait.

From the boot of my car, I selected a clipboard on which there was a wad of paper, a hard hat with HSE in big letters on the front and an ID badge in a plastic clip-on holder. I had learned long ago that a person with a clipboard is universally accepted as rightfully belonging wherever they happened to be, but also that the Health and Safety Executive could absolutely go wherever they pleased, without warning, without permission and then demand answers from the persons they encountered without needing to justify asking them. The ID was fake and had taken me about ten minutes to make at home. I had bought the sticker for the hat online. I had only used the disguise once before, but with complete success, so I had no qualms about using it now. If all else failed a confident manner would see me through.

The Mill had been added to over its century of life. There was a huge brick building in the centre of everything else, which I assumed housed the furnaces had been designed with architectural consideration and not just function. It had high windows stretching over several stories, a tile roof, and cast-iron guttering. All of it had elegant features, flowers cast into the downpipes, fleur-de-lis in the stone around the windows, additional lines here and there. It would most likely be missing from a modern construction where cost might dictate these minor additions are ignored. The central brick building dominated the site but there were many, many smaller buildings surrounding it, huge silver pipes joining many of them. I picked out a building that I guessed was a cooling tower, there were piles and piles of steel beams in several areas and enormous overhead cranes to carry the steel about the place and to the dockside. As I watched, a ship was being loaded by a ship-to-shore crane.

In general, the mill looked empty and I wondered if that was just because it was so big that you could employ ten thousand people and never see them. It appeared more likely though that the mill could be doing better. Mrs. Barker had said that was what the new owner, Brett believed. I saw old plant equipment that looked like it needed to be replaced and it was idle when it ought to be busy doing something if the mill was also busy.

I wandered through an open roller-shutter door into the main building. There were at least workers in here and there was activity. I got a few glances, but nothing more than that. I had been wandering for a good ten minutes and it was time I went back to reception and met with Ronald. I went via the car once more to dump my disguise in the boot.

The reception was plush, they had spent some money on it and it stood out as an oddity against all the dirty industrial landscape around it.

The whole front was glass panels from the double-height roof to the floor. The doors opened automatically as I approached them with a swishing sound. Then closed behind me as I walked over an enormous mat emblazoned with the legend, "Welcome to Barker Mill. The Home of Steel". I continued onto a marble floor where my footsteps echoed across the room in the otherwise silent space. I could see the two young ladies on reception talking, but their voices did not carry at all.

I was greeted professionally by a pretty, blond lady. I was expected, and Mr. Drake would be back shortly. He had been waiting but had been called away to tend to something. Could I please fill in the visitors' book while I waited for him and take a seat on the right? I could help myself to tea or coffee from the machine in the waiting area should I wish to.

I waited only a minute or so before an older chap came into reception. He had thinning grey hair that was several weeks past needing a cut, large brushy eyebrows that had retained his original black hair colour and looked to be trying to join in the middle, and watery, steel-blue eyes that looked tired. He had on a poorly fitting pair of grey trousers with a belt cinched in to keep them up. The belt itself had lost the shiny black surface leather around the buckle from the many years of being done up and undone. On his feet were workers steel toe-capped boots which looked almost new, as did the luminous yellow jacket he wore. The jacket had Barker Steel written on the back. To finish off his outfit, he had a shirt and tie under the jacket. The tie had many stains, a couple of burn holes and my guess was that he wore the same one every day and the thought to buy a new one never occurred to him. He was perhaps seventy years old and walked with a spritely pace.

I watched as he neared the desk where the two ladies were sitting. The one I had spoken with nodded in my direction at which he looked up and headed over to meet me.

I stood up before he arrived and extended my hand as I moved towards him, 'Ronald Drake?'

'Yes sir, that be I.' He shook my hand with a firm grasp, which I liked.

'Thank you for meeting with me at such short notice, Mr. Drake.'

'That is not a problem at all, sir. Always happy to help. Besides Mrs. Barker asked in person and I likes to keep the Barkers happy,' he said all this with a smile, he seemed a jovial sort. 'Shall we walk while we talk? I understand you wish to see some of the Phantom marks.'

'Yes indeed. Can we start with the office in which Mr. Barker died?'

'Of course. Right this way please, sir.' Ronald pointed to a door leading out of the back of reception and led the way towards and then out of it. The door led outside again where it had started to drizzle lightly. The fine, mist-like rain would soak through one's clothes if exposed for long enough but transitioning between buildings as we were it posed no concern. We followed a yellow safety walkway from the back of reception across a large yard and into another building. This building looked old, perhaps as old as the main mill building and as we passed through the front door I realised this would have been the original reception. The desk was still there with several other fittings.

We crossed through the room and went up a flight of stairs, which opened out onto a wide corridor with offices on both sides. Some of the offices had windows along one wall which allowed me to see in as we passed. I was following a pace behind Ronald and trying to take in as much as I could. It was late afternoon on a Thursday and there were plenty of people working on whatever it was they were doing. Was the mill in trouble? Did it have a shaky future? I had too little information at this point to tell.

'Here you are, sir. This was Mr. Barker's office. I suppose it still is actually, although it is a different Mr. Barker now.' Ronald opened the door, which was unlocked and stood to one side, so that I could go in first.

'Where is the current Mr. Barker? Is he not in work today?' The office was empty. The computer screen had timed out and switched itself off and there was no coffee mug sitting empty on a coaster nor any smell of coffee. He could be a tea man, but my guess was that no one had been in the office today.

'Mr. Barker comes and goes without my permission, sir.'

I nodded. Of course.

'Is he away from the mill often?'

'I couldn't say, sir.' I looked at Ronald. He was very clearly not saying what he wanted to say. I suspected this might be because we were stood in the firm's main office building and perhaps he was diplomatically not saying anything negative about the owner. Very wise. I would ask again later when we had moved elsewhere.

I had no real interest in the office except for the door frame where I could now see the burnt handprint. I examined it closely. The door and the frame were oak if my knowledge of wood was enough to go by. On the left, as one entered, just lower than my eye height was a distinct four fingers, thumb and palm print burned into the wood of the frame. Staring at it now, running my fingers over it and giving it an experimental sniff, I was trying to work out how the effect had been achieved. My first thought was a viscous flammable gel could be moulded into the shape and set alight, it would burn briefly and leave the print. There was no smell of an accelerant that I believed would still be present though. I needed to give it further consideration. I took a few photographs.

'Where to next please, Mr. Drake?' I asked, smiling at my guide.

'This way, young sir,' he replied amiably, then turned and made his way back along the corridor to the stairs.

Once outside, I decided to press him for some more information, 'Ronald, I can tell that you are not a fan of the new owner. I am curious to hear why.' He did not speak but instead looked around as if checking to see if there were persons within earshot.

'Not here,' he said and quickened his pace as we headed for the foundry building.

We crossed between buildings and turned a corner to find ourselves at the opposite end of the foundry to the one I had gone in. Still following the yellow safety path, we entered via a small door in the side of the building. It was warmer at this end of the building and I was assailed with the smell of tortured metal as soon as we went inside. It was not a smell I knew, yet it was somehow still familiar as if I had encountered it before. I wracked my brain, insisting it deliver the information to me but all I could come up with was being in the machine shop at my school where we had heated metal up and whacked it with a hammer or drilled holes in it etcetera.

There were lots of shadows from the machinery as the overhead lighting failed to create enough illumination to penetrate in some areas. We were walking along a corridor formed between some of this machinery now. Above us were walkways where the floor was a mesh panel of some kind. The mesh allowed light to come down, but from my perspective it allowed me to see up into the pipework above. I had no idea what any of the machinery was for or what it did or how long it might have been standing in its current position. From its aged appearance, I suspected that much of what I was seeing would have been the original installation. Ronald reached a staircase, also made of steel mesh, and began to climb. At roughly three metres above the shop floor, we stepped off the staircase and onto a walkway that took us across the expanse of the foundry. From my vantage point, I could see workers performing numerous activities, their little white hardhats moving around below me.

I paused to watch the molten steel being poured. I was transfixed by the beauty and horror of it. I knew very little about steel, but I did know that it was one of the most recyclable substances on the planet, even when rusty it could be melted down, turned back into steel once more and used for whatever purpose one chose. The soft orange glow emanating from the furnace closest to me, cast gloriously playful shadows against the walls and would kill anyone who got too close.

'Nearly there, sir.' said Ronald, who had noticed my motion had stalled and had come back for me. I nodded and followed him once more. We got to the end of the walkway and stepped into the darkness at the other side of the building. Ronald turned a corner, descended a short flight of concrete steps in a brick corridor and fetched up to a door set into the wall.

He pointed to the wall next to the door. A blackened but faded handprint, just like the one in the frame of the owner's office door could be seen. There was some graffiti near to it which I tried to read but could make no sense of. However, I could read where someone had written the year 1954 just below the handprint.

'Old Sam was here when this happened, Mr. Michaels,' Ronald told me.

I took a picture of the handprint. 'Old Sam?'

'I'll take you to see him now. Three lads were badly injured when a walkway came loose and fell to the ground.' A horrifying thought. 'The mesh panels had been tampered with. As they walked across the void the floor just came away beneath them. Old Sam was a young man at that time and was working right down by Furnace A that you were just looking at. He saw the whole thing.'

Ronald led me around more corridors, down some more stairs and I was as thoroughly lost as I could have been by the time we arrived at a small door in what I thought was an outer wall. Ronald opened the door and I expected daylight from outside to stream in. Instead, we were met with the gloom of a small room.

'Now we can talk, Mr. Michaels. Here, in Old Sam's boiler room we will not be disturbed.' We were clearly not in a boiler room, but I already had enough questions without adding to them with trivial ones. The room was a box about six metres square in which there was various junk stacked and a wall of lockers facing us about halfway across the room from where we stood. Ronald was already crossing the room. As he reached the lockers he vanished from view, a pace later I saw where he had gone.

The lockers overlapped in the middle to create a small gap through which a person could go if they turned sideways. I slipped through and found myself in a den of sorts. There were comfy chairs arranged around a coffee table, another table against one wall on which a kettle and mugs sat and either side of it was a non-matching pair of free-standing lamps casting light and creating shadows. None of the chairs matched either. I guessed that all the furniture had been brought in by people who were throwing them out and that this was a worker's escape that the bosses didn't know about.

Asleep on a brown, corduroy armchair was an elderly gentleman that I was certain would introduce himself as Old Sam. There were a few wisps of white hair left on his head and liver spots adorning his pate and hands. If I had to guess his age, it would be over eighty. He was wearing a pair of Barker Steel overalls.

'Old Sam!' yelled Ronald from right next to me, making me jump. Old Sam didn't twitch. 'He's getting on now,' Ronald said. 'He should probably retire but Mr. Barker, the previous Mr. Barker that is, never once suggested that he should, so Old Sam just kept on turning up for work each day. He was my shift supervisor when I started in 1965. I was fifteen then, we started younger in those days and he had been here a decade already.' Ronald crossed the room and gave Old Sam's arm a shake which brought the chap out of his slumber and back to blearily blinking consciousness.

'What?' Old Sam wiped some drool from his mouth. 'What do you want, Ron?'

'This gentleman is here to investigate the Phantom, Sam. Mrs. Barker sent him.' Old Sam stared at me, taking me in. Sizing me up perhaps.

'Another one?' asked Old Sam. 'We only just had an investigation.'

'The last investigation was in the seventies, Sam,' replied Ronald with some exasperation in his voice. 'Look, never mind that. Tell Mr. Michaels about the Phantom.'

Ronald sat himself down in the chair adjacent to Old Sam, so I took this as a cue and took a seat myself. Old Sam levered himself up so that he was sitting straight in his chair, wiped his chops again, scratched his head and said, 'Okay, Ron. Okay.'

For the next thirty minutes, I listened patiently while the two gentlemen regaled me with various tales about the Phantom. Both had joined the Mill because that was what everyone in the local area did. They both had family members or friends that already worked there, so had second-hand stories to tell that they had heard from the previous generation. In Old Sam's case, his grandfather had also worked at the Mill and had been one of those employed when it first opened. The Phantom was deemed to be responsible for dozens of acts over the last hundred years. Some events were mere pranks where light bulbs would be taken from an area causing the night shift to have to shut down, but in most cases, the Phantom attack was more serious, often leading to machinery damage, injuries and in two different instances the death of a worker or workers. The Phantom had been seen on several occasions. I remembered the photograph I had found during my initial internet search earlier this afternoon. On each occasion, the Phantom was described as a cloaked figure that moved silently, had glowing eyes and vanished at will whenever anyone tried to follow it.

'I saw it myself,' Old Sam confided at one point, leaning right in to make and hold eye contact so that I knew he meant it. 'It was in the rafters above A furnace.' As I watched, his eyes went up and right indicating he was engaging the memory portion of his brain. Had they gone up and left he would have been engaging his imagination which would have told me he was making it up. 'It was July 5th, 1954. It was Friday afternoon and we were close to the end of the shift. The crew was making the last steel of the shift and I could almost taste the beer at the working men's club. Barry and me. That's Barry Dunford I mean, well we were hoping to court these two girls, Margaret Miller, that's the shift supervisor's daughter and Susie Watts. Susie, well she had a small mole on her left hip...'

'Sam,' interrupted Ronald. 'The Phantom?'

'Oh yeah. Where was I? Well, I was a new lad at the time and still learning, so I was being taught about the degassing rig at the time. Suddenly everyone was running, and I thought they were playing some kind of trick on me. I was left at the degassing rig because someone had to stay and everyone else ran off because there were injured people, although I did not know that at the time.'

As I listened, I could feel myself being pulled into the story. If he was making it up he was doing a convincing job. I interrupted him a couple of times to ask a question. I have learned that people making things up cannot suddenly add tiny details and it exposes the lie. Old Sam though was recalling the story from memory, including seeing the Phantom and following it. He explained how he had left the degassing rig and climbed up into the rafters and how he had burned his fingers on the handprint the Phantom left.

'That was a scary moment I can tell you,' he concluded, then slumped back into his chair as if retelling the story had exhausted him.

I had been making notes throughout and had already formed several theories. I was certain of course that there was no Phantom, but it also seemed likely that Old Sam had seen something. I also had a feeling that he was holding something back, that there was a vital element of the story he had not shared with me.

'What do you think caused the walkway to fall, Sam?'

'It was the Phantom.' He looked at me with worried eyes when he said it.

'Is that what everyone thought at the time? That it was the Phantom and not some unfortunate industrial accident?' I asked.

'Oh no, Mr. Michaels. The fixings had been sawn right through. It was the handy work of the Phantom and no mistake. The handprint on the wall told us clearly enough but they wasted their time on a full investigation anyway,' he trailed off again.

'Tell me then, please. What do you think the Phantom is?' I was thoroughly curious to hear his answer.

'Well, I don't rightly know what to believe, sir. Some say it is a restless spirit of a worker killed when the Mill was being built. He is trapped here because he fell into the concrete foundations and is still there to this day.'

Ronald chipped in then, 'I heard it was the original Mr. Barker's business partner and that Mr. Barker murdered him rather than share the Mill. Now he haunts us all.'

I noted their theories then swung the conversation in a new direction and back to a question I had already asked. 'Ronald, I asked you earlier about the new Mr. Barker. You declined to answer at the time, but I feel you have an opinion you would like to share.' I left him to answer. Mrs. Barker had basically accused the man of murder. I felt it entirely possible she would be right, but I wanted to build up a picture and reach a conclusion based on facts.

The two men glanced at each other for a moment before Ronald spoke, 'I'll say this, Mr. Michaels: the new owner wants rid of us older chaps. I don't think we have long left here with him in charge.'

'Why is that?'

'He wants to sell the mill, Mr. Michaels. That's what I hear anyway.'

Old Sam took up the discussion. 'My granddaughter Kerry works in the top corridor - puzzle palace I calls it. Well, she overhears things and once she overheard the new Mr. Barker and the old Mr. Barker shouting in the owner's office. New Mr. Barker was quite vocal about how old the workforce is, how old and broken down the equipment is, how the mill makes very little profit. Kerry told me that he also said it was about time the old Mr. Barker got out of the way so that the new Mr. Barker could bring about some long overdue change.' Old Sam sat back in the chair as he fell silent.

Ronald put a steadying hand on Old Sam's shoulder in support and turned his face to me. 'Perhaps the Phantom will get him, Mr. Michaels.' The way he said it sounded like a suggestion or a prediction like it was something that could come to pass if he just wished hard enough for it. A brief chill passed down my spine and I snapped my notebook shut to break the moment.

'Gentlemen, I must thank you for your time, it has been invaluable.' I had taken a lot in over the last couple of hours and now needed to sift through my notes, write down my thoughts and start my investigation proper. I would need to come back to the Mill undoubtedly, but my watch told me the time was 1847hrs, so I had kept Ronald way past his allotted finishing time and it was time to let him go. 'Would you be so kind as to escort me back to reception, Ronald?' I indicated about the room. 'I have become somewhat disoriented.'

'Of course, sir. I would not want you wandering around the mill unaccompanied anyway. Some fool was in by B Furnace earlier this afternoon actually, just before you arrived in fact. That's why I was late meeting you. I went looking for him. The boys said the idiot was wandering around with a clipboard and a hat that said HSE.'

My cheeks wanted to colour, so I focused on not letting them. If Ronald knew it had been me he gave no indication, but I made a mental note to reconsider the HSE disguise.

We bid Old Sam good evening and set off on a winding route back to reception. It was a good thing I had Ronald as a guide as I would otherwise have needed to find the Thames just, so I could orientate myself.

Ten minutes later Ronald had me back at reception where I gave him a business card and asked him to call me if he thought of anything I might need to know. He headed off to his car and I went to mine at the far end of the car park where I had left it.

My House Thursday 7th October 2015hrs

The drive home had been swift and painless. The traffic out of Dartford had already peaked and was dwindling by the time I joined it so that I got home in less than half the time it had taken me to get there. To fill the time though, I went back over the events of the last few hours. Mrs. Barker seemed genuine in her belief that her husband had been murdered and in her grief. It was something of an odd case for me because I was not actually investigating the Phantom, I was looking into whether her husband had died of natural causes. The Phantom felt like nothing more than a red herring at this point. Still, since the paranormal is codswallop this case had precisely the same amount of it as any other I took on. Unintentionally, I found myself thinking about Amanda's role in the forthcoming investigation, how I would deploy her and how much time we would spend together. This inevitably led me to consider whether our time together would yield any kind of romance between us. I saw it happen all the time on TV cop shows, inevitable sparks between the two sexy detectives. The more reasonable part of my brain assured me this was pure fantasy though. Not only that, the continuing desperate hope that I could win Amanda's heart would torture me as she dated other men oblivious to my feelings. The option to tell her how I felt had two alternate endings. She runs into my arms or the far more likely version where it all becomes very awkward and weird and we cannot work together. The logical course of action, I assured myself was to pursue someone else. Hayley at the coffee shop, Natasha at the pub, Poison in the bookshop. All had suggested I was on their list of things to do. Poison and Hayley especially. I continued to ponder my options for the rest of the drive, slowly convincing myself that I would be less distracted by thoughts of Amanda if I were finally getting some action elsewhere. Typically, though, I had not arrived at a decision by the time I got home and started my evening routine.

It was well after dinner time as far as the dogs were concerned, so they had fallen hungrily into their kibble before I could put it on the floor. They were now asleep either side of me as I was sitting on the sofa. I had a few items on my to-do list, such as call my mother and make sure I avoid her plan to have me organise a baby shower, go through my notes on the

Phantom case, work out my next move and call Amanda so I could discuss it with her. The most pressing on my list though was eating. I had eaten an apple since lunch time and I was registering empty.

I eased myself out from between the slumbering hounds and headed to the kitchen. Perpetually fighting taste over nutrition, I wanted a juicy, fat, cheeseburger with bacon and cheese covered fries. I rarely bought the ingredients to create such a feast though, knowing that temptation was far harder to succumb to if one did not have such things to hand. I settled on a compromise that ticked enough boxes from both taste and nutrition camps and made a turkey burger with sweet potato fries. The fries were oven baked and I used a wholemeal roll with no mayonnaise. First Dozer and then Bull had come through to the kitchen to investigate whether I had something extra for them to eat. I tossed them each a thick slice of carrot and watched as they trotted happily away to devour their prizes in private.

While my burger had sizzled in the pan, I continued to consider my relationship options. I dismissed the notion of falling into bed with Poison. There were several reasons why I shouldn't. At my decision, Mr. Wriggly folded his arms and turned his back on me grumpily. Natasha felt like an obvious choice, but also like I was settling for the silver medal because I could not win the gold. Acknowledging that made me uncomfortable, but since I had no way of contacting her it was a moot point. This left Hayley. Part of my brain categorised her as the bronze medal. I told that part to shut up though. Hayley was lovely. What she appeared to be offering in terms of a relationship was not exactly what I was looking for, but since beggars cannot be choosers and I wanted to avoid getting to the point where I was begging, she made perfect sense. Anyway, all I was proposing to do was go out on a date for some dinner or something. I decided that I would visit Hayley in the next day or so and ask her to join me for dinner. There, decision made. Unless, of course, I could get hold of Natasha. She had given me her number, which I had promptly lost, so the ball was in my court, but I was unable to do anything with it.

I checked the fries and flipped the burger. Maybe I would talk to the chaps about it at the pub tomorrow. Get a steer from them. And maybe I would see Natasha there anyway, and if it felt right I could ask her out in person. I had a few minutes before the food would be ready to eat, so I called my mother on her house phone. She answered on the third ring by reciting the phone number as usual.

'Good evening, mother.' I replied.

'Oh. Hello, Tempest. What can I do for you?'

'The baby shower, mother.'

'What about it?'

'It is not a task that falls within my skill set.' I heard my mother open her mouth to speak, so I pressed on quickly. 'However, I realise that whenever I tell you I cannot do something, I just wind up doing it anyway. So, I might as well just accept my fate and help you plan it.'

'Oh, you are a good boy.' The truth was that my mother was rubbish at organising anything that did not take place at the church hall. If I refused to get involved, my sister would end up there with her friends eating soggy egg sandwiches and singing baby themed hymns.

'Yes, mother.' I replied neutrally. 'Have you already thought about what you want to do? Has Rachael said anything? Or given you any ideas about what she wants? Does she even know you are doing this?'

'Rachael was here today actually, so I have a full list of things that she wants and places that she thinks we could have it.' I sighed in relief. Half the battle was won if Rachael had already given mother a list. There remained a distinct chance that left alone my mother would ignore all the requests and do it the way she felt it should be done. I would need to remain involved, but the task was less complex than I feared it might be. I listened while mother recited the list to me and we made a brief plan for me to free up some time in the next couple of days. I could take her to see some of the suggested venues and help with booking flowers and cakes and food etcetera. No date was set. It was left to me to call her in a day or so to arrange it when I had wrestled my diary under control. I had expressed that I had just taken on a major new case, but it was obvious from my mother's tone that my sister's baby shower was more important.

My food was ready to eat, and I was hungry, so I promised once again to make some time and that I would call her soon. Then, thankfully, I disconnected. It was not that I disliked my mother, or disliked spending time with her. It was just that she was a little bit demanding, expected everyone to dance to her tune with no concept that anyone might have anything better to do and that she was generally a pain in the backside. Nevertheless, she was still my mother, the only one I had, and combined with my father, with whom she still lived, I could say that I had great parents.

I was sitting at the breakfast bar in my kitchen leafing through a food magazine while I ate. As always, the enjoyable bit of consuming the meal took a fraction of the time to prepare it, but it was tasty and nutritious and well worth the effort.

There had been a light drizzle earlier and the pavements outside were wet. Despite this, the rain appeared to have passed and it was a pleasant enough evening. The dogs needed some exercise, so I clipped their leads on and headed out on our usual route around the village. Periodically, they would stop to sniff something or urinate on a lamppost that had been urinated on by dogs ever since it was erected.

We reached the park in the centre of the village and I unclipped them from their tethers, so they could run free and search for squirrels. I took out my phone and called Amanda.

She answered on the third ring. 'Tempest. Good evening.'

'Hi, Amanda. Good evening to you. How was your day?' I enquired.

'Perfectly acceptable, thank you. Do we have a case?' she asked, straight to the point.

'Indeed, we do. I met with Mrs. Barker, widow of the late owner of Barker Mill. She is convinced her husband was murdered despite the coroners' report claiming natural causes and believes it was the heir Brett Barker that did it.' I paused while I checked that I could still see both dogs. Bull emerged from behind a tree to join his brother.

Amanda spoke before I could continue. 'What about the Phantom?'

'Well, there is something going on at that Mill. I am just not sure what it is. The likely explanation is that someone once saw a shadow and convinced themselves it was a figure. Since then superstition has caused people to blame accidents on a mysterious cloaked figure.'

'You do not sound as certain as you usually do.'

She was right. 'There is some physical evidence, burnt handprints, and the eyewitness reports sounded more convincing than usual. Like I said, there is something going on at that steel mill. We have been hired to investigate her husband's death though, not the Phantom. So, that is what we need to focus on. Are you available tomorrow?'

'Yes. I have a shift tomorrow evening, so I will need to get away by late afternoon, say around four o'clock so that I can get a few hours' sleep before I start. Otherwise, I am good to go.'

'Super. I have a couple of people to interview already but we should get started early and see them later. Can you come to my place at 0800hrs?'

'Sure.'

'Then I will see you in the morning.' I had bid her good evening and disconnected just in time to see Bull shoot after a rabbit that had popped up in a nearby bush. I yelled his name in the vain hope that he might halt his charge. I might just have well have attempted to use *the force* for all the impact it had. Thankfully, I managed to snag him as he popped back out of the bush still wagging his tail and snuffling the dirt where he had first spotted it. The rabbit had doubtless sought refuge back down his hole, so I was lucky the tiny dog was not halfway down the hole himself.

Tethered once again to their leads, I led the two of them out of the park and back to the house. It was mid-evening, the day seemed to have been quite long already, so I would be bound for bed before very long.

First, though, I needed to spend some time going over the large pack of paperwork I had been given at the Mill. It was bound in plain brown paper and labelled only with, "FAO Tempest Michaels". I knew already that the pack contained financial reports and other drab documents pertaining to Brett Barker's affairs. I was not going to have any trouble getting to sleep.

Starting the Investigation. Friday, 8th October 0713hrs

I awoke to find the utterly boring financial statements I had been reading through last night still lying on the bed. I had fallen asleep reading. Across the bed, the duvet moved slightly, and a small black nose peeked out: A Dachshund coming to snorkel depth. An odd thing about Dachshunds is they love to burrow. They will burrow anywhere they can. I don't mean they dig a maze of warrens under my garden, but in the house, they go under pillows, under blankets, under a sweatshirt if I discard it on the floor. They will stay like that for hours, reaching what I would expect to be an uncomfortable temperature, yet it appears to be their preferred state.

The nose belonged to Dozer. He peered at me suspiciously, wondering if I would make him get up just because I was awake, but his concerns were for naught. The clock told me it was 0713hrs, which constituted a lie in for me. I considered the day ahead for a few lazy minutes still tucked under my warm bedding. I had a new case to pursue. I had a new partner, which ought to mean that the firm would solve more cases and make more money. I was seriously considering getting a part time admin assistant and the thought of not having to do all the paperwork was joyous.

This morning I had Amanda coming to the house to go over what I knew about the Barker Mill case so far. Then we would be off to interview the chap that had been dismissed under suspicion of being the Phantom, and then to see Brett Barker hopefully. I wanted to interview the chap that had been fired simply because I needed to eliminate him. That he might be guilty of any involvement in the death of George Barker never entered my mind. I was just being thorough and building a complete picture of the events surrounding the death. I suppose though that he might have a grudge against the old man. Anyway, I was off to interview him with Amanda and I wanted to meet Brett Barker, the man my client was convinced had murdered her husband. How he had pulled that off I had no idea. Yet. He might be entirely innocent. The death might yet prove to be natural causes. But then what was with the Phantom and the burning handprint on the door frame. Something was amiss at the Mill. I did not like things that were amiss. I did not like mysteries with ridiculous supernatural explanations. It was time then, to find some answers. I swung my legs out of bed and followed them to the bathroom for a shower and shave. Amanda would be here soon enough, and the day was beckoning.

Forty-seven minutes later the doorbell chimed to announce the arrival of someone that wished to enter my abode and the dogs burst into their usual fit of barking.

By then I was showered, shaved, dressed and fed. The dogs had been out and had eaten and the day had begun.

I opened the door to find Amanda on my doorstep as expected. As always, she looked fantastic in everyday clothes. Today she was wearing, knee-high black, leather boots with stretchy black leggings, not the cheap kind though, her leggings looked like they came from Hobbs or Laura Ashley. Her perfect chest was clad in another stretchy fabric. Unadorned with a logo declaring the designer, it was a long sleeved deep red roll neck top that somehow made her boobs look bigger. At least, to me they did, as I tried my hardest not to notice how they pushed the unzipped portion of her black leather jacket apart like two faces peeking between closed curtains.

'Good morning.' I managed, stepping away from the door to let her in. The dogs were shut in the kitchen so that she could come in without having to step over them.

'Good morning, Tempest.' She smiled her ever winning smile.

'Shall I open this?' she asked, one hand on the kitchen door handle. The dogs had gone silent or at least had stopped barking and were sniffing underneath the door, probably already aware that they knew the person on the other side. I nodded and watched as the two sausage-shaped fools climbed over each other to get out the door first.

To stop them jumping up at her legs, Amanda crouched down to pet them. They both rolled onto their backs to have her scratch their undercarriage. She cooed at them for a minute before standing back up, and contented, they trotted off to their bed in the lounge.

Amanda followed me into the office where I had already printed off a ream of information regarding the Mill and the persons of interest. I found photographs of Mrs. Barker, her late husband George and the new owner Brett just by exploring the internet. I had printed off pictures of the Mill from the outside and some shots of the inside, plus the picture of the Phantom and the shots of the burnt handprint. Some were already pinned to the cork board in my office/dining room, those that were still on the table I swept up and added to the board while Amanda took off her jacket and began to study them.

'This is Brett Barker?' she asked, indicating his picture. 'Good looking.' she said when I nodded. Was he? I guess she would be a better judge than me on male attractiveness. To me, he looked like a bloke, but I suppose, now that I was considering it, he had good hair, a strong jaw and a certain muscular athleticism to his figure. Amanda was still staring at his picture. I decided that I hated him and suddenly hoped he was guilty.

'Shall I make tea?' I asked, already on my way out the door. I wanted one, so the kettle was going on anyway, but she called after me that a tea sounded great.

A few minutes later, two mugs steamed on the dining table while we sat, and I brought her up to date on what I knew so far. It did not take long. I tried to avoid conjecture at this point of a case as early conclusions tended to prove themselves false. The plan for the day was to interview Owen Larkin, the young executive that had been fired by Mr. Barker over suspicion of sabotage and to revisit the Mill to interview Brett Barker. I had emailed Mrs. Barker last night requesting her assistance in setting up the appointment with Brett. I expected the new Mill owner to be resistant to interview and suspicious of my purpose. Whether that would prove to be the case I was yet to find out, but Mrs. Barker had assured me he would make himself available today and his PA would contact me later to advise a time.

Owen Larkin lived in Crayford, a few miles and a town over from Dartford but on the same strip of river. His address I had obtained from reception at the Mill, they had been instructed by Mrs. Barker to give me their full cooperation. They did not, however, have a phone number for him, so I was going to wing it and try to catch him at home. It was 0855hrs, we had finished our tea, let the dogs into the garden for a quick pee and were heading to Crayford right now.

On LinkedIn Owen Larkin was still listed as working at Barker Mill in the role of Vice President of Business Development. I had no idea what that title meant, but my assumption was that since he had not updated his professional profile with a new role he had probably not yet been reemployed and was thus to be found at home. It was a guess, but as we pulled up to his address it was clear I was right.

Owen Larkin Interview. Friday, 8th October 0932hrs

I had a picture of Owen Larkin, so could match the face of the man stood stretching on his doorstep to the one in my hand. Dressed in sports gear, yet devoid of perspiration, he looked like he was about to go for a run.

It was 0932hrs on a Friday morning and the street was largely deserted, the absent cars having been used to take their owners to work. Owen Larkin lived on a street of small, but neat terrace houses. Front gardens were well kept and most had a short brick wall bordering the pavement with a well-clipped hedge framed just above it. Outside some houses, the hedge needed a trim and in others, there was no hedge, but in general, the street was pleasant and today the sun was shining down with a warm October radiance.

With a plethora of options for a parking spot, I parked right in front of the house with the passenger's door to the pavement. It was an unconscious act based on placing the lady against the kerb so that she did not have to step into the road and avoid cars. However, the accidental result was that Owen, who had been just setting off on his run, ground to a halt at the sight of the pretty blond waving at him.

'Owen Larkin?' she asked through her open window, already knowing the answer. 'Could I trouble you for a minute of your time?'

His motion arrested, he was still moving toward the car and beginning to bend down when Amanda opened the door and stepped out. I laughed at how instantly hooked he had been. Amanda is stunning to look at and had probably shot him her best smile. I would have been equally hooked had she called out to me in the street. It might be fun to run an experiment to see how many men could ignore her.

While I was getting out of the driver's seat and coming around to join them on the pavement, Amanda took his hand and shook it. He was not tall, perhaps five feet nine inches. I knew his age to be twenty-nine, he had an MBA from a London Business School and he was single, so far as I could tell.

'Good morning.' Amanda said. 'We need to ask you a few questions about the Mill, shall we go inside?' Amanda had put an arm out to guide him back towards his house and had asked the question as if it were happening anyway and his acquiescence was a foregone conclusion. As it turned out she was right, and he allowed her to guide him to his house.

'This is my colleague, Tempest Michaels.' she said, indicating to me as we went into his house. 'I am Amanda Harper.'

'Err, hello.' he replied weakly. 'What did you say this was about?'

'Mostly this is about Barker Mill, Mr. Larkin. Thank you for agreeing to answer our questions.'

'But,' he began, but she cut him off before he could catch up with himself and realise he had not agreed to anything of the sort.

Amanda had flipped open a notepad, as had I. She clicked her pen to make the nib appear and fixed him with a smile once more. 'You were dismissed from your job on September 2nd. Is that correct?'

'Um, yes.'

'Can you tell me about that, please? What led to the dismissal?'

'I'm sorry.' Owen started. 'Why is it that I need to answer your questions today?' It appeared that the spell Amanda casts on men is temporary as Owen had found his brain now.

'We are investigating the murder of George Barker on behalf of Mrs. Barker.' I replied. He turned to look at me properly for the first time.

'You think he was murdered?'

'Mrs. Barker does, and she has hired Amanda and me to determine how, and then who perpetrated the crime.'

He seemed to consider this for a moment. 'I read that it was natural causes.' He said more to himself than to us. He was deep in thought. Then a lightbulb came on in his head, his face showing it as surprise. 'So, you are here because you think I could have done it.' He exclaimed with worried excitement.

'Not exactly.' Amanda answered. 'You could have cause for grievance and that might act as a motive. We are simply being thorough though and need to speak with you to eliminate you from our enquiries.' It was a textbook answer designed to alleviate any worry that we might be on to him. We needed him to talk for exactly the reason Amanda just said, but he could be guilty, as much as anyone else could at this stage. 'Can you tell us about your role at the Mill? You worked directly for Brett Barker, didn't you?'

She was trying a new tack, getting him talking about a safer subject.

'Yes, I did. Brett and I were working on big plans for the future...' he stopped mid-sentence.

'Go on.' Amanda encouraged.

'I'm afraid that is all I can tell you.' he answered.

'Why is that?' she asked, probing for more. His reluctance to talk about his role at the Mill was suspicious.

'Is Brett looking to close the Mill?' I asked directly.

Instead of answering he closed his lips tight and mimed locking them with a key and throwing the key away. Amanda and I both made a note on our pads.

Amanda changed tack again. 'How long have you known Brett?'

'Since Eton. Since we were eleven. We met on our first day in fact.' Back on safer ground, he had started talking.

'And you followed him to Barker Mill?'

'Brett and I had similar interests. We went to the same Oxford college, read the same Bachelor's degrees and he offered me a job long before we graduated.'

'How did your dismissal come about?' she asked, swinging back to her original question.

'I was framed for an accident I had nothing to do with and fired without the chance to defend myself. That is what happened.' snapped Owen, finally displaying some emotion. Clearly, the incident still angered him. It was my experience that people, in general, like to talk about anything unfair that ever happens to them. They will tell anyone, encouraging the listener to agree that they were treated unfairly as if this in some way confirms that they were indeed always in the right. Owen was no different, so for the next five minutes he talked animatedly about how he had no idea how the crane safety lockouts came to be in the boot of his car, and that he never even went onto the shop floor to have been able to get them and had no knowledge of the equipment so didn't even know what they did. He had some colourful things to say about the former Mr. Barker, pausing at one point so that Amanda and I could write down, "miserable old wanker". A term that Owen was very definite about.

'You received a healthy severance did you not?' I asked.

'I did. But only when I threatened to sue for unfair dismissal. It was Brett that sorted me out. He just went over the old man's head.'

'Brett Barker?' Amanda confirmed.

'The very man.'

'Tell me about Brett Barker, Owen.' He turned to face me when I spoke.

'Brett Barker is a visionary. He is the right man to lead the firm to its new future.' He had said firm, not mill I noted.

'What future would that be, Owen?' I asked.

Owen closed his mouth and did the thing with the lock and key on his lips again. The impression I got was that he knew he had said too much. Then he changed his mind and spoke, 'That is not for you to know.'

'Why is that?' pressed Amanda.

Owen refused to answer.

Amanda and I continued to ask questions for almost an hour. When at one point he seemed to be getting impatient, Amanda asked him if he would be a darling and make some tea. When she smiled at him he had decided that tea sounded a great idea and had scampered off to his kitchen. This gave Amanda and I a few moments to converse.

'What do you think?' she asked me once we heard noises coming from the kitchen.

'I think he was innocent of the crime he was dismissed for but is up to something now. He and Brett were colluding on something. I heard rumour that he planned to close the Mill because it is losing money. How much truth there is to that I cannot yet tell. It looks run down though. The equipment is old, the staff are old. At least the ones I met were.

Amanda opened her mouth to speak but was silenced by my phone ringing. The number that came up was a Dartford prefix but not one my phone recognised. I answered, 'Blue Moon Investigations. Tempest Michaels speaking.'

'Please hold.' Came the response, after which the voice went away, leaving me with little choice but to hold.

After a second or so, and just when I was considering not holding at all, I was connected with a new voice. This one sounded young, engaging and female, where the former voice had just sounded grumpy, old and womanly. 'Mr. Michaels?'

'Yes. Speaking.'

'I am calling on behalf of Mr. Barker to advise you that you have a meeting this afternoon at one o'clock. The meeting will last thirty minutes. Please ensure you arrive early so that you do not miss your slot.'

'Very good.' I replied.

'Thank you, Mr. Michaels. The meeting will take place in Mr. Barker's office. You can get directions to it from reception. One o'clock. Please be punctual.' she disconnected. There was no attempt to get my opinion on whether the meeting time suited me. It seemed likely that Brett Barker liked to play power games and did this to everyone. I had met people like him before and had always found them quite ridiculous. I wanted to meet with him though, so ducking the meeting or turning up deliberately late, would most likely not work in my favour. I had no interest in playing his games. If there was indeed a game to play because he was involved in this mystery, then I would win later, not now.

Chat with Poison. Friday, 8th October 1100hrs

We left Owen at 1035hrs and went back to my office. I left Amanda there to do some research and go through emails so that she could familiarise herself with the enquiries I receive. I excused myself and set off to attend to a task for myself.

Just around the corner from my office is an occult bookshop that sells rare books, graphic novels, film and TV memorabilia, and comics. Basically, it sells anything that had a tangible link to the paranormal world. The bookshop is called Mystery Men and is run by Frank Decaux, a small, mousy man with the heart of a lion. I had discovered his bravery quite recently when he accompanied Big Ben and me on a case that put us into direct contact with a cult of vampire-wannabe idiots that had promptly tried to kill us. Frank was nevertheless completely mad and believed everything supernatural existed with a foaming-at-the-mouth fervour.

He has an assistant in the shop who goes by the name Poison. Her real name is Ivy Wong, she is nineteen years old, super-hot and believes I saved her life when I blundered blindly into a serial killer just as he was about to bite out her throat a few days ago. Poison had kissed me with great passion a day or so before, and then immediately after that incident and had made it very clear that I was to use her as my sex toy whenever I wanted to. While this seemed like an offer I should not refuse, the age gap bothered me, and I was already drawn to other women. For several days I had tussled with the idea of just succumbing to her advances, but the decision to pursue Hayley dictated that I had to say no to Poison. At least for now. The two ladies worked less than fifty metres from each other and my life was complex enough without trying to sleep with two ladies at the same time.

An unpleasant task ahead of me, I headed to the bookshop to speak with Poison and somehow let her down gently. On my way, I wondered if she had ever had a man tell her no before. Would she cry? Would she kick me in the nuts? Neither eventuality was palatable, but before I could formulate how to phrase my thoughts on the matter I was at the building that housed the shop and heading up the narrow stairs that led to it.

Poison was behind the counter reading a book. There were no customers in the shop and she smiled at me as I came through the door.

'Hi, Tempest.' She beamed.

'Good morning, Poison. All alone up here?'

'Frank is out at an auction, some rare book he wants.' She moved away from the counter and came towards me. 'It does mean we have some privacy though.'

'That is what I came here to discuss actually.' I said, keeping my tone flat. 'I cannot give you want you want I'm afraid.' I had to get the words out before the sexlicious strumpet coming towards me closed the distance, got her hands on me and made me forget the purpose of my visit. She came to rest just inches from me and tilted her head up to meet my gaze.

'What do you mean, Tempest?' she asked, disappointment in her voice.

'I cannot be in a relationship with you.'

'Why ever not?' she asked.

'For several reasons.' I answered and then slumped against a bookcase as I tried to arrange my thoughts into a coherent reason that would make sense to her. 'Most of which are confusing even to me. Our age difference bothers me, I guess that is the biggest reason. I am old enough to be your father.'

'My father is fifty-six, Tempest and therefore old enough to be your father. And I am not a little girl. Do I look like a little girl?' She pushed her shoulders back as she said it which inevitably pushed her boobs out.

'No, you most assuredly do not. But the age gap is still there, and I cannot get away from it. But beyond that, I am interested in someone else.' I realised as I said it that I meant Amanda and not Hayley. There were other reasons why I should not become involved with Poison such as she worked for Frank and I felt there it would be poor form to fool around

68

with his employee. It would be fooling around too I acknowledged. Sex with Poison would most likely be incredible, her body suggested it would be, but I could not envisage a relationship forming afterward.

'So, Mr. Michaels.' Poison started, taking her time over what she had to say. 'I turn twenty in a few weeks and will no longer be a teenager. The age gap will remain the same but the concern you have should diminish as I age, and it becomes less significant.' She took my right hand in both of hers. 'So here is the deal. I will leave you alone for now so that you can let your current love interest play its course. I am not going anywhere though. I owe you my life.' I opened my mouth to speak but she silenced me with a hand to my mouth. 'I do, Tempest. Despite your protestations and I plan to repay you. You can have me anytime you want me. Call me, come find me, send a note for me. Whatever you choose to do, when you want me I will be your plaything.'

The voice from my pants was going nuts but I could not think of anything to say. I worried that I might have dribbled a bit but also worried that the tightening sensation coming from below my belt was going to be visible to her and that she might think it was there as a demonstration of wilful intent on my behalf. It was entirely involuntary. A chap simply cannot listen to an attractive lady tell him to *get it here* and not have his body react.

Poison sighed, reached up to put her hands behind my head and kissed me lightly on the lips. For a moment, I thought she was going to try to deepen the kiss, but she pulled away and took a step back.

'I should go.' I said, thankful that she hadn't noticed the uncomfortable bulge in my trousers.

'I'll see you soon enough, Tempest. You might want to take care of that before you go out in the street.' she said nodding her head at my groin.

Bugger.

Back at the office a few minutes later, everything south of my belt was back to normal and calm. Amanda was sitting behind my desk using the computer. She looked up as I came in.

'We should go.' I said, 'We have an hour to get to Dartford but need to park and get through reception at the Mill etcetera, and who knows what traffic might be doing.'

'Yes. Time to go.' She picked up her handbag, grabbed her phone from the desk where it had been sitting next to the mouse and stood up. 'You get some weird emails, Tempest.'

'Yes, I do.'

Barker Mill with Brett Barker. Friday, 8th October 1250hrs

The drive to Dartford had been uneventful. We were once again tucked into the close confines of my little, red Porsche Boxster but it only took twenty-three minutes to get to the Mill. On the way, she had asked me more about how I thought she and I would operate together, whether we would take separate cases or work on singular cases together. I had expressed that we should let the workload and the nature of each case dictate how we needed to operate. Some cases would be simple and could be dealt with by either one of us. Other cases would require a lot of research, such as the death of Mr. Barker and we would pull together to try to solve them.

Amanda had read through the day's emails. It was the first time she had seen them, although I had probably described some of them to her before. She seemed a little surprised at the stupidity of some of our potential clients.

Now at the Mill again, I parked closer to the reception entrance than I had the day before. The sky was overcast, robbing us of our shadows and it threatened to rain.

The same two ladies were on reception. They had us sign in as guests and wait for someone to come down from the main office to collect us. The clock on the wall in reception claimed it was 1247hrs. It was a few minutes late, my watch assured me it was more accurately 1253hrs. Since we were expected at 1300hrs sharp, I expected Mr. Barker to be running on time and I was not disappointed. An attractive young lady in a short-skirted business suit came to collect us at 1255hrs (according to my watch, not the clock on the wall).

She did not bother to introduce herself, she simply said, 'Mr. Barker is expecting you now.' She checked to see that we were getting up to follow her and led the way back to the office where I had been yesterday. As we crossed the yard outside, sticking strictly to the yellow safety path, the first few spots of rain began to fall. They changed the tarmac from dark

71

grey to a glistening black in tiny circles as each one landed. Soon enough they would begin to join up.

The door to Brett Barker's office was closed, the young lady knocked, paused and opened it. The door swung wide as she stepped inside and out of the way to reveal directly in front of us the new owner of Barker Mill. He was already standing up and coming around the desk to greet us. I gave him some points for this as I had wondered if he would remain behind it.

He crossed the room, buttoning his jacket as he came, but he had not actually looked at us until right then. His face, which was ridiculously handsome, froze momentarily as he saw Amanda. I suppose he was expecting just a chap and had he checked out the Blue Moon investigation Agency website he would have found just me listed. So, here I was accompanied by the strikingly delicious blonde and it had caught him briefly off guard.

He recovered quickly though, a warm smile spreading across his face.

'Good afternoon.' he said, his educated accent everything I had expected it to be. Not that it offended me in any way, I found it pleasing to listen to people enunciate their words correctly. 'Tempest Michaels, of course.' he said, shaking my hand with a firm, manly grip. 'And this is?'

'Amanda Harper.' Amanda said, offering her hand to be shaken.

We had all met in the centre of the room in front of the large desk that dominated it. The young lady that had led us up here had quietly closed the door behind us and slipped out. Brett Barker had Amanda's hand in both of his and was staring into her eyes. He was still smiling his best smile and kept glancing to me and then back to stare at Amanda. He appeared to catch himself in the act before it became odd and let her hand go.

'Please take a seat.' he said looking directly at Amanda. 'Each of you.' he concluded, remembering me.

We were both sitting in large oak chairs that were positioned to face the desk obliquely from the right while Brett went back around the desk to his chair. He picked up a red stress ball as he went.

'So, I believe my late Grandfather's wife has employed you to investigate whether he was killed by the Phantom or indeed died of natural causes like the coroner says.'

Amanda stayed quiet, so I could field the question and when I spoke he finally turned his gaze towards me. 'Do you believe your Grandfather died of natural causes?' I wanted to see how he reacted to a direct question about the death. It was entirely possible that he was guilty but equally likely that he was not. Would he give us some indication?

'Of course, I do.' he snapped. 'The old fool had a terrible heart, was way past retirement age, worked too many hours, and refused to let me take over the operation so that he could have an easier life.'

'Why?' I asked getting the quizzical face I wanted as Brett waited for me to expand my question. 'Why did he refuse to hand over power to you?' This was a harsh question which I hoped would expose some raw emotion and frustration.

I poised my pen, ready to write while he glanced between Amanda and me looking a little uncomfortable. Was he trying to decide how to answer? Probably.

'Mr. Michaels, I am not sure what Margaret might have told you, but I am under no obligation to answer any of your questions. I agreed to this meeting largely to indulge my curiosity. She has not spoken the words directly to me, however, it is my assumption that she believes I am the one that has somehow convinced him to die of natural causes.'

Amanda and I stayed quiet. He was talking. Despite saying that he did not feel he needed to answer our questions he suddenly felt like sharing and the longer he talked the more he would tell us.

'Let me state for the record that I did not kill my Grandfather.'

'Where were you on the night that he died?' I asked.

'I refer you back to my previous statement about having no obligation to answer any questions.'

'No alibi.' I said aloud as I wrote on my pad.

'Why would I need an alibi?' he chuckled, his brow wrinkling in a display designed to indicate the concept was preposterous.

'What is your relationship with Margaret like?'

Brett drummed his fingers on the desk a few times while he stared out of the window. 'Alright. I'll tell you what, Mr. Michaels. I will indulge you a few questions. It feels a bit like therapy. Margaret and I have never really got on. She is poorly qualified to be the financial director of any firm, let alone a multi-million-pound operation such as this. She gained her position through marriage and I have been vocal about her inappropriate employment for years. We live in the same house, yet rarely see each other and we manage to remain professionally civil.'

'Will she maintain her position now?' I asked.

'Do you mean, will I force her out now that I am in charge? No. I would not stoop so low. Besides she retains a small portion of shares in the business that were gifted to her years ago by my grandfather. Unless she opts to sell them or gets locked up I am stuck with her.'

'What was that about being locked up?' Amanda asked.

'An old clause in the Barker Mill share ownership contract. The shares pass from heir to heir. Only ten percent can ever be sold, given or traded to anyone else and it must be someone from the Barker family that receives them. The only way for the heir to lose control of the shares, and thus the Mill itself, is to commit a crime and be incarcerated. The clause was written in at the behest of my great-great-grandfather when his son, my great-grandfather was found guilty of embezzling to support a gambling habit.'

'You gave Owen Larkin a large payout after he was dismissed. Why is that?' Amanda asked, changing the subject.

74

'Owen is innocent.'

'You seem very sure.'

'Sure enough.' he replied, fixing her with a smile.

'Why is that?' I asked.

Brett sighed and looked away from her again. 'Owen and I have been working together for years now. I trust no one more than him. He is as invested in the future of the Mill as I am.'

'So, how do you explain the components found in his car?' I checked back through my note. 'Crane safety lockouts. They sound like a vital piece of safety equipment.'

He switched his gaze from Amanda to me. 'I don't explain it. I have not the slightest idea who put those in Owen's car and nor does Owen.'

I changed tack again. 'The Mill has suffered a spate of bad luck accidents which some are claiming to be the work of the Phantom. Then your grandfather dies and a burnt handprint, the calling card of the Phantom, is found near his body. What do you think is going on?'

He considered this for a second looking directly at me. 'Are you asking me if I think there is a phantom haunting my Mill? I don't. I do however think that someone is deliberately breaking equipment. I have had to enforce a total system check before every piece of equipment is turned on. Productivity is down by almost forty percent.'

'If someone is doing this, do you have a theory why?'

'Not until I work out who. It could be a disgruntled employee, someone overlooked for promotion. If I overlook the burnt handprint it could all be a coincidence.' He seemed ruffled suddenly. Angry.

I nodded to Amanda to continue the questioning.

She checked her notes then looked up. 'It has been claimed that your grandfather was considering someone else to succeed him as heir to the Mill. Why would he do that?'

'My Grandfather and I did not agree on certain principles regarding how the Mill should be run, where its future lies and what we need to be doing to ensure the future prosperity of the Barker family.' It felt like a rehearsed answer, but he had taken his time to deliver it as if he needed to think about what to say. Was the pause rehearsed also?

'Are you not concerned that this makes you a suspect?' I asked. Then I saw the trap coming.

'A suspect in a natural death. Are you a fool man?' Brett was clever enough to have led me into the question and like a fool, I had swum after the bait. He turned his gaze firmly towards Amanda. 'Do you have any more questions for me?' he asked, smiling. He had essentially dismissed me.

Amanda and I conferred briefly but decided we did not have anything more at that time. We got up to leave but Brett then asked a question that surprised me.

'What are your rates?'

'Excuse me?'

'Your rates, Mr. Michaels. If I wished to engage your services to find the Phantom.' He was serious.

I was already stood, so while I was putting my notebook away I outlined what I charge but added on a healthy twenty percent just because I felt like it.

He nodded his understanding but left it at that.

A few minutes later Amanda and I were heading back to the car and out of the Mill.

Research at Home. Friday, 8th October 1443hrs

I dropped Amanda back at her car and she took herself home. She had a shift this evening and was going to get a few hours of sleep first. I waved her goodbye and headed into my house. I did the usual routine with the dogs and made myself a cup of tea.

I had not yet read much of the phone-book-thick file I had been given on Brett Barker. My feeble attempt at scrutinising the documents last night had achieved very little before the sweet comfort of sleep had wound its soothing grip around me and pulled me down.

Now that I had met the man and instantly learned to thoroughly dislike him, I felt a renewed energy and vigour with which to attack the file.

I was sitting on the sofa with a pile of documents on my left side. I had a notepad and pen on my right. Planning to be thorough, I would work my way through the pile, transferring the read documents to the right where they would form a new, inverted pile to keep them in their original order. In the notepad, I would make inscriptions regarding anything I found noteworthy or anything I did not understand or wanted to research.

I picked up the first file from the top of the pile. It was a series of school reports from Eton. Quite what I might glean from his school days I could not fathom, but I opened it and started to read. I did not get more than a few words in though before I felt the uncomfortable sensation of being watched. I turned my head to the left where I found Bull standing with his front paws on top of the pile of documents. He did not bother to wag his tail and his expression, if one cared to translate it said, 'I know that you know where the biscuits are, but I know where your shoes are so perhaps you should find the biscuits and I will not have to find your shoes.'

I glanced to my right. Dozer was stood on my notebook. A classic pincer movement. He tilted his head slightly to the side as I looked at him. His expression said, 'Noms?' He was less articulate than his brother.

A minute later, I was settling back into my seat and picking up the Eton school report once more. The dogs had devoured their biscuits and already taken themselves to bed.

For the next three hours, except for bathroom breaks, tea making time and the obligatory letting the dogs in the garden to chase birds, I studied the boring pile of documents. I had made just over two A4 pages of notes. Little things had stood out and were possibly of some significance, but if I had hoped for a piece of evidence that would get him convicted, then I was to be disappointed. He had been expelled from Eton, caught in possession of marijuana before he completed his A levels but had finished his pre-university education at Harrow. There was clearly plenty of money to be spent on the heir. He had then been arrested bringing a small amount of marijuana into the country from Amsterdam in his early twenties but had gained a double first from Oxford and had a guaranteed future at his family's firm, so he probably felt he could break a few rules and get away with it.

I had gone through ten years of company credit card statements, personal credit card statements and other information contained in the pack. There were some large sums that seemed anomalous. I had looked one up and It turned out to be a membership to a porn site. Vanilla porn though, nothing weird. Another, quite recent transaction had been a large and very exact sum to a pharmaceutical firm. I had made a note to investigate what they did so I could determine if it was of any significance.

The research dutifully done, I stretched in place on the sofa and checked my watch: 1748hrs. Surprisingly the dogs had slept through their dinner time which was rigidly set at 1700hrs. It only shifted from this appointed hour if I was late getting home or was going to be out and might feed them slightly early.

I was also in need of sustenance. I usually had a hearty meal on Friday as I was going to the pub and wanted something to slow down the alcohol absorption. I was not sure if it worked like that. Nevertheless, going to the pub on an empty stomach always resulted in reaching my limit sooner than intended so I maintained the practice.

Friday night at the pub was a habit I had fallen into rather than chosen. I lived in a quiet country village and very much liked that it had a pub. In the summer, people would sit in the garden outside enjoying their drinks in the sun. Patrons would come not only from the village but also from the surrounding villages. Nearby there was a historic Abbey which attracted tourists and it was not uncommon to find small parties electing to take refreshment at the pub before moving on. It was called The Dirty Habit after all. In the winter, when it was cold enough, the Pub Landlord would light an open fire. The flickering firelight and the sound and smell it gave off sparked romantic notions in my head.

One glorious evening, not long after I had moved to the village, it had snowed. Snow, a worthwhile amount of it anyway, was rare in the South East of England. However, that evening it had fallen to form a blanket about four inches deep transforming the look, feel and the sound of the village. I had wandered happily around to the pub, carrying the dogs instead of letting them walk, as their undercarriage was dragging in the snow. I had fallen in love with the place right there and then.

It had been my first visit to the pub and I had met two chaps that night - Basic and Brian Clinton and right there the Friday night pub crew had been created. Now it was Friday night again and I was looking forward to the routine of it.

At the pub. Friday, 8th October 1926hrs

Dinner had been chicken and black bean enchiladas with a side of steamed brown rice and fresh avocado. The dogs devoured a can of chicken flavour pedigree chum. Now that all three of us were suitably replete we were winding our way through the streets to the pub. All thoughts of work, Brett Barker, the Phantom or anything to do with that or any other case had been banished from my mind. I was focused on getting my lips to a cold, clear glass of lager. A thought occurred to me then, which was that I needed to talk to my sister before I did anything about her baby shower. I pulled out my phone and with one hand still holding the dog leads, I managed to send her a short text message asking if she could meet me this weekend to discuss it.

Her answer came back almost immediately, confirming that she would come to my house the following afternoon at three o'clock unless she heard from me that I was unavailable.

I text back that it worked fine for me and put my phone away. The pub was in sight.

I was hoping to see Natasha the barmaid tonight. A little over a week ago we had enjoyed lunch together and she had kissed me. It was not planned. The lunch that is, not the kiss. I had bumped into her near my office in Rochester where I had been on my way to get some lunch for myself. I had invited her along. Anyway, Natasha was the Friday night barmaid at the pub, she was absolutely gorgeous, educated, well-spoken and ticked every box I could come up with if a chap was allowed to walk around with a checklist for prospective mates. I had been fantasising about her for months and suddenly I was in with a serious chance. Then, after she had given me her number I couldn't find it and last Friday she had not been at the pub. Now, more than a week had gone past since she had pressed her lips to mine and told me the ball was in my court. I felt an overwhelming urge to speak with her. I had already implored the Landlord to give me her mobile number, but the look I got from him told me I was not the first that had asked for it.

Bull and Dozer quickened their pace as we neared the pub and pulled me over the threshold into the welcoming, alcohol-scented walls of The Dirty Habit.

Of Natasha, there was no sign. Behind the bar, the Landlord was pulling a jar of ale for one of the regulars whose name I could not remember. To my right, Basic, Hilary and, Jagjit were already sitting at our usual table.

'Wotcha, Tempest.' Jagjit said in greeting. Similar salutations came from the others.

'Any sign of Ben?' I enquired.

'No. Late as usual. Probably trying to wash off the stench of sex again.' said Hilary.

I nodded agreement. 'My round.' I announced and headed to the bar. Before I got there, Big Ben came through the door behind me.

'Sorry I'm late, chaps. I passed a mirror and got stuck for a bit admiring myself. You know how it is. Oh, no you probably don't, do you?'

'Sit down, dickface.' Jagjit said laughing. Big Ben cracked a smile and took a seat.

I went to the bar. The chaps at the table behind me were a mix of characters. I met Jagjit Singh when I was four years old on the day I started school. We had hit it off and had played together at the weekends as kids do. When I left the Army and bought my own house it was serendipity that caused me to buy one just around the corner from the house his parents had moved to a few years before. Jagjit worked in real estate sales of some kind in the city. Hilary, whose real name was Brian Clinton also worked in sales but was the manager of a telemarketing firm nearby. He was kind of skinny and scrawny – the type of shape that my mother would say needed to eat a meat pie. He was the only married one of the group and the only one with kids unless Big Ben had a few out there. It was entirely possible that he did as Big Ben was a force of nature placed on the earth by God to shag women. That was what he claimed

81

anyway. Big Ben stood six feet and seven inches tall. He was all lean, hard muscle and he was unfairly good-looking. He also had money. Not millions, but enough that he didn't bother to work and thus could invest time and effort in his main hobby of... you guessed it – shagging women. To Big Ben's right, was Basic. His actual name was James Burnham but at some point in the past someone had given him a nickname and it had stuck. Now even he introduced himself as Basic. The nickname fitted him because he was thick. Proper thick. Like I.Q. somewhere in the high forties thick. He was also built like a bear, but he would not hurt a fly and was at the pub with us every Friday night. He had come along on capers with me a couple of times when I needed some extra muscle.

When I returned to the table a few minutes later with five fresh pints of lager Big Ben was giving Jagjit advice on pick-up lines.

'The thing to know is that every chat up line in the book has been used to death so you need to come up with something original.' I set the drinks out on the table. Jagjit, Hilary and Basic each still had some left of the previous pint, so I lined their new ones up behind their half-drained glasses. Big Ben and I had yet to quench our thirst. No surprise then that Big Ben paused to take a long draught of his as I put it down.

'So, what do you do?' asked Hilary.

'I have several tactics to deploy depending on the calibre of the prey and what mood I am in. One method that often works is to strike with a shock tactic statement that gets their attention.' Big Ben answered.

'Such as?' I asked.

'Well, my current favourite is to announce that the first time I sleep with a girl I am always impressed by just how far a vagina can stretch to accommodate me.'

'Wow.' Jagjit said.

Hilary just looked stunned.

'And that works?' I asked.

'Generally, yes. The lady or ladies are either horrified, in which case I have blown my chance, or they are not, in which case I am pretty much guaranteed to be in.'

'I'm not sure I am brave enough to try that tactic.' said Jagjit.

'I'm not sure you should try.' said Hilary.

'Nor me.' I added.

'So, moving on.' Jagjit started, changing the subject. 'I didn't yet tell you all about the new love interest Tempest has attracted.' I had my drink to my lips as Jagjit spoke and could not swallow fast enough to interrupt him.

'Oh, really?' asked Big Ben looking at me.

'Really.' replied Jagjit. 'The delightful Debbie came by the house on Sunday night. She was wearing only lingerie, heels and a coat.' I stayed quiet waiting for Jagjit to deliver his punchline.

Then I was going to punch him.

'Excuse me. How did this snippet not crop up in conversation over the last few days?' Big Ben asked me quite seriously like I had been holding back important facts. Jagjit butted in before I could answer, tactilely putting his hand on my forearm as if acting as defensive spokesman.

'Well, Ben, the thing is, Debbie has a mustache like Lando Calrissian.' Laughed Jagjit before regaling the entire table with the tale of how he had screamed and nearly wet himself when he opened the door to her. I then had to explain how it had come about due to my mother ambushing me with a blind date when I had gone for dinner at my parent's house. Debbie is a girl that I knew twenty-five years ago growing up. Back then she was ok to look at, she had filled out a little, which wasn't an insurmountable issue, but the facial hair was a bit off-putting.

Big Ben turned to me, put his pint down and for once posed a serious question. 'What are you going to do about the girl situation? You seem to suddenly have options and don't know what to do about them. I could give you my advice,'

'But since you would shag them all at the same time, in the same bed and then shoot off to shag their sisters as well, we can pretty much skip that part of the conversation.' I interrupted.

'Weak.' Big Ben said shaking his head sadly. 'Just weak. But since it's you, you shandy-sniffing butt weasel, I suppose you should pick one and focus on her.'

'So, which one?' asked Hilary, who had been quiet throughout this exchange and never got involved in conversations about single women because his wife told him he was not allowed to.

'Yeah. Which one, Tempest?' asked Big Ben.

I shrugged, acknowledging that I just did not know the answer to the question. I stayed quiet for a second considering how to frame my answer but instead elected to use the assembled group as a sounding board. 'Ok, so I have one girl that is clearly interested, but in my opinion too young for me.'

'Poison.' stated Jagjit.

'Yes. Miss Ivy Wong, AKA Poison. I could engage in good old, honest naked fun with her.'

'Damn right.' said Big Ben.

'But.' I accentuated the *but* hard and said it twice. 'But, I cannot work out what I do with her after the naked fun.'

'More naked fun, silly.'

'Yes, thank you, Ben.' I replied. 'Seriously though, I like her. She is undeniably hot in a fitness model meets Victoria's Secret model way, but at nineteen I cannot see the two of us engaging in anything other than naked fun and I will continue to interact with her and her boss afterward.

Let's just scratch her from the list for now.' I took a sip of beer before continuing. 'Next up is Hayley from the coffee shop,'

'Describe her.' Big Ben demanded.

'Okay. She is mid-twenties.'

'Shag her.' he instructed.

'Is slim but curvy,'

'Shag her.'

'has a pretty face and delicate hands,'

'Anoint her with your sticky goo.'

'and sent me a text saying she just wants some cock.'

'Give me her number, shag someone else.' Big Ben concluded.

'Ben, I am not sure that you are being much help.' said Hilary. He was right of course but helping had never been Big Ben's intention. His plan was to annoy me because he is an utter git.

'The option to shag her does appeal actually.' I conceded. 'She is lovely and clearly wants an uncomplicated arrangement.'

'Sounds like a win to me.' said Jagjit. 'Why are you holding back?'

'Amanda.' I answered simply. It was an honest answer and I knew it. 'Also, I don't just want a shag. I am not in my twenties anymore, the need to rampantly sow my seed might still call to me at times, but I can barely hear it over the desire to have something more.'

'Something more... what?' Big Ben wanted to know.

'Something more relationshippy. Something where we spend time together not having sex, where we might take a holiday together or go to a garden centre to pick out shrubs.'

Big Ben had a look on his face as if someone had just suggested being a eunuch might be fun and he should give it a go. 'What. The hell. Is. The matter. With you?'

'There is nothing the matter with Tempest.' Hilary said, 'He wants what most men except you want: A girlfriend.'

'So, why don't you shag Amanda then?' asked Big Ben.

'Because Amanda,' I paused for effect, 'does not appear to want to shag me.'

'Have you asked her?'

Before I can answer, the door behind me opened with the tell-tale rush of cooler air and I watched as across the table the colour drained from Jagjit's face.

I turned my head to see who it was and there was Debbie in the doorway, silhouetted by the streetlight outside. I was just a few feet from her and effectively trapped.

'Hey, baby.' she murmured, locking eyes with me and smouldering with passion.

'Hey, baby!' replied Big Ben getting up. He flashed her a smile, 'Might I buy you a drink?'

'Goodness, you are a big one.' she replied taking in Big Ben's height and musculature.

In typical Big Ben style, he replied with, 'You should see me naked if you think I look big now.' Then he took her unresisting hand and led her to the bar. She didn't even look in my direction as she went. I was eclipsed by the promise of a greater prize. Suddenly realising I was holding my breath I exhaled and felt myself slump.

'Who is that?' whispered Hilary from across the table.

'That is Debbie.' answered Jagjit.

'My God.' Hilary said taking her in. 'What is Ben doing?'

'Taking one for the team I think.'

At the bar, the Landlord dutifully placed a drink in front of Debbie, a white wine spritzer by the look of it. Big Ben leaned forward and said something quietly to her then headed back over to our table.

'Right, knob jockey. You are going to owe me one for this. Honestly, I am not sure my dick is ready to tackle anything less than a nine and Debbie scores a three, so if I snap my dick off you need to be ready to listen to a lot of women complaining.'

'What are you going to do now?' I asked.

'Take her home and shag her I guess. Make it so she never thinks about you again.'

'But you were going to crash at mine, so have already been drinking. Can you drive?'

'I have not yet finished my first pint. As long as I don't have any more I will be fine.' He answered.

With that, he went back to the bar where Debbie was waiting patiently. I watched as he whispered something to her, then stared horrified as she grabbed his wrist and dragged him towards the door. My gumption finally caught up with me at that point. While I might be horrified at any notion of being near to or even interacting with Debbie, I could not contemplate sleep tonight knowing the fate I had allowed Big Ben to consign himself to just to save me.

'I might need a hand here.' I said to the table as I stood up.

Debbie and Big Ben had just passed us and were out the door of the small pub already. 'I can't let you do it, Ben.' I said loud enough to arrest their motion.

He pulled away from Debbie and came back towards the safety of the pub. As he neared though he slowed and leaned down so we could talk quietly in a huddle.

'What are you doing, mate?' he asked. 'Will this get her off your back?'

'Maybe.'

'Only maybe?'

'Yeah. No guarantee that I can see.'

'Damn. Well, too late now.'

'You have to be kidding.' Jagjit chipped in.

'I'll just have to set some ground rules I guess.' Big Ben said, looking less certain now.

'Are you sure you want to do this?' I asked.

'Mate, I would rather ask the cute girl at the pharmacy for petite size condoms.' He looked as scared as I was feeling.

Behind him Debbie was pulling her coat tighter around herself, it was cool out and a breeze had blown through the car park chilling us all.

Big Ben stood up straight, set his jaw and turned to go. Crazy or not he had decided to see the task through. I threw myself at him and tackled him to the ground.

'Goodness boys. There is no need to fight over me.' Debbie said.

Big Ben had come to rest face down with his hands beneath his chest as if he was about to perform a press up. I was untangling my arms from his legs where I had landed partially on top of him. We both looked up at her.

'You can both have me.' Debbie added.

'Screw that.' I heard Jagjit say from behind me.

Big Ben and I agreed wholeheartedly with that sentiment, throwing ourselves upwards off the ground and making a scramble to get back inside the pub. Jagjit, Hilary, and Basic blocked our way causing a logjam as we shoved them roughly through the aperture in a desperate bid to escape the horny plus-size woman outside.

I tumbled through the doorway into the warmth and relative safety inside still pushing Jagjit ahead of me. I tripped and fell on the sill of the door, drawing the attention of the old lady who had already chastised me once for leaving the door open. She just looked down at me and tutted.

As I began to get up from the slightly moist and sticky carpet, I heard a quiet yelp from Big Ben. I shot my head around to look over my shoulder at the doorway behind me. He was half in, half out of the door, but he was horizontal and gripping the corner of the fruit machine positioned by it with both hands. His legs were outside the door somewhere.

We locked eyes. 'Help?' he mouthed somewhat impatiently as if I should already be off my arse and doing something.

As I stood up, I could see that Debbie had hold of his ankles and was pulling him back outside. Hilary was staring in mute horror and neither Jagjit nor Basic had even noticed.

'Fellas!' I yelled. 'Grab an arm!'

Grasping Big Ben around his shoulders so I had a good grip, I tugged him away from the fruit machine which allowed him to lock his arms around my torso. He looked into my eyes, 'Don't let go.' he pleaded.

'Let him go.' Debbie demanded, tugging at his legs. There were four men trying to pull Big Ben back into the supposed security of the pub and just one Debbie was holding her own against us. She did have a lot of mass and a low centre of gravity on her side though. 'He is coming with me!' she shouted between grunted breaths.

'No, he isn't.' I insisted. The ridiculous tug of war continued as a car pulled into the carpark. A couple in their twenties got out, looked at us inquiringly and sidestepped cautiously past us to get into the pub.

Momentarily distracted by their passing, Debbie's grip loosened. With a final yank, Big Ben was free. We tumbled back into the pub in a pile out of breath on the carpet.

'My round?' I asked feebly lying on my back. I had someone's feet on me and my head was lying on someone else's hip.

'Someone's round, that's for sure. I need a double.' Hilary answered.

My Parent's House. Saturday, 9th October 0951hrs

I usually spent Sunday afternoon at my parents' house, but mum wanted me to help shift some heavy plants around in the garden as they were to be bedded down in the greenhouse for winter, so was going over now instead. Quite why she went to the trouble of growing plants that could not tolerate the English winter I could not understand. I had, however, given up arguing about it many years ago. If I failed to help the task would simply fall to my father and he would struggle to complete it by himself. Between us, it would be easy.

I had taken the dogs for a pleasant early morning walk across the vineyards and had some breakfast but had done little more than that before setting off for their house. They only lived a few miles away, so with the dogs in a neat pile on the passenger seat, I headed there taking the scenic, countryside route rather than the faster hop down the motorway.

My parents were pretty good fun although my mother was disappointed that I had not supplied grandchildren yet and clearly felt my priorities were wrong because I ought to be impregnating someone surely. Marriage first of course and I got the impression that my mother did not care who I married just as long as I just got on with it. She was also not entirely content with my job. She did not exactly disapprove of my line of work but would much rather I do something that she could talk about in public without people asking her if she was serious.

In contrast, my father was a delight. He was relaxed about just about everything, though I suspected that if my mother had been equally as relaxed, and as much fun as my father, then growing up there would have been too little discipline.

The drive to their house had taken just a few minutes and as usual, as I swung into the street the two dogs popped their heads up attentively. They always knew they were arriving at my parent's house and I remain curious about whether it was smell or sound or some kind of dog GPS system that told them where they were.

Parking outside their house, I remembered that the last time I was there mother had ambushed me with Debbie, the rather calorie enhanced sex pest that had sought me out at the pub last night and had previously turned up at my house in her underwear. She was not the first instance of my mother attempting to mate me off but had been by far the scariest proposition thus far. I felt confident that mother would not try the same trick again so soon, but just in case, I crept up to their front window and looked through it to scan the potential battleground. They were, however, both absent and were most likely already in the back garden getting started on the task planned for the morning.

I went around the back of the house, following the dogs as they had shot off ahead of me. My parents were not in the garden though, they were still in the house. I could see dad washing up dishes at the kitchen sink. He looked up and spotted me when Bull barked at the back door. He waved a soapy mitt, grabbed a small towel to dry his hands and disappeared from view. He reappeared a few seconds later in the dining room and opened the door which was locked from the inside.

Both dogs barrelled past him and headed for the kitchen, always on the hunt for food. Finding none, they soon whizzed by us heading deeper into the house to look for my mother, just in case she had some food for them.

'Hey, dad, how's it going?' I asked.

'Pretty good, kid.'

'What you been up to?'

'I tried out some frontin' in the hood yesterday.'

I gave him my most quizzical single eyebrow lift.

He gave me a grin. 'A young gentleman was rapping about it on the radio. He made it sound most entertaining, so I gave it a go. It seemed that all I needed was a Bentley with some bitches in the back. I had to make do with the Ford Escort and your mother and I may have not quite achieved the effect he intended as, to be honest, it was pretty much like any other journey with your mum. Still, the intention was there and that has to count for something.'

'How did I turn out so normal, dad?'

'Honestly boy, I have no idea.' he laughed.

Mother arrived carrying Dozer. He was upside down and being cradled like a baby. He was clearly quite content with this arrangement and looked to be going to sleep as she stroked his belly.

'Good morning, Tempest.'

'Good morning, mother.' The pleasantries concluded I turned to dad. 'Shall we get started?' I asked.

'I'll just finish washing up the breakfast things. Then I'll be out.'

'Haven't you finished that yet, Michael?' my mother asked.

'Clearly not, you cantankerous old bag.' replied my father smiling. He headed for the kitchen, keeping a close eye on his wife and leaping out of the way of the inevitable and well-earned kick when it came.

A short while later, both of us were beginning to perspire from the effort of shifting the heavy flower pots with their large plants in. Mother was directing our efforts from the comfort of a garden chair while continuing to stroke Dozer, who was at least now the right way up and sprawled asleep on her lap.

The task of getting the plants in before the first frosts of late autumn damaged the tender stems, took little more than two hours, but I was glad to be finished. Mother had supplied tea and biscuits while we worked. Now we were sweeping the remains of a few fallen leaves and cooling down. It was cool enough outside that we needed a jumper or jacket, but the heavy lifting had dictated we strip down to t-shirts. Now that we had stopped all the heavy lifting the cool air was nipping at our exposed skin.

'Let's get inside.' I suggested.

'Agreed.' Dad said. Mother was already inside.

'Would you boys like a sandwich?' My mother called out from the kitchen as we went in.

'Cheese and pickle.' My father replied.

'Not for me, thank you.' I said after a brief consideration of my options. I was going to use the fact that it was lunchtime and that I was hungry as an excuse to visit the coffee shop near my office and I would ask Hayley to accompany me on a date.

I kissed my mother, shook my father's hand and shooed the dogs out to the car.

Grabbing Life by the Balls (AKA growing a set). Saturday, 9th October 1257hrs

I checked my watch: 1257hrs. It seemed like a perfectly good time to get some lunch. Lunch was usually something healthy that I had prepared in advance as it is all too easy to encounter unnecessary calories and eating out or eating on the run just encourages that to happen. In my fridge at home, I had some fruit, a home-made granola bar, water and a Tupperware pot filled with a vegan salad. It was left over from yesterday when I had not managed to fit my lunch in. Rather than go home for it though, I was going for lunch at the coffee house in Rochester. It was time to deal with an altogether different need.

I had parked my car in its usual spot behind my office and left the dogs on the passenger seat rather than take them to the coffee shop. I was sure they would be welcome but rather too distracted by all the people and food. It was cool enough that I had no concern about leaving the dogs in the car for a short period. They would just sleep.

Hayley worked at the coffee shop. The two of us had been flirting harmlessly for months until a week or so ago when the flirting amped up a notch. We had exchanged numbers and Hayley had enquired if she could use my penis as a pogo stick. Hayley it seemed, knew what she wanted and was not inclined to dither about making her desires known. I had failed to commit to her request thus far because foolishly I had been pinning my hopes on Amanda wanting the same. Now though, Amanda worked for me and the chance of wearing her as a hat seemed not only less likely, but now also the other side of some invisible employee/employer barrier.

It had been a dry year for me so far. Big Ben assured it was because I am a complete wazzock when it comes to women and that I have missed plenty of opportunities. Big Ben though would have shagged Hayley, Amanda, their sisters and their mothers the day he met them and thought nothing more about them, so his advice was parked and would stay that way. As I headed across the street, I wondered what I should say to Hayley. I didn't need to launch a charm offensive to woo her, nor did I need to play coy. Perhaps I could just enquire if she was available for a date later that week? It seemed too passive, she is a strong woman that knows her own mind and has already made her intentions clear. So, I should be assertive and tell her the time has come for her to get a damned good seeing to. Or was that just too laddish?

My idle musing had led me across the street and into the coffee shop. It was busy today. I rarely go in, other than first thing in the morning, so I was not used to seeing the lunchtime crowd. I joined the queue behind a pair of chaps in work fatigues, their cargo pants worn from use and dotted here and there with paint or other fluids that had stuck or stained but had no negative effect on the usefulness of the garment.

Hayley appeared from the kitchen bearing two plates on which were what looked like toasted sandwiches. My stomach growled as the scent assailed my nostrils. Perhaps my diet could allow me such an indulgence for once. I had seen on their menu a salt beef sandwich, which I knew was a hefty offering, loaded with slice after slice of beef and swiss cheese plus mustard and pickles. I would compensate by hitting the gym again tonight and drinking water instead of getting the hot chocolate I had planned.

I tried to catch Hayley's eye as she went past. She was oblivious to my presence though. The queue moved forward and I with it. I estimated my wait would be no longer than two minutes before I was ordering. Hayley swept past on the other side of the shop once more and disappeared into the kitchen to collect the next order. Now that I thought of it, lunchtime was probably the worst time to talk to her as they were so busy. It did not matter though, if I failed to speak with her now I would come back later. Texting works just fine but, and forgive me if this is old-fashioned, if you intend to invite a young lady out then one should do so in person.

I reached the front of the queue and ordered a large bottle of sparkling water with a glass and ice and the sandwich to eat in. I was handed a little stand thing with a number on it so that my food order could be brought to my table. I took it and my beverage to the nearest available seat and plopped myself down to wait.

The wait was no more than a few minutes, my patience rewarded with Hayley herself bringing my sandwich out. I saw her coming and was watching for the moment when she recognised me. It happened only after she paused to scan the room for the order number on my table. Having seen it, she looked at me and her face lit up in what appeared to be genuine pleasure. This certainly boosted my ego.

'Hello, Tempest.' she purred at me as she neared.

'Hello, lovely.' I answered meaning it. Hayley had on her usual work clothes combination of jeans, t-shirt, and trainers with an apron tied around her waist. The t-shirt had a coffee stain above her left breast and several grease spots dotted about. Despite the unflattering clothes she looked knockout still. Her hair was a deep lustrous brunette that fell to well below her shoulders. It was tied up today in a loose swirl. Her eyes, set just a few inches above her gloriously full smile, were a deep chocolate brown and seemed to dance with perpetual pleasure. Hayley was full of curves rather than lean or athletic and the whole package was just so enticing.

Hayley placed the sandwich in front of me and sat down in the chair next to me. Customers be damned. 'So, what brings you in here today, Tempest?' her voice was deliberately demure.

I had always loved the flirting game. Even if I had never been great at converting the flirting into something more, I was good at this bit. 'Dear lady, I am here only for you.' It might be a line, but it was also true. 'I have resisted the need to be close to you for too long, so perhaps it is now time to end the flirting and spend some time together.'

Hayley's eyes dilated as I spoke, they were locked with mine and as I watched the tip of her sexy tongue darted out to wet her lips. It might have been an unconscious act, but it went straight to my groin where someone was already beginning to stir. She had been sitting with her back against the chair and one leg crossed over the other. She uncrossed them now and leaned forward to bring her face close to mine. She placed a warm, small hand on my right thigh and whispered 'I'm going to sit on your face the first chance I get. Text me.'

My pulse hammered out a quick staccato beat at the thought and Mr. Wriggly did his famous submarine impression and went *up periscope*. Hayley stood, brushed her lips against my cheek as she went and headed back to the kitchen without another glance.

Well, goodness, I was horny now. My pulse was returning to normal, but I dared not get out of my seat lest I scare small children with the lump in my trousers. I swigged some water and tucked into my sandwich. Reflecting on it later, the sandwich itself was glorious, but at the time it never registered as my thoughts were so focused on the potentially very naked and willing Hayley.

My Sister. Saturday, 9th October 1415hrs

I had taken my time leaving the coffee shop, but as expected, the dogs had barely registered that I had been gone and were asleep in a ball on the passenger seat where I had left them. As I opened the door to my car, I was rewarded with the joyful scent of warm furry creatures. Before I pulled away I had duly sent a text to Hayley inviting her to join me tonight for dinner out. I suggested we eat at 2000hrs tonight. Her reply had come back in less than a minute, sent from the kitchen where she was still invisibly working. It thanked me for the invite, accepted and advised me that she would pick me up from my house.

A date with Hayley tonight. It was an exciting prospect which was greatly distracting me from the task of driving my car. I chastised myself for daydreaming and gave myself a mental shake. Thinking more clearly now, instead of fantasising about Hayley taking her knickers off, I called a restaurant I knew served great food and reserved a table.

Pulling onto the drive at my house, I sent a fresh text, 'Dear Hayley, I have reserved a table at the Wild Oak in Aylesford for 2000hrs. I look forward to seeing you this evening.'

The Wild Oak in nearby village Aylesford was a gastro-pub where I had eaten a few times. It was well known in the area and I was surprised to have been able to get a table. The food was excellent and expensive enough to give the impression one was not skimping, while also not so outrageously expensive that the cost could barely be justified. They served a lot of locally sourced game and fish paired with seasonal vegetables. The lighting and tables were arranged to create the impression of intimacy even when surrounded by other diners. I was already looking forward to it.

It occurred to me that Hayley may very well wish to come to my house after dinner. I kept the place tidy but was a little paranoid that it may smell of dog without me noticing as I would be oblivious to the smell. I decided a thirty-minute blitz clean would do no harm, but as my sister, Rachael was due soon I would leave the polish, duster and vacuum cleaner out to remind me. A text pinged through to my phone just as I was getting the vacuum cleaner out of its cupboard. I snagged it from the counter and, pleased to see that it was from Hayley, opened the message to read it.

'Thank you for booking dinner. I will pick you up at 715. Xx.' I translated it into proper time: 1915hrs. Hayley wanted to pick me up rather than the other way around.

I saw no reason to argue so acknowledged with a quick, 'See you then. X.' I had already spent enough time daydreaming about what might happen after dinner given some of the things Hayley had already said to me, so I did my best to put thoughts of rampant gorilla sex from my head and got the Barker Mill case file out.

My thoughts kept returning to Hayley though and the very real possibility that she and I might have sex at some point in the not too distant future. I was finding this thoroughly distracting. Distracting to the point that I had read the same passage three times now without taking anything in. I was reading a brief history of the Barker Steel Mill which I had found online. Thus far it had not told me anything of worth, but I was trying to absorb as much information as possible as one never knows what might be the missing clue. Of course, tonight I would be out with Hayley. Two minutes later, I realised that once again I had drifted off to the place where Hayley was laying on my bed wearing nothing but high heels and a thong and beckoning with a finger that I join her.

I chastised myself for my teenage levels of horniness but abandoned my reading. Perhaps I should get the housework done now. I set about polishing the worktops and windowsills in each room. My activities attracted a suspicious eye from Bull - he was not keen on activity. Dusting complete, I turned on the vacuum cleaner. None of these tasks required my brain so I could idly fantasise about naked women without it affecting my work and, in the hope, that I might get over it before Rachael turned up with her kids.

Naturally then, my next thought then was of Amanda laying on my bed wearing nothing but heels and a thong, her heavy chest heaving in anticipation of imminent fondling. I jumped as the vacuum cleaner ate the bottom edge of a curtain and began to drag it inside. Suddenly back in the real world, the vacuum cleaner was starting to lift off the ground as it pulled more of the floor-length curtain inside. Panicked slightly, I yanked it back but succeeded only in pulling the curtain rail loose from its mooring above the window. The doorbell chimed, and I was surprised I could hear it over the vacuum cleaner which was now making a grinding noise. It was beginning to choke on my curtain, which untethered on one side had offered the hungry machine more free material to gobble up.

Finally, my brain caught up and I switched the machine off, ending its reign of terror. The curtain rail was hanging down at an angle from the side still attached. I would need to take the whole thing off and fix it later. On the carpet, the guilty looking vacuum cleaner had over a foot of material inside it. I hoped it was not destroyed. The doorbell went again. I left the evil vacuum cleaner where it was with a pointless threat to deal with it later.

I was expecting my sister. Sure enough, there was a Rachael sized blob through the frosted glass flanked by two smaller blobs on either side. I shooed the dogs out of the way and opened the door. There was my twin sister, standing on the doorstep with her children. At six months pregnant she was sporting a considerable bump but somehow still looked tall, slim and athletic. It had often been said that I had got the brains while she got the figure and looks. Growing up we had both been in sports clubs, martial arts clubs etcetera and had both competed in and out of school. It was Rachael though that brought home the trophies, rarely me. She had gone on to compete briefly for a National gymnastics squad when she left school. Then she met a man, dropped everything to get married and before too long the children started arriving. Her employment history was brief and mostly listed retail work. In contrast, I had gathered letters to list after my name from various centres of education and had pursued a career. The children had both arrived during periods when I was out of the country on operations in some drab part of the world, so I had seen neither as a small baby and had until this year spent so little time in the UK that they barely knew who I was. Now though, I was the strange uncle that caught ghosts, or so it seemed that was their understanding. It was close enough.

'Hello, Fallon. Hello, Martha.' I greeted the two children. Fallon was four and still holding mummy's hand. He was a little wet around his nose and face in the way that some children perpetually are. Martha was six going on forty-five and too old to hold mummy's hand now.

'Hello, Tempest.' said my sister while my nephew and niece continued to stare wordlessly at me.

'Would you like to come in?' I asked

'That would be better than staying outside.' she replied flippantly. The kids needed no further instruction. Fallon let go of his mother's hand and disappeared into the house under my left arm. Martha went past me on the right. Before Rachael could waddle across the short distance to the house they had opened the kitchen door and were already giggling at the dogs.

Rachael and I air kissed as I closed the door behind her. It was only the second time she had come to my house. She lived with her husband near his family in Hampshire. I had yet to visit their house and had not seen or spoken to her husband Chris in what was probably two years now.

'Good to see you, sis. Would you like a tea?'

'Yes please.' she answered following me through to the kitchen.

'Do the children drink tea?'

'Not really. Juice or water mostly.'

'How about coke?' I offered after a fast mental-tally of the soft drink options in my house. I drank tea or water and only had coke in the house because it went so well with rum.

Rachael answered my question with a hard, 'No. They will be bouncing off the walls if you give them coke.'

I considered that I might like to see that. It sounded fun. 'I have water then.' Was what I said though. I took two small glasses from a cupboard and handed Rachael drinks for the children while the kettle began bubbling behind me.

'Is the garden safe?' she asked.

'In what way? It has no escape routes if that is what you mean. I have to keep all holes in the fence smaller than a Dachshund can fit through or they would be off adventuring in seconds.'

'Kids?' Rachael yelled through to the lounge where the kids and dogs had gone. 'Take the dogs in the garden.' The instruction was delivered in a tone that held no option for bartering, discussing or arguing. Only mothers and Sergeant Majors could achieve that tone in my experience.

I moved to the patio door and watched as the dogs plopped over the sill followed closely by the children. Then Bull spotted a squirrel on the ground across the garden and attempted to break the land speed record to get to it. Both of my dogs had a thing about squirrels. I could not work out if they felt it was some form of personal insult that a squirrel would come into the garden, or whether it was something else, but they went after them as if they were balls thrown by God.

The children had yet to take off their coats, so would be sufficiently warm running around and playing among the trees and bushes outside.

Rachael was finishing making the teas when I got back to the kitchen. 'Got any biscuits?' she asked, levering herself back onto a tall stool at the breakfast bar.

Eating sugary treats was rare for me but I was partial to a thick chocolate chunk cookie, so produced a tin of them from a drawer and offered her first pick.

'Did mum ask you to organise the baby shower?' she asked.

'Yup.'

Rachael sighed. 'I even told her not to.' she said munching her biscuit. A few crumbs had dropped and were sitting on top of her bump. 'It was all her idea you know.'

'Really? Mother gave me the distinct impression that you had asked her.'

'Nope. Well, sort of I suppose. We were talking about the baby and she asked when I would be visiting and then asked if I wanted a baby shower. It was obvious she wanted me to have one, so she could show off a grandchild to her friends. I accepted the inevitable and asked if she wanted to organise something when I next visited.'

I chuckled. That did sound like mum.

'So, since it is happening anyway. What sort of event do you want?' Rachael was munching again so the question hung for a moment while she tried to clear her mouth. I pressed on with my plan rather than wait for her. 'I was planning to find a quiet venue that caters so that you avoid mum's soggy egg sandwiches and heavy pastries. It would be arranged for a weekend during daylight hours and I would invite a limited number of your friends plus mum's collection of old ladies.'

'That sounds perfect. Thank you, Tempest.'

'No problem. I already have a place picked out. I just need to speak with them and see when they have availability. I'll let you know what I organise.' I sipped my tea as Rachael dunked what must have been her fourth or fifth biscuit in hers. I guess growing a baby makes you hungry. 'I am going to need a list of the friends you wish to invite with email addresses and phone numbers. It would help, I suspect if you email them to me and cc all of them on the email, so they will have a clue who I am when I make contact.'

Rachael chuckled. 'Still struggling to talk to women, Tempest? How is it that you are so awkward with girls when you are so good looking?'

'I don't struggle to talk to women.' I corrected her. 'I struggle to translate talking into anything else.'

A scream from outside split the air. I was off my stool and moving in a fraction of a heartbeat. Rachael didn't react at all. 'They are just playing.'

she said dipping another biscuit in her still warm tea. 'That was Martha's over-excited scream.'

Out of the window, I could see the children chasing the dogs around a tree. I sat back down.

'What was I saying?' I asked myself more than her.

'You were lying to me about how you can actually talk to girls.'

I opened my mouth to protest but she cut me off. 'Don't worry. Most of the girls I wish to invite already know you. We went to school with some of them.'

'Okay.' I said weakly, unsure who she might be referring to and still smarting about her comment on my ability with ladies. A thought occurred to me. 'I have a date in a few hours actually.'

'No, you don't.' she replied without looking up.

'Yes, I do.' I snapped back.

'Okay then. I'll bite,' she replied though she clearly didn't believe me.

'Her name is Hayley. She works at the coffee shop near my office.'

'And you asked her out?' Rachael asked, her voice ripe with disbelief.

'Mostly.' I conceded now unsure what had actually happened.

'Good. Just don't tell mum. You know how desperate she is for you to produce an heir.'

I nodded. It was wise advice.

Rachael and I continued to chat for another hour. The patio doors burst open at one point. The dogs and children arriving in the kitchen moments later with the scent of autumn on their clothes and fur. The kids drained their glasses of water and snagged a chocolate cookie for each hand. The dogs drank from their water bowl and to keep things even I gave them a gravy bone each.

'The dog did a poo,' Martha announced.

'They do that,' Rachael replied.

With no other news to report, Martha, Fallon and the dogs went back outside. Through the window, we could see them grabbing piles of fallen leaves and throwing them high in the air to run underneath as they fell. The action was accompanied by squeals of laughter and excitement and the odd bark from a dog.

All too soon, Rachael said it was time to go. The children groaned but conceded and suddenly the house was quiet.

Too quiet.

I turned on the TV for some noise and set about getting ready for my date

A date with Hayley. Saturday, 9th October 1845hrs

Hayley wanted to pick me up at my house. I had thought it a little odd when she suggested it but dismissed the thought as old-fashioned bordering on sexist. It didn't bother me that she was the one taking me out. Why would it? I was a fan of strong, independent women after all.

I shot my cuff to check my watch only to find that I had not put it on yet. I pulled my phone from its back pocket hiding place instead: 1845hrs. She was not due for half an hour yet, so I had plenty of time to finish getting dressed.

Mildly concerned about spinach between my teeth or the risk of bad breath, I had reserved brushing, flossing and mouth washing until the last minute. It seemed last minute enough now so I headed upstairs to the bathroom. I took my shirt off as I went to eliminate the chance of dripping toothpaste on it and hung it on the end of the stair banister.

In the bathroom, I posed shirtless in front of the mirror, flexed my arms a few times inspecting the musculature critically. I didn't feel like I was getting old, grey hair had yet to come and I was keeping body fat mostly at bay. I slapped my stomach where a light covering of unnecessary fat ruined my abs and told myself to stop overthinking life. I could lose the fat if I really wanted to, but to achieve that I would have to pin my diet back to the point that it would bother me. It seemed unnecessary. I gave myself a mental slap and opened the bathroom cabinet. Then the doorbell went.

The dogs, who had undoubtedly been asleep on the sofa, burst to life in a fit of barking. I could hear them rush through the house to arrive, skidding to a halt, at the front door. I wanted to make whomever it was wait, but the dogs would continue to make noise and there were babies in nearby houses who might be sleeping at this time. It was better that I just answer the door.

I snagged my shirt on my way down the stairs and threw it on without doing it up. Through the frosted glass of the front door, I could see the figure was a woman and it looked very much to me that the distorted silhouette was Hayley.

Bull and Dozer were going nuts at my feet, so I shooed them back into the kitchen and shut the door. Then quickly checked myself in the mirror in the hall to make sure I did not have anything sticking to my face or hanging from my nose. Satisfied, I opened the door.

Hayley was wearing a figure-hugging pair of skinny jeans which made her legs look longer than they were, a pair of Mary Janes with a two-inch heel in bright blue and a matching blue three quarter length leather jacket over a white satin halter neck top. She looked stunning.

I knew she was attractive, I had always been interested, but I realised now that I had only ever seen her in work clothes with an apron around her waist. A short, quiet noise of excitement came from just below my belt.

'Hello, Hayley. You look stunning,' I said being honest. 'Would you like to come in?'

'I'm a little early. Sorry,' she replied taking in my bare feet and open shirt.

'That's okay, I'm nearly ready. If you can give me a couple of minutes we can go.' I stepped away from the door so that she could come in. As I shut the door, the dogs started up barking again. 'I will have to let them out. Is that okay?'

'Of course, Tempest. I am dying to see them anyway.'

'Just watch out for them in case they claw your legs or leave nose prints on your clothes.' I opened the kitchen door and the pair of idiots fell out as one mass of black and tan fur with eight legs and two tails. They were both trying to occupy the same space so were essentially both simultaneously trying to stand on the other's back. Propelling themselves forward anyway, they ran right into Hayley's legs and started trying to climb them. Hayley bent down to coo and fuss them, so the pair rolled onto their backs for tummy tickles. They were so fearsome.

'I will be just a few minutes,' I assured Hayley as I headed for the stairs.

'Please don't rush, I will be just fine here with your lovely dogs.'

Back upstairs I could hear Hayley talking to the dogs in a typical childish voice that one uses on pets. I did the same thing myself. I set about cleaning my teeth but with a greater sense of urgency that I had intended as I did not wish to keep the lady waiting.

Teeth cleaned, hair tidied, and aftershave applied, I wandered through to the bedroom to get my shoes and buttoned my shirt as I went. In total, I had probably taken about five minutes and I was looking forward to a few hours spent in the company of an attractive woman. It had been several months since I had gone on an actual date and longer than that since I had engaged in any nocturnal, naked activity. Mr. Wriggly was very conscious of this fact and had been reminding me all day.

As I came down the stairs, I could see that Hayley and the dogs were no longer in the entrance hallway. I checked quickly in the dining room/office, but they were not there so I moved through the house to the kitchen, which was also empty and then into the lounge.

In the middle of the lounge, stood in front of the mantelpiece was Hayley, no longer wearing her skinny jeans and jacket combo. Instead, she was in bright white, very sexy lingerie, stockings and all and still wearing the heels.

Mr. Wriggly made a noise that sounded pretty much exactly like a rule does when a school child twangs it off the edge of their desk while holding it down and creating a reverberation with the free end. Kind of a boooinngggoooinggoooiinng noise as he changed state from sleepy passiveness to determined aggression in about half a heartbeat. Visually, it would have been much like a party blower unfurling. I could hear him mustering the rowers up to ramming speed.

As I watched, she took off her bra, letting it fall from her fingertips to the carpet. Then she crossed the room and began to kiss me. The remainder of my evening was, shall we say eventful and entertaining.

A Rude Awakening. Sunday, 10th October 0815hrs

I awoke to a hammering on the door and the dogs barking incessantly downstairs. I was on the wrong side of my bed and momentarily disoriented until Hayley sat up next to me, her breasts demanding my attention as the covers fell away from them.

'Good morning,' I said with a smile remembering the night before. Then smiling again as I re-categorized my memory to be of the early evening, late evening, night and early morning before. My belly rumbled its emptiness as dinner had simply never happened.

'Err, Hi,' Hayley replied, squinting a little. 'What is all that noise?'

'The terrible attack dogs reacting to someone knocking on the door. I had better go and see who it is.' I hopped out of bed unashamedly naked and grabbed jogging bottoms and a t-shirt. I pulled them on, leaned over to kiss Hayley quickly and headed along the corridor to go downstairs.

The dogs were both spinning in place, wagging their tails and doing their best to block my way so that I had to pick them both up first and deposit them in the kitchen before I could answer the door.

I yelled out, 'Won't be a moment,' as I went by the front door to get rid of the dogs, then hurried back to answer it. On my doorstep was Amanda looking lovely as usual and I felt a sudden pang of guilt over having sex with Hayley even though I knew it was entirely irrational. 'What's up?' I asked her.

'Sorry for the early intrusion. I have been trying to get you for hours. There was a phantom attack at the Mill.'

'Oh,' I said dumbly. 'I was, um, busy. Otherwise engaged.' I hazarded.

'Hello,' came Hayley's voice from behind me.

Amanda was now looking over my shoulder at Hayley who had appeared at the bottom of the stairs wearing my shirt from last night. It was buttoned up using only two buttons so that the slightest movement would reveal her private topiary.

'Hello,' said Amanda politely. 'Shall I come back later?' she asked looking at me. Her tone was a little snippy.

'Perhaps I could meet you at the office in thirty minutes? I could do with a shower.'

'I bet you could,' she said. Again, it was a snippy retort but then she seemed to recover her composure. 'Of course, Tempest. Sorry. I didn't think this through and it was rude of me to be hammering on your door so early. I have never asked you if you had a girlfriend.'

Hayley had wandered through to the kitchen where I could hear the kettle beginning to make noise.

Amanda said, 'I'll, err. I'll go. sorry. I'll see you at the office later then?' she seemed embarrassed now.

'Thirty minutes. I'll see you there.'

'Okay.' She turned to go but then a thought occurred to me.

'How did you find out?' I asked. 'How did you know there had been an attack?'

'Brett called me. He wants us to take the case and find the Phantom.' This was unexpected. The hiring us bit, not the bit where he called Amanda. He had been dribbling at her from the moment we went into his office yesterday. I elected to not say anything about Brett.

'Okay. Well, that is a development. I will be as quick as I can.'

Amanda went back down the path from my house to the road. I saw her getting into her car as I closed my front door. I went into the kitchen where Hayley was searching through cupboards for something. She was standing on tippy-toes to investigate the top shelf and the shirt was riding up to reveal her peach shaped bum cheeks. A glow of desire shot through me.

112

'Where do you keep your teabags?' she asked. I walked over to her, spun her around and kissed her.

'Forget the tea,' I murmured as I grabbed her waist and lifted her onto the breakfast bar. There was no resistance and I silently admonished myself as I undid the shirt buttons and accepted that I was probably not going to get to the office in thirty minutes.

The Office. Sunday, 10th October 0903hrs

I pulled into my parking space at 0903hrs. I had taken forty-three
minutes and was hoping that Amanda would be cool about it. It was
unusual for me to arrive late anywhere, but then it was unusual for me to
have sex and one had caused the other. I had checked my phone when
Hayley and I had finally come up for air, there were thirteen missed calls
from Amanda over a two-hour span starting at 0518hrs. She had also left
text messages telling me what she was calling for, but I had missed it all as
my phone had been downstairs and switched to silent.

I had left Hayley at my house rather than hurry her up and kick her out.
When I left, she was still wearing my shirt and drinking tea on the sofa
with both my dogs. I had promised to call her later, skipped breakfast
because there simply wasn't time and had run out the door peeling a
banana as I went. In the car, during the short ride to the office, I replayed
the previous night. It had, quite simply, been fantastic. Hayley has a great
body and knows how to have sex. She had been thoroughly enthusiastic,
knew exactly what she wanted and exactly what I would want her to do.
However, now that I was no longer in her company, I found that I wasn't
thinking about her so much as I was yet again thinking about Amanda.

Fortunately, it was a short drive to my office, so I could not dwell on
the confusing complexities of my desires for very long. I ran up the stairs
to my office. Amanda was sitting at my desk using the computer. 'Good
morning,' I called as I went past her to the kettle and cups in the corner by
the window. 'Do you fancy a tea?'

'Yes, please,' she said nothing else while I filled the kettle and set out
two mugs but was clearly waiting to speak when turned around.

'Everything okay?' I enquired.

'Err, Yes. Only no, sort of. I feel bad about this morning. I had no idea
you would have company. Is that your girlfriend? No, sorry. Forget I
asked. It's none of my business.' Amanda was blushing now. It was the
first time I had seen her flustered. 'Sorry. I'm being odd. Can we just focus
on work?'

114

'The young lady you met is Hayley. I need to tell you that because she works in the coffee shop across the street and you will almost certainly bump into her at some point working here.'

'Oh. Okay.'

'She is not my girlfriend. Actually, I don't know what she is, or how she would class herself if I were to ask her to.' I thought about that for a second myself. 'Perhaps focussing on work is what we should do.' I handed Amanda a mug of tea and went over to see what she was doing on the computer. I didn't want to talk to her about Hayley.

Setting her tea down, Amanda said, 'I have been researching the Phantom, trying to correlate the attacks with other events at the mill or events in the Barker family. I wondered if I might find a link between the chaps that have been injured or killed and something else that was going on at the time. So far nothing, but with one hundred years of history to dredge through it might take a while.'

'Tell me about the attack last night.' I requested.

'As I understand it, a couple of lads saw something and went to investigate what it was. They came across the Phantom going into a building, gave chase and got hurt. One of them has a burn to his upper arm where the Phantom touched him.'

'Really? Is it bad?' I asked.

'Bad enough, I think. He is still in hospital, so we can visit him and get a better account of the events. I got his mobile number and name out of the ladies on reception at the mill. The name is,' I watched as she lifted a piece of paper to read the note on the page underneath, 'Chris Partridge. The other guy got away without being injured but we will need to speak to him as well to corroborate the story or give an alternate account.'

'It sounds like you are on top of everything. What hospital is he in?'

'Dartford general.'

'Okay. Do you want to visit the mill first or the hospital?'

'Brett asked how soon we could start the case. I did not confirm we would take it, I figured I needed to talk to you first, but he is very much expecting us to be back in his office tomorrow morning to discuss the case.'

I took a slurp of tea and let the hot liquid warm my insides for a moment while I thought about it. I didn't like Brett Barker, he a was a classist git, but that was not a good reason not to take his money or to refuse to pursue a potentially prominent case and solve a hundred-year-old mystery. 'Okay,' I concluded. 'I don't think the Phantom case and the death of Mr. Barker are linked. Whoever killed George Barker was not playing at being the Phantom one hundred years ago, and whoever is playing the part of the Phantom now is still operating even though Mr. Barker is dead.

'That makes sense,' Amanda agreed.

I downed the rest of my tea. 'I guess we need to go see the poor chap in hospital, visit Brett Barker to officially accept the case and agree on costs before we start looking into the Phantom properly.'

'Have you given any more thought to hiring an assistant to handle paperwork, emails and phone calls?' she asked.

'I have actually,' I replied. 'I even looked at where to place the advert. The Weald World have a job page on which I can run an advert for free. We can do that now if you like.' I had been considering the merits of an assistant for some time. My initial plan had been to hire a person that could help with research, do some paperwork and sift emails and calls, but then Amanda said she wanted to work for me and suddenly I had a partner. She would share the burden of the growing workload and do the research with me or even have her own cases, so the nature of the assistant role had changed or perhaps increased in its necessity.

Amanda and I spent a few minutes crafting a job description after which we did a quick spell check and sent it to the website. A second or so later a note pinged back to say our advert had been sent for review and would be live within the hour.

Dartford A&E. Sunday, 10th October 1200hrs

'We need to visit the chap in hospital, yes?' Amanda asked.

'That is our natural next step. We are still stumbling around in the dark trying to piece bits together at the moment. Chris Partridge, that was his name, wasn't it?'

'I believe so.'

'He ought to be able to provide us with a new perspective,' I continued. 'He came into direct contact with the Phantom. Physical contact in which he got injured. I want to hear exactly what he saw.'

Amanda had offered to drive, and I saw no reason to argue so we were whizzing up the M2 motorway to Dartford in her nippy little Mini Cooper just a few minutes later. It was the first time I had ever been in a Mini. A fact which I had never given any thought to before, but now struck me as odd given how many of them were on the road. The Mini was a masterpiece of design and a British automobile icon from the sixties. This was the relaunched version that BMW brought out two decades ago. I knew there were several different derivatives available now, but this was the original two-door un-mucked-about-with design and was nearly new. I liked it. It sounded good. It felt, from my passenger seat, as if the steering and handling were crisp and Amanda clearly enjoyed being at the wheel.

'I do almost all my driving around town,' she had said when I asked her about the car. 'So, it rarely gets a decent run. It feels nice to let her stretch her legs.'

'I notice a gym bag on the back seat, do you work out often?' I asked to make conversation.

'Three or four times a week I guess, depending on my shift pattern. They have a small weights room at the station that someone put in years ago, but I go to SupaGym in town. The one by the clock tower.'

'Oh, Yes. I know it. Is it expensive?'

'I don't think so. There are cheaper options but SupaGym has lots of classes at times that suit me, so I think it is my best option. You clearly workout,' she said glancing at me. 'Which gym do you go to?'

'A small place on the Aylesford Industrial Estate called Meatheads. It has nothing fancy and everything I need. The type of gym that puts sawdust on the floor to absorb the blood and sweat.'

'Sounds delightful,' Amanda said while wrinkling her nose in disgust.

'I would love to be able to never go again, but I would be fat within a month.' We continued talking about nothing much at all for a few more minutes.

The hospital Chris Partridge had been taken to was on the outskirts of Dartford where it bordered Crayford and was just a couple of minutes ahead of us now. Amanda put her indicator on and moved to the offramp to leave the bypass. I had not been to Dartford General before, neither had Amanda she said, so we followed the road signs to find first it and then its car park. The car park was a multi-story affair, but we were able to park on the ground floor as there were plenty of parking spaces available.

Inside reception, Amanda showed the middle-aged and rather portly gentleman on reception her police ID and was immediately given the exact whereabouts of the person she wanted to visit. We set off to the burns unit in the direction he had indicated. The hospital was colour coded, the walls of different areas painted to match the colours on the map. We were looking for the red area.

Amanda had helpfully found and printed a picture of him this morning and pulled that from her bag now. We walked along fresh, shiny corridors. Skylights and full-length windows let in plenty of light. There were people bustling in both directions and when we reached an intersection there were people crossing through the flow and getting caught up as they tried to weave between the continuous stream of human traffic. Dartford General was a new, purpose-built hospital with wide corridors and automatic doors. We passed through Radiology and X-ray and then maternity following the signs onwards to our destination. We reached a vaulted atrium where a coffee shop, newspaper and magazine stand and gift shop were located. It was all rather nice I suppose, but it was still a hospital, so unless you were here to have a baby I doubted many came here for joyous events.

We reached the burns unit easily enough, Amanda flashed her ID at the desk once more and was pointed further into the ward.

Chris Partridge was sitting up in bed talking to another man who had his back to us as we approached. Chris was wearing jogging bottoms and a t-shirt, his right arm was bandaged from the elbow upwards, the dressing protruding from his sleeve. He looked up as we approached, and I saw his attention focus on Amanda. His eyes widened slightly, then I saw very visibly his eyes look down from her face to her chest, pause there and then go back to her face. It was something I had never seen before and I wondered what that was like for a woman. I brought his attention back to me.

'Good afternoon, Mr. Partridge. My name is Tempest Michaels, this is my associate Amanda Harper.'

The chap that had been sitting with his back to us turned around and leaned back in his seat, then interrupted me before I could say anything else.

'My Lord. Look, Chris. It's an angel come to take you away.' He was looking Amanda up and down.

'She can take me anywhere she wants,' he replied from the bed. They were both young men, perhaps mid-twenties and full of life. Which is to say, they were acting like lads, full of bravado and ready to outdo any other lads around them. They were not being very gentlemanly. I automatically opened my mouth to berate and belittle them both but caught myself before speaking. Amanda would most likely handle this herself and did not need me.

Looking bored, Amanda leaned forward so that her boobs were right in front of the seated man's face. He would be able to see down her top. She looked across at Chris on the bed.

120

'If you two virgins need to see some tits, then here they are. See them?' The boys were looking a little surprised, but the seated chap had a growing smile on his face. Amanda put a hand out to rest it lightly on the edge of the chair between his legs.

The seated man turned, smiling to his friend on the bed and was about to say something that he undoubtedly thought funny when her hand shot forward and grabbed his scrotum. His smile vanished instantly, replaced by a look of shock and terror.

'What's the matter?' she asked. 'Not had a lady touch you down there before?' she looked across at Chris again. The jovial look had disappeared from his face also. 'Now then, chaps.' The seated man tried to squirm away but stopped as I watched her grip tighten. 'We are going to have a little chat about what happened last night, what you saw etcetera and at no point during our little chat will either one of you look at my tits. Is that clear?'

On the bed, Chris remained silent. In the chair, the chap moved his head to glance across at his friend, probably for moral support but his attention swung immediately back to Amanda when she gave another little squeeze. 'I asked you a question,' she reminded him.

'Yes. Yes! Just please let go.' She didn't. Instead, she looked across at Chris and raised her eyebrows in question. He nodded and was very definitely looking at her face when he did so.

Amanda took a last look down her own top and seeming satisfied stood back up finally releasing her handful of balls.

'So, as I was saying, chaps,' I restarted. 'My name is Tempest Michaels, you seem to have gotten acquainted with my colleague Amanda Harper. We have been engaged by Barker Mill to investigate the Phantom sightings and your assault last night. Kindly sit back and pay attention because we have a few questions.'

'Let's start with your name,' Amanda asked the seated man who was now nursing his testicles.

He looked up. 'Err, Gary Mitchell?' he hazarded as if unsure himself.

'You were with Chris last night, were you not?' she asked

'I was,' he replied. He was a much meeker version of the Gary that had been sitting there when we came in. It was a neat trick, subduing them the way she had. I was impressed but acknowledged that it was not something I could learn. I suspected that if I tried such a tactic a fight would quickly ensue.

For the next forty-three minutes, we both asked the pair questions about what they had seen, what had then happened, how the injury came about and most importantly what they thought they had encountered. We had both looked up at one point and demanded Chris repeat what he had just said.

'I said: it smelled like a girl.'

'In what way did it smell like a girl?' We might be onto something here.

'You know those cheap as anything Katy Price perfumes you can buy in Wilkinsons or the supermarket? Well, she smelled like one of those. I have dated girls that wear them, so I recognised it because you cannot get the smell out of your clothes even after your mum washes them.'

'You think the Phantom is a girl?' I asked.

'Oh. Well, I hadn't thought about it until now.' His face coloured and he paused to scratch his head for a moment while thinking how to answer. Then he looked across at Gary to gauge his opinion.

'No good asking me, mate, I never got close to it. I chased after you when you said you saw it.'

'Gary, did you actually see the Phantom?' I asked.

'Well, no. Not exactly.'

'Yes, you did!' Chris insisted. 'I spotted it by the offices and pointed it out to you and we chased after it as it headed into the pump room.'

'Sorry, mate. You said that you saw it and that was good enough for me at the time, but all I saw was something moving in the dark. It was over one hundred metres away, I couldn't really see what it was.'

Chris looked exasperated. He started waving his injured arm around. 'Then how did I get this?'

It was a really good question and one that I wanted an answer to. 'Amanda would you be so kind as to take Gary for some refreshments?' I wanted to have Chris in isolation for a while. See if I could dig down to the truth. Maybe the wound was self-inflicted, and he was looking for attention and infamy. 'I am sure Gary can regale you with his version of events over a coffee.'

'Come along then, Gary.' Amanda smiled at him and extended her hand for him to take. Gary smiled a big lecherous grin, then remembered his aching testicles and reset his face to neutral. He stood up, making sure he was looking at anything in the room but Amanda's ample chest and followed her, not looking at her bum, back out of the ward.

I took a seat where Gary had been and took my time getting comfortable. I had a feeling that Chris had made the whole thing up. If he had, then he would now be worried about the truth being revealed, so I made him wait. If he was lying he would be squirming inside.

I settled into the chair, arranged my notebook and pen and fixed him with my best anti-nonsense stare. 'Why don't you tell me all about what you think you saw last night and how you came to get the burn on your arm?'

Chris stared at me for a second, I think he could tell I was now dubious about his story, then laid his head back onto the pillow so that he was gazing at the ceiling and I could not see his eyes. Then he began telling me his tale. He had been finishing his shift, but he and Gary had upset Mr. Stewart, their shift supervisor earlier that day so had been put onto cleaning duty. They had been outside sweeping and weeding for an hour after everyone else had finished and gone home. They knew that if they didn't get the job done properly he would just have them back late on Friday which would mess with going to the pub, so they just got on with it.

Heading to his car, Chris had seen, clear as anything, a figure wearing a floor-length black cloak, complete with a hood, coming out of the main office building. It came out of the main doors and turned in the direction of the mill buildings.

He pointed and yelled to Gary and took off towards it. I interrupted him to ask him why. His simple reply was that he saw the Phantom. The Phantom ran from them and headed into the pump room. I would look up where the pump room was later. Chris got there ahead of Gary, but once inside he and Gary could not see the Phantom and could hear nothing but their own breathing and an occasional gurgle from a pipe.

They had elected to split up to search the room. He said the room was really big when I asked him about it. I didn't know what really big meant as big is not exactly a standard unit of measure. Prompting a better description, he said the room was large enough that they had lost sight of each other very quickly once they split up to search it. Chris and Gary had been able to talk to each other though by shouting. At this point, Chris admitted that Gary had asked if he was sure he had seen anything and had suggested they call it a night and get home. Chris said he knew what he had seen and wanted to look a little longer. The pump room was filled with equipment and pipes and had elevated walkways over several levels linked by cat ladders and staircases. He estimated that he had searched for about ten minutes and was about to give up when the attack happened. He was still talking to Gary, so could tell that he was back at the door they had come in through, waiting for him and getting impatient.

The Phantom had struck from behind by whacking him in the back of the head, perhaps with an elbow, but then he had felt blinding pain searing into his right arm where the Phantom had grabbed him. He had screamed in pain and fallen to the ground which was where Gary had found him a few seconds later. When Chris looked around the phantom was gone.

I looked down at my notes. I needed to speak with Amanda to see if Gary had any thoughts on the matter, but my gut reaction was that Chris was making it up and had planned to give himself a cool wound but had got it wrong and really burned his arm. I had asked him some questions which I thought would expose whether he was lying or not, such as how tall it was, did it speak or make a noise, could you see its feet when it was running away from you. Chris though was able to answer all the questions. The Phantom must be about six feet tall he told me because it was silhouetted against the door of the pump room door as it went it and he could gauge the height from that. It had not spoken at any point and it was too dark for him to see its feet. His actual answer was that it appeared to be floating across the ground at speed and he could not hear its footsteps, but I was convinced the answer was an embellishment.

I did have one more question though. 'Chris, you appear to be the first person that has ever come into physical contact with the Phantom and lived. Given your unique perspective, who or what do you think it is?'

'Dude,' he started, fixing me with a serious look, 'I have not the faintest idea.'

I thanked him for his time and left him. I spotted Amanda as soon as I went into the coffee shop area. She was alone at a table at the edge of the coffee shop area and was fiddling with her phone. She looked up as I approached but did not move to get up. I placed myself in the chair opposite her. 'How did it go with Gary? Did he have anything to say that would be of interest?'

'He apologised for ogling me. Said he was just being laddish because he was with his mate and then he asked me out.' Amanda seemed to get propositioned a lot. 'I declined by the way. Otherwise, he had very little to say that was of use. He hadn't seen anything except what he thought was possibly a shadow moving. Chris had shouted something and started running so he had run after him. It was only when they got to the pump room that Chris had briefly explained what he had seen. They went inside and split up and the next thing he knew Chris was yelling. When he found him the shirt he was wearing was smouldering around his right bicep and he was yelling that he had been attacked by the Phantom.' Amanda flicked through her notes to see if there was anything key that she had missed. 'That's about it,' she concluded.

I thought for a moment. The account by Chris was unconvincing but it had been told in a convincing manner. It was mostly corroborated by Gary, so I was willing to believe that Chris had indeed seen a person dressed as the Phantom and had chased after it. The element I was most curious about was how the wound had been inflicted. I had asked Chris about this but all he had been able to tell me was that he had been grabbed around the bicep by a hand that did not feel human, he had said not made of flesh, and a terrible burning sensation had been immediate. He had described the hand as incredibly hot. I mimicked grasping my right bicep with my left hand.

I needed to ask another question and would need to head back to the ward to do so. Before I did though I intended to listen in to the conversation the two lads would have when Gary got back there.

When I had been sitting in the chair next to the bed I had attached a small one-way radio microphone to the underside of the chair. If Gary and Chris had been making the whole thing up, either for attention or for some other reason, the first thing they would do is discuss in hushed tones how well they had kept their story together or variations on that theme. I had the radio thingy linked to an app on my phone which I had produced from my bag and was now opening.

I set the phone on the table between Amanda and I. 'Would you like to hear what the chaps are saying now they are back to together?' I pressed the button that would set the speaker working.

They were laughing when the speaker came to life but then Gary spoke. 'I tell you, mate, I would give my right nut to get my hands on her tits.' I looked up at Amanda and felt my face instantly flush. 'They must be at least a double D. I bet a fella is risking a sprained tongue taking those on.' I stabbed the phone with an embarrassed finger to close the app. Suddenly it was very quiet at our table and I was struggling to find something to say.

Amanda rescued me - sort of. 'Boys talk about tits, Tempest. Boys look at tits, boys think about tits and boys cannot seem to get enough of tits. Tits, titties, tits. Apparently, I have quite the pair.'

126

I figured that what I was supposed to do at this point was agree with her and provide a seriously manly comment about boys to make me seem so much more the mature gentleman and not one of the lads. However, my head was completely filled with images of tits now. I was almost straining the muscles in my neck to ensure I did not glance at hers, but then conscious that I was not looking at them my rebellious libido insisted I try to remember exactly what they looked like. I have no idea what they look like I argued because she is always dressed. Ha, ha. My libido replied and instantly supplied an imagined image of Amanda in black lingerie so insignificant I could probably swallow it without needing a glass of water. Her fabulous breasts were barely contained by the cups of her bra and were heaving with every breath.

'Are you okay, Tempest?' Amanda asked snapping me back to reality. 'You went very quiet and still, but your lips were moving.'

I had an erection. Mr. Wriggly was very much ready for action – gun loaded and looking for someone to shoot. 'Err, yes. Sorry. I was, um, thinking about a theory I have.' Cool and suave I was not. Flustered and certain that she could see my penis straining against the front of my trousers I needed to distract myself, but her breasts were still right there in front of me. 'I have a question about the wound. I want to see if they took a picture of it. Won't be a moment.' With that, I grabbed my bag and swung speedily out of my chair so that I was facing away from her and had my bag hanging over my groin. I did not want some child pointing at my pants and asking, "What's wrong with that man, mummy?"

I made it back to the ward without incident and by then the head of steam Mr. Wriggly had built up had dissipated. Chris did indeed have a picture of the wound on his phone and it answered a question. The handprint was quite clear, I could see four fingers and a thumb. It had been a right hand that had grabbed him, which meant that it could not have been self-inflicted. I thanked Chris for his time and for sending me the picture, which might prove to be a key piece of evidence later. I retrieved the radio piece from under Gary's chair. They both looked thoroughly shocked that I had bugged their conversation. I would play it back later to make sure that they had not discussed anything other than

Amanda's amazing chest, but I suspected that I would hear nothing of worth.

I met Amanda back at the coffee shop and we headed out of the hospital.

There was silence in the car for a minute while neither of us spoke. I checked my watch: 1503hrs. My stomach rumbled meaningfully and quite audibly in the quiet of the car. I put my hand to it in a reflex reaction as if the action would quieten it.

'Are you okay?' Amanda enquired.

'Just hungry. I skipped a couple of meals and appear to now be running on empty.' Hayley had ruined my dinner plans last night, not that I was going to lodge a complaint. Then Amanda showed up this morning and breakfast had not been achieved either. I could not remember the last time I had skipped two meals, but it must have occurred back when I was in the Army and such things could just happen because you were cut off from an easy to access food supply.

'Okay,' Was all Amanda had to say in reply. I guess it was obvious why I had missed my meals and she was delicately avoiding the subject.

I took a bottle of water from my bag, drank a large draught from it and hoped it would be sufficient for now.

The Office. Sunday, 10th October 1537hrs

Amanda had dropped me back at the office and headed off home. She was tired from working two jobs and I expected that in the same position I would also want to have a bath and put my feet up. I considered briefly going via the coffee shop opposite my office as my mental clock told me Hayley would be working now, but the consideration started an internal debate about what was the cool thing to do. If I went to see her today was I a bit desperate for attention or recognition? Hayley was quite clear that she did not want a boyfriend, but was that just what a girl said when she was being cool about it all and now that we had slept together was the situation changed? I honestly had no idea and was giving myself a headache trying to work out the permutations. I gave up and went home for a cup of tea.

As I pulled up to my house, my watch claimed it was 1537hrs, my stomach told me that breakfast was quite some time ago. Then I remembered that I had missed breakfast because Hayley had been there, and my brain had lost control of my motor function when Mr. Wriggly grabbed the wheel and steered it towards Boobyville.

Then I wondered if Hayley was still here, which caused a definite twitch from just below my belt. I looked back at the road but could not see a car I did not recognise. Nevertheless, I called out as I went through the door just in case.

No answer was returned. However, I was met at the door as always by a tangle of black as tan as my two Dachshunds fought to get to me. I stepped over them to get into the house then knelt to fuss them both. Bull climbed onto my knee in a bid to lick my face, so I offered him my chin and was rewarded with the warm, damp flannel that was his tongue. Always the chin, never the lips, as a Dachshund will happily lick your teeth given the chance. Dozer had flipped over onto his back, so I could scratch his belly. No matter whether my life was stormy or calm, these two were a reassuring rock of love that I could anchor myself to.

I stood up again and let them into the back garden, whereupon they spotted a cat walking along the back fence and tore across the lawn as fast as their little legs could propel them, barking all the way. The cat largely ignored them but did at least pause to make sure they had not learned to climb the fence since yesterday. I left them to voice their displeasure at the intruder and went to my kitchen to find the kettle.

With the kettle getting excited behind me. I opened the fridge, snagged the carton of milk for my tea and had a rummage. I needed something for lunch. Electing to make a hearty vegetable omelette, I took spinach, mushrooms, peppers etcetera from the drawer in my fridge and carried them to the counter.

Was that a buttock print I could see?

The counter had been put to alternate use this morning and not been touched since. I would not call myself a clean freak, others might, but I kept the house neat and tidy and above all sanitary, so the veggies went back into the fridge with a groan from my belly. My hunger would have to wait a few seconds longer while I cleaned the surface.

Thirty minutes later a nearly clean plate was going into the dishwasher and food was no longer a primary demand. The dogs had come back inside, eaten a few slices of carrot as a treat and taken themselves off to bed once more.

It was 1621hrs. I had the evening to myself. I found it to be one of the great pleasures of being single and having my own place. I could do what I want when I want. Outside it was just beginning to get dark. Full dark was more than an hour away, but I was a fan of the autumn twilights, so I called the dogs, inviting them to come for a walk. In response, I got the usual silence. Rather than call them again I took a pace to my right and opened the fridge. I could not tell whether it was the displacement of air as the door opened that they react to, or the sound of the light bulb in the fridge coming on, but they could hear it over the TV, a thunderstorm and perhaps even Armageddon. Even when fully asleep, the two Dachshunds would appear if I opened the fridge, so half a heartbeat later eight paws skidded to a stop at my feet. Chuckling to myself, I took their bowls from the cupboard, gave them a slightly early dinner then snagged their collars and leads.

Outside in the cool air, I took them on the long, northern route out of the village that would sweep around the top edge of the vineyards. There were still blackberries in the hedgerow. I stopped to pick and eat a few while the dogs snuffled around my feet. The grape vines themselves had been picked clean recently by the owners. The grapes no doubt already on the way to becoming wine.

On my way back into the village, I considered the merits of a Sunday evening drink at the pub. I had not been to the gym for a couple of days, so I felt that I really should find the time to fit in a decent workout tonight. The truth though, was that I really didn't want to. I was tired. I recognised that I was making excuses, but I still wanted to have a drink in a quiet relaxed atmosphere, instead of an exhausting hour of lifting weights. I was still arguing with myself when I got to the pub on my way home. Bull and Dozer pulled me across the carpark and I failed to resist.

The pub was almost empty. A few regulars nodded a greeting as I went in. The landlord was already reaching for a glass before I got to the bar, so I needed only to nod as he indicated the tap for my usual beverage. The cold liquid was exchanged for a crisp ten pounds note and I suddenly realised just how ready for a drink I was. I downed over half the pint in my first draught. I took a packet of pork scratchings to share with the dogs and settled into a sagging, but comfortable sofa in the far corner of the pub.

Using my phone, I attended to a piece of business I might otherwise forget and sent an invitation email to the list of friends Rachael had sent me. It was an easy task, but the message was sadly lacking in any real detail as I had yet to book a venue. Lacking that particularly important piece of information, I instead requested that they leave a hole in their Saturday early afternoon and advised that the baby shower would be at a venue in Rochester.

Ninety minutes, three pints and a second bag of pork scratchings later I was still berating myself as I ran a bath. It was 1907hrs. I was going to get a bath, watch a movie on the sofa with the two dogs and get an early night. I would go to the gym in the morning.

Self-Flagellation. Monday, 11th October 0530hrs

I had not set an alarm, I never do, but I awoke at almost exactly 0530hrs just as I had planned. I was still berating myself for the extra calories I had taken in the previous evening. Pointless calories in the form of beer which were completely counterintuitive to my healthy diet and exercise regime. I was about to get up and spend an hour burning calories at the gym but considered myself already in deficit through my poor choices last night.

I had packed my gym bag before I went to bed and had laid out my clothes ready to go. I got out of bed determined to hammer out a really good workout this morning.

An hour and a half later I was coming back through my front door exhausted but elated having achieved that aim. As punishment for the beer, I had performed one of my most brutal routines. I simply selected ten exercises that I could perform sequentially without a break and which would work every body part. I then performed as many sets as I could. Between each sequence of one hundred exercises, ten sets of ten exercises, I would give myself a break to take on water and wipe off the sweat. I had managed seven complete sets this morning, almost seven hundred exercises as I had started to fail towards the end of the last one. Then I had promptly collapsed on the gym floor in a heap of panting jelly. A few of the regular gym goers, people I saw most weeks, had observed my routine and nodded in acknowledgement of someone really going for it.

Arriving inside my house, I had hustled to the loo with almost two litres of water planning its escape route from my bladder. It was 0715hrs as I scooped the dogs from the top of the stairs and sent them to do their business in the garden. Watching them disappear across the lawn, I noted that the grass was getting long and there were a lot of leaves down. I made a mental note to find some time for gardening soon.

In the kitchen, I prepared a healthy breakfast using vegetables, fruit, and eggs then headed for the shower.

Amanda and I were seeing Brett Barker at 1030hrs, so I had plenty of time before I needed to leave the house. We were meeting at the office in Rochester. I was teaching myself to call it *the* office and not *my* office now that there were two of us working there. By 0843hrs I had tidied my house, put some laundry on, walked the dogs and driven to work. I was feeling alert and empowered by my early morning workout and very much ready to catch a phantom and solve the mystery of George Barker's death. Whether there was any link between the two I did not know. It was not something I would rule out, but it certainly felt like I was getting a two-for-one deal as both cases involved the same people, same business, and the same locations.

I opened the door that leads up the stairs to my office then changed my mind and went to get coffee. Yesterday I had avoided going to the coffee shop through confusion about how Hayley would view my presence there so soon after spending the night together. Today though it was a working day and thus completely normal that I would be there buying coffee. Content that I had it all worked out, I went in.

I could not see her behind the counter though and as I queued for several minutes to place my order she did not appear. I ordered coffee for both Amanda and I then asked Sharon, my server if Hayley was indeed working today.

'Nah, got the day off,' she replied without looking up. Sharon handed me the beverages and moved on to the next customer.

I left the coffee shop and crossed the street. As I neared the office, Amanda was just getting out of her car.

'Good morning,' she called.

'Hey there,' I replied holding up her coffee cup. 'I got you coffee.'

'Ooh, super,' She took the offered cup from me and tentatively sipped the hot, bitter liquid.

'Our advert for an admin assistant went live already. I checked this morning.'

'Yes, I saw that too,' she replied. 'I wonder if anyone will apply.'

'I guess we shall see.' The conversation had taken us up the stairs and into the office. I checked my watch: Bang on 0900hrs. 'We should not wait too long before setting off. The roads into Dartford could be hell at this time of day on a Monday.'

Amanda had taken the lid off her cup and was blowing on the liquid to cool it. Her luscious lips bore a faint trace of pink lipstick and they formed a perfect 'O' as she did so. I had to look away for fear I might just lean in and kiss her.

She sipped at the coffee and put the lid back on, content that it was now at drinking temperature.

'Shall we go then?' she asked.

Neither one of us had even put our bags down.

'We can do. You will need to drive though. My car does not have cup holders.'

'Really?' she asked, her brow wrinkling. 'What kind of car does not have cup holders?'

'Sleek, sexy, German sports cars I guess.'

She shrugged and fished for her keys while turning to go. I locked up and followed her down the stairs. We got into her car, placed our coffees in the very convenient cup holders and off we went back to Barker Mill.

Barker Mill Again. Monday, 11ᵗʰ October 1012hrs

We arrived back at the Mill at 1012hrs. Today though, in contrast to any days before it, the car park had in it two news crews with vans and all the antenna and paraphernalia needed for outside broadcasting. I wanted to avoid the press if I could, so we parked in the exact same spot as we had the day before, grabbed our bits and dashed into reception where the girl from Friday was stood talking to the two ladies behind the desk.

This was my third visit in the last few days, so I knew the drill and just got on with filling in the visitors' book and taking my visitors' badge. I had to ask Amanda for her car registration number for the form although I had no idea what they used the information for.

The young lady escorted us out of reception via the back door and across the yard, sticking to all the yellow walkways, then into the building that housed the main offices. The door to Brett Barker's office was closed again but as we approached I could hear him shouting at someone.

The young lady made an apologetic face and we waited outside until we heard him slam the phone down a few seconds later. She knocked, he spoke, we went in. He looked flustered and guiltily I liked it.

'Please come in,' he ushered with his left hand to the two chairs we had sat in yesterday. 'Work stuff,' he said gesturing to the phone by way of explanation.

Amanda took the chair nearest the desk, but I picked the other one up and moved it across to the other side of the room, so we now formed a vee in front of his desk and he would have to swing his head back and forth to speak with us like he was watching tennis. I wondered if he would object, at which point I would have claimed a headache and wanted my back to the light from his window. However, if the change bothered him he gave no indication.

'Mr. Barker,' I began, all professional polish applied. 'I believe you wish to engage our services to catch the Phantom.'

135

He squirmed a little in his seat. 'Yes, yes I do. But look, I wish to go on record stating that there is no bloody Phantom haunting this steel mill. However, there is someone playing bloody silly games and I want them caught.'

'You think it a simple act of vandalism from a member of staff? Or could this be something more sinister than that?' I asked.

'Such as what?'

'Are there rival mills that want you out of business? Is the sabotage to your equipment actually to cover up a different crime?' I watched as his face coloured slightly. It was momentary, and I had to commend him for his control. Yet the involuntary reaction was definitely there.

'No. I mean, I don't know,' he stuttered. 'This is why I need you to investigate and find the culprit, the criminal. Whatever. That is what you do, isn't it?'

'The police do not have the resources to commit to crimes of this nature,' Amanda said.

'So, in essence, yes. This is what we do,' I answered. 'I will find your Phantom, Mr. Barker. But I will need full access to freely move around every area of the Mill and may need to bring in a team. Can you make arrangements for this?'

He reached for his phone and when a voice answered he instructed them to fetch someone to his office. He had said the name, but I did not catch it. He put the phone down, the conversation clearly over and looked back at me. 'You will need to inform me when you plan to be here so that I can alert security.'

I spent the next few minutes going through my standard explanation of fees and expenses. I made it clear that the very nature of the case and its mysterious circumstances made the length of time it would take to reach a conclusion unpredictable. This was the first time Amanda had heard my speech and I noticed that she was taking hurried notes.

'Is there anything else I need to know, Mr. Barker? Anything you think might be relevant? Any suspicion you may have as to who might be responsible or why?'

He gave it a second or so with his head down in thought. His decision though was that there was nothing he could think of. I noted that I could not see what his face was doing when he put his head down.

I slipped my notebook and pen back into my bag and got up to leave. Amanda did likewise, and Brett came around his desk once more to shake our hands.

'I wonder if I might detain you for a moment, Miss Harper?' he said. She looked at me instead of answering, I was not sure what I was supposed to say. I didn't own her, and she didn't need my protection.

'I'll be outside.' I said over my shoulder as I went out the door. Brett closed it behind me.

A moment later the door opened again, and Amanda came out. I glanced in the room to see Brett retreating behind his desk then got moving down the corridor as Amanda had not waited for me and I was several paces behind.

Desperately curious about what Brett had wanted to see her in private for, I kept my mouth shut and played it cool, hoping she would tell me anyway.

Cool guy, that's me alright.

Putting my phone away in my bag, I walked into a doorframe.

'Are you alright?' Amanda asked, a quizzical eyebrow raised.

'Yup,' I was rubbing my head where I had hit it.

'Brett asked me out,' Amanda informed me matter-of-factly. 'I am not sure why he felt he needed to do that in private.'

Same reason I would, I thought. 'So that when you knock him back he does not have to have others see it happen.'

'I said yes.'

Nuts.

'But only after the cases are concluded. He is one of the primary suspects after all.'

'That he is,' I agreed, hoping desperately that he was guilty.

'Cute though.'

I hated him.

We exited the building on our way back to the car and went back through reception, so we could hand over our badges and sign out once more in the visitors' book. I had forgotten about the press though and two steps into reception we were spotted and then recognised. I watched the realisation spread as the first person saw me, nudge the chap next to him who then grabbed the lady with the microphone in her hand and suddenly they swung into action as one lump because they suddenly had a new angle to their story. It took two seconds and I had nowhere to hide.

'Tempest Michaels,' yelled the lady in the suit with the microphone, trying to get my attention as I returned my badge. 'Tempest Michaels,' she called again when I did not instantly respond.

I handed the badge to the lady behind reception, noting that it was the same lady every time I came in and wondered how many hours she worked. I resigned myself to my fate and turned around to face the reporter. Over her shoulder, I saw that the other crew of reporters were outside the glass front of reception and had also spotted me.

'Yes. It is I,' I said with a touch of flamboyance. I had no idea how to handle reporters, so I was guessing that if I gave them some cooperation they might treat me kindly. I was probably fooling myself. 'How may I assist you?'

The microphone was thrust in my face while a chap with a boom brought another one to hover above my face and a third chap with a shoulder mounted camera lined up to shoot the event. 'Are you here to catch the Phantom?' the lady asked. She was mid to late twenties and quite petite. Her attire was camera ready business suit and good coat and she was attractive while wearing minimal makeup.

'You have me at a loss, you appear to know my name, but forgot to introduce yourself.'

'Sarah Gainsworth, Channel Six news. Are you investigating the Phantom, Mr. Michaels?' She appeared to be all about hurrying and I then realised why: The other team of reporters was setting up now just behind them and she wanted an exclusive.

'I can confirm that I have been engaged to investigate the Phantom of Barker Mill,' I answered calmly.

'What do you think the Phantom is?' she asked next.

'I expect the Phantom is a man,' my simple answer. 'There will be no ghostly apparition at the conclusion to this case, just a man in a costume.'

'Then how do you explain the one-hundred-year history of sightings, attacks, and unexplained events?'

'It is quite simple. Someone partly glimpses a figure, there is a strange or unexplained incident, a shadow is seen for a moment only and can be anything. The legend of the Barker Mill Phantom is just one example of people making an explanation for something they have seen and not been able to explain. The Loch Ness Monster is perhaps the best-known example of this phenomenon.'

The second squad shoved their version of Sarah Gainsworth forward and a fresh microphone was thrust under my chin. 'How soon will you catch the Phantom?' she asked.

I flapped my mouth for a second trying to form my next sentence... and then a fight broke out. Looking back, I am not sure exactly what the catalyst was. I think one cameraman got in front of the other cameraman, and when one shoved the other, someone else got knocked and it pretty much descended into a pitched battle from there.

I felt a tug on my shirt sleeve and turned to see Amanda. She was pulling me away from the action and any foolish idea I might have to sort it out.

'Let's go,' she mouthed at me. So, we did. Leaving the camera crews to their business.

Amanda ran for her car, plipping it open as she went, and we piled in. I don't know if evasive driving is standard police training, but she nailed the pedal and had us out of the car park like she was driving a stunt car in the Italian Job. Half a mile later she calmed it down and settled in with the traffic on the bypass around Dartford.

'That ever happen to you before?' she asked.

'Goodness me, which bit? The crazy fighting to get to me? The being recognised? Or the being interviewed by the press? Because no to the first two and yes to the last. That was something of a surprise.'

'Okay,' she said, eyes on the road. 'I supposed your picture got put about quite a bit last week with the vampire thing.'

'I assume that is why they recognised me.'

'Something to be prepared for in future I guess.'

Publicity. I read once that there was no such thing as bad publicity, but I doubted that was actually true. We fell into silence which extended for a few minutes before I felt the need to strike up a conversation.

'You have a shift this afternoon, do you not?'

'I do. Three o'clock to midnight.' The hours sounded decidedly unfriendly to me.

'Do you want to drop me back at the office? I will get stuck into the Phantom case I think.'

'What will you do?' she asked.

'I am not sure. There is something screwy going on at the mill, but unlike many of my cases, there is no obvious explanation that I can see yet. This will all be the work of one person, almost certainly someone motivated to put the mill out of business or something. It could be someone with a grudge against the Barker family. I believe I will need to stake out the mill itself at night, my hope with that strategy is that I will get lucky and catch someone in the act. But I will be interviewing a lot of staff in a bid to expose any little secrets, get a general impression of how the staff feels – the underlying current if you like. I think I will start though with Owen Larkin. Something about him is off so I will watch him for a while.'

'He was not telling us the truth, that is for sure,' Amanda agreed.

'I also need to keep going with the investigation into the death of George Barker. We are being paid to find out whether he did die of natural causes and what part the Phantom might have played, so I will be making daily reports to Mrs. Barker.'

'What is your gut telling you? Was he murdered?'

'Yes, I think so. Quite cleverly though and I don't yet have the slightest idea how. I cannot work out if the burnt handprint on the doorframe of his office is a red herring or if it means something. It is the bit that I cannot fit to anything else. Was it intentional and left there by the killer? Or opportunistic and left there by someone acting independently? Or did someone leave it there as deliberate misdirection?'

'The coroner recorded the death as natural causes. You will need a solid case to prove otherwise.'

'I have no doubt you are right. Why was he not taking his heart meds though? He had a bad heart and a stressful, demanding job. It could be called suicide if he was doing it intentionally.'

'One has to ask who had most to benefit from his death. Motivation and opportunity will guide us, just the same as it will in the Phantom case.'

'I agree. That puts your future boyfriend Brett firmly in the frame though.'

Amanda turned her head to look at me. Her expression was surprise mixed with displeasure. She was reacting to me referring to Brett as her future boyfriend and she was right. I was being childish.

'Sorry.' I said, looking at her now instead of the road ahead of us. 'That was daft. I don't know why I said it.'

'Tempest.'

'Yes?'

'I have a question.'

'Okay.'

'Do you fancy me?' The question was asked softly like she was trying to be kind to a small child and extract a truth they might not give up if they thought it would land them in trouble.

My face coloured. I had no idea how to answer the question. I wanted to blurt out the truth: that I was utterly, utterly besotted by her, but I couldn't get my lips to move.

'I ask because I saw that you have me listed on your phone as PC Hotstuff.'

Oh, God.

'And I catch you looking at me – like, a lot.'

Ground swallow me now.

I was staring at the carpet trying to form a coherent sentence. Beside me in the driver's seat, both physically and metaphorically, Amanda kept quiet and waited for me to answer.

I finally found some gumption. 'I. I, ah. The PC Hotstuff thing I put into my phone when I didn't know your name. I never got around to changing it.' This bit was true. 'But... I find you attractive. It would be ridiculous for me to deny it, I guess. I am a single heterosexual man and you are a very attractive single woman and, honestly, it didn't help when you kissed me.'

'I kissed you?' she was frowning, trying to remember having done so.

'In my house. In front of my mother. Remember?'

'Oh. Oh, yes. But that was just a peck on the lips to trick your mother.'

Try telling Mr. Wriggly that.

'I am a man. We are easily confused.' I was still struggling to express myself but needed to regain some control of the situation. 'Look. This is not going to be an issue. I had a totally normal reaction to meeting an attractive woman. We work together now. We didn't then. Things have changed.'

'Are you attracted to... sorry, I cannot remember her name. The girl from the coffee shop.'

'Hayley? Mr. Wriggly is.'

'Mr. Wriggly?'

Oh, my Lord I just said that out loud.

'Who is...' she tailed off as her cheeks started to flush. 'Oh. Silly question,' she said putting two and two together. 'I have never heard of one called that before.'

I considered just getting out of the car. We were doing seventy miles per hour, but it still seemed to be a better option than staying where I was.

'It won't be a problem,' I said again.

The rest of the journey was quiet and uncomfortable. As she dropped me off by my car we both sort of mumbled a goodbye and avoided looking at one another. She did not look back as she drove off. I stood in the car park pondering my life. I would not indulge myself enough to allow self-pity in, but I was a little miffed at how unable I was to manage something as simple as my own love life. I had finally ended my dry spell only hours ago. The woman involved was an absolute delight, but even trying my damnedest, I could not shift my infatuation with Amanda. I had intended to keep it under wraps, but she was savvy enough to see through me. Perhaps though, what I thought passed for calm, suaveness came across as dribbling stupidity to Amanda.

Amanda was… I didn't even have the words. There were women everywhere and she stood out like a beacon in the dark among them. She could have any man she wanted, and I suppose Brett Barker was proving that point. He was better looking than me, a little younger, a little trimmer and a multi-millionaire with his own helicopter. He probably had his own plane and private island as well. It was a package I could not compete with. Finding evidence to prove he had killed his grandfather might not make Amanda fall into my arms but it felt like a good idea anyway.

I headed up to my office. I was going to get my teeth into this case and crack it. I was going to put thoughts of Amanda out of my mind and I was going to be the man I wanted to be, dammit. Then maybe I would deserve Amanda.

I sat at my desk and plotted a brief plan of what I would do for the next few days. The plan would be reactive depending on what I found out along the way.

My first task was to stake out Owen Larkin. Then tonight, I would stake out the Mill. Tomorrow, I would meet with Mrs. Barker and ask her about the other person her husband considered as the alternative heir to the Mill.

I checked my watch, did some mental calculation, and headed home to walk the dogs.

Staking out Owen Larkin. Monday, 11th October 1402hrs

I parked my car across the street from Owen Larkin's house and wondered, not for the first time if my car was too distinctive for being unobtrusive. Bright red, sleek and sporty, the 2009 Porsche Boxster S with a full Porsche body kit and a big spoiler on its back end, was a car I would glance at or would remember having seen. Maybe I needed a Ford or a Vauxhall so that I could blend in better. Too late now though, so I sat in my car and watched his house.

This was not my first stake out, but I had only felt the need to commit to them a handful of times before. I was thankful for this as they are boring, and I have a natural inclination to go to sleep, making the very act of staking someone or somewhere out quite pointless. However, there was something off about Owen Larkin and I wanted to devote some time to watching him.

His car was parked on the road in front of his house. I had found out what car he owned by getting Amanda to do a quick search. The police have access to some very useful information. If his car was there, I expected that he would be also but there was nothing happening, so I waited.

To pass the time, I called Frank.

'Tempest,' he answered. 'Unexpected pleasure. What can I do for you?'

'Good afternoon, Frank. What do you know about the Phantom of Barker Mill?' I asked.

'Ooh, research,' he responded excitedly. 'It is not a subject I have read much about although it does appear in a few books I have on my shelf. Britain's most haunted buildings by Edgar Toomly has a section about it. I shall see what can find and get back to you.'

'Thank you, Frank.'

'Will you be in later?'

'I'm not sure what my movements might be, so you will be best to call first.'

Frank disconnected, and I went back to staring out of my window hopelessly hoping something would happen. I took to theorising what might have happened when there had been a Phantom attack. Old Sam told me about his mate Barry and Mr. Miller the shift supervisor. That particular incident was over fifty years ago now, so the trail was quite cold, but Old Sam's mate might still be alive and able to answer questions. I doubted I would be able to delve much further back than that and still be able to find persons to interview so it was my oldest available incident and, as such, formed a start point of sorts.

The Phantom was either shadows or superstition or more likely it had started out as a shadow, a half-seen something that an excitable individual had then embellished to create a fanciful story. It might have started as a bit of a laugh but from it, the story of the Phantom had grown and soon it was a popular way to explain mistakes: What happened to this broken equipment? Oh, it must have been the Phantom. The individual that had broken it thus gets off scot free. But after that, I felt it entirely plausible that people had used the story of the Phantom to cover up more sinister events. If you had a love rival and wanted them out of the way you could saw through some walkway bolts and then arrange for the intended victim to go across the walkway. Would anyone even look at whether there was a culprit? Or would the Phantom be instantly blamed by one and all?

One stage further was to assume that people might dress up as the Phantom. It was described in very loose terms after all - cloaked figure all in black. Not hard to replicate. Satisfied that I had fleshed out some basic ideas for how the Phantom sightings had stretched over a century, I glanced down at the clock. I had been staking out Owen Larkin's house for twelve minutes. It felt like three hours.

Two more minutes dragged by slowly.

'Stuff this,' I said out loud and turned on the ignition. I checked the road before pulling out to see there was a car approaching. I recognised the driver. It was Owen Larkin. I had not considered that he might have more than one car.

I slunk down a little in my seat, turned off the ignition and watched. The car went past mine and on further down the road until the driver found a parking space large enough to accommodate his car. A few seconds later he emerged onto the pavement and walked briskly in my direction. He had his phone to his right ear and was talking loudly and with great animation. He was clearly agitated.

As I listened, I realised he was talking to Brett Barker. It was obvious in fact because he referred to him by name more than once.

'It wasn't me, Brett. I didn't go to the mill on Saturday night.'

This was getting interesting. As he passed me by and went up his driveway I eased out of my car keeping as quiet as I could. I was wearing brogues that would make too much noise on the road and paths, so I slipped them off and deposited them in my car, then crossed the road keeping low in just my socks.

Owen Larkin was good enough to have grown a hedge that shielded me from view but allowed noise to penetrate. Overhearing his conversation was easy. Then I heard the door open and as I peered through the trees I could see Owen was stood halfway through his door. He was listening to Brett on the other end of the call again.

'Yes.'

A pause while he listened

'Make sure Furnace B is out of action.

A pause.

'Ok. I'll do it tonight.'

A pause.

'Yes. You told me that already.'

A pause.

'I don't think we need to worry about Tempest Michaels. He clearly has no idea what happened to your grandfather.' Then Owen laughed. A shared joke of some kind. 'Well, your grandfather had it coming, but there is no chance they will ever tie it to you.'

This was solid gold!

'Okay. I'll see you tomorrow.'

A pause.

'Yes.' Then he disconnected. I was still crouching behind a bush.

'What are you doing?' asked a voice from behind me. The voice belonged to a little old lady walking her equally old Jack Russell. I turned in horror at the question. It was loud enough for Owen to have heard and through the tiny gaps in his hedge, I could see him looking in my direction now. He knew my voice! I could not dare to answer the lady. It seemed rude but, in my hesitation, Owen appeared to be moving back towards the street from his front door.

Needing to move fast and not sure how to do so without exposing myself, I took a few fast steps and dived through the neat hedge of his next-door neighbour. I came to rest just as I heard heavy footsteps hit the pavement where I had been. I held my breath, waiting for Owen to spot me, finally exhaling thirty seconds later when I heard the front door close. The old lady had found me boring thankfully and had gone on her way.

I needed to get up and get moving, the full realisation of what I had just heard now hitting me. Owen Larkin *was* the Phantom, he had been guilty all along and his actions were being orchestrated by Brett Barker himself. Not only that but he had suggested that Brett was guilty of his grandfather's murder. I didn't know what they were up to with all the Phantom nonsense, but Owen was going to be at the Mill tonight to perform some task at furnace B. Now that the street was quiet again I risked a glance over the short hedge I had hidden behind to make sure

Owen was not looking out his front window. I could neither see nor hear anyone moving, so I got up, maintained a crouch until I was back out onto the street then ran across the road and dived into my car.

Tea and Biscuits Monday, 11th October 1607hrs

The mill was so vast I needed everyone I could get my hands on to help me cover it if we were to catch Owen Larkin in the act. On my way home, I had called Big Ben and Amanda and then Jagjit and Basic and finally Frank. They were all up for a bit of Ghostbusting and Frank had assured me Poison would be coming too. The exception was Amanda who was on shift tonight. I called her, not because I wanted to see if she could join us, but because I specifically didn't want to call her. It felt cowardly to avoid speaking with her now, so I had set my jaw and made the call. I told her what I had heard and what I planned to do. Surprisingly though, Amanda questioned whether going into the mill to catch Owen was a good idea.

She also could not believe that Brett was behind the crimes. 'Brett hired us, Tempest.'

'I cannot explain his strategy, Amanda. However, I heard what I heard. Owen is hitting the mill tonight on the instruction of Brett Barker.'

'Are you going to clear it with anyone that you will be at the mill tonight? You cannot ask for Brett's permission to be there.'

'I don't want people to know we are coming. I do not know who else is involved so I cannot speak to anyone. Except maybe Mrs. Barker.'

'Well look, Tempest. Basically, if you do not have permission to be on the premises you will be breaking and entering. Even if you do not break anything in the process.'

'Understood. I think you are worrying needlessly. If we catch Owen Larkin the Phantom case will be sewn up – case solved in record time. Faced with taking the blame himself, Owen will implicate Brett and I expect to be able to ascertain then whether Mr. George Barker was murdered and how.'

'Tempest, I am advising against this course of action.'

I was struggling for words. I was going. I knew it was the right thing to do and my best chance to catch the man responsible. Catch Owen sabotaging the mill and dressed as a Phantom and there would be little he could do to wiggle free.

'I fail to see the flaw in my logic, Amanda. I will call you when we catch him.' I heard Amanda sigh at the other end of the line. She had no further warnings to give though so she wished me luck, which sounded quite forced and false and she disconnected.

I counted my team. I had seven live bodies. It was far too few, but it was what I had.

I had a stack of simple two-way radios that I had bought from a sale of Army goods more than a decade ago. At the time, I thought I might just be able to flog them on for a profit as they had been virtually giving them away but had never actually got around to doing so. Now they were in a box in my loft gathering dust and should only require a charge to make them functional.

The loose plan was to get to the mill early, spread out with large fields of vision around and between the various building so we could watch most entry points and thus spy the perpetrator arriving or leaving. Brett had told Owen he wanted it done tonight which to me meant after dark when the mill was shut down and there was no one there. As a former employee, Owen would know his way around the mill and probably had been given keys or passes or whatever by Brett so that he could get in. I was making assumptions, but they felt sound.

Catching him in the act, together with my testimony that I had overheard Brett issuing him with instruction to sabotage equipment, ought to be sufficient to wrap up the case. However, I expected that Owen would cave in and give us the full story. Better yet, Amanda still had her police ID and was still actually a police officer, so could arrest him and hand him over to the local police once we had what information we needed. What would the full story be though? Had they also conspired to kill the late George Barker also? Honestly, at this point, I still had no idea how they had achieved it, although I could easily convince myself the two crimes were connected and perpetrated by the same person or persons. It would be nice to wrap up both cases together and get a fat cheque from

Mrs. Barker. Hold on though, Brett had taken the firm on to catch the Phantom. When I proved that he was orchestrating the Phantom's actions would I still get paid? Who would I send the invoice to? You should have taken a fee upfront, Tempest. Silly boy.

Never mind though. A case is a case and I wanted to solve this one.

I was nearing my house and felt the usual elation I get when I can feel a case coming together. I had never expected to find solving silly mysteries so gratifying.

I turned the final corner into my street and saw my parent's car parked in front of my house. This was not particularly unusual, they lived only a few miles away and liked to borrow the dogs to go for a walk in the countryside. I had given them a key when I moved in, so on occasion, which is to say every other week or so, they would just turn up. If I was in, we would have a cup of tea and a chat and we might all go out for a walk together. If I was out, as I had been when they arrived today, they would simply take the dogs and head off into the local countryside by themselves. I was being a bit too generous there. More typically mother would spend half an hour weeding my garden, so she could moan at me for not staying on top of it and then she would take the dogs for a walk and would return via the village pub for an industrial strength gin.

I parked beside their car and went inside. In a rare change from the usual, no dogs came rushing to greet me. I went to the kitchen window and peered around the back garden. Since they were not there either, my parents must be out walking them and would return soon enough. I flicked the kettle on to make myself a cup of tea and headed to the loft.

I believed that I knew where the box of radios was in my loft, but I was wrong, and it took five minutes of searching under other items to reveal their location. I bumped my head twice on wooden trusses during my rummage and found an old Play Station 2 that I had not seen in years but brought out of the attic with me anyway. It would be fun to play some of the old games on it, maybe have a lad's night with Mortal Kombat and Need for Speed. I took it and the radios back downstairs and set the kettle to boil again.

While the tea infused, I dusted the radios off and plugged each one into the base charging unit I had got with it. In all, I had twelve radios and eleven of them showed the little red light to indicate they were charging but not charged. They would display a green light when they were fully charged, which if my memory was correct, would take about three hours. I poked the twelfth radio with my technology ignorant fingers, but it steadfastly refused to be raised from its dormant state.

Behind me, the front door opened as my parents returned with the dogs. They all spotted me at once, the little dog's tails prescribing a fast arc as they strained at their leads to get to me.

'Hiya, kid,' my dad called through.

'Hello, Father. Hello, mother. Did you have a nice walk?' The dogs were finally released from their leads and shot across the kitchen floor. I knelt to pet them.

'It is a lovely Autumn day, Tempest,' said my mother. 'We found some late blackberries so picked and ate them off the bush.'

'Sounds nice.' Which it did. I lived in a lovely area surrounded by fields and vineyards on rolling hills that provided wonderful views out across the countryside. 'Would you like a cup of tea?' I enquired.

'Now that sounds nice,' my dad said so the kettle was pressed into action once more.

'What is going on with these?' asked my Dad pointing at the radios.

'I have a Phantom to catch tonight.' I replied in a husky, vaudeville-stage voice while wiggling my eyebrows mysteriously. He looked at me quizzically, indulging me like one might a simple person. I gave up trying to be theatrical. 'There is a fellow dressing up and sabotaging the Barker Steel Mill. I believe he will strike again tonight. The mill is vast, so I have a gang of us going up there, so we can spread out and cover as much ground as we can.' I sipped my tea. 'I think it will be an easy task this time.' The last time I had involved my friends in one of my excursions we had all got into an enormous fight that was probably more accurately described as a riot and then we all got arrested.

'How many in your team?' my dad asked.

'Seven. Not really enough given the ground we need to cover but we will make it work.' I could see my dad was counting the radios.

'Hmm. So, is this Phantom chap dangerous would you say?'

'Hard to tell. Anyone can be dangerous if they are armed, but the short answer is that I don't think so. The chap I am now convinced is acting as the Phantom is a young executive type and not much bigger in height than mum. His movements are being controlled by someone else, but that person will most likely not be there, so it is just the one man to catch. He will be outnumbered, so I expect him to just surrender when we corner him.

My dad made a thoughtful noise, 'Hmm.'

We drank our tea along with a handful of dunking biscuits from the tin I keep in the cupboard for guests. Dunking biscuits are a *thing of beauty* my dad had once observed when I was a child on his knee. I could still hear the echo of it every time the tin came out. It was a warm and pleasant memory.

We sat on the sofas in my lounge and talked about what was happening in the news and whether we would get together for dinner at their house this coming weekend. It was not long though before mother brought up the topic of the baby shower.

'I had a quick chat with some of the other grandmothers I know, and I think I will get by just fine without your help. So, you are off the hook.' It sounded like a disaster in the making. I had not told her that Rachael had visited me and clearly Rachael had not done so either. The event was planned now but I played along rather than give mother the impression she was not needed.

'Jolly good, mother. What do you have planned?'

Mother's face beamed though as she prepared to tell me all about her exciting plans. 'Well, Tempest. Margaret Wilson, you know... from the church. Well, she said that she threw a baby shower for her daughter, Sarah, you know... from the church. And they had it at her house and she invited friends and family and they all made gifts for the baby and drank nice wine and Margaret made sandwiches and quiche and...'

The noise of mother speaking was becoming a drone and I needed to stop her, ask some clarifying questions and convince her to abandon any derivative of this plan that she might have. Unfortunately, once in full flow mother was a lot like an ocean liner; hard to stop, dangerous to get in front of and if you tried to affect a turn it would take a while before she even noticed.

I looked at dad. He just shrugged at me. Helpful.

I raised a hand. Like a child.

'... but she did say it was a bit crowded at her house and if she were doing it again she would use the church hall.' Mother finally noticed my raised hand which had now been in the air so long I was holding it aloft with my other hand. 'Did you want to ask a question, dear?'

I put my hands back in my lap. 'I have a few items on your list to discuss. You plan to all drink wine, yet the mother-to-be, for whom the party is being thrown is not able to drink...'

'She can have a small one,' mother complained.

'No, she cannot, mother and I suspect that her friends would slap the drink from her hand if they saw her with it.'

'I had a small brandy every night when I was pregnant with the two of you,' mother claimed defiantly.

'That explains a lot, mother. Nevertheless, pregnant mothers do not drink because they understand what it does to the foetus, so we need to consider the impact on the guest of honour if everyone else is to drink. I would suggest non-alcoholic drinks only.' Mother was muttering under her breath. I pressed on. 'Then you mentioned *making* gifts. Are you talking about knitting clothes and blankets for the baby?'

'Yes, dear. So much nicer than buying something from a store.'

I doubted my sister would agree but accepted that it was going to take some clever diplomatic skills to get this message into mum's brain. 'Hmmm,' I started, knowing I would need to play my hand very carefully. 'I wonder if perhaps we should at least explore some alternate options and see what Racheal thinks of them. Do you have a list of her friends to invite?

'No. Not yet.'

'Then I will have her email me a list tonight with phone numbers. That way we can do a head count and see if they will all fit in your house.' Mother acknowledged that element of my plan with a nod of her head. I was on safe ground if I suggested doing anything with a computer as she hated technology. I pressed my advantage. 'You do realise that you will have days of preparing food and then all the cleaning and washing up afterward.' It was actual washing up too as mother's hate of technology extended to dishwashers also.

'That's what I have your father for,' she said grinning at him. He made an exaggerated sad and hurt face.

'Yes, mother. I am sure he is already looking forward to it. However, I can send her a few images of alternate venues just in case she has something else in mind and perhaps we can avoid having dad standing in the kitchen for several hours.'

'That will all cost money, Tempest.'

'Which I will pay as my baby shower gift.' Even though I was fairly certain men did not traditionally give gifts for baby showers, this seemed like the most efficient way of avoiding a tearful sister sitting sharing soggy egg sandwiches with her friends, shoehorned into my parent's lounge.

The discussion ranged for a few minutes more while we finished our tea and biscuits. Like a boxer sparring with a particularly gifted opponent,

I danced around the topic of gifts but could not find an opening where I could strike. In the end, I gave up. I had scored some points, although with my mother one had to do it so surreptitiously that she thought any new idea was, in fact, hers all along. In essence, I quit while I was ahead and left the remaining topics to be broached another time.

I had one more question though. 'When is it to be?' Mother looked at me blankly. 'The party, mother. What date?'

'Oh, next Saturday.'

'Of course, it is.' I already knew all of this. My purpose in asking the question was simply to check mother was not organising something completely different.

Just then my phone rang. It was Jagjit, so I answered. He wanted to confirm the time and place we were meeting and if it was okay to bring Hilary along. Hilary's real name was Brian Clinton, but... well, guys are dicks basically. Anyway, Hilary was one of the regular Friday night pub chaps and had spoken before about coming along on one of my capers just because all the other chaps had. I had never pursued it with him because I suspected his wife would not let him, but if he was free to come the extra pair of eyes would help. I confirmed all the details and disconnected.

Mum and dad were gathering their things to leave. I hooked a finger through the three empty mugs and grabbed the biscuit tin with my other hand.

I saw them to the door and bid them a pleasant evening. The Dachshunds were in their bed with just the tip of one tail showing out from beneath the blankets. I liked to believe that goodbyes made them melancholy and that this was the reason they greeted people but never saw them off. It was more likely though that they knew there was no food in it for them so saw no reason to move.

I closed the front door on the cool October air and went upstairs to get ready. Then heard a knock at my front door again. Mother must have forgotten to tell me or ask me something. I opened the door expecting to

157

see her, so was momentarily caught out when I found Frank outside. His arms were full of books and folders in which sheets of paper had been stuffed.

'Hello, Frank.'

'Phantom,' he said giving no further explanation. He sort of indicated the arm full of books with his head so that I would understand that they were about the Phantom. He was loaded down by them, the awkward stack threatening to slide out of his control at any moment.

'Is that all you could find? I joked.

'Oh, goodness me, no. I have twice this much still in the car. Your dad is getting it for me.'

Sure enough, coming down the path towards my house was my father carrying another stack of books.

'And there's more,' Frank beamed.

I took the pile he was holding from him and deposited them in the kitchen while he went back for more. Dad came through the door a second or so later to dump the second pile on my kitchen counter.

'He is an entertaining fellow,' dad said, referring to Frank. 'Is that the bookshop owner you were telling me about.'

'The very same.'

'Is he safe?'

'I think so. He just has an alternate view to most people. Frank sees a shadow and assumes it has been caused by an evil spirit left on earth in the aftermath of a battle between a fairy prince and a goblin wizard.'

'What is all this then?' Dad asked, indicating the pile of books?'

'It is research into the Phantom of Barker Mill,' Frank said, coming through the door, his arms full of yet more books. 'It is also evidence of other phantoms gathered over several centuries, catalogued material on

158

the theories regarding why phantoms form, what motivates them, how to fight or repel them and the third pile that I am holding now provides alternate theories on what the entity might be.' He dumped the heavy pile of books on the kitchen counter next to the other two. Sticking out of the pages were dozens of little, coloured flags where he had no doubt marked a passage that was pertinent to the case in hand.

'Michael,' yelled my mother from the front door.

'Coming, dear,' he replied to his ever-patient wife who had been made to wait and was now keen to get home to the snooker or something. 'Catch you later, kid.' he said on his way out of the door.

'So, Frank. What have you got for me?'

'Perhaps, Tempest, I should start by laying some groundwork definitions. Please tell me if I am teaching you to suck eggs. A phantom is the spirit of a dead person believed by some to visit the living as a pale, almost transparent form of a person, animal, or other object. It comes from the ancient Greek word phantazein which means image or apparition. Phantoms differ from ghosts in that they are always grounded to a specific place. Tragedy or trauma, not necessarily one that causes their death, but one that becomes the focal point of their life, fixes their ethereal form to that place. Acts as an anchor if you like. There are many famous reports of phantoms in the UK. When one considers the whole planet, the numbers of recorded incidents becomes immeasurable.'

Frank paused while he fished out a particularly thick book. 'Here, in Baron's Guide to the Dead he has recorded phantoms in different categories. There is a whole section on phantoms that haunt roads. The records do not go back very far, of course, little more than a century and most are linked to fatal car accidents. There are a few reports of much older phantoms on our roads such as this one,' he indicated with his finger, 'which is a Phantom monk that appears on the A6003 near Corby. Baron suggests that he found evidence of his appearance recorded as far back as 1514. It is most likely that the road he was killed on was a bridle path that became a major thoroughfare and then a road as the years went on. This one,' he pointed again, 'is on Bluebell Hill just a few miles away.'

I leaned in to read the passage. The author claimed there was a phantom that appeared as the image of a woman in a bridal gown. She would jump in front of cars, causing drivers to swerve and in some cases crash, but she would then vanish. She was always seen in the same spot and the reports went back decades.

'Moray and Blithe write about the Phantom of Barker Mill in some detail. I think they have the best report although it is an old one. They became involved in 1912 when two workers were killed. Archibald Quibly asked them to chronicle his investigation.'

Frank droned on for long enough for me to make tea, drink it and consider making another. There was a lot of information if one cared to do the research. He gave me alternate theories regarding lore on phantoms, what the different researchers thought the Phantom of Barker Mill's origins might be and even a few ideas about how to trap it.

'What do *you* think it is?' I asked, more to indulge him than out of any sense of curiosity. I thought Frank was harmless but also completely bonkers. I indulged him because I liked to hear alternate theories. They made me consider mine and in doing so sometimes forced me to form new ideas.

'It is probably a classic phantom. Very possibly the spectral image of the first Mr. Barker's business partner.'

'Or?' He had made the last statement in a manner that suggested he thought it might be something else.

'Well,' he started, 'I think,' he was really drawing this out. 'That you have a much bigger problem.'

'In what way?'

'Some of the evidence points to this being a phantasm.' Frank had locked eyes with me, he was trying to convey how serious he thought this was.

'And the difference is?' I asked.

Frank rolled his eyes. 'Phantoms are not exactly benevolent, but they are also not known to be violent. This one is. Only a few days ago another man was burned in an attack. Phantasms have been recorded as the most violent of all apparitions. Well, behind wraiths of course.'

'Of course.' I echoed.

'So, I think the Phantom of Barker Mill is actually a phantasm. A particularly nasty one. Prone to violent acts and not to be underestimated.'

Trouble at Mill. Monday, 11th October 1950hrs

Rather than take my car, which only had two seats, I had arranged for Big Ben to pick me up. We then collected Frank and Poison as they lived quite close to one another and headed to Dartford with a car full.

Big Ben and I were wearing our usual outfit for such activities which was an all-black set of combat-style fatigues with black combat boots, black, fingerless gloves with Kevlar knuckles and a vest that had Kevlar plates in and pockets to the front in which useful items went. I had instructed everyone else to wear black as we wanted to merge into the shadows and be invisible. In a bid to make sure they did, I had made it sound like we were carrying out a daring raid inside enemy lines. I had told Frank to come dressed as Batman, then, after I had put down the phone, realised my mistake and fretted for the next two hours that he might do exactly as instructed.

Luckily, he had not taken my instruction literally so was wearing hues of black and grey - a hoody over a Black Sabbath t-shirt. Poison, the athletic little minx that she was, had on sports gear. It was all black including her trainers, but as was often her way, her midriff was showing. I acknowledged that her stomach was a flat, wondrous canvass that ought to be displayed, but it would reflect any light and reveal her position. I elected to not worry too much about it.

On the way there, I had regaled the car occupants with what I had learned about the Phantom so far.

'So, the Phantom is Owen Larkin?' asked Big Ben in confirmation. 'Why don't we just have Amanda arrest him at his house?'

'Because if we catch him in the act it will be very hard for him to deny his guilt. Currently, all we have is my testimony that I heard Owen and Brett Barker talking about the Phantom. If it went to court, any decent lawyer would rip the case apart and I always try to present the client with a watertight solution.'

'But isn't the client in this case also the man behind it all?' asked Poison.

'Well, I admit I am a little confused by Brett Barker's move to hire me to solve the Phantom's identity if he is the one pulling his strings. I think the answer to the why of that will be solved this evening if we catch Owen.'

The forming up point I had chosen was the car park of a large national supermarket chain. It was situated on the other side of the road from the Mill so provided a good field of vision to the front gate. The overhead lights of the carpark provided illumination for the shoppers going to and from their cars and held back the inky gloom in every parking space and trolley park save for the corner that I had chosen to gather in. Here, two broken lights close together gave us the shadows I wanted.

The seven of us were performing final preparations for what I worried might be a long operation. It was 2007hrs, so the last shift of the day could be seen leaving the Mill on the opposite side of the road.

My team looked like a poor man's paramilitary group when viewed together. Everyone was in black as instructed, everyone had a radio clipped to their belt with a mouthpiece extension clipped onto their jacket collar and most were wearing some kind of tough army-style boot. If one ignored the radio and viewed the chaps separately they just looked like they had made lazy wardrobe choices, except for Poison who always wore black and managed to make it look like a kaleidoscope of colour just by being in it. Big Ben and I were the problem, I suppose. Our matching Kevlar body armour vests and combat outfits needed only to be accessorised with an additional cape and pointed-ear cowl and either one of us could be Batman. I was fervently hoping the supermarket did not have cameras on the car park that were being monitored inside, as a contingent of anti-terrorist police descending on us would make a swift end to the evening.

I handed out a tin of black face paint for the team to remove the shine from their faces and expected to have to convince them to use it, but they each took to the task with glee, applying it to each other and checking their faces in the reflection of car windows. Apart from also handing out a couple of oversize black hoodies, one to cover shiny black letters on

Hilary's coat and one to just cover Poison up a bit, I had no other wardrobe tasks to perform. We were ready.

I had game-played Owen's actions in my head and believed he was most likely to wait until the Mill was empty before he ventured in. From the supermarket carpark, I would see him if he arrived early. What he might do though is enter the Mill by an alternate entrance, so it was time to get moving.

The Mill had no night time security, just an entry code to make the front gate open at night. Their lax security has allowed me to see and commit the entry code to memory on my first visit.

'Okay, chaps,' I started. 'With luck, this will be a short mission.' I held up a photograph of Owen to show them all. 'This is the man that has been acting as the Phantom. He has been sabotaging Mill equipment and is responsible for injuring at least one person. I want you all to consider him as dangerous.'

'Tempest I can only stay a couple of hours,' said Hilary. 'My wife will not tolerate me being out all night.'

'Fair enough mate.' I replied. Next to me, Big Ben had started humming something.

'Tempest,' a voice called from behind me. My heart actually stopped, I swear. I turned around slowly to find my parents walking across the car park towards me. 'Cooee, Tempest,' my mother called again.

'What are you doing here?' I asked them as they reached the group.

'You said you needed a big team for tonight,' chipped in my dad. 'So, we thought we could help.'

I gave myself a mental slap. I was struggling to find a reason why they could not help but I had nothing. They were old but not decrepit, they could run, and they had working eyes and ears. Besides they were already here so it would be hard to turn them away. They were even wearing black, although my mother's sweatshirt had kittens on the front of it.

I hung my head in defeat for a second. Then lifted it back up with a happy expression showing instead. 'Great, we could use the extra eyes. Ben, can you grab two more radios please?'

While Big Ben was opening the boot of his car, I produced the black face paint again and offered it to my parents.

'Ooh, Michael. Wait until I tell the ladies at the church,' mother said excitedly.

'I suspect, mother that you have the wrong idea about how this evening will go. This is a stakeout in the belief that the person pretending to be the Phantom will show up. But what that means is we will be quietly tucked into dark corners doing nothing but quietly watching until he shows himself. That might be hours,' I warned.

'Oh hush, Tempest,' said my mother with a smile. 'You are always off on some adventure. Always chasing some villain and getting yourself in the papers. And who knows? Maybe with us here you will avoid getting arrested for once.'

I took a radio from Big Ben's offered hand and clipped it to my mother's waistband, then threaded the microphone wire up through her sweatshirt and clipped it just under her chin. Next to her Big Ben did the same with my father. We demonstrated quickly how they worked.

Not willing to have my parents operate as a couple, I split them up, suffering the unfortunate task of pairing my mother with myself. I opened the map of the Mill once more and added a new spot for the extra team to watch from.

Then my mother and I, Poison and Jagjit, Hilary and Basic and finally Big Ben, my Father, and Frank slipped across the road when a gap between cars appeared and headed to the Mill. The gate entry number worked as it should, and we were in and fanning out.

Strict radio silence was the instruction until movement is spotted.

I had selected for my mother and me a position on the far side of the Mill. We were exposed in the security lights as we crossed the car park,

165

there was no way to avoid this, but once we reached the buildings there were ample shadows into which I disappeared. I had taken my mother's hand to make sure she stuck with me, but I could feel her dragging behind me slightly now. I turned to see her fiddling with her handbag, trying to get something out of it.

'What are you doing, mother?'

'I brought a torch with me, love,' she said pulling a Maglite from her bag and switching it on. The beam of light instantly pierced the gloom I was relying on for stealthy movement.

I grabbed for it and switched it off. 'Mother,' I started, hearing the desperate pleading in my voice already. 'We are supposed to be invisible. We need to be quiet, we need to get to our viewpoint without tipping off the Phantom and when we get there we need to remain unseen. No torches. No phones. No humming hymns if you get bored. Do you understand?'

'Well, I don't think you need to be so snippy, Tempest. If I fall over in the dark I will make plenty of noise.' My right eye twitched.

'Just follow where I go, and I will avoid any trip hazards. Okay?'

Mother said nothing, clearly a little ticked. I took her hand again, forcedly smiled at her and set off again.

The radio crackled quietly to life. 'Ben's team in position,' came Big Ben's voice.

'Hilary and Basic in position,' a few seconds later.

I replied to both with, 'Roger. Out.' Just then we turned the final corner and I could see where I intended to go. I hugged the shadow at the edge of the building, watching silently for a moment. The best position for us was against the building opposite. It backed onto the water and from the leading edge, we had a clear view down two sides of the mill main building and to several other buildings exposed on this side of the Mill. To get there we would have to cross through the lit area again.

A minute went past. 'What are we doing, Tempest?' asked my mother at normal volume, the sound echoing against the dark.

'Mother!' I whispered with as much inflection as I could muster at low volume. 'At night noise carries further. Near to water, it carries even further. You must whisper. Like I am. Get it?'

'Okay,' she replied with an exasperated face. 'Are you going to be this pernickety about everything?' I ignored the question, grabbed her hand and pulled her across the distance between the two buildings at a jog.

The radio crackled to life again as Poison reported that she and Jagjit had got to their position. We settled into the recess a doorway provided and allowed the dark to envelope us. Swinging my head back and forth, I could not see a way that Owen would be able to approach without us seeing him and if he was already here he could not leave without showing himself. So, my only hope was that he did not decide to disobey Brett and fail to show tonight.

Time began to stretch out. Anyone that has performed a task that involves little movement and little talking and where you have almost nothing to watch will understand just how slow the clock hands move. As a soldier, I had performed guard duty in the middle of the night, by myself and with nothing to watch on several occasions. One gets practiced at ignoring the boredom.

'How long will this take do you think?' asked my mother. I checked my watch; three minutes had elapsed. I had expected her to crack sooner.

'Movement. Stand by.' The radio squawked quietly. It was Big Ben. I had positioned Big Ben on the opposite side of the main Mill building to us. At a run, which would be a walk if my mother was involved, it would take at least two minutes to reach him. There was no reason to go anywhere yet though. I waited for him to confirm what he was seeing.

'I have a figure wearing a black cloak. Moving north in front of the mill. Do we pursue or observe?'

'Observe for now. Let me know if he goes inside,' I replied.

'It just vanished!' Frank exclaimed with utter glee. I ignored him, waiting for Big Ben to report again.

'Erm, Frank is right. I don't see him now. He went into a shadow cast by a lamppost and did not come out the other side,' Big Ben said, whispering quietly into his microphone.

'I can see someone. I think,' Jagjit announced. I waited again for him to update us all. 'Okay, we have a cloaked figure moving away from the mill towards reception.'

I worked the map in my head. It could not be right. The two points where the Phantom had been sighted were at least three hundred metres apart, but the reports had come in mere seconds from each other. 'Jagjit, what are you seeing?' I asked.

'Hard to tell.' he answered. 'It is definitely a person and I think they are wearing a long cloak, but they are a good two hundred metres from us and mostly in the shadow. I only saw it because I sneezed and when the figure turned to look in our direction light caught on something it is carrying.'

'Where is it now?'

'I.... don't know.' There was a pause.

'We are moving position, Tempest,' Poison answered. 'It may have gone into a building.'

'Or, it may have vanished,' said Frank in a happy voice. Frank would like nothing more than to find a real supernatural creature that defied any explanation I could give.

'Urh, Tempest?' the new voice was Basic. 'Urh, there is something here as well.'

'Hilary, what do you see?' I asked, knowing that I would get a better description from him than I would from Basic.

'Well, I would say I was looking at a Phantom.' On my mental map of the Mill grounds, the apparition had now been spotted at three different sites that were separated by hundreds of metres all within the space of thirty seconds.

'Tempest, this is a free forming phantasm,' said Frank. There was utter conviction and a touch of terror in his voice. 'Tempest, these things attach themselves to a specific place or object and they never leave. It is always a tragedy that anchors them, and they can be dangerously protective. No wonder there have been injuries.'

'Frank, I think it more likely that we are chasing shadows.' Frank would always believe a completely nuts explanation over one that made sense. 'Let's not get spooked, everyone. Who is seeing what now?'

'I just saw something move past a window. It is inside the mill. I'm going in,' announced Big Ben. 'Frank and your dad can stay here to observe in case anything else comes along.'

'No, Ben. Observe only for now.' I didn't want him inside in the dark by himself. Better to wait until Owen came out and we could corner him as a team. This would be difficult though if everyone was seeing something different.

'He's gone,' said Frank meaning Big Ben.

'Let's go,' said mum as she left the darkness that kept us hidden and headed back towards the front of the Mill.

This was getting to be bothersome.

'I just caught sight of it again, Tempest,' Poison's voice told us through the radio. 'It is heading for the office block, I think.'

'She is right, Tempest. There is definitely someone or something here.' I quickened my pace. Everything was happening on the other side of the building. 'We are following,' Jagjit said and I imagined he and Poison sneaking along behind whoever it was they were now tailing.

'Don't get too close,' warned Frank.

'What do we do?' asked Hilary.

'Stay where you are for now.'

'But… I mean, what do we do about the Phantom we have here? It is walking right towards us.' Hilary sounded quite nervous.

This was getting ridiculous. Suddenly, everyone was seeing shadows. I was seeing nothing. I had no way of knowing if anyone of them had seen anything or if they were all seeing something. The team was spread out, starting to sound scared and I could not get to any of them quickly without abandoning mother and running, which was not an option. My anger was rising, I could feel it beginning to wilt my calm, attacking my ability to control the situation evolving around me. I had not felt this since operations in Iraq. It is desperately helpless feeling for a commander. You have multiple reports to filter and assess with only seconds to make a decision that may determine whether people - your people, get hurt or not.

I forced the helpless feeling back down, crushing it with my determination to seize back the initiative. 'Guys, this is what we are going to do.' I was nearing the front of the mill now. My pensionable aged mother beginning to puff beside me, but it meant I would be able to see Poison and Jagjit soon and if necessary leave mum behind without losing sight of her. 'The Phantom is not… whatever Frank said it was.'

'A free-forming phantasm. Not to be underestimated,' he chipped in helpfully.

'Yes. Thank you, Frank. It is just a man. His name is Owen Larkin and he is not a threat. I cannot tell what each of you is seeing but it is time to put an end to this sham. Hilary, Basic, I want you to approach whatever it is you are seeing and confront it verbally. Issue a challenge. Tell it to stop. If it runs, tell us then chase it. Poison, Jagjit, same for you. I am moving towards your position now so will come to you. Dad, Frank, go to the building entrance that Ben went in through and call for him. Do not go further into the mill looking for him. Everyone got that?'

170

I got a round of acknowledgements and yesses back. Then I hit the corner of the Mill and emerged from the darker side into the better-lit front area. The car park, reception, and main office building were all now visible.

I turned to face my mother. 'I am going to catch up with Poison and Jagjit, I think they may actually have something. Just keep coming back towards the car park and stay in the light where others can see you please.'

'Okay, Tempest,' she replied. Whether she would do it or not remained to be seen. I needed to get to where the Phantom was though, so I broke into a run. I could see Jagjit and Poison ahead of me as they moved between buildings and were illuminated by the overhead lights.

Then there was an explosion of noise over the radio which carried Big Ben's voice. The sentence we heard was somewhat unbalanced in favour of words starting with an F or a C. For brevity I shall record that he said, 'Argh. Man down.'

'Tempest, it ran. We are chasing it,' said Hilary between laboured breaths.

'Son, I'm going in to find Benjamin,' my dad informed me.

'Tempest, it went into the office building,' reported Jagjit.

'Ben, talk to me,' I had a man hurt, he had to take priority.

'The little git kicked me in the nuts,' he managed between breaths that carried the sound of his pain.

I had stopped my run towards Jagjit and Poison, indecision ruling my motions. I needed to be three places simultaneously. I could not achieve that, so I just had to trust the team and hope that no one else got hurt. I thought better of that plan instantly, not the trusting part, but the bit where I used hope as a strategy to avoid injury for my team.

'Right. Jagjit and Poison, abandon your Phantom and head towards the mill. Pick up my mother on the way and meet me where Big Ben's team

171

was located. Stay in the light. Hilary, same for you. Come to us. This situation is now too dangerous, so we are going to regroup and abort.'

I started running to where Frank and my dad should be. Jagjit and Poison should be behind me and Hilary with Basic should be coming at me from the other end of the mill. Perhaps twenty seconds and one hundred metres later I was closing in on Frank and my dad.

'Ben? Are you going to live?' I asked as I ran.

'Yeah. My nuts hurt, that's all. It is nothing a face full of boobs wouldn't fix. The guy caught me by surprise.'

'Who is talking about boobs? Is that you, Benjamin?' my mother asked, her tone chiding.

I elected to ignore her. I spotted Frank and slowed my pace. He was holding a door open, presumably to allow some light to penetrate the gloom inside. He had seen me coming and spoken to my dad who now emerged with Big Ben. He was cupping his testicles and was slightly bent over, still feeling the deeply imbedded pain is his abdomen no doubt.

Beyond them came the sound of someone running. The others heard it at the same time, I saw their heads snap around as one towards the noise. From the gloom came a fluttering black cloak running full tilt between the buildings. Air drag from running had pulled the hood back to reveal the out-of-breath face of Owen Larkin.

Gotcha.

Behind Owen, both Basic and Hilary were chasing but did not seem to be making up any ground. I calmly strolled to the middle of the narrow path that ran between the buildings and extended my arm for him to halt. I saw no reason to make a fight of this. He was outnumbered and surrounded and caught in the act. I was sure he would surrender.

Sure enough, he spotted me and began to slow his pace. Then, from my right, my father ran along a raised walkway, probably put there for off-loading trucks and threw himself off to perform a flying tackle. He crashed into Owen, who had the barest moment to react. The two of them crashed to the ground.

'Oh God, my hip!' my dad yelled, rolling on the ground. 'Oh, my word.'

'Are you alright, Dear?' my mother asked, just arriving.

Owen was getting up. 'Are you quite done?' he asked at a shout.

'Language, young man,' said my mother.

'I might argue that this is, in fact, the correct time for the use of expletives,' I ventured. My right eye twitched again.

Hilary and Basic arrived to join us all crowded around Owen. They were both out of breath. I wondered when Hilary had last had to run anywhere.

'Hey, guys. How are you both doing?' I asked them.

I got a thumbs-up from Basic. Hilary was inspecting his trousers though. 'I tore my trousers on something. My wife is going to do her nut.' There wasn't much I could say to that. I chose to ignore it. I could hear Big Ben humming again. I knew the tune but could not name it.

'Tempest,' Jagjit's voice came over the radio. 'We still have someone at the offices.' I thought they were on their way to me.

'Who are all these people?' Owen asked, looking around at the assembled team.

I held up my index finger. 'One moment please?' Then into the radio, 'Jagjit, what have you got? We have the Phantom here.'

'I haven't managed to get close enough yet, but we followed a person in a black cloak into the office building. I don't know where they went but we searched downstairs and found nothing, so we are heading upstairs now.'

'Be careful, okay? Owen Larkin is the Phantom and we have him here.'

'Yes, well done.' Owen said in response. It seemed like an odd answer to give in his situation. I looked at his face. It held no fear, no concern that he was in any kind of trouble. I did not like how calm he seemed.

I continued talking to Jagjit and Poison. 'Just don't scare anyone that might just be working late. Okay?'

'Okay,' they both answered together.

On the ground, my dad was pulling himself together. No lasting damage then. Around him, Hilary and Basic were still heaving ragged breaths in and Big Ben was rubbing his groin.

I focused on Owen. 'Owen you know who I am and that I have been employed by Mrs. Barker to investigate the circumstances of her husband's death. I have also been engaged to investigate the Phantom and its recent spate of activities by Brett Barker.' I watched, expecting his face to colour, but it did not. He continued to look serenely calm as if he was the one in charge of this situation. 'I have no authority to arrest you though and you are free to go now that I have a number of witnesses that will testify to seeing you here after work hours, trespassing on mill property and dressed as the Phantom.'

'I might be free to go, but I would not be so sure that you are,' he leered at me, his face a smile and then we all heard the sirens.

'Tempest, we have a problem,' Jagjit said over the radio. 'There is a lady here. She says she is working late and that we are trespassing. Also, I can see lots of police arriving at the gates.'

Just then an alarm sounded inside the mill. Big Ben was closest, so without prompting he crossed to the building and pushed open the door to peek inside. 'There is a fire,' he announced cheerfully.

'What have you done?' I demanded of Owen.

'I have no idea what you are talking about. I am here legitimately. You are the ones trespassing. Maybe you did something.' He was still grinning; it was beginning to unnerve me.

The police were now entering the grounds of the Mill, we could hear them approaching, their sirens bouncing off the walls as they came between the buildings.

'What do we do?' asked Poison over the radio.

'Come to us,' I replied. 'Comply with any instructions the police may give you.' I was getting a sinking feeling deep in the pit of my stomach. Owen seemed all too confident.

'Tempest, what is happening?' asked my mother. I thought I knew the answer, but I was afraid to say it in case I was right. My brain was telling me that I had been set up, that Brett and Owen had played me, and we were all about to get arrested. I looked around at the team. They were all here voluntarily, I had made no promises to them about what would happen this evening or how events might turn out. However, I had not warned them that my ego might lead them into a trap or that the great Tempest Michaels might get them all arrested again.

Behind me, cars screeched to a halt and armed police officers spilled out shouting instructions.

The eyes of my team were all swinging from the police to me and back to the police. 'Everyone do as they say.' It was the only advice I could give.

Owen knelt on the ground next to me obeying the same instructions, but where we all looked sick or stunned or frightened, he was still grinning. As the police approached us, weapons trained at our bodies, I heard the whump of a small explosion from within the Mill.

Super.

'Oh, God. My wife is going to kill me,' wailed Hilary. Behind me, Big Ben was humming again, and I finally worked out what the tune was - 99 Problems by Jay-Zee.

99 problems, but a bitch ain't one.

A night in the Cells. Monday, October 11th 2115hrs

Having offered no resistance, the process of arresting us, cuffing us and loading us into a van had taken no time at all. Poison and Jagjit were brought out to join us. Owen however, was released once he had identified himself to them. It was clear that he had been the one that had contacted the police. He must have done so some time ago as it was an armed response unit that had arrived to deal with us. The first realisation led to the second, which was that the whole thing had been a trap. A trap laid by Brett and Owen and sprung by my own stupidity.

As the police had shouted orders and rounded us up, I had tried protesting that we were there on behalf of Mrs. Barker. It was a futile effort though as they were going to take us away to sort it out regardless of what I said. For that matter though I had not alerted any mill staff or Mrs. Barker that we were going to be on the property, we had gained entry by using a pin code that I should not have, we were dressed like a paramilitary group and the mill was now on fire.

Just before they closed the back doors of the van, I saw a fireman emerge from the Mill and overheard him telling the police that the fire was out. How significant it had been I did not know. Owen had set it though. I was certain of that.

Mum was crying gently on my dad's shoulder. He was quietly consoling her. I felt miserable, but when he caught my eye dad gave me a cheeky grin and a wink.

During the ride to the police station, I had a few minutes to role-play different scenarios in my head. I kept coming back to the inescapable conclusion that Brett and Owen had known I was outside Owen's house and they had staged the argument so that I would hear it and fall into their trap. It might have been a hastily ventured idea on their part when I was spotted in my car near Owen's property. They had relied on my gullibility and were now probably doing high-fives and toasting themselves. We would be cleared of the charges, I was fairly certain of that. Fairly certain. Mrs. Barker would get involved, but I would struggle to prove that it was not my team that had set the fire.

I was now more certain than ever that Brett was guilty of sabotaging the mill. I knew not why yet, but whatever the reason was, it seemed likely to be the same reason for causing the death of his Grandfather. My position was greatly weakened, my resolve was not. I was going to get Brett Barker.

Damned right I was.

Outside Dartford Police Station. Tuesday, 12th October 0647hrs

My one phone call had been to Amanda. She had listened to my requests then promised to make the necessary calls to get my family and friends released and the situation cleared up. I thanked her for doing what she could to get my parents out swiftly. Amanda knew many of the police at the Dartford Station, so would be putting in some calls and driving up to Dartford herself to grease the wheels.

Being led back to the cells, I passed Big Ben and told him Amanda was on her way. His response had been, 'Boobs mate, they work like Mastercard: everywhere and all the time. She will have us out in no time.'

No time turned out to be ten hours. I could not tell if that was swift or not, but we were released without charge in the end at 0647hrs. It had taken the intervention of Mrs. Barker to finally convince whomever it was making the decisions that they had nothing to hold us for. Mrs. Barker had stated that she had no intention of pursuing any charges and had claimed that we were on the site legitimately. I would thank her for that later when I called to apologise for the embarrassment. What I could not fathom was why Brett Barker had not overruled her or given his opinion. He had taken me off the playing board with a very effective move, but was now letting me go?

As I came out of the Station, everyone was there waiting for me. I felt utterly miserable and embarrassed. Ashamed maybe. My mum was there, she had spent the night in a police cell, something I am sure she never envisaged happening at any point in her life. I didn't know what to say to any of them, but how to begin to make this up to my mother was beyond my comprehension at this point.

There were a few steps down to the street level where my friends and parents had gathered. I descended them and my mother stepped forward to meet me. I wondered if she was going to slap my face and berate me. I steeled myself for the blow which I knew would sting my conscience more than my skin, but it did not come.

Instead, my mother hugged me. 'That was different,' she said smiling. 'Wait until I tell the ladies at the church.'

'You are not upset?' I asked confused.

'Well, I was a bit last night. It was a bit of a shock, but now I have so much to tell everyone. Real action and adventure. Breaking and entering, chasing ghosts, getting arrested. I can write to all my pen pals. Usually, I tell them rubbish about how the garden is doing and I have my rotten cousin Kathlyn in Australia who always has something interesting to brag about. Let her see if she can top this!' Mum seemed positively reinvigorated by the drama of the last few hours.

'Come on, Michael,' she said grabbing my dad's hand gleefully. 'Get me home. I have a task for you.' I did not wish to think too hard about what that task might be. She pulled him across the road towards the train station where she probably intended to get a cab back to where we had all left our cars. Dad had glanced in my direction as his arm was being yanked, he sort of shrugged and grinned and then was gone.

I looked at the rest of the group. Frank and Poison, Jagjit, Hilary, Big Ben and Basic. They mostly looked tired. We were all still wearing our clothes from last night, we had been fed, but it was not food that one would willingly eat unless hungry, so at the top of my to-do list, other than find Brett Barker and shove a bowling ball up his arse, was to get a shower and try to remove the scuzzy feeling. I expected that the others felt the same.

'Chaps we got royally screwed last night. You probably gathered that we walked into a trap. The chap we were looking for was there only to draw us in.'

'What about the figure Poison and I were following?' Jagjit asked.

'Yeah, there is something that does not add up, Tempest,' Big Ben chipped in. 'The person I followed into the Mill was over six feet tall. Owen is several inches shorter.'

'Are you sure?' I asked. 'It was dark inside the mill; he could have been standing on something. How certain are you that it was not Owen Larkin?'

'The figure we were following was also over six feet tall and was wearing a black cloak. I don't know where that person went, but I could smell them,' Poison answered. 'They went inside the main office building and the only person we found in there was the girl upstairs working late.'

'Yeah, I covered the exits while Poison searched, so unless they went out a window they never left, and we didn't find them,' said Jagjit.

'You didn't find them because they were never there,' Frank said. 'We were chasing a phantasm. Probably a dangerous one which can take physical form at will. It attacked Big Ben and led Poison and Jagjit away. It can manifest in multiple locations at once. If I had thought to bring the right equipment with me, I could have recorded the levels of psychokinetic energy and maybe photographed its ethereal image to separate the physical form from the spirit inside.' He paused to make sure we were all taking in how serious the situation had been. 'The appearance of Owen Larkin at the same time is nothing more than coincidence. We would most likely have seen and followed the phantasm no matter when we went to the mill.'

Just then Amanda pulled up. She parked on the double yellow lines in front of the Station. I suspected that not even police officers are allowed to do that. She got out of the car. Her face was displaying an overabundance of displeasure. It was not a look I liked on her. I had never seen her upset before. She was still completely gorgeous, just in an angry, I'm going to kick someone in the nuts kind of way.

'Good morning, Amanda,' I ventured. I received a scowl in return.

'I believe my ride is here,' I said to the group. 'I'm sorry about the night in the cells. Sorry to you Frank because your shop is closed, and you should be there and not here. Sorry to you Hilary because I know you are going to catch hell from your wife. She hates me anyway, so you can just blame me.' He just shrugged. 'Basic, please say sorry to you mum from me. I know she looks to you for help around the house.'

180

They all told me that it was not my fault, even though we all knew it was. They were a good bunch.

'I cannot park here for long, Tempest,' Amanda said loud enough to be heard over the others. 'Someone will come out and move me along.'

'Chaps get a taxi back to your cars and send me the bill. Okay?'

They nodded, and I opened the door to Amanda's car. Big Ben dived past me and into the back seat. 'There are five of them, so they can fit into one cab,' he said by way of explanation.

I then had to wait on the pavement while Big Ben attempted to fold himself into the back of Amanda's Mini Cooper. It was not designed for a man with a six-foot seven-inch-tall, two hundred and fifty-pound frame. He tried several positions but, in the end, gave up and laid sideways across the seats with a seat belt looped around his waist.

I got in. Amanda got in and we pulled into traffic just as an angry looking desk sergeant was coming down the steps towards us.

'I'm ready for it,' I said as we set off. I was due a large helping of I told you so. I figured I might as well get it over with.

'I'm ready for it too?' Big Ben chipped in from the back seat sounding hopeful.

'Ready for what?' Amanda asked me. 'Ready for me to berate you for doing something you should not have? What would that achieve?'

'Okay. Then...'

'But you should have listened to me, you idiot.'

'Yeah., said Big Ben helpfully.

'You think Brett walked you into a trap, but you have no evidence to support that.'

'But...'

'Everything you told me is circumstantial. Owen has been given his old job back - that proves nothing. Owen and Brett were discussing sabotaging the mill - only you heard it and they can deny it easily. The facts are that you led a group onto private property without permission to be there. Used a stolen code to gain access, then terrorised a member of staff who was working late.' She took a breath so that I could respond. I opened my mouth, but she cut me off. 'You would not believe the strings I had to pull to get you out in such a short span of time. Honestly, if Mrs. Barker had not lied and stated that you were there on her behalf, I doubt I would have got you out at all. Why did you not call her like you said you would?'

She paused again. I checked to see if she was going to start speaking once more. Decided she was going to let me speak and attempted to answer her most recent question.

'I...'

'Of course, this all ignores that fact that I have already quit my job and now work for you. When you embarrass yourself like this, you embarrass me as well.'

'Yeah,' said Big Ben in the back again. I could hear him grinning at my expense.

Amanda cut her eyes to her rear-view mirror. 'And you can shut up. You big stupid lump of meat. You are not without blame here.'

'If I may?' I interjected quickly. 'You are drifting.' With Amanda staring at Big Ben she was no longer paying attention to the road and we were in traffic. Her car was at the edge of its lane and about to enter the one next to it. A horn blared.

'Damn it!' she swore, yanking the wheel to bring the car back to where it should be. 'Sorry,' she mumbled quietly, acknowledging her driving rather than apologising for berating me. 'Ben, can you shift to the side? You are blocking my view.'

'Babe, I am the view.'

'I'm sorry too,' I replied to Amanda, ignoring Big Ben's enormous ego. 'I genuinely forgot to call Mrs. Barker last night. I was too swept up by the excitement of the case. I am sorry that this might reflect badly on you.'

'You make a habit of getting arrested,' she said. I could see though that the suppressed anger had been vented. She was calm again.

'I do,' I admitted. 'Honestly, I am not sure how I achieve it. Does it work in my favour that I have never been charged?'

'Not really.'

We sat in silence for a few minutes. Amanda drove, I stewed over how I had been so easily fooled by Brett, and Big Ben... well, who knows what Big Ben was thinking, it probably involved having sex though.

It was Amanda that broke the silence. She looked at Big Ben in her rear-view mirror. 'So, Ben. It seems you and I are going to end up working together on a semi-regular basis. Why don't you tell me something about yourself?' she encouraged.

Big Ben appeared to give the question some thought before answering. 'I get my balls waxed every other Thursday by a young lady that is also called Amanda.' Big Ben left it at that, undoubtedly awaiting her response.

'I meant, tell me something interesting,' Amanda replied deadpan.

Here's something I know about Big Ben. For him, women fell into four categories:

1. Women I have slept with
2. Women I am going to sleep with
3. Relatives
4. Women who are too old, too young, lesbians and the truly odd ones that don't want to sleep with me.

Amanda was in category four. I think this was largely because Amanda was a ten on the scale of zero to hot and was well practiced at deflecting the efforts of men that only wanted to shag her because she is beautiful.

Big Ben appeared to be struggling for a suitable topic. I elected to help him out. 'Ben plays the saxophone. Actually, he plays it really rather well.'

'Now that is interesting,' said Amanda. 'What got you into that?'

'Girls like it. Charms the pants right off them,' he answered.

'Right,' Amanda replied. 'I am given to understand that you are something of a player. What is it that you look for in a relationship?'

'A relationship?' Big Ben had said the words as if they were uncomfortable in his mouth and he wanted them out as quickly as possible. 'Generally, I look for a way out.'

'So, you just move from girl to girl, never worried that you may have already met *the one*?' she asked.

'Hell, no. Honestly, I don't believe in *the one*. Please understand there is nothing misogynistic about my actions. I do not pretend that I intend to do anything other than ruin them for all other men and move on. I am very open about my one night only policy.'

'And women actually agree to sleep with you?' she said incredulously.

'An abundance of them,' I chipped in a degree of glumness in my voice.

'How on earth do you convince them?'

'Convince them? Babe, I don't have to convince them. They have formed a queue and taken numbers. How do I put this in simple terms?' he asked and made a humming noise. 'For a lot of women, present company clearly accepted, a night with me is a lottery win.'

Amanda made a scoffing noise.

'I understand your disbelief, but the evidence stacks on my side. Some people are good at maths, some are good at writing. Some people have a physical skill that makes them Premiership football players or the lead England fast bowler. I have a body and loins that were put on this planet to make ladies moan in pleasure.'

Amanda did not look convinced.

'Let me put it this way. If this were Harry Potter, my Patronus would be a giant cock.'

Her bottom jaw fell open. She was staring at Big Ben in the rear-view mirror and trying to work out if he was pulling her leg.

'Sooo,' I said, scrambling for a new topic.

Much of the rest of the short journey back to Big Ben's car in the supermarket carpark was conducted in silence. As she pulled up next to the car, Big Ben and I thanked her and got out. I was tired from a lack of sleep and needed to eat, shower and distract myself with some ordinary working day activities.

Amanda's car peeled away and disappeared out of the car park. Big Ben shrugged wordlessly at me. The meaning of which was indecipherable but may have been, "Women!" or, "Shall we go?" but he did not appear to be looking for a response, so I climbed in and promptly fell asleep, waking as he pulled up at my house. I thanked him and waved him off.

Interviewing an Admin Assistant. Tuesday, 13th October 0900hrs

Having not returned home last night no one had let the dogs out and I was greeted by a couple of neat little parcels on my dining room carpet. The boys appeared from the living room looking a little sheepish. I patted them both and apologised for not getting home for them. I felt bad. They had probably paced and paced until they decided they could no longer hold it. I let them outside and made them an extra special apology breakfast of scrambled eggs.

When they were finished with their food, I gave them a helping of milk then clipped their leads on and took them for a good walk. Only once I was content that they were properly dealt with did I sort myself out.

By 0900hrs, I was just pulling into my parking space behind the office. The fatigue from a poor night's sleep had retreated under a barrage of hearty breakfast and hot shower. I felt fresh and relaxed although still ready to murder when I remembered Brett Barker.

As I approached my office from behind the building, I wondered what might be causing the susurration I could hear. The cause, I learned as I turned the corner and my office door could be seen, was the muted voices of a hundred or so people lining up outside my door.

When Amanda suggested I hire an admin assistant to sift emails and perform other basic office admin tasks, I had acknowledged that she was right. It had already been my plan, I just had not done anything about it until two days ago when I had placed the advert on the jobs page of the website for The Weald World. In the excitement of yesterday, I had forgotten about it. I had expected applications to come by email and had feared that there might not be very many.

The advert read:

Administrative assistant required. Part time flexible hours, circa 20 hours per week. Applicants must be computer literate, familiar with Office software, able to work alone and have a solutions-based attitude.

The ad went on to state salary range, desired qualifications, the location of the job and name of the business.

I stared at the line for a moment, my mouth open and my feet motionless while I took in the sight. Backed up along the building, leading away from my office door and down Rochester High Street was a queue of people dressed as Jedi, wizards (I could tell by the hats, wands and in several cases rather convincing beards), vampires, Ghostbusters and Bram Stoker-looking crazies for as far as I could see. They were leaning against the wall or fiddling with their phones or sipping coffee from the coffee shop across the street. They were young and old, men and women, short, tall, fat, thin, different races and I had invited every one of these nut bags to interview for the admin assistant job.

I could not see to get into my office without them seeing me, but the chance to turn around and run away was lost as someone at the front spotted me and my presence went through the line like a ripple. Sighing deeply, I gave myself a mental slap and accepted my fate.

'Good morning,' I said to those near the front as I drew my keys and opened the door. 'I will need a minute and the office is too small to accommodate more than one interviewee at a time so please wait here and I will come to fetch you in a minute.' I said to the chap at the front. He was dressed rather oddly, and I suspected it was supposed to be a Batman costume. Its homemade nature - the cape appeared to be a black bin bag, made it a little hard to tell.

I trudged up the stairs to my office, banged my head on the door frame a few times, collected myself and went inside. I prayed the phone would ring with an urgent matter to which I would have no option to attend but it resiliently defied me with its silence. I put my bag down, switched my mobile phone to silent and turned around to go back downstairs and fetch the first applicant. At that point, I jumped out of my skin because the Batman, or whatever he was supposed to be, was already stood in my doorway.

'You see that?' he asked in a voice he was forcing to be deep and husky. He sounded like a crap version of Darth Vader doing a Batman

187

impression. 'Have you ever witnessed anyone move more silently than that? I can sneak up on anyone. That is why they call me the slug.'

So, not Batman then.

'Tell me you don't need a sidekick with a skill like that.' This guy had crazy eyes and they were bugging out of his head.

'I don't need a sidekick full stop, I'm afraid. I need an administrative assistant that can answer emails, sort files and prepare invoices.'

'Really?' he said in a normal voice. He sounded both incredulous and disappointed. 'I thought that was just superhero code. Are you sure you don't need the world's most silent sidekick?'

'Quite sure, I'm afraid.'

'Oh.'

'Do you have any experience with office administration?' I asked although I was sure I already knew the answer.

'Erm,' he started, 'not really. I expected to be fighting creatures of the night with you. I slept outside all night to make sure I was the first one through the door this morning.'

'Well, I commend you for your determination, but I don't fight creatures of the night. I solve cases that people believe have a supernatural explanation and what I need is an office assistant to handle the paperwork.' The slug looked a little despondent and I was beginning to feel sorry for him. 'I tell you what, leave me your email address and if I ever need your particular set of skills I will call you.'

'Really?' he brightened.

'Absolutely.'

Anything to get you out of my office, you total, grade A nut bag.

He scribbled his email address on a noticeboard and skipped back down the stairs. From my position stood near the door in my small office,

I could see the next in line peer around the corner, come to a decision and head up the stairs towards me.

From my vantage point above him, I could see that he was wearing a suit. A good start, I thought. He also had on a tie, his shoes looked new and neat and his hair was elegantly styled with a side parting.

This could be much better.

As he reached the top of the stairs I took a step forward to shake his hand, but no hand was offered in return. Instead, he grasped the front of his suit with both hands then he yanked hard and ripped his entire outfit off as one, to reveal a Spiderman outfit beneath. He then reached behind his head to pull the face piece down to cover his features.

Perfect.

I had to commend him for his efforts. The suit had clearly been carefully tailored so he could rip it off as one and must have taken some time and effort to create. In addition, although I suspected one could buy such things online, the Spiderman outfit was also utterly convincing, and it fit him well.

There was no getting away from the fact that this was precisely not what I wanted to hire though. So, I skipped formalities and got to the point. 'I need an office admin assistant, not a Spiderman wannabe. Is there any chance you can wear sensible clothes and perform mundane office tasks?'

'Are you kidding? You have Spiderman in front of you and you want me to answer the phone and take notes?' He was completely serious.

'It seems prudent to point out that I advertised for a part time administrative assistant, not Spiderman.'

'Well yes, but any fool can hire an office clerk. What you need is a crime fighting partner, someone who has superhuman strength and isn't afraid to trade blows with evil villains.' I was finding it quite distracting that I could not see his eyes at all and when he spoke I could not see his mouth, only the face mask moving. I gave him another look. He was not very muscular.

Curious now I decided to test him. 'So, with your superhuman strength, how many press ups would you say you can perform?'

'All of them!' he shot back.

'Okay, Spiderman. Crack on.' I took a seat by the window, so he would have the whole office floorspace on which to impress me.

'Err. Ok,' he said, sounding decidedly less certain now. He fell forward into a traditional press up position and started actually doing press ups.

'I'll count for you,' I offered and began to call them out. 'Two, three, Four, Five, Six, Seven, Eight.' The next one came a little slower than the previous ones. 'Niiiine,' I counted as he slowly rose back to the start position. He went down again, got about halfway back up and the T of ten died on my lips.

He collapsed on the carpet breathing hard. 'I think,' he managed between breaths, 'that I have to be actually fighting crime,' more breaths, 'for the superhuman strength to work.'

I had pandered to his fantasy for long enough. 'I don't think this will work out. I need an office assistant. Really that's all I need. Thank you for coming in.' I didn't leave him room to present an argument but offered my hand to get him back up. I gave him his discarded business suit as I showed him towards the door. 'Send the next one up, won't you?' I asked of his back as he descended the stairs.

I checked my watch to see how much time I had wasted already and sitting down behind my desk ready for the next candidate. The next chap through the door was wearing a poor-quality black suit and had a very chunky but battered looking briefcase in his left hand. His hair was thinning, and his waist was expanding as one sees in so many middle-aged men. Despite his suit and hair and waist he had a professionally broad smile and came right at me to shake my hand.

'Reg Parker,' he said introducing himself. He placed the briefcase on my desk, popped the clips to open it and swung it around to face me. 'I have for you, Mr. Michaels, every piece of high tech ghost-hunting and supernatural detection equipment you could possibly want.' He proceeded to point out and name the gadgets in the case. 'EMF meter, full spectrum camera, EVP recorder, NVGs, motion sensors able to detect ethereal matter.'

Inside the case was an array of gadgets, some that I recognised, such as night vision goggles, but most were odd looking and obscure with a dubious number of buttons and LEDs. I picked up the set of NVGs.

'Best that money can buy,' Reg told me, lying though his teeth. They were old British military issue circa 1990. I had worn the exact same model a few times back in the day. They looked serviceable, but such things were not hard to come by anymore. I put them back in the case, my brief curiosity satisfied. 'They are not all that special compared with some of my more specialist equipment,' he said, selecting an odd-looking box with a small screen. He flicked it on and to me, it looked like a cheap oscilloscope. The analogue screen could have been taken from a 1970s television except it was only two inches square. He extended two antennae from the top, the old slide out chrome type one would find on an analogue radio thirty years ago. High-tech this was not.

'What does it do, Mr Parker?' I genuinely wanted to hear the codswallop that he had prepared to explain the item.

'The latest in PKE – that is Parapsychotic kinetic energy detecting equipment.'

Wrong, I thought to myself, certain the correct term is Psychokinetic Energy.

'What this sweet thing will do is allow you to find the source of the ghost's energy, the point that is anchoring it to the earth still. Once found you can destroy the object it has linked itself to and free it to enter the spirit realm. I am happy to give you a full demonstration of each piece of equipment once the purchase is made.

I had to hand it to Reg - he was utterly fluent in talking rubbish. The meaningless words just fell from his mouth and he delivered them with such conviction. It was entertaining, but I felt that I had better things to do with my time.

'Mr. Parker, I am curious to hear how much of this equipment you sell.'

'It would depend on whether you wanted the figure for the domestic market or global sales.' Again, there was not the slightest hesitation in his lie. I could really admire salespeople. 'Now, I can offer you today an introductory discount of fifty percent if you spend over £2500.00 and take out finance.' He paused for effect before delivering the killer line. 'This is a one day offer only though. I'm afraid I have several customers waiting and quite limited stock because it is in such high demand.'

'Two thousand five hundred pounds. You cannot take a penny less?'

'No hard bargaining I'm afraid, Mr. Michaels. I can see you are a savvy customer, but these are rare items. I have the finance paperwork right here. Shall we get started?'

'I'm afraid it is just too much money for me, Mr. Parker.'

'Oh. Err, are you sure.' He looked unsure for the first time since entering my office.

'Quite sure. You did say you had other customers waiting. Perhaps they will have more secure funds than I.'

'But, the finance, Mr. Michaels. Very affordable repayments,' he said with a smile.

'Perhaps you should leave me your card. That way I can contact you if I need any of these items.'

'Supply and demand, sir. If you need it at a rush it will cost more.'

'I will take the risk.'

Reg looked as if he were going to restart with a fresh tactic, but either he realised it was pointless or perhaps conceded to himself that he had a case full of crap and had not been able to swindle me and so should move on. Whatever the case was, he gave up and put his sad collection of worthless electronics away.

'You cannot blame a chap for trying,' he said as he took his briefcase and headed back out the door and down the stairs.

I decided I had wasted enough time. The endless line of candidates I had seen outside seemed unlikely to yield a worthwhile employee. It was the first time I had ever interviewed someone for a job. I didn't count Amanda. I had been erring on the polite side and holding my tongue instead of telling the crazies what I thought. I had done that for long enough though.

As I got to the top of the stairs and started down them the door to the bottom opened and a middle-aged woman entered. She was dressed as the fifth incarnation of Dr. Who - the one that Peter Davidson played. She even had a cricket bat under her left arm.

I held out a warning hand for her to stop. 'Hell, no,' I told her dismissively, as I brushed past her and out into the street.

It was cool out today and overcast. It threatened to rain again although it was currently dry. The line of applicants for my crappy admin assistant role had grown. I estimated that there must be over one hundred people and they were all wearing costumes of some kind or were desperately odd looking. What I mean by that is they appeared to have not checked themselves in a mirror. Ever. They had crazy hair, their clothes in general not only failed to coordinate but also appeared to have escaped from a prior century. I am not one to follow, or even advocate following fashion, nor do I think vanity is something to be admired. But, come on guys.

I was being watched by the people standing in line. Most were giving me an engaging smile, some were dressed as warriors and were trying to look tough. One, a young lady, blew me a kiss and flicked her head to make her hair move. It was probably supposed to be sexy, but it caught in the beard of the chap behind her who was dressed as a wizard. I ignored the pair while they tried to untangle themselves. I took two steps out into the street so that more of the line could see me and raised my hands.

193

'I am Tempest Michaels. I advertised for an administrative assistant. That is the only job on offer today. The job involves managing emails, answering the phone and some filing. Nothing else.' I could see there were going to be questions. 'There is no ghostbusting to be had, no fighting the forces of evil. I am not looking to employ someone to help me battle witchcraft or prevent a coming alien invasion.' Some of the hands that had been beginning to rise had gone back down. 'Unless you are here to interview for a job that involves a bit of typing, dealing with invoices and sifting emails, please leave.'

No one moved for several seconds and I thought I was going to have to reinforce the concept somehow. Then a Mace Windu lookalike gave up brandishing his very authentic looking purple lightsabre, switched it off and began trudging away. It opened a floodgate. Soon the costume party was drifting down Rochester High street, some towards Chatham, some towards the bridge over the muddy river Medway and perhaps onwards towards Strood. Others crossed the road and went into the coffee shop. Just one chap came directly towards me. He was dressed in an outfit that would not have seemed unusual were it not for the company that he had just been keeping. Coming through the crowd of Jedi, wizards, knights, Ghostbusters etcetera I took more notice and could see that his suit was in fact not so much a suit, which of course it was, but it was a suit from two hundred years ago, complete with pocket watch, greatcoat and a swagger stick with a polished chrome knob in his right hand. His face was full of knowing importance. Clearly, my instructions did not apply to him, or at least that was what he believed. I realised he was dressed as Sherlock Holmes. Or better yet as Basil Rathbone dressed to play Sherlock Holmes.

'I can perform all the tasks you have demanded,' he said, his voice a soothing baritone.

'You have other skills that you wish to be considered though?' I coaxed.

'Indeed. You may recognise me. I am a famous detective. My death was reported in 1893. However, I survived the fall from the Reichenbach falls and was transported forward in time to find myself here. My name is

Sherlock Holmes and I am here to offer you my skills to solve the cases that will baffle you.'

I looked past him. As the crowd dispersed and the numbers thinned I was left with just one in the queue. A man in his early twenties. He looked vaguely familiar. I turned my attention back to the man in front of me. I had an urge to be abrupt and rude, it seemed the swiftest method of ending this exchange. It was not in my nature to do so though. Instead, I smiled politely. 'I'm afraid I would find myself as the weaker part of such a partnership and that does not appeal. I am sure you understand.'

Thankfully he nodded. I extended my hand, we shook, and I stepped around him and towards the young man who was now stood just a few feet from the door that led to my office.

'Shall we get started?' I asked and ushered him towards the door. I went up the stairs quickly, taking my jacket off as I went. 'Please come in. Take a seat.'

The chap came in behind me and took the seat in front of my desk as I went around to sit behind it. 'Good morning. As you are the only candidate that has survived the initial filtering process the job is now yours provided you can demonstrate sufficient aptitude. Can I assume you speak English?'

'Yes. Very much so.' His accent was local. I was glad for it. It would not have mattered if the chap had been Ukrainian, or Polish or even French, nevertheless I was pleased that English was his native language.

'Here is my keyboard,' I said passing it to him and swivelling the screen so that he could see it. 'Please navigate to Microsoft word and write a passage about what you had for breakfast this morning.'

He took the keyboard and mouse and got going. I had him perform a few other basic tasks just to reassure myself he was capable. I asked him questions as he was doing it. Why he was interested in the job? How was it that he was available? What other experience he had and what other jobs he had held? I wanted to make sure he could speak articulately and answer questions while he was typing. Five minutes after he walked into my office I could not find anything further to ask him or any further tasks to set him and not a single reason why I should not employ him.

'I just realised that I have not yet asked you your name.'

He did not reply immediately though. He was sitting, looking at me with his head cocked slightly to one side as if he wanted to ask a question rather than introduce himself.

'And your name is?' I prompted.

'Jim Butterworth.'

Jim Butterworth. The name sounded familiar. I knew it from somewhere. Where did I know it from? My brain was attempting to connect the two dots but could not quite make them touch.

'You might know me better as Demedicus.'

Bingo! Ding, ding, ding, ding, ding.

Now I knew why he looked familiar. Three weeks ago, I had been called by his grandmother who had been convinced he was a vampire. She had wanted me to kill him. He was no longer dressed as a vampire though. The last time I had seen him his finger nails had been painted black, he had been wearing eyeliner and he had convinced himself that he was a vampire. He was living in a basement, sleeping in a coffin and had threatened to kill me for disturbing his slumber.

'Right. Well, thank you for coming in. You look very different.' He was wearing normal person clothes. A pair of grey trousers, black shoes, a white shirt and a coat.

Are you still living with your Grandmother?' I asked

'Err, no. No, Granny kicked me out.'

'Oh.'

'Yes. I am living with my boyfriend now. I hope that doesn't bother you.

'I cannot imagine why it would,' I said. There are millions of gay people. The world is filled with people of different race, religion, gender. They are separated and connected by their interests, beliefs, hopes, and dreams. I wished them all every happiness and generally hoped they would leave me alone and stop killing one another.

'This is a new thing actually.' I guess James wanted to tell me about it even though I had not prompted more information. 'After you killed our master, Ambrogio.'

'I didn't kill him, James. He died attempting to escape justice and after he had given me a sound beating.'

'Yes, sorry. Anyway, you did us all a favour killing him. After that the club fell apart and I decided I didn't want to be a vampire anymore and that made me question some other decisions and I realised that I am LGBT.'

Probably not all four at the same time I suspected. Maybe not L at all - equipment deficiency and all that.

'Is there anything else you want to know?' he asked looking a little sheepish as if he now felt that he had told me far more than I needed to know.

'When can you start?'

It turned out he had nothing planned for the rest of the day, so we discussed pay and hours and probation period. I had read all about such things this morning while I was eating my breakfast so that I had a slight idea what I ought to pay and how I should manage an employee. Then I left him sitting at my desk sifting emails while I went to the bank.

Spectral Dog Case. Tuesday, 12th October 1100hrs

When I got back to the office, James was on the phone. He was diligently taking notes on a pad I kept on the desk, the phone trapped between his shoulder and ear to leave his hands free.

I listened to his half of the conversation, giving him the space to do his job. I acknowledged that I was impressed - not only was he doing a good job, but he had grasped the task without being prompted and sounded confident on the phone.

'So, this was Saturday?' He made a note. 'And you have not seen him since then?' Another note and a pause while he listened. 'Can we go back to the bit about the dog please?' A pause, 'Yes.' Pause. 'Yes.' Pause. 'The size of a horse. Yes, I think I have that. Mrs. Collins can I place you on hold for one moment while I confer with my colleague?'

James put his hand over the speaker and stared at the phone base unit hopefully searching for a hold button that was not there. I had not seen the need to buy a phone with lots of functions. In fact, I had not bought a phone at all but had taken an old one out of my attic. He accepted that his search was fruitless and looked up at me.

'Do you want to take this call? I'm not really sure what I am doing. The lady...' he looked down at the pad. 'Mrs. Collins, her husband has disappeared, and she thinks he has been eaten by a spectral dog.'

I motioned for him to hand over the phone.

'Mrs. Collins, this is Tempest Michaels. I am the lead investigator and owner of Blue Moon Investigations. You say that your husband has disappeared?'

The lady's name was Carol Collins, her husband had gone missing three days ago but, of course, the police had done little to follow up on the missing person report. This would not have attracted my attention nor given her cause to seek out a paranormal investigator, it was the clearly defined, glowing spectral dog on the CCTV camera at her husband's breakers yard that got me involved.

The couple owned a breakers yard in Gillingham where they dismantled old cars and made a profit from selling off parts and recycling plastics, steel etcetera. Her husband was the gaffer and she did the books and they employed a few lads that operated the machinery and drove the vehicles. Her husband had simply failed to come home one night. She had not worried at first. He often came home late because he had a late collection or delivery or went via the pub for a few drinks, then came in after she had gone to bed for the night. When he was not there in the morning she started to panic though and then she got a call from Malcolm - one of the lads at the yard, who had arrived to open up and found it still open. Her husband's car was still there but there was no sign of him. They did, however, find blood on the ground in the yard.

The police were called and confirmed the blood was human. There was no body though and no other evidence to work with. Mrs. Collins said she was deeply worried that something had happened to him, but he had no enemies. They had no real rivals, certainly none that would stoop to murder to eliminate the competition, so she could not imagine what might have happened. The police had assured her they would give it their full attention and had immediately looked at the CCTV footage from the previous night. There were only a couple of cameras, so what one could see of the premises was limited. They whizzed through until someone yelled out as a blur went past the camera.

When they backed the tape up and advanced it at regular speed what everyone watching had seen was an enormous glowing dog walk past the camera. I could understand instantly why she had called me for help. The police would carry on with their investigation but were not going to look into the possibility that a ghost dog had eaten her husband.

There was not much the police could do as the dog did not appear to be breaking any laws. They had searched for it at the premises where not only could the dog not be found but no trace of it either. The dog was clearly massive, on the short clip we saw it walked in front of a Vauxhall Corsa and was not much lower at its shoulder than the roof of the car.

To her credit, Mrs. Collins did not seem convinced that it was a ghost dog, but she wisely had no intention of finding out for herself what it was. She wanted it dealt with before it damaged the business or scared off her staff and she wanted her husband back if at all possible, please.

I noted down all of this, committing much of the detail to memory, wrote down her address and agreed to meet her in an hour. I put the phone down.

James was sitting in the chair behind the desk, his hands folded in his lap. He was looking up at me expectantly, either waiting for an instruction or for me to tell him what I was going to do.

'Well done, James. You handled that phone call in a very professional manner.' Credit where it is due. I worried that I just sounded patronising. It was my first time being a boss. I had subordinates when I was in the Army, but this was different. Suddenly, I had two employees. Not that Amanda was really my subordinate. I dismissed my concerns, I was the owner of the business, so as long as I could manage to be in charge without being a dick about it I should be fine.

'So, what now?' James asked.

I looked at my watch. The time was 1117hrs. We had agreed to part-time hours where James would work five days per week between 0900hrs and 1300hrs and would on request work on a Saturday if the business was busy. He had been employed for all of about forty minutes so far and I had not really set him any tasks.

'I think,' I said as I opened the desk drawer and dug around in it, 'that you should knock off for today and start in earnest tomorrow at 0900hrs. I will, of course, pay you in full for today.' I found what I was looking for and produced a spare set of keys. One key opened the door from the street at the bottom of the stairs, the other opened my office door, which I never locked. My reasoning was that if someone broke their way in through the bottom door they would just do the same at the top of the stairs rather than be put off by a second locked door and I would have two broken doors to replace.

I did not have to convince James to take the rest of the day off. He was gone in a flash. I settled into the still warm desk chair and opened a search engine. I was glad of this new case, I needed a distraction from the embarrassment of being suckered by Brett Barker. I looked for the breakers yard business. I found a listing for them that gave a phone number and address, but they had no website. The search did show them on a map though. I clicked on the image, allowed it to open to full page size and scrolled down to zoom out. The business was located well away from houses and residential property, down a narrow looking lane near to the riverfront. It was not far from the Strand outdoor leisure park I had been taken to as a child. I wondered what that place looked like now. A memory of chasing my sister through the kiddie's pool surfaced. I smiled at the image of childhood happiness and innocence but then remembered how that had been replaced by adult problems like Brett Barker and my smile, rather than fading, got screwed up and thrown in a corner in anger.

Bother.

I was wallowing. It had been hours since I was released from custody. I had heard nothing from Brett Barker or Owen Larkin or even Mrs. Barker, but I was still employed to solve the mystery of the Phantom for Brett and to work out for Mrs. Barker who had killed her husband. I was quite very ready to prove that it was Brett Barker behind everything and that he was guilty of murder. I just had no start point currently.

I slapped myself in the face, a physical action to break my mental focus.

Come back to Brett Barker later. Deal with the spectral dog.

I left the office and went to see Mrs. Collins.

The House of Mrs. Collins. Tuesday, October 12th 1215hrs

The address she had given me was for her house, also in Gillingham. I knew the area a little and could identify where her road was. It was all terraced houses in that area, which would often mean that parking was difficult. But at lunchtime on a Tuesday I should be okay.

I cruised along her street, taking in the house numbers until I found hers. There was nowhere to park despite my expectations, but I found a spot around the corner. Her house was coated in render and painted a soft magnolia colour with contrasting toffee brown on the stone features around the windows, front door and on the guttering. The front garden was tiny and sported a pair of rose bushes, one each side of the front bay window. Leading from the street to her door, was a chequerboard path of black and white tiles. A few of them were broken yet most were intact, and I had to wonder how long the path had been there. If it was an original feature, it was most likely over one hundred years and counting. Pretty good workmanship and made to last.

I walked down it and rang the bell. Through the small panel of frosted glass, a shadow could be seen moving. Seconds later the door was opened by a lady. She introduced herself as Carol Collins. I showed her my card and she welcomed me inside.

Over the next hour, Mrs. Collins told me everything she knew, showed me the CCTV footage several times and introduced me to her two employees, Barry and Malcolm, who were politely waiting in her lounge when I arrived.

The CCTV footage was compelling. In the short clip where the dog appeared, it wandered from left to right in front of several dead cars that provided a reference for its size, but it paused at one point and looked directly at the camera. Its eyes were twin glowing orbs of evil, at least that was how Mrs. Collins described them. I was certain it was just the ambient light bouncing off the tapetum lucidum, a reflective layer in many animal's eyes. I had to admit though that the effect was convincing and would have been at home on a horror movie special effect. The dog's fur was definitely glowing, it made the creature appear translucent as if one could see through it.

Mrs. Collins expressed that she was too scared of whatever it was to go investigating for herself, so she had sent in Barry and Malcolm. Two nights ago, they had volunteered to go to the yard. Mrs. Collins had kept the yard shut since her husband had gone missing, so no one had been there since the police had left. The two chaps returned terrified an hour later with a tale of being chased by a hell-hound and barely escaping with their lives.

They regaled me with the same story, telling me to be wise and never go to the yard after dark. Malcolm wanted the whole thing to be sold off.

'You should sell it, Carol,' Malcolm said to his employer.

'How can I? What will you and Barry do for a living?'

'Oh, don't worry about us. We will land on our feet somewhere. It's just not going to be the same without Edgar there anyway.'

'But he might be just fine, Malcolm. Mr. Michaels doesn't think it is a ghost dog. Do you, Mr. Michaels?'

'Well...'

Malcolm cut me off before I could speak. 'If you wait, the value will just keep going down and you will get nothing for it.'

Carol seemed to be deliberating. 'What if Edgar turns up? He could just be hurt somewhere. It happens all the time.'

'He would understand, Carol,' Malcolm said. 'You have to sell as quickly as you can before the press gets hold of the story. Once that happens no one will buy it.' Malcolm was pressing the idea of selling the business quite hard. I made a note on my pad. If their behaviour was suspicious then Mrs. Collins was not picking up on it.

I left Mrs. Collins with her two employees and headed to the breakers yard. Notwithstanding Malcolm's warning, I felt quite inclined to go there at night. I would need a partner for the event and one or two items to aid me in capturing the dog if indeed there was one there. That I had seen it on TV did nothing to make me believe I would see it again.

I had been hired to rid her of the spectral hound and to determine if her husband had been dragged to hell. My theory was that the Mrs. Collins' husband had simply absconded. They owned the breakers yard between them, so if he elected to leave her he probably wanted her to give up her half of the business, a goal he was unlikely to achieve if she was the woman scorned and wanted to cut his nuts off and boil them in vinegar. What had tipped me off was her two employees Barry and Malcolm. They had put on an impressive performance playing the part of two men completely terrified by the spectral hound. It had convinced Mrs. Collins that what she had seen on CCTV was in fact real. When I ruled out the chance that the creature was a ghost dog or some other supernatural apparition the obvious conclusion was that they were in on it. Barry and Malcolm were not the only employees at the yard, but they were the longest serving. "They have been with Edgar since the start." Mrs. Collins had told me. My guess was that their loyalty lay with Mr. Collins. More than anything though it had been Malcolm's continual assurance that the best thing she could do was sell, even at a reduced or below market price.

The drive to the yard took me less than five minutes although I had to get out and walk the last five hundred metres because the road was full of terrible potholes and I was driving a low-slung Porsche. The road only led to the breakers yard, which explained the lack of upkeep and repairs. To either side, piles of litter fought weeds for dominance. I passed abandoned white goods, tyres and every manner of vehicle component.

I was wearing Italian leather loafers that were not designed for their current use, but I refused to tiptoe too daintily around the puddles, mud and oil spills. I would clean them later instead of being precious about getting them dirty.

I arrived at the yard gates. To my left and right stretched fencing that had seen far better days. It was intact though and had a good layer of barbed wire at the top which looked like a recent addition. Inside the yard, the tarmac road continued for about thirty metres to terminate at a portacabin - the office no doubt. All around the site, what I could see of it anyway, were old, broken cars stacked in piles. One atop the other and four, five or even six deep in places. They had been piled up to make lines so that the gaps between looked like corridors.

I watched for a few minutes, but no dog the size of a Rhinoceros wandered past. I whistled and tried, 'Here boy,' a few times. Still nothing. I gave up and headed home.

I got back to my car, took a rag out of the boot and wiped the worst of the muck from my shoes before I got in. Heading back out towards Gillingham and home I placed a call to Big Ben.

The display screen in my car showed the call connecting. He picked up on the first ring.

'Alright, bender. What's up?' Big Ben was such a delight.

'I have a job for you, mate. We need to catch a giant spectral dog that is haunting a breakers yard in Gillingham. Can you fit that in between women tomorrow?' I asked.

'Sounds like fun. Count me in.'

'I need you to do something else first.'

'Name it.'

'I am sure you must have a few lady vets in your back catalogue. You are always bragging about how they all leave you grateful for the experience and begging for more so now you get to prove it. We need a couple of things that might be difficult to obtain without a bit of inside help.' I stopped talking then because I had just seen something and needed to go back and look again. 'Hold on a second mate.'

I slowed the car and swung it around in a big loop to go back over my tracks. The crappy road that led to the Breakers Yard was accessed through an industrial estate. I was almost out of it when I had spotted a business name. I pulled my car in front of it now and took a picture with my phone. Palmer Pharmaceuticals was housed in a squat brick building perhaps ten metres square over two stories. This was an old industrial estate from the seventies when the businesses were proper individual buildings in contrast to the modern version which was generally lines of units inside a single larger building. There were a few cars in the car park, but it did not look like it sold anything from the premises unlike most of the businesses around it. Perhaps then it was simply a cheap rent from which they could conduct their enterprise and their goods were sold via third parties.

I scratched my head. I was staring at the name of the business because it meant something important. I could not work out what though. The information would not coalesce into something meaningful. I said the name over out loud a few times. That made no difference either, so I filed it away to research later.

'Dude are you ok?' asked Big Ben. 'I can hear you mumbling something.'

'Does Palmer Pharmaceutical mean anything to you?' I asked.

'I don't think so,' he answered after a pause.

I put the car into reverse, swung it around again and pointed the bonnet back in the direction of home. 'So, here is what I need you to get...'

The Killer Clue. Tuesday, October 12th 1617hrs

I got home soon enough but did that thing where you have driven somewhere and then have no memory of the journey as if you have been on autopilot instead. I had been thinking about the pharmacy. It meant something, but I didn't know what and had been wracking my brains to make a connection.

I was getting nothing. Perhaps it would come to me if I got on with something else. I was out of the car and opening the door to my house. Bull and Dozer were excited to see me as always. I patted them each and let them in the garden, I stood on the patio watching them snuffle in the bushes. They showed no sign of wanting to come back inside, so I went to fetch a cup of tea thinking I could sit outside with them or maybe throw a ball if either of them felt inclined to chase it.

I left the patio door open despite the cool air, hoping that this would impart to the dogs the message that I would return shortly. From the kitchen window, I watched Bull disappear behind the greenhouse as the kettle boiled. He emerged the other side just as the kettle reached a full violent boil and flicked its own switch off.

Water poured, I opened the drawer next to me for a teaspoon and the dots I could not join together five minutes ago aligned themselves in my head and solved the Barker Mill case in one hit.

In the drawer, my hand was hovering over the small spoons and next to them was a packet of painkiller tablets I had bought whenever I had last suffered a headache. Palmer Pharmaceutical made pills. That was the connection. I picked the packet up forgot my tea entirely and rushed through to the office.

To the left of my desk was a pile of unfiled paperwork. I had yet to work out what I ought to do with old case files. My head said they had no purpose after each case was closed and that if I held onto everything I would soon be paying for offsite storage. Furthermore, I would spend all too long organising and storing the files rather than doing investigative work. The piles of paper had not yet grown to such a proportion that I could not ignore them though so that was what I had been doing. Right at the top, because it was a chronological pile was the Brett Barker file. I pulled it onto my desk and started leafing slowly through it. Less than five minutes later I pushed back in my chair and sat there jubilantly holding the smoking gun.

In my hand were copies of Brett Barker's business finances that Mrs. Barker had provided. Among the many pages were his company credit card statements and there on June 5th was a payment of twenty thousand pounds to Martin Wilkins. I had been curious about it at the time, as it was such a large and exact amount, and I had performed a brief search to find that Martin worked at Palmer Pharmaceuticals. I did not know what the money had been for, but I had a pretty good idea.

I went onto a search engine and looked the firm up. Lining up the crosshairs on Brett Barker had not taken very long at all. Palmer Pharmaceuticals made a wide range of medical treatments administered in pill form. Among them was Captopril. George Barker had been taking Captopril to control a heart condition and I was willing to bet that Brett Barker had bought a supply of the packets with a placebo inside instead of the real drug. He could swap the old man's pills over, they would look exactly the same but do nothing to aid his failing heart.

It was not solid evidence. However, I was certain it was enough to make people look further. I had him. I just needed something more so that I could remove any ambiguity – like a note from Brett plotting the whole thing. That would be nice, but was unlikely, so it was time to act in a calm and strategic manner.

I called Amanda. Her phone rang for some time before it connected to her messaging service. I elected to disconnect and leave her a text instead. The text simply told her that I had evidence that Brett was guilty, and she needed to call me.

I would call her again in a few minutes if I did not hear from her and keep trying her number until I was successfully connected. I needed to call Mrs. Barker though, so I tackled that next.

Mrs. Barker must have assigned my mobile number to her phone as she answered with, 'Good evening, Mr Michaels?'

'Good evening, Mrs. Barker,' I started. 'I believe I have found the evidence that implicates Brett in your husband's death.'

I heard her catch her breath, the noise suggesting that I was delivering news that was very exciting. 'I am glad to hear it, Mr. Michaels. After last night's debacle, I was considering releasing you from the contract. What is it that you have found?' she asked.

'Evidence that he has been substituting your husband's heart medication. It is circumstantial evidence at this time leaving me to find something more concrete before I go to the police. I need to search his rooms at the house as well as his office at the mill. Does he have any other property or hideaway locations where he might stash something?'

'Not that I am aware of, but I will give that some thought.'

'What I am looking for initially may be in his wing of the house and I do not wish to tip him off that we are searching, so I need you to provide me with free access to his rooms. Can you do that?'

'Of course, Mr. Michaels. Brett will leave the house at eight o'clock tomorrow morning, as usual, to go to work. I can let you into his wing of the residence any time after that.'

'Very good, Mrs. Barker. If I do not find what I am looking for there we may need to search his office or car.

'What time should I expect you?' she asked.

I ran the question through my head quickly. I was keen to get on this right now, but the task had to wait until Brett was going to be out of the way for a few hours. If there was evidence in his apartment I expected it to be hard to find. Probably hidden. I still hadn't spoken with Amanda and I wanted her there for several reasons. 'Shall we say 1100hrs?' I offered.

'You mean eleven o'clock?' she clarified, sounding confused.

'Yes, Mrs. Barker. Eleven o'clock. If I need to change that time I will inform you.' My phone vibrated in my hand to indicate another caller was trying to connect. Pulling the phone from my ear I saw that it was Amanda. 'I have another call, Mrs. Barker. Please excuse me, I will see you tomorrow at eleven o'clock.'

'Good evening, Mr. Michaels.' She hung up.

'Amanda?' I said quickly punching the answer button on my phone to switch between calls.

'Tempest.'

'Hi.'

'Hi.'

'Err, sorry. This conversation got lost somewhere. I was just on the phone to Mrs. Barker. I believe Brett bought fake heart meds and substituted them for his grandfather's. I intend to look for additional evidence of this in his wing of the Barker house tomorrow morning and need our help.' I let that statement hang for a moment. 'I think he really did it.' I added as I knew Amanda was less inclined to believe the handsome, super-rich beau was guilty.

'Okay. What did you find?' she asked.

'There is a transaction a few months ago in his financial records where he paid twenty thousand pounds to a Martin Wilkins. Martin Wilkins works at Palmer Pharmaceuticals and Palmer Pharmaceuticals make Captopril. You are going to tell me that this is circumstantial, but we must follow this up. If we find anything else, bearing in mind I intend to find and quiz Martin Wilkins, then we have him.

'What are you asking me?'

'I am going to the Barker mansion tomorrow at 1100hrs. Mrs. Barker will let me into his wing of the building so no warrant to search the premises is required or anything else that might hinder the chain of evidence should we find what I am looking for. I want you to come with me though to corroborate what I find, call in the detectives who will catalogue and record the evidence and to make the arrest if we can find what we need.'

I could hear her thinking. She made small noises as she mulled the idea over. Was I asking a lot? I did not think that I was and there was no risk to her that I could see. 'Okay.' She said having arrived at the same conclusion. 'We search his place and if we find anything I will make the appropriate calls. This needs to be done right.'

'Deal,' I replied, cheering silently. I was going anyway but having Amanda along would speed up the search and make any evidence found more legitimate.

'Will you be at the office?' she asked.

'Yes. Meet me there?'

'I'll be there by ten.' She disconnected.

I put my phone down. Then realised I was not yet finished. I had loosely organised to raid the Breakers yard with Ben tomorrow night. Was that still a good idea? Probably not. I did not want to run the risk that I was tied up still dealing with the Phantom case.

I picked up my phone once more and placed a call to Big Ben.

'Dude,' he answered sounding a little out of breath.

'Hold fire on that gear I asked you to get, mate. We need to postpone the raid for a day or so.'

'Okay.'

'Okay? Really? No questions to clarify why or what has changed?'

'Well, I would take an interest in your stuff but then I would be ignoring the two naked girls that are currently waiting for me upstairs.'

I had no idea if he was lying or telling me the truth. It seemed entirely possible he was being honest though.

'Well, we still need the gear, just not tonight.'

'No problem. I have it already. I went to visit the vet lady like you suggested and she was just finishing her surgical shift for the day, so she brought it to my house and decided to stay for a shag.'

'Then where did the second girl come from?' I asked, thinking I had caught him out.

'There was too much gear for her to carry so she brought her vet nurse with her,' he explained as if it were obvious. I really hated him sometimes. Mr. Wriggly echoed the sentiment. 'Got to go. Talk later.' He hung up, leaving me with imagined images of the impending shagfest at his place flashing through my mind.

Git.

I checked my watch. It was very nearly 1700hrs. My stomach growled, politely reminding me that I needed to eat. I called the dogs in for their dinner. Then looked up a number for Palmer Pharmaceuticals and dialled it.

It connected almost immediately. 'Palmer Pharmaceuticals, Good afternoon.' A man's voice.

'Good afternoon.' I started wondering what approach would get me the information I wanted. I went with the direct question first. 'This is Dr. Edwards of Dawlish Medical Supplies. Can I speak with Martin Wilkins please?'

I was half expecting to be asked what my call was pertaining to but after a very short pause his voice came back with, 'I'll put you through now.'

Pleased that I was going to get to question the chap and be able to hear from his reaction whether he was indeed guilty of supplying Brett Barker with dodgy drugs I was surprised to hear a woman's voice instead.

'Good afternoon. How can I help?' It always annoyed me that receptionist staff would put a call through without telling the next person

212

in line what the caller wanted thus forcing them to start their explanation all over again.

'Good afternoon. My name is Dr. Edwards. I was hoping to speak with Martin Wilkins.'

'Can I ask what it is pertaining to?' She was rude enough to see no need to introduce herself.

'It is a long-running matter that he and I have been working on together?'

'Really?' she said, her voice full of disbelief. 'You have been discussing a long-running matter with the office mail boy? I hardly think so.' I was going about it badly, but I was getting information nevertheless.

I tried a new tack, taking some of the polish out of my voice and allowing in some local guttural drawl. 'Okay. You got me. I'm his mate, Dave. Is he there?'

'You are not his mate. I doubt your name is even Dave. Martin Wilkins quit his job here four months ago. I shall assume you are another debt collector after money that he owes someone. Please do not call again.' She hung up abruptly.

The short phone call had not given me what I wanted, which was to talk to Martin and pin him down so that I could force him to meet with me. He might be key to proving Brett's guilt. I had however, found out plenty about him. I performed some internet searches, but he was not on Facebook and although I could find some limited information about him I could not find a photograph or where he was currently employed.

I fixed myself some food and turned on the TV. There was not much more I could do tonight.

My New Office Assistant. Wednesday, 13th October 0857hrs

As it was my business, I came and went from the office as I pleased and rarely kept exact office hours because I had no need to. If I had no case to pursue and I felt like a lie in or wanted to spend longer in the gym I simply did so. Only once had this practice caught me out when I had arrived at the office at around 0930hrs to find a client waiting. The client had elected to come to the office rather than email or call because, like so many others with a genuine case, he had felt he would sound like a mental patient through any medium other than in person.

This morning, I had risen and walked the dogs and eaten a nutritious breakfast all before 0800hrs. Then I had sat on my sofa with Bull on my lap watching breakfast news when I remembered that I now had an employee at the office and ought to be there before him.

As it turned out, I got to the office only just before 0900hrs and in my rush skipped my usual routine of going via the coffee shop to get a beverage, read the free paper and maybe flirt with Hayley. Going through the bottom office door at 0857hrs, I could see that the office light was on. James had beaten me in, opened up and was already at it.

However, when I got to the top of the stairs what I saw was a young lady where James should be sitting. She wore a pair of thin-framed, designer glasses and she had loose curls of blond hair cascading over one shoulder. I could not see much of her face from the door, it was covered by her hair, but she looked up as I came in.

'Good morning, boss,' she said in a man's voice.

OMG. It's James.

'You look a little stunned, boss. Is there something wrong?' he asked, the voice sounding completely alien coming from the cherry red lips. My brain was working overtime to keep my mouth from speaking as I was not sure what words might come out of it. I was not bothered that my new assistant liked to wear ladies clothing. Well, not exactly. I had always held with the opinion that people should be allowed to do as they please provided their actions do not negatively affect others. My brain though was struggling to accept the image and the sound had been generated in the same place. It was like watching someone play the trumpet but hearing the noise of a piano come from it. The disturbing part was that James as a girl was not unattractive. If I passed him/her in the way, I might glance twice.

'Err, good morning, James.

'It's, um. It's Jane,' he/she replied with some hesitation.

'I'm sorry?'

'I have two personalities fighting for dominance,' he/she said with a little more confidence as if they were rehearsed words that had been said in explanation many times before. 'You know my male side, James. Well, this is my feminine persona, Jane.'

I like to think that I am hard to shock. I have seen a lot of the world's ugly bits, been exposed to the dregs of mankind etcetera and it was not so much that my new employee's habits were shocking; they were not. I had not anticipated them though. I was having trouble making my jaw work. I wanted to ask if I needed to stock the toilet with feminine products for his/her needs.

In the end, I went with, 'Jolly good, James. I mean, Jane.'

'Would you like a coffee?' he/she asked.

'Err, yes. I suppose I would.'

This was an unexpected or at least unplanned benefit. I had hired an assistant to perform tasks that were taking up too much of my time. Time that I felt would be better spent engaged in more profitable endeavours. Fetching me coffee was not one of them. However, I saw no reason why I could not fetch the coffee on occasion so that the task was reciprocal. Perhaps Amanda would also want coffee and thus the three of us could take turns. Anyway, coffee sounded good, so I pulled a fresh ten pounds note from my wallet and gave Jane my order.

Jane collected her handbag from the floor by the desk, dropped her phone into it and left the office, shrugging on her coat as she did.

I settled into the chair behind the desk, finding it still warm from her bottom and scanned my emails. This was something I would do less and less now I suppose as I would be training Jane/James to identify which emails or calls were of merit.

Less than two minutes after she had left the office, I heard the door at the bottom of the stairs open again to herald her return. Surely, she had not been gone long enough to have even got to the coffee shop, so had she forgotten my very simple order or was there something else forcing her premature return?

It was not Jane though, but Big Ben's grinning head that appeared around my door frame. 'Alright, nosher?' he asked

'Generally, in England, people start with good morning,' I responded.

'Only because they lack imagination and panache.'

'Good morning, Ben. What are you doing here?' I checked my watch: 0911hrs. 'Are you not normally in bed underneath a supermodel at this time of the day?'

'That would not be unusual, but last night's shag was an air hostess and she had a flight this morning. She left in the middle of the night.'

'I guess that sounds entirely plausible. It fails to explain your presence here though. Not that you are not welcome, of course.'

'I have a golf game and got the time wrong, so I am out of the house an hour early with nothing to do. Your office is on the way, so I decided to stop off here, get some breakfast in one of the many delightful shops and pop in to annoy you.' Big Ben had been leaning against the office door frame until now but finally came in and flopped into one of the chairs by the window.

Then he stopped, sniffing the air experimentally. 'Hold on. I can smell perfume.' he sniffed deeply and wiggled his nose about a bit. 'That's

Princess by Vera Wang. High-end stuff mate, not your average high street brand. Rich client in this morning already?' he asked.

I was impressed by his olfactory system. 'How can you possibly tell the brand and bottle?' I asked.

'How? It has a very oriental flower centred scent. Launched in 2006 it celebrates youth and femininity as its top notes deliver aquatic nuances with the pure and sharp scents of water lily, apple, mandarin and apricot but the heart of the perfume is composed of guava, tiare flower, tuberose and a touch of dark chocolate. The base notes, if one can discern them, deliver traces of vanilla and amber. It is quite distinct from anything else on the market.'

My mouth was hanging open. I had known Big Ben for years and this was the most articulate he had ever been about anything. I could not discern one perfume from another. I struggled to tell my own collection of aftershaves apart.

Big Ben was looking at me as a teacher might to a dull student. 'You have to know your enemy, mate. Otherwise what chance do you have of defeating her?'

I was still a little stunned. 'Actually, you are smelling my new assistant,' I managed.

Big Ben sat bolt upright, leaning forward in his chair to lock eyes with me. A devilish grin on his face. 'Did you go and hire a saucy young assistant to shag?'

'Ah, not exactly.'

'Is she really hot? She is, isn't she? You hired a sexy minxette and were not even going to tell me. Did you shag her at the interview or afterward?'

'It is not really like that, Ben.'

'In what way?' he asked, face all quizzical.

'Well, to start with Jane is…' But then I stopped myself. 'It would not be appropriate for me to have anything other than a professional relationship with her. We are going to work together. Possibly for years if she proves worthy of retaining and wishes to stay, so I am afraid I can report that no shagging has or will take place.'

'Well, nuts to that. I shall assume that since you have not placed dibs on her that I am free to give her a jolly good ploughing myself.' It was a statement of intent, not a question.

'I think I hear her returning with coffee now, so feel free to work your undeniable charm.' I was failing to keep the mirth from my face, but if he had noticed it there he was not reacting to it.

'Watch and learn, Padawan.' Big Ben stood up as we listened to Jane coming up the stairs. He took off his jacket, revealing his muscular frame sheathed in a short-sleeved polo beneath. Standing in place, he pumped his muscles a few times and felt his teeth to ensure there was nothing stuck in them.

Jane reached the top of the stairs where I met her to take my coffee and make the introduction. 'Jane, this is, Ben. He is an old friend of mine and often contracts for the firm when I have dangerous work or need the extra muscle.' I indicated his impressive arms.

Big Ben took a step forward and extended his hand towards Jane who took it gently. Big Ben had an engaging smile set firmly in place. 'Good morning, Jane. This is an unexpected surprise. Tempest always surrounds himself with the most beautiful women.'

'Thank you very much,' Jane replied in her best bass-baritone.

My face was beginning to hurt from holding in my smirk. I watched as Big Ben's confident smile froze in place. He looked down at the hand he was holding and saw that it was not the delicate feminine one he ought to see but was instead quite meaty and manly with some hair on the knuckles. He looked back up at Jane's face, taking in the Adam's apple on the way. The frozen smile fell away as if it were held there by marionette strings that had just been severed.

'Is everything alright?' I asked him.

His mouth flapped open and closed a couple of times and he withdrew his hand. 'Err, yes,' he managed. 'Yes, of course. Are you pre, or post-op?' he asked Jane. He recovered well, I'll give him that.

'Neither, actually,' Jane replied. 'I just have two versions of myself. One female, one male, but all male genitalia.' Jane looked down at the coffee cup she now held with both hands then looked back up at Big Ben in a shy way, sort of peering through her blonde hair and idly dragging one long fingernail around the top of the plastic cup lid. 'I am available, actually. If you would like to take me out sometime.' Somehow, he had managed to make his deep voice sound quite demure.

Big Ben's face was fighting with itself to decide which expression should be displayed. Horror and revulsion were being beaten down by suave coolness, but they were there in the background nonetheless. 'I'll pass I think. I'm strictly no sausage.' He checked his watch. 'Better go in fact. I don't want to keep the chaps waiting and miss our tee time.' He reached behind him to snag his jacket from the chair, slipped into it and squeezed past me to get to the door. He whispered, 'You are a dick,' on his way past.

I chuckled to myself. That had been fun, but I suspected he would get his own back at some point.

'Will there be much of that?' Jane asked.

'Much of what?'

'You using my female side to surprise your friends?' I hadn't thought about this from Jane's point of view. 'I just want to know so that I can be prepared.'

'Jane, please accept my apologies. That was entirely unplanned, and I failed to consider your emotions. I have no plan to spring anything like that on you again. Thank you for playing along though.'

'I thought he might recognise me. I don't think I look all that different as a girl.'

219

'Well, you do.'

Raid on Brett Barker. Wednesday, 13th October 1100hrs

As promised, Amanda arrived at 1000hrs almost exactly. She had called from the car with the intention that I would come down to meet her outside. Instead, I invited her up to the office explaining that I had hired an assistant for the firm.

At 1003hrs Amanda could be heard climbing the stairs. She entered the office with a breezy, 'Good morning.'

'Hey there. How are you this morning?' I replied with genuine interest. I was in a good mood and looking forward to ruining Brett Barker's day. Amanda and I had been on edge for a few days now. It started with her running into Hayley at my place on Sunday, had not improved with me getting arrested on Monday, and the discussion about my feelings regarding her did nothing to improve matters.

'I'm fine, Tempest,' she replied. She was taking off her jacket and had her back to me when she said it.

'Uh-oh,' I said.

'Uh-oh?'

'I know I seem generally confused around women, but I have enough ex-girlfriends to know where the term *fine* sits on the scale.'

'What do you mean?' she asked, her expression turning stony.

I suddenly felt like a pit was opening beneath me. Pressing on presented itself as the safest option. 'Women, in general, have a scale of contentment. It goes in descending order like this: Great, good, okay, not okay, I hate you, fine. When a girl says *I'm fine* a chap should look for a shield or leave the area.'

'That is absolutely dead on correct,' said Jane speaking for the first time in front of Amanda.

'Whoa!' said Amanda. She was now staring at Jane.

'Hi,' said Jane. 'I'm Jane.' She got up from behind the desk and came around to shake Amanda's hand.

'Pleased to meet you. I'm Amanda, the other detective here.'

'We should go,' I said butting in. 'You ladies can get to know each other later.'

I sort of pushed Amanda back out the office door forcing her to release Jane's hand which she was still gripping in wonder.

In the car park, Amanda managed to throw off her initial shock. 'You know that Jane is a guy, right?'

'Of course. He was a guy when I hired him. Then when he turned up for work today he was no longer James but was Jane instead. I was a little thrown by it, but I don't think it makes much difference if he comes to work in boxer shorts or balancing his junk in a silk thong. If he can manage the office paperwork, emails and calls then he can stay.'

'He smells good.'

'It's Princess by Vera Wang,' I replied with knowing authority.

Amanda stared at me, clearly wondering how I could possibly know what perfume he/she was wearing.

'Know your enemy?' I tried. She raised one eyebrow inviting me to try again. 'Big Ben came by right before you and instantly knew what it was.'

'Right. It makes sense that he would be able to tell perfumes apart. Did he hit on her?'

'Yup. Funniest five minutes of my life.'

We got into her car during the exchange and pulled out of the car park. We were once again on our way to Dartford where I hoped to find the vital piece of evidence I needed to nail Brett Barker for his grandfather's death.

'You seem rather chipper this morning.' Observed Amanda as she cut her eyes to me. She had not bothered to respond to my thoughts on what the term *fine* meant but was clearly still not entirely happy with me.

I decided to smile back anyway. 'I am still irked that I walked into Brett's trap on Monday and I am pleased that he appears to be guilty after all. I am allowing myself to revel in the sweet joy of righteous revenge. I realise that it was I that walked into the trap, it is all on me, but I also think he is guilty and it looks like I can prove it. The money paid to Martin Wilkins ought to be sufficient to get the police involved once more and to have them investigate further.

'We should speak with Mr. Wilkins first.'

'I tried. He no longer works at Palmer Pharmaceuticals and I have not been able to track him down yet. The police will find him if we give them sufficient cause to look for him.'

'So, why not hand what you have over to them now?' she asked.

'Because the bank transaction is not enough by itself. If I find something to corroborate my theory I can hand over a solved case. If I find nothing, then I will have to hand them what I have but given his arrogance and confidence I believe he will still have something we can use to nail him, and my bet is we will find it in his house.'

'You don't like him. Why is that?'

'Apart from because he got my mum thrown into a cell for the night?' My smile had gone now. Why did I take such issue with Brett Barker? He had not actually done anything to me. He was desperately over privileged and offensively arrogant, but I met plenty of people like that. He was a criminal, but I came across plenty of those as well. He had hit on Amanda and that was where my loathing has started.

'Nearly there,' Amanda announced to break my train of thought. Sure enough, we were pulling off the motorway and closing in on the Barker Mansion.

Amanda had remained quiet for the last couple of miles while I was deep in thought about Brett Barker and my dislike for him. I had a question for her now though. 'What are *your* thoughts on Brett Barker? You seemed to hit it off. If he were not guilty of murder would you entertain seeing him socially?'

'Would I go on a date with the handsome, athletic, single multi-millionaire?'

'Fair point,' I conceded.

Amanda swung her car into the drive, through the vast gates, and down the long driveway to the house. We passed under the canopy of trees that stood like sentries lining the route on either side.

'Is that a zebra?' Amanda asked, staring out of the window.

'They have a small herd.'

'I like him more all the time.'

As we pulled in front of the house, Mrs. Barker stepped out to greet us in person.

'Good morning, Mrs. Barker,' I said as I got out of the car and shook her hand. 'This is my colleague Amanda Harper.' Amanda was coming around the car and extended her own hand.

'Good morning,' she said.

'Good morning. Are you the police officer?' Mrs. Barker asked.

'I am. For a few more days at least.' Amanda replied.

'Very good. I have a key to the north wing. That's Brett's area of the house,' she added in explanation. 'Do you need to do anything first, or can we begin?' Mrs. Barker seemed heady with excitement and eager for us to get on with it.

I looked across at Amanda. 'Is there anything?'

'We have the homeowner's permission to search. That pretty much ticks every box from a legal standpoint. There are no formalities to observe so we can just start,' she replied.

I turned back to Mrs. Barker. 'Please show us the way.' She spun back towards the house leaving us to catch up.

As we crossed the vast gravel drive, she had questions. 'What exactly are you looking for?'

'Evidence, to put it simply. Any correspondence, either by email or otherwise between him and persons at Palmer Pharmaceuticals. Any physical evidence.'

'Like what?' she asked.

'Like boxes of pills with the fake drug inside would be good.' I said as a joke but refrained from laughing. 'Anything that will give rise to have the police reopen the case and conduct a proper criminal investigation.' I was checking Amanda's expression to see if she disagreed or felt I was being overly optimistic. If she had any thoughts on the matter her face was not showing them.

Mrs. Barker led us into the house through the main doors and across the marble of the atrium to the left-hand side of the grand staircase. As we climbed the stairs, I began to worry that I might not find anything today. It felt like a very real possibility. Brett may have never brought anything incriminating into the house. Or his office for that matter. Would the testimony of Martin Wilkins be sufficient? Not that I had his testimony or had even been able to talk to him. If he no longer worked at Palmer Pharmaceutical would I be able to track him down? Would the police reopen the case with just a credit card payment that looked a bit fishy?

As I was pondering whether I had been over exuberant in my desire to search his rooms we arrived at them. Mrs. Barker inserted a mortice key into a relatively unassuming, but still large, solid oak door and pushed it open in front of her. Amanda followed her in with me trailing behind.

The room on the other side of the door was another atrium or lobby - it was not a room to be lived in but one to be passed through. The cool, sleek marble floor had a pair of matching leather sofas arranged to face each other. They were set in the middle of the room with a chrome and glass coffee table between them. On the coffee table was a copy of the Financial Times, which had clearly been read or at least opened, a copy of the Economist and a vase containing an arrangement of white lilies. The walls were panelled to a height of about six feet with ornate oak. Above the oak was a burgundy wallpaper that probably cost more per square metre than my car. Everything in the room was perfect: Perfectly arranged, perfectly considered to match or contrast with the other items and perfect in its condition. It was a room that trumpeted opulence. I have never stayed at a penthouse suite in a top-flight hotel, but I imagined this would be what I ought to expect if I did. Mrs. Barker seemed not to notice, her perception of such things clearly different from mine after years of seeing it every day.

Amanda let out a quiet whistle of impressed appreciation. 'Where do we start?' she asked.

I asked Mrs. Barker, 'How many rooms are there?'

'In this wing of the house? I do not know. There are seven bedrooms, and each has a private bathroom and dressing room adjoining so that is twenty-one. Then there is a library, billiard room, kitchen and two dining rooms.'

'Two dining rooms?' Amanda asked.

'Formal and informal,' Mrs. Barker replied in a tone that suggested it was perfectly obvious why there would be two dining rooms. 'There will also be a cinema room, several lounging rooms plus offices and rooms such as this one. It has been years since I came in here, so I cannot be certain, but I would hazard a guess at perhaps thirty-five rooms.'

Inside my head, I said *wow*. 'I propose we start with the most likely places to yield a result. Does he have a personal computer here?'

'Yes, of course.'

'Amanda do you want to tackle his computer or get started on the physical search?'

'I'll take the physical search, thank you. I looked at a man's browser history once and it scarred me for life.'

'Can you show us the computer, please?'

Mrs. Barker advised me that she didn't know where his computer was, reminding me again that she not been in his wing of the house in years. She nevertheless found it on her first attempt in a room set up as an office. A few seconds later I was at the keyboard.

I expected to find his computer was password protected and it was, but like many people, his built-in security demanded he change the password every few weeks. After a while, he had run out of easy to remember words or number/letter combinations and had been forced to concoct less memorable ones. His password was not on a post-it note in the first drawer I opened, or the second drawer or the third but was under the keyboard itself.

While I was sitting at the desk, Amanda busied herself opening drawers and cupboards in a methodical manner. This was my first ever house search. I discounted those I had conducted as a soldier in places like Northern Ireland and Iraq but had elected to not tell Amanda and had read up on the subject last night: Good old Google. I was watching how she performed the task so that I could copy her movements and look like I knew what I was doing.

By 1330hrs, some two and a half hours later, my stomach was beginning to grumble, and we had found nothing of any worth. Brett was either meticulous about erasing his browser history or had erased it recently by chance. His emails, the few of them I found, showed correspondence with a small group of old university buddies with whom he was planning a skiing trip. There were some personal banking transaction emails and a few Amazon purchase and dispatch notifications. Nothing pertaining to the case though.

Amanda had searched a stack of rooms and I had joined her after accepting the computer was going to give me nothing. There were still toilets and a few rooms left that looked like no one had ever lived in them, but we were running out of places to look.

Mrs. Barker had left us to complete our task but had sent a servant up with refreshments. A cold lunch was waiting for us back in the marble-floored entrance room. In lieu of anything more productive to do, I announced to Amanda that I was going to get something to eat and left Amanda looking through a cabinet in the bathroom adjoining his bedroom.

On the coffee table was a spread of cold cuts and sliced cheeses, pastries, cakes and biscuits and a selection of what appeared to be freshly baked bread rolls. I selected a seeded wholemeal bap, split it in half with my fingers and made a sandwich. I assembled a plate of food and relaxed on a couch expecting Amanda to join me shortly. As I munched, I posed to myself the question of where would I be if I was an incriminating piece of evidence?

'Tempest.' Amanda's voice echoed through from somewhere in the house. Rather than shout a response I put my plate down and got up to find her.

Amanda was still sitting on the bathroom tile where I had left her. 'I leaned on the bottom of the cabinet to lever myself up and it moved under my hand. It has a false bottom.' She lifted what I had assumed to be the base of the cupboard under the sink and there, in the gap underneath were packets and packets of Captopril. 'I cannot tell if they are the real pills or the fake ones or a mix of both but here is your smoking gun.' She looked unhappy. I told myself it was probably just fatigue and elected to ignore it.

'That's it then,' I said.

'I guess it is.'

Mrs. Barker chose that moment to check on our progress. 'Hello?' she called. 'Mr. Michaels?'

'In here,' I called back then exited the room to stand in the corridor and make myself visible.

She followed me into the bathroom. 'Goodness,' she exclaimed as Amanda showed her the pills. 'Is that George's heart medication?' she asked.

'It would appear to be,' I answered her.

'Is that sufficient for a conviction?' she asked us, eager to hear the answer.

I looked at Amanda for her to answer. 'For a conviction? That I cannot say, but it is enough for me to call in a forensics team. I need to make a phone call,' she said levering herself off the tile and pulling out her phone. 'I must insist you both vacate the room. No one can touch this now until it has all been formally catalogued. Mrs. Barker, I'm afraid you are likely to have police swarming all over the house for much of the rest of the day.'

If that prospect bothered her, she showed no sign. Her mood was gleeful. She thanked me several times as we walked back to the entrance room then left me there advising that she needed to attend to something else. Satisfied that I had met the terms of my contract I wandered back to my lunch. Picking up my plate again I sank down into one of Brett's luxurious sofas and cared not if I spilled crumbs. Brett was guilty. I smiled to myself like the Grinch at Christmas.

Within the hour I was a sideline attraction. I was still sitting on the sofa but where I had started out alone there were now a dozen or more people going back and forth through the room. They were conducting a search of the house focused almost exclusively on his rooms and I was waiting for Amanda. She had requested that she be allowed to make the arrest like it was a perk she had earned. A mark of respect perhaps for solving a crime that was otherwise going to go without investigation.

There was a plain clothes Detective Inspector on the scene, who had agreed she could and was now on the opposite side of the room briefing her. I could easily hear their conversation. She would meet two uniformed officers at Barker Mill where they expected to find Brett. After she made the arrest they would take him into custody. A further forensics team would then conduct a search of his offices for further evidence.

I had been largely ignored throughout all of this. It did not bother me. I had considered asking if there was anything I could do to help, yet I had not done so as I was convinced the answer would be negative. More than anything, I was looking forward to getting the arrest over with and to getting home. The adrenalin rush of finding exactly what I was looking for, and in that moment knowing I had solved the case, had drained away and left me tired. I was surplus to requirement for the arrest, but Amanda was my ride home, so I was stuck waiting for her until the task was done.

As she chatted with the Chief Inspector I wondered why she was so keen to make the arrest herself. A few more minutes ticked by as people bustled past me paying me no heed. Just as I was going to take myself outside for a change of scenery Amanda shook the Chief Inspector's hand and headed my way.

'Let's go,' she said not bothering to pause as she went out the door.

'Okay,' I replied to her back as it disappeared around the doorframe, flailing in my attempt to get my fat bum off the low sofa quickly.

I ran to catch up. 'All done here?' I asked rhetorically.

'We need to get to the mill fast. The uniforms are already there so I have maybe fifteen minutes before they perform the arrest without me.'

'Why are you so keen to do it? I thought you liked him.'

'He appears to be guilty of murder, Tempest. Any interest he may have shown me is of no further concern. Plus, this will be my first arrest ever and since I only have a few days left in the police I feel like this is my last chance.'

Silently I noted that she had managed to be in the police for years without making an arrest. Was that even slightly normal? Were there other officers that could boast the same?

Outside it had begun to drizzle lightly. A fine misty rain fell from the dank grey sky. I turned my face up and let it wet my face.

'Are you ok?' Amanda asked, paused half in, half out of her car.

'Oh, Yes,' I replied. 'I am just pausing to mark the moment.'

'We have to go,' said Amanda. She got in the car and started the engine.

As I crossed the short distance to the car I looked back at the Barker Mansion, trying to commit the image to my memory. I doubted I would ever see it again.

Neither of us spoke on the way to the Mill. I had no idea what Amanda was thinking. She might still be annoyed with me, but whether this was because she thought I was in love with her and had employed her as a move to get close to her, or if it was indirectly aimed at me because she was interested in Brett Barker and was on her way to arrest him I could not tell. It might be neither and she was simply nervous because she was about to perform her first arrest. I kept quiet though rather than encourage conversation.

My phone pinged quietly in my pocket. As I read the message I suddenly had something to talk about.

'Amanda, I have a text message that has come through with no number on it. I didn't know that was possible, but the message claims that Brett has a false panel in the wall of his office and we will find the Phantom outfit in there.'

'Let me see,' she demanded.

I handed her the phone, which she stared at for a few seconds reading the text for herself. I watched her eyes flick across the words then revert to watching the road ahead.

'I guess we will find out soon enough,' was all she said.

The Arrest. Wednesday, 13th October 1527 hrs

There were indeed uniforms waiting for us at the Barker Mill. Several of them in fact as if the pair assigned to the task had brought some mates along because they had nothing better to do. A white panel van with police markings was parked next to the two squad cars – probably the forensics chaps. The office building that overlooked the car park had faces peering through the windows.

The rain had picked up. It covered the windows in running lines of water, turning the faces into indistinguishable blobs. In deference to the rain, they were all staying inside despite their curiosity.

Amanda introduced herself and then me. After an initial handshake, I was once again side-lined as surplus to requirement and I considered staying in her car and having a snooze. Curiosity won in the end, so I trailed after the group heading towards the main office building.

Taking charge, Amanda explained where Brett worked and where we would most likely find him then led the assembled group past reception and directly towards his office.

Inside the building, for the umpteenth time in the last week, I followed them upstairs knowing exactly where they were going but with no purpose of my own. As Amanda strode towards the end of the upstairs corridor and Brett's closed office door, I stopped by a water cooler and got myself a drink. The office staff had all stopped work and were staring at the police. Some of them stood up for a better view.

No one moved to make any attempt to stop Amanda or the two uniforms flanking her or the two forensics guys as she opened his office door and went in. From my vantage point down the corridor, I saw the surprise on his face. The door closed. I sipped my water.

Less than a minute later the door opened again, and Brett came out in cuffs with one of the uniformed officers guiding him from behind with a hand on his shoulder.

Brett was led along the corridor where I was leaning on the water cooler. He did not make eye contact with me or acknowledge me in any way.

The office door opened again, and Amanda came out. I pushed myself upright and met her halfway down the corridor before she could close the distance to me.

'All done?' I asked her.

'No. This is going to take a while longer. Bryan, one of the forensics guys already found the hidden compartment in Brett's office. There was a cloak hanging up and a steel hand thing that has clearly been exposed to some heat – the hot glove thing you described. Bryan said it looks like it has burnt flesh on it.'

My mouth made an 'O'. Was Brett the Phantom as well?

'Can I see it?'

'I took a picture,' she offered. It showed a crude hand that could be held by a handle at one end. The handle appeared to have a lever on it to flex the fingers. The fingers were articulated at each knuckle. It was chunky looking and could be held at a point where the wrist should be. The handle, I could not tell from the photograph, so I was making guesses, would be made from asbestos or some other kind of insulating material so that the device could be held once heated.

'What on earth was he thinking, keeping it in his office?'

'He immediately claimed that he had never seen it before and had no idea the compartment it was in even existed.'

Amanda wanted to stay to wrap things up, but I was done. I was playing no part in current events and had not been involved for a couple of hours now. My time was precious enough that I had no intention of squandering it sitting around waiting for Amanda. I bid her goodbye, promised to catch up later and caught a cab to Dartford train station with the insistent rain now beating against the windscreen.

Luck was on my side for there was a train just pulling into the platform as I was handed my ticket. I boarded the carriage, musing that I could not remember the last time I had taken a train anywhere. It would probably have been to take a trip into central London some years ago as it was the one place only a fool or the very knowledgeable tried to drive and park.

I fell asleep on the train with my face against the window and awoke through pure luck as I arrived at Rochester station. I walked from there to my office in the rain to retrieve my car. A little more than an hour and a half after making my decision to leave the mill, I arrived back home. The rain still fell, gurgling into the drains. It would sweep the autumn leaves before it, convincing the last few leaves clinging to their summer homes to give in and vacate the premises until next year. Autumn was my favourite time of the year, but it always heralded the bleakness of winter.

As I walked up to my front door my phone pinged to announce a text message. I glanced at the screen to see that Amanda had replied to the message I had sent her from the train. I had wondered how she was getting on at the mill, but she had already left by the time I asked and was home. She got back before me. Had I bothered to wait...

Oh well.

It was 1743hrs and once again the dogs were overdue for their dinner. The rain looked like it was clearing. If it stopped, I would take the chaps out and let them chase bunnies at the park. I allowed myself a smile at another case closed and another cheque in the post. I opened my door and went inside.

Training Jane/James. Thursday, 14th October 0900hrs

I got to work the next day wondering if my assistant would be a boy or a girl today. I was early, so I ducked into the coffee shop to get a drink on my way to the office. Hayley, who I had hoped to bump into was absent. I asked one of her colleagues as she served me if Hayley would be in later. Sharon, according to the name tag told me that Hayley had a day off. I swore in my head and pulled out my phone to text her. Sharon handed me my skinny americano with a shot of hazelnut which I took to a table while I tried to work out what to write.

'Hi, Tempest.'

I looked up to find Jane, not James looking down at me.

'I felt like getting a coffee on my way to work and was going to pick up one for you. I see you already have one though,' she said.

'I do. I have not yet taken the first sip though. Grab yours, I'll wait for you,' I suggested.

Jane smiled and headed over to the counter.

I started with, *"Hi, Hayley."* Then deleted Hayley and wrote, *"Sexy."* Instead. Then deleted that and wrote, *"Sex bomb."* Still not satisfied with the first two words I just wrote her name.

"I held off messaging you for a few days because I am still not sure what sort of relationship you want. The other night was fantastic and would very much like to repeat the event any time you wish. I am mildly," I crossed out mildly. *"I am concerned that I should have messaged you sooner so please forgive me if I have misread your cues. You did, however, make it clear that you wanted hassle-free sex, so I have kept my distance this week."*

I pressed send and away the text flew.

Waiting for Jane to return, I remembered that I had still not booked the venue for the baby shower that was in two days. The realisation gave me a moment of panic. I wanted to book a local place, local to where I was currently sitting that is. There are several tea rooms in Rochester, all of which are nice but there was one I had visited on a lunch date some time ago. I had spotted that it had a private function room and I knew it was very cute and served excellent food in very sensible portions.

I pulled up a search engine on my phone, then changed my mind. I didn't want to call them. I needed their function room at short notice, so needed to discuss face to face when they could fit the party in and maybe grease a palm in the process.

Jane returned, daintily sipping her coffee and holding a little paper bag that most likely contained a cake of some kind. She was wearing ladies leather gloves in a pastel blue that matched her winter coat and scarf. I really wanted to know where a transvestite bought such items. Probably the internet, but I wondered if they were expensive as they were clearly designed to look like women's items while being able to fit a man. The gloves especially must have been hard to come by.

'I have to run an errand,' I told her as I got up. 'Are you okay to open up?'

'Of course.'

'I should not be long, but please go through the latest emails and messages. I will take you through financing and invoices when I get there.'

'Okay, boss,' she replied with a smile.

I held the coffee shop door open for her and closed it behind me. Jane crossed the road towards the office, fumbling in her Radley messenger bag for her keys. I turned left and headed to The Queen Victoria Tea Rooms.

I got back to the office forty minutes later. Booking the baby shower had taken longer than I had expected, but it had also proven to be cheaper than I had budgeted for, and it was now pretty much organised.

Food, location, decoration all done. I followed up the email I sent to Rachael's friends on Sunday night with a new email updating them with the venue address, a link to The Queen Victoria Tea Rooms website and advice on what time to arrive and where to park in case they were unfamiliar with the location. I also called mum so that she could handle the ladies she was bringing along.

Upstairs in the office, Jane was sitting at the desk, one hand on the mouse and staring intently at the computer screen. She did not look up when I came in, but she did speak.

'Have you read anything about clowns recently?

'Clowns?'

'Yeah. I read something in the paper last week about clowns being spotted late at night, in places one should not see a clown and how the clowns were not very friendly looking. Then there were reports of girls being chased by clowns and then last night a young married couple was chased. The man challenged the pair of clowns that were following them, and he was stabbed.'

I had read similarly worrying reports but had not seen this most recent one.

'Anyway, you have an email from a woman who claims her brother has joined a clown cult. She spells it K-L-O-W-N though. She wants you to investigate and bring him back.'

A cult of Klowns. It sounded harmless enough, I felt like making jokes about the activities the klown cult might get up to. Throwing buckets of water that turned out to be filled with confetti, or practicing falling over their own huge feet. Did their uniform come with a spinning bow tie? I held back though and asked to see the email.

'I printed you a copy,' Jane said holding up a sheet of paper.

Dear Sir,

I am writing to beg for your help. A week ago, my brother disappeared, but the police do not class him as a missing person because he is still answering his phone and sending text messages. He met someone and has run a way to become a klown. He has changed his name and says that he is not coming home until their mission is complete. I don't know what his mission might be, but I have seen reports of klowns scaring and now attacking people and I think he is somehow mixed up in it all.

He is a good boy. Can you find him and bring him home?

I read the email twice. It was my kind of work. Sort of. It certainly had the weird element going on.

'Please contact her and set up an appointment.'

'When for?'

'Monday, if that works for her. I can go to her or she can come here. Whichever suits her best,' I answered after a few seconds of deliberation.

'I will set up a diary on your email system and link it to your phone so that I don't need to call you every time I need to organise your movements.' Jane's ability to organise my work activities combined with a natural confidence to do so was impressing me.

'Any other emails of interest?' I asked.

'Um, all of them?' she hazarded, clearly unsure what the right answer was.

'Doubtful. I have not read them, but typically I get maybe one enquiry a day that has some merit to it.' Jane looked confused. 'Why don't you pick one that you believe we should consider? Then we can go through it together.' I wanted Jane to be able to sift the email and phone enquiries and spot the stupid ones and the ones that I could make money from.

'Okay,' she said fiddling with the mouse to scroll through the emails. 'How about this one? Geoff Gudeon of Mereworth reports that his girlfriend may be suffering from the early stages of a werewolf curse. He believes that it may be linked with moon patterns as every few weeks her behaviour shifts.' I waited while Jane read a little more to herself. 'He goes on to say that for a week she becomes unpleasant, difficult to please, grouchy etcetera. She has not yet started to growl, and her teeth have not grown, but he is concerned that he may be living with a woman that is going to change into a werewolf at the next full moon. Does he need to be scared?'

I eyed Jane suspiciously in case she was yanking my chain. 'Seriously?' I asked. 'The man's girlfriend gets bad PMS and turns into a bitch. Case solved. If we charge him for providing an answer to his daft question it would be swindling him. Next one.'

'Oh. Um.' More mouse fiddling. 'Here is one that sounds serious.'

'Hit me.'

'Sandra Gross thinks she was hypnotised into being a zombie.'

I opened my mouth to dismiss it as ridiculous hokum. The lady had most likely had gone to a crappy hypnotist show with a few friends, had imbibed one too many cocktails or had dropped a pill, but instead of voicing my opinion I found that I wanted to hear more.

'What else does she write.'

'Sandra tells us that she went to a show by the Great Howsini, then there is a whole bit about how she was approached after the show because she was *just right* for being hypnotised. The Great Howsini wanted to conduct some experimental sessions with her among some other special persons. The sessions would be free. Blah, blah, blah. Then she says that she went to the session but when she came around from being hypnotised she had lost five hours and was in a car park in Pluckley, miles from where she had started out. Blah, blah, blah, no memory of getting there but she had an overwhelming sense of wanting to eat human flesh.' Jane looked up from reading the screen. 'What do you think?'

'I think there might be something to it. Please file it somewhere to be considered later.'

Jane and I went through a few more of the email enquiries that had been received in the last twenty-four hours. I explained that I needed her to view each with the very simple standpoint that there was no paranormal and so every single case had a perfectly ordinary explanation. Jane seemed dubious, a trait that I had to forgive. I had learned that most people had a willingness to accept, to a greater or lesser extent, bizarre answers to quandaries that had ordinary explanations. To assist her I wrote, "There is no paranormal" on the board opposite the desk in large letters.

'Shall we go through the financial stuff?'

'Sure thing,' she replied.

For the next hour, I went over the firm's finances, the paperwork, how to produce invoices etcetera. It was dry, but necessary stuff. The task complete, I had run out of routine things to show her. I checked my watch: 1137hrs. The spectral dog case needed to be pursued and I needed to perform some research, so I might as well do it here with Jane and show her a skill that might prove helpful later.

'Shove over,' I said while coming around the desk. I grabbed one of the chairs from by the window and plonked it down next to her as she slid her chair away from the keyboard.

My intention was to resolve the case, in part at least, by catching the spectral dog. With the pooch out of the way, there would be no reason for Mrs. Collins not to reopen the business. This would not determine where her husband had got to, but I was betting that he was alive and well and staying somewhere else. He had not been eaten by a ghost dog after all. So, where was he?

I performed some internet searches with Jane watching and we found out a little bit about the man. Mrs. Collins had given me a photograph upon my request. His age was recorded as fifty-eight so the picture I had was maybe ten years old - he still had mostly brown hair in it. He did not appear in any social media but there had been a couple of newspaper articles about his business when it had been investigated for illegally tipping scrap parts in the countryside. The report did not say whether the allegations had been proven true or not. Mr. Collins was overweight but not obese. Like most men, he was carrying a good few extra pounds around his waist. Regular trips to the pub would do that. He was a big man though, broad-shouldered and tall at over six feet by my estimation. He had probably been considered good looking when he was younger and might still be so by women of a similar age.

An hour of searching the internet gave me nothing helpful. I explained to Jane that at this stage of a case I had to feel my way around. Using the standard assumption that there was nothing supernatural going on I would form a theory based on what else could have happened and then explore those options. I believed that if Mr. Collins was not at home and was not spending money on his credit card – he was not - I had Mrs. Collins check every day - then he had to be shacked up somewhere. He could be staying at a mate's house, but it felt more likely that he had a lady on the side and he was with her. Mrs. Collins told me that he regularly worked late and very often came home later because he was going via the pub. The pub then, if indeed he had ever been going there, was a next most sensible place to visit. The public house was called The Morning Star. I had to look up where it was. Getting there would be easy enough and it was only a few miles away.

Before I went to the pub I needed to go home, have some lunch and take the dogs for a walk. I left Jane to lock up, saying that I would see her the next morning.

On the way home, I called Jagjit and asked to borrow his car. I would need it tonight. He drove a large utility vehicle and the large load bed in the rear would be used to transport the dog to a safe place if we were successful in catching it.

I tasked Big Ben with obtaining an animal control pole from the vet lady. I probably could have bought one, but I had no desire to buy things when I could borrow them, and I doubted I would need it again any time soon, if ever. I also told him to get drugs that we could use to knock the beast out with. It was a cliché, but I intended to feed it a steak loaded with the drug and allow it to knock itself out. If the CCTV footage was anything to go by, the dog was big and big dogs are strong and have big teeth. Dealing with a sleeping giant hellhound felt safer.

I got home at 1316hrs. The dogs were waiting as always. In contrast to recent days, the sun was shining, so we went straight out for a walk. The pair of tiny dogs pulled at their leads, each trying to get to the next smell first. I followed them where they wanted to go, feeling relaxed and happy. The dogs usually calmed or soothed whatever troubles might be bothering me.

The circuitous route around the village led me back to my house at 1357hrs. I made a wholemeal chicken wrap loaded with raw vegetables, shook some hot sauce on to it to keep my metabolism firing and emptied the washing machine. Basic tasks complete, I checked myself in the mirror to make sure that I did not have food stuck to my teeth or dribble on my collar then headed out to see if I could track down the missing Mr. Edgar Collins.

The Morning Star Public House. Thursday, 15th October 1517hrs

Finding the pub had been simple enough, I had just followed the satnav. It was formed from an end of terrace house as the row of houses met the corner formed by the confluence of two roads, Barnes Street and Maple Road. It was poorly kept, the paint was flaking from the walls and the window frames, several panes of glass were broken and had been taped back together, and in front and just to the side of the main door was a stain where someone had recently vomited. Whoever had been tasked with cleaning it up had done a poor job. In general, it was a bit cruddy looking.

I pushed the door open. Inside was not much better. It was mid-afternoon on a Friday and there were more people inside than there ought to be. Perhaps I was being prejudiced. Whatever the case, there were more than twenty chaps of varying ages stood around the bar or sitting at the tables drinking beer or ale. Most of them looked up as I entered. I was inappropriately dressed and stood out wearing smart office clothes where they were all in working clothes. I elected to ignore the stares and proceeded to the bar.

The gentleman behind the counter radiated a personality that made me confident he was the Landlord. I ordered a pint of lager and asked him if he was.

'I am indeed,' he replied. 'Is there something I can help you with?' he asked, giving me an easy opener.

I produced the picture of Mr. Collins. 'I am looking for my uncle,' I lied. 'I have been in the army overseas for years. Now I am back and as I don't have much family I was hoping to reconnect with Uncle Ed. I was a boy the last time I saw him, and he used to drink here, so this is the start point of my search.'

If he questioned the story he showed no sign of it. He took the picture I was showing him, peered at it squinting, swore and then looked around for his glasses which were on a string around his neck. Finally finding them, he still had to move the picture towards his face and away from it to bring it into focus. 'Oh, its Eddie.' he said. 'We don't see him much.' He took a couple of paces along the bar and shouted through a gap in the wall, 'Rita.' A few seconds ticked by with no reply so he tried again, 'Rita, my love.'

'What?' a distant female voice came back.

'When did you last see, Eddie?'

'Who?'

'Eddie?'

'Eddie who?' It seemed like this might go on for a while. I took a sip of my pint. I didn't really want a beer at this time of the day, or even this time of the week but it seemed appropriate to order a drink since I was in a bar.

A lady, whom I assumed was Rita, appeared from the gap in the wall, wiping her hands on a pinny around her waist. Like the Landlord, she looked like she could wrestle drunks out the door and probably open a beer bottle with her bum if required.

'What are you on about, you daft old bugger?' she asked.

'Eddie,' he started again, this time showing her the picture, 'when did you last see him in here?'

She took the photograph and examined it. 'Who wants to know?'

'His nephew,' he explained pointing at me. I smiled back.

'He was in here for a bit last week with Sharon. Or was that the week before?' she asked herself. 'No, I think it was last week, maybe on Thursday night. They stopped for a drink and then went again.' I was focussing on the name Sharon and wishing I had a photograph of Mrs. Collins to show them so that I could confirm by elimination that he had another lady. It had been my original theory after all.

'Do you know if he lives around here then?' I asked.

'Sorry, love,' Rita replied, 'that I cannot help you with.'

'You said he was here with Sharon. I know he remarried but I thought her name was Louise. I am probably wrong though. Is she a tall lady with blonde hair?'

'What, Sharon? No, love. Sharon is short, fat, and ugly.' She laughed as if she had said something particularly funny.

I had picked a description that was very much not Mrs. Collins just in case it was his wife that had been in with him and the Landlady just had the name wrong. Short, fat and ugly might be a harsh, if accurate description, but it was not Mrs. Collins. I thanked her and the Landlord for their time and took the photograph back. Rita disappeared back through the hole in the wall and the Landlord moved off to serve another customer.

I took a sip of my drink. Edgar Collins was having an affair, that much seemed certain now. He had kept it from his wife for however long it had been going on but was now most likely shacked up permanently with the new woman. So, I knew why he was missing, but not where he was and still had no idea what part the dog played in this. His disappearance and the spectral dog showing up could not be a coincidence. With luck, I would catch the dog tonight, get Mrs. Collins and her employees back to work and in so doing would flush out her husband. If not, then I felt certain I could perform some non-paranormal investigating and find the address for the short, fat ugly Sharon and in turn, assuming I was right, Edgar Collins.

I had downed less than half of the pint of lager. Quite sufficient I felt. I tapped my pockets to confirm I had my wallet, phone, and keys and left the pub quite happily behind me.

My watch ticked through 1600hrs as I was getting into my car. I was leaving my visit to the breakers yard until it was dark. I had been there during the day and had seen nothing. I was guessing again, but my guess was that Edgar or one of his chaps was bringing the dogs in at night. I debated setting up an observation post to film that person delivering the dogs, but the equipment I owned was not sophisticated enough. I could

245

therefore only hope to catch them by jumping out from my hiding place when they were doing so. Of course, they were not committing a crime. If it was Edgar setting the dogs then it was technically his property, so all I could do was report back to Mrs. Collins.

The internal debate left me getting to the yard once it was dark, letting ourselves in and seeing if anything happened. We might not get lucky on the first night and I would have to rethink the plan if we struck out for more than a couple of nights in a row. I had a good feeling though, so I gave Big Ben a call, told him what time I would collect him and outlined the plan.

I had a few hours to kill, but plenty of housework and other mundane tasks to keep me busy. It would be action time soon enough and I was looking forward to a bit of night time sneaking around.

Junkyard Dog Thursday 14th October 1937hrs

I collected Jagjit's car after he finished work. He was good enough to call and let me know it was available. He still lived with his parents, or at least had moved back in after a brief and disappointing marriage. Their place was walking distance from my house, so I took the dogs with me and they rode home on the passenger's seat.

That was two hours ago. Since then I had dressed in my usual black combat gear, eaten a light meal – nothing heavy in case this evening involved a lot of strenuous activity and had gone to collect Big Ben.

We had arrived at the breakers yard after dark and waited for thirty minutes to allow our night vision to settle before we had used the key Mrs Collins had provided to slip in through the front gate. Once inside I shut the gate behind us and made sure it would not swing open again. I believed there was a large dog here, that it might be dangerous and thus wanted to ensure it did not escape and wreak havoc elsewhere. Big Ben and I had poked around for a minute or so hoping to spot the dog. He was carrying the animal control pole he borrowed from the vet lady. I wanted two, but she only had two and needed to keep hold of one just in case she needed it. Big Ben did not expand on that, but I supposed that a vet might sometimes be brought a feral dog or cat and need to pin it in a safe manner.

'I'm bored with this,' Big Ben had announced after the first minute of searching the yard. 'Here pooch! Here poochy, poochy, poochy!' he called loudly while making little whistle come-to-me noises.

It had not been the greatest idea as seconds later the world's largest dog came barking, growling and bounding around the corner ahead of us. It was picking up speed, heading straight for us and did not appear willing to negotiate the terms of its surrender.

'Wowza!' Big Ben uttered. Then he turned and ran. At least I am guessing that he then turned and ran because I had already done so, had covered ten metres and was accelerating away from him. It was not going to take the dog long to cover the distance to where we had been, and outrunning it held little hope as a strategy. When Big Ben caught up to me a few paces later I yelled, 'Climb!' and headed for the nearest bank of cars.

It was a breakers yard so there were maybe a thousand or so battered and beaten looking cars piled one atop the other arranged in vaguely neat piles and lines so that it formed a maze of sorts. It probably only seemed like a maze because I had never been inside before and in the daylight, there would in fact be clearly defined and obvious paths through the yard.

I leapt onto the bonnet of something bright yellow then grasped the front tyre of the car next to and one layer above it and swung myself up onto its bonnet. Not convinced this was high enough yet I went a further level up, scraping my left arm against something sharp as I did so. Now three cars up and thinking that I was probably out of reach I stopped climbing and turned to see where the dog was. The answer to that question was that it was at the line of cars running parallel to the one I had climbed trying to eat Big Ben.

'Get the hell off me,' Big Ben yelled with his usual gusto. The dog tried to snap at his feet as he scrambled a little higher. We locked eyes for a second and he grinned at me. 'That's a real dog Tempest, definitely not a ghost, I could feel its breath on my leg when it tried to bite me, and I have slobber on my trousers.'

'That bit was never in doubt. You think we are high enough here?'

'I reckon so,' Big Ben said. I watched as he wiped his hands on his trousers, probably to remove grease or dirt and keep his grip ready. 'Where is the steak?' he called across to me. We were perhaps eight feet apart with the dog circling around beneath Big Ben.

The almost cartoon like plan was to load a steak up with the drug and hope that the dog ate it. I was not one for using hope as a strategy, so we had brought the animal control pole along as well. I had abandoned the pole while running away like a little girl though. It had seemed unlikely I could climb the cars while holding it anyway so now it was ten metres away laying uselessly on the ground.

I had a small back pack hooked over my shoulders in which was a Tupperware type box containing the steak. The drug was already applied by use of a hypodermic needle to get it right into the meat, so I fished the box out and threw it across to Big Ben.

He caught it one handed despite the poor light, opened it, and as the dog, which was now stood on its hind legs to stretch up for him again, took its next lunge, he dropped it into its mouth.

Dogasaurus swallowed the meat almost without acknowledging that it had something it its mouth and never once took its gaze off Big Ben. The vet had assured him the dose would knock out but would not endanger the animal so that we could attach a muzzle, collar, animal control pole etcetera and take it to the local RSPCA centre. Apparently, she had not said how long the anaesthetic would take to knock the animal out though and he had failed to ask.

The enormous, gently glowing dog circled for a bit, looked at me briefly and then resumed trying to find a way to get to Big Ben.

'Ah, Tempest,' Big Ben called across the void.

'Yes, mate.'

'My um. My right hand is going numb.'

I considered that for a second. 'Did you handle the steak or just tip it out?'

'I grabbed hold of the damned thing. My hand is really going numb.'

'Then let us hope our canine friend here is feeling the same effect.'

The dog chose that point to stop trying to climb the cars under Big Ben. It dropped back down onto all fours, shook its head a few times, like one might if one was feeling a little fuzzy and let out a bark.

I said, 'I think we have a result.'

'Good because my forearm is numb now and I can't feel my fingers anymore.'

The giant dog shook its head once more then wandered away from us, its quarry forgotten. 'Can you climb down?' I asked.

'It seems only my right arm is affected so I will be fine one handed. If the tiny amount I got on my skin is anything to go by the dog will not get far.'

'Well just in case I'm coming over to give you a hand.' I said as I swung off the cars and landed neatly on the ground. Two paces across the path between the line of cars and I was underneath Big Ben. I was redundant though as Big Ben swung his legs over the edge of the car he was on and dropped to the ground just as I had.

As he stood back up he was holding his right arm with his left and looking at his hand. 'I have a cut on my hand,' Big Ben said as he turned his hand over to show me. 'I must have snagged it on something when I climbed the cars.'

'I did the same. Plenty of sharp items in the dark I guess. Shall we find the dog?' I was about to set off to see where dogasaurus had got to when it came back around the corner ahead of us.

'Oh nuts,' hissed Big Ben and half a breath later we were both running once more.

We rounded a corner and found ourselves in a dead end. Ahead of us were cars piled high on our left and right... and also right in front of us because we had run into a dead end. I was concerned about the dead bit of that phrase. My pulse hammered out a quick warning, but the problem also presented an opportunity. Beside me Big Ben slowed slightly as he too saw that we had nowhere to go. I grabbed his elbow and pointed to the way out.

The dog was gaining on us, the steak seemed to have had no effect thus far except to numb Big Ben's hand. We got to the end of the corridor of cars to find we had nowhere left to run, we had seconds before the dog would be upon us. So, we did what the dog could not do; we opened the doors of the Volvo estate in front of us and then closed them again. The dog slammed into the car as we slid out the other side. I was tempted to stroll away with as much nonchalance as I could muster but prudence dictated we continue running. We turned another corner and could see the fence that marked the edge of the yard. I got there first, hit the fence to slow myself and ducked down behind the mangled wreck of an old Ford Mondeo.

Big Ben slammed himself into the fence next to me and crouched down to minimise his visibility.

'Do you think we lost it?' I asked.

'Doubtful,' he answered. 'I don't think hiding works all that well with dogs.' I had to concede the point.

'Any idea what kind of dog it is? You got a better look at it than me.'

'Some kind of cross between an Anatolian Karabash and a stegosaurus I think. Whatever it is, it is mean and nasty and generally unhappy to see us.' he replied.

'Did you see it eat the steak? One bite and swallow - just like that. The thing must have a throat my leg would go down without touching the sides.'

'I know a few girls like that.' A typical Big Ben response.

'I thought you said the steak would knock it out.'

'Tempest, there was enough Propofol on that steak to drop a cow.' Big Ben and I had gone through the dosage instructions the lady vet had left, and had then used it all anyway.

'I suppose we did put more on than she suggested. Unless she messed up the instructions the dog might actually be something other than a dog,' I speculated.

'You mean it might actually be a spectral dog? That is what we were sent here to find,' Big Ben asked being flippant.

'I meant more that it might actually be part stegosaurus, but let's just give it a minute and see whether it comes looking for us.' A minute passed

251

by and nothing of interest happened. 'I'm going to take a peek,' I said sidling to the edge of the car and peering around it. It was dark in the breakers yard and given the nature of the business it was sited well away from houses and streetlighting that may have provided some background light. Now that I was peering further and further around the car, I could see something lying on the ground close to the portable cabin that I assumed served as an office. Was it a dog? It was something and it was not moving but I could not see enough in the dim light to tell what it was with any degree of certainty. I briefly considered getting the torch from my webb belt but knew it would kill my night sight instantly.

'Anything?' asked Big Ben from right by my ear.

I elected then to end the silliness of hiding behind cars and stood up. 'I think that is a dog laying on the dirt in front of the cabin.' I pointed so he could form an opinion also.

Standing up to join me Big Ben squinted his eyes in the dark and shrugged. 'It could be. It could be a crumbled cardboard box just as easily.'

'Let's go find out then.' With that I set off to investigate. Two seconds and six paces later both Big Ben and I could see that the shape on the ground was indeed a dog. It was laying with its back to where we had been hiding. Its paws were stretched out perpendicular to its body pointing away from us as we approached while its head was tucked down towards its chest. It did not move as we neared it thankfully, so I knelt to check it was alive.

Stood over the inert form of the giant, shaggy-haired dog I rubbed my hand over its fur and lifted it up to inspect it. The palm of my hand was now glowing. I gave my hand a sniff. 'Luminous liquid,' I stated. 'The same stuff they put in glow sticks.'

'Mydery tholved,' replied Big Ben still holding his arm.

'Mydery tholved? Are you okay?'

'I veel a liddle odd. My dongue hath gone to thleep,' he replied.

I stood up concerned and had a look at Big Ben's eyes. They were difficult to see in the dark, so I grabbed his shoulder and swung him around, so the moon was on his face. He was dribbling slightly. A thought occurred to me. 'Did you lick the wound on your hand?'

'Oh vuck!' I accepted this as admission of guilt. His hand was bleeding from a cut which was probably where the anaesthetic had entered his blood stream to start with and now he had put the wound to his mouth and gotten more anaesthetic from his skin.

'We had better wrap this up and get you out of here before you keel over. Perhaps you should sit down mate.' I was not particularly concerned about him, the dose he had given himself could not be that strong. I was more worried about having to deal with the dog/dinosaur by myself. I swung my back pack off and onto the ground in front of me, zipped it open and fished out a large muzzle which Big Ben had also borrowed from the vet.

I shuffled a pace over on my knees and tried to slip it onto the dog's snout. I was interrupted in my task by a crashing noise behind me. I did not need to turn around to know what it was. I finished forcing the muzzle onto dogasaurus, secured it with the buckle around the back of its head and felt marginally safer.

Then I swung myself around on the ground to face back to were Big Ben had been standing. He was, of course, no longer standing. He was flat out on his back and clearly no longer conscious. The anaesthetic was strong stuff. The problem now though was that Big Ben must weigh two hundred and fifty pounds or something around that mark. At six feet seven inches tall and all solid, honed muscle, he was significantly bigger than I, and as a dead weight he was going to be hard to move. I invited him along on this caper because I expected to have to carry the dog to the car and wanted his help. I might be able to drag the dog to the car, but there was no chance I would be able to lift it up to the car's flat bed.

I tussled briefly with the best way of tackling this and settled on going to get the car and bringing it to them. If I could not lift either of them perhaps the minor dose that Big Ben had inadvertently administered to himself would wear off soon enough. Otherwise I was going to have to wait it out.

Standing up, I patted my front right pocket to make the keys were still in there but something moving caught my attention. My heart skipped, and my breath caught as right in front of me, not more than ten feet away was a second giant dog. It was gently glowing like the first one and very much not drugged.

It grinned at me a big doggy grin. I watched as the muscles in its shoulders bunched, it was going to lunge. Why had I just assumed there was one dog? It had not occurred to me at any point that there might be a second dog. Or were there three or four?

How ever many there were, I was suddenly in big trouble. The animal control pole was off to my left, Big Ben was unconscious just to my right and the dog could cover the ground in a few bounds. Caught in a hopeless situation, the only sensible or logical option that gave me any hope of survival was to leave the dog to go for Big Ben while I grabbed the pole and gave myself the chance to get it under control.

The dog made its move, bursting into motion off its back feet. Logic went to hell as I threw myself over Big Ben to protect his inert form. He was too easy a target and had no way to defend himself. I had dived on top of him, protecting his head and neck with my own which left them now exposed. Thinking quickly, with maybe half a second before the enormous hound bit me I ran a quick inventory check to see what I could use against it. Would I be able to twist and stab it or beat it once it had its jaws on me? I had no idea, but I felt it arrive above me right then, so I was going to find out!

Steeling myself for the pain I needed to endure, I physically jumped when the dog licked my ear. Then it nudged my head with its giant nose. The damned thing wasn't dangerous at all! It was breathing in my ear, big huffing breaths of an excited, playful dog.

I rolled over, taking myself off Big Ben and there was the dog, staring down at me just a few inches away. It wagged its tail and cocked its head to one side.

'Hey doggy,' I said in what I hoped was an engaging tone. 'Would you like to play fetch?' I patted my webb belt, found nothing of use so scouted around until I found a discarded plastic jerry can. The can was bigger than one of my own dogs but probably about right for dogasaurus here. I shook it a few times to make sure he was watching then threw it and watched as he bounded off into the dark.

The plan had been to catch the dog as a start point because I had erroneously assumed it was going to be dangerous rather than playful. Revealing the perfectly ordinary and not even slightly paranormal nature of the dog would have allowed Mrs Collins to return to work and I had planned to then follow the movements of Barry and Malcolm in the belief that they would lead me to the errant Mr Collins. Case solved, fee paid. Super.

That was still more or less the plan, but I had some time to kill now while I waited for Big Ben to come around. Together we could shift the unconscious dog to the truck, load the other, quite playful dog into the cab and head back to the RSPCA centre where I planned to drop them off until their owner came forward.

Fortunately, I didn't have to wait too long but my wait was not ended by Big Ben coming around but by approaching headlights. The long winding lane that led to the yard gave me plenty of notice before the vehicle arrived. I used the time for hiding and setting up a camera. The approaching headlights had nothing else in this direction that they could have been coming to so upon spotting them I had run back to the car to collect a bag from the back seat and to pull the car around the corner where it could not be seen. I dragged Big Ben out of sight behind the cabin but left the unconscious dogasaurus where it lay. The camera had an infrared setting that would pick up everything despite the lack of light. I had bought it when I bought most of my gear back when I made the decision to go into private investigations. I had used it only a couple of times, but it was still a worthwhile investment. I climbed onto the roof of the cabin and positioned the camera at the leading edge so that it would record whomever was approaching. I stayed on the roof to remain hidden myself and because it gave me a good vantage point over most of the yard.

I settled down to wait. The approaching car turned its headlights off perhaps two hundred metres before it got to the yard. Were they trying to be stealthy? If so, then why?

I flattened myself to the roof and hoped that Big Ben would not pick the next couple of minutes as his time to regain consciousness. Flattening myself to the roof was almost certainly unnecessary, it was rare for people to look up, or to look for danger, or even to really take in their surroundings. All I needed to do to stay invisible was not move.

Two car doors thunked shut one after the other. A few moments later I was rewarded with the sight of Malcolm approaching. He was carrying a large torch which kicked out some powerful light. He was swinging it about, aiming it here and there. The second figure I had not met before, but I knew who it was because Mrs Collins had shown me a photograph. That Mr Collins was here now solved the case essentially, it certainly proved several elements of my theory to be correct and since I had been engaged to catch a spectral hound and solve the mystery of where her husband had gone I would be able to provide a complete report tonight.

'Fluffy!' shouted Malcolm, clearly calling a dog, 'Susan!' Were the giant dogs really called Fluffy and Susan? If so, which was which? 'Come on dogs,' he called again and this time one of the giant hounds bounded out of the dark.

Then it was the turn of Mr Collins to speak, 'You can come out now, we know you are here.' He stood with his arms folded, clearly feeling confident. 'You are not the first to break in here looking for cash, but there is nothing here for you to find. If you are hiding from the dogs you can come out now, they won't hurt you.'

I was ready to jump down from my position, staying there until they left was not an option, but I wondered what else he might say if I left him to ramble for a few more minutes.

'Fluffy!' Malcolm called again.

When Fluffy failed to appear and no one answered, Mr Collins's request for the intruder to come forward they advanced again. They were roughly twenty metres away and coming directly towards the cabin I was laying on top of. A few paces later and Malcolm spotted the second dog. He seemed genuinely concerned as he rushed forward falling to his knees by its head. I could hear him clearly from my position. 'Fluffy my baby, what have they done to you? If they have hurt, you I will track them down and make them pay.'

'Never mind the damned dog, Malcolm.'

'Never mind the dog? Never mind the dog?' Malcolm roared from his position near the unconscious pooch. 'This is all your fault! The dog should be at home with me not locked in your junk yard while you shack up with another woman and swindle your wife out of her half of the business.' Malcolm was still on the ground checking the dog over. He appeared to have contented himself that the dog was just knocked out and was stroking its head. 'I don't know how you talked me into this, I swear.'

'I didn't talk you into it. I'm your boss, I gave you an order. Simple.' Mr Collins could not see the storm cloud brewing, but I could. Malcolm was attached to his dogs, I knew how he felt. The dogs were his to love and protect and he was unhappy at how things had turned out. I watched as he carefully laid the big dog's head back on the ground and got to his feet.

'You gave me an order, did you?' Malcolm was not a small man and he was looking ready to throw some weight around.

Mr Collins noticed his employee's tone for the first time and suddenly looking less confident. 'Now then, Malcolm. Let us not get excited. We still have intruders to find.'

'Well, maybe I don't want to find them anymore. Maybe I ought to call Mrs Collins and tell her what I know.'

'Now let's not do anything rash, Malcolm,' said Mr Collins.

'Maybe I should tell Mrs Collins about the secret account and the other set of books that the tax people don't know about.'

'You wouldn't dare,' spluttered Mr Collins.

'Or maybe you should make me your new partner in the business being as how loyal I have been to you all these years.' Malcolm had moved to stand right in front of his boss. He towered over him now being quietly threatening.

'Yes, Malcolm. Yes. I'm sure we can come to some arrangement.' Mr Collins was stammering a little.

Beneath me in the dark, Big Ben groaned and both men swung their heads towards the noise. It was time to show myself, but I was not quick enough to prevent what happened next.

Malcom took a step forward, flicked his big torch on and shone it in the general direction of Big Ben. Mr Collins also had a torch, a three-cell steel Maglite. I had not seen it until now as he had not turned it on and I was only seeing it now because he had raised it above his head.

'No!' I shouted. It was the only thing I could do but the only effect it had was to make Malcolm look up at me on top of the cabin. Behind him, Mr Collins took a step forward and smashed the Maglite down onto Malcolm's skull. Malcolm dropped like a stone.

I threw myself off the cabin before Mr Collins could follow the first blow up with another and hoped that Malcolm's skull was as thick as it looked. I landed two-footed, rolled to absorb the impact and came up into a run. Mr Collins was only a few metres away, but the Maglite had reached the apex of its upward swing again and I could tell I wasn't going to cover the distance in time. He had murder in mind and did not seem even aware that I was present.

I was about to yell at him again in the vain hope that I might disturb his aim, but I didn't bother for I could see there was no need. The makeshift club swung cruelly downwards and stopped halfway as Susan caught it in her mouth. Susan had seen her stricken master and stepped in to save him. In the pale moonlight, Mr Collins looked shocked. He had committed his body to the swing so as his arm had stopped, the rest of his upper body had spun savagely about that point. He was now hanging under the dog, Maglite still in his hand as he stared up at the dog's face with a slack jaw.

The dog then shook its enormous head back and forth a few times and Mr Collins screamed. I know this about dogs from owning a few over the years: when they bite you, it hurts. I have only ever been bitten by accident, while playing with them as they had lunged for and missed a toy. On one occasion, a Labrador of mine bit my right hand and I could not hold a pen for a week. I suspected this was something more convincing than that.

I skidded to a halt next to Mr Collins and Susan. 'Make it let go! Make it let go!' Mr Collins appealed. I guess the pain was sufficient that he didn't care why a chap had appeared out of the dark wearing black combat fatigues, he just wanted help.

'Hello, Susan,' I soothed. The dog looked at me, its expression impossible to read. I reached out to stroke its ear, believing that it would either let me do so and perhaps I could slowly convince it to open its mouth, or it would see me as a threat, spit out Mr Collins and bite my face off.

Thankfully it went with option one. I scratched its right ear and cooed at it. 'Perhaps you should drop the torch, Mr Collins.' I suggested. He was still gripping it hard in his hand despite the dog's mouth around his wrist. He did so, the torch clunking onto earth worn hard by the passing of countless heavy vehicles.

'Did I miss something?' asked Big Ben from behind me.

'Kind of. How are you feeling?' I enquired.

'Who are you people?' asked Mr Collins still hanging from the dog's mouth.

Ignoring him, Big Ben replied to my question 'I have a fuzzy head and I can taste twiglets, but otherwise I appear to be fine.'

'Can you check out Malcolm while I catch you up then, mate? He took a nasty blow to the back of his head.'

Big Ben knelt to examine the inert form. 'He's alive. Got a cracking lump on the side of his skull though and it is bleeding quite convincingly,' he advised after a few moments of scrutiny.

'Call an ambulance please, Ben. I think it's time we wrapped this up.'

The dog continued to hold Mr Collins between his teeth. Every now and then Mr Collins would try to wriggle free and would be rewarded with Susan just increasing her grip a little as a warning. Mr Collins would squeal then settle and the cycle would repeat. I could not convince Susan to give up her prize and if I am honest I didn't actually try very hard to make her.

A little less than thirty minutes later, an ambulance arrived along with the police and shortly afterwards a police animal control unit. For once, I didn't know any of the police and for once they didn't arrest me. Mr Collins had screamed blue murder at them, accusing us of breaking in which had forced him to respond by coming to the yard. He then claimed we had attacked him and his employee and it was us that had caused the injuries paramedics were treating Malcolm for now. The police had looked at us seriously for a moment and probably would have arrested us had I not got Mrs Collins on the phone. As joint owner of the business she had given us a key, so we were not now intruders but two persons with a legal entitlement to be where we were. To finish the game though, I retrieved the camera, took it back to the start and showed the police what had really happened.

They took Mr Collins away, put Malcolm into an ambulance and the two dogs were being handled by police animal specialists as Big Ben and I left.

Another case solved, Mrs Collins had been over the moon to find out that her husband was cheating on her. She referred to him as a useless piece of limp meat. Retribution seemed likely to ensue.

It was now 2118hrs according to my watch. I had to wipe dirt from the face of it when I lifted my cuff to check the time. Diving around in the dirt had unavoidable side effects and this was probably the dirtiest, oiliest dirt I would be able to find for miles around. I looked at my clothes. They were black, so the dirt did not show, but I could tell it was there.

Nevertheless, Big Ben and I were going to the pub next. I had asked Big Ben if he felt he should see a doctor, but I knew what his answer would be before I asked it. Had he said yes, I would have known he was feeling really bad. He made the point that there wasn't anything they could do except keep him in for observation and that this would be a waste of both his time and the NHS resources.

We arrived at Jagjit's car, spun it around on the path sending debris shooting into the bushes and left the breakers yard behind us. I was driving. Obviously. And I felt inclined to have a heavy right foot. It was not unusual for Big Ben and I to grab a beer for an after-action-review and I could hear the cold, amber liquid calling me.

The Bit of New Information Thursday October 14th 2157hrs

We parked Jagjit's car back on his drive and knocked on the door to hand over the keys. Fortunately, Jagjit answered the door so we avoided having to explain to his parents why we were covered in dirt and had ripped clothes and bloody bandages.

'Hey, Tempest, Ben,' Jagjit said as he opened the door. 'Tough night?' Jagjit was wearing dinosaur pyjamas and was eating from a family sized bag of hula hoops. They were beef flavour. He offered the bag to Big Ben and me but we both politely declined. He had crumbs on his top.

'It was eventful,' I replied. 'Thanks for the loan of your car. We didn't need it in the end.'

'Oh, really?' he asked. 'Did you not catch the dog?'

'We did.'

'Dog would be a loose term,' Big Ben said, 'and there was two of them. Big ugly things.'

'Yes. Well, we were able to get out alive and the case appears to be solved,' I concluded.

'Ben and I are going for a pint if you fancy joining us?'

'I had better not, guys. I have a big meeting in the morning. Actually, that reminds me. I forgot that I have something to tell you.'

'Oh, really? What is it?'

'The lady you have been solving the Phantom case for. It turns out she is the big new client the partners at my firm are all excited about.'

My curiosity was piqued. 'Tell me more please.'

'Not much more to tell,' he replied between munching crisps. 'She has a big lump of riverside land. She and the partners are looking to turn it into a whole bunch of luxury homes looking out over the Thames. It should be worth mazillions.'

'Mrs Barker?'

'Yes, Mrs Margaret Barker.'

'Definitely the same one that I have been working for.'

'One hundred percent, mate. Why?'

Why? I wasn't sure exactly, but this was important somehow.

Big Ben and I bid Jagjit good night and with a plan to see him tomorrow anyway we set off for a well-earned drink. We walked the half mile to the pub via my house. My two miniature Dachshunds had heard me coming down the path to the house and were scrambling to get out of the door to greet me as I was trying to get in. 'Hello chaps,' I said as I scooped them both, so I could get past them to grab their leads.

They both stopped and sniffed deeply at my clothing then eyes me suspiciously. I knew why. They did this every time I came home with the smell of another dog on me. They were jealous types. Bull eyed me disapprovingly, then as a pair, they left me to offer their affection to Big Ben instead – the dog version of a cold shoulder.

A minute later I had them both secured. They had snuffled excitedly around Big Ben's feet while he gave them both a pat and a scratch. I was taking them to the pub and they understood enough of what I said to forgive me for cheating on them with another dog. Now they were straining at their leads to get to the destination. I needed no such encouragement.

Big Ben reached the pub door first and opened it with a flourish. All conversation ceased briefly as the patrons stared at the two guys dressed in black SWAT gear now stood in the pub doorway.

'Shut the door. You are letting the cold in,' instructed Madge from her seat near the door. Madge was a pub regular, the type that you get in every village ale house that had been alive longer than anyone else and thus knows everyone and their business.

We did as instructed. I pulled a chair out for Big Ben to sit, he still looked a little woozy. I hooked the dog leads around a table leg to stop them wandering off and took a step towards the bar. I stopped there though and turned back to Big Ben. 'What do you want to drink mate? You still look a little off balance.'

'Hmmm,' he replied thoughtfully. 'I am not one hundred percent yet, I'll give you that. Maybe just a beer.'

'How about a non-alcoholic beer?' I ventured.

'Mate,' he replied, turning to lock eyes with me, 'drinking non-alcoholic beer is like going down on your sister: it might taste kind of the same, but it is just plain wrong.' Big Ben had a knack for analogy that often impressed and horrified at the same time.

'A beer then?' I confirmed and headed to the bar.

Big Ben and I had put away three pints in very quick succession whereupon he had taken the sensible route and jogged home. It was a solid five miles to his penthouse apartment in town and would take him perhaps forty minutes. It was safer and more responsible than me dropping him off. He could have taken a cab, but he believed the exercise would help to straighten out his head. I would not recommend everyone jog home late at night through dark countryside paths but in Big Ben's case he was probably the most dangerous thing out there.

I had stayed for one more pint, because it felt right to do so, then had thanked the Landlord and had taken myself home. I walked through to the kitchen and snagged the dogs a gravy bone each. The gravy bones were inhaled as only a dog can, leaving two tiny faces looking up at me in the hope there might be more yet.

I went through the house performing some basic tidying up. I took the clean dishes out of the dishwasher and put them away. There was ironing to do, I fleetingly considered tackling it now, but my brain was fuzzy from a few hurried pints and I was dirty from the night's fun and games at the breakers yard.

I snagged two more gravy bones to the staccato rhythm of tails beating excitedly and headed upstairs to get a shower before bed with the funny little dogs following.

As I got in to bed I remembered that the Ashes cricket match was starting shortly. It was in Australia this year so coverage did not begin until nearly midnight. I put the television in my bedroom on and turned it down to quiet. My brain was itching because of what Jagjit had told me. The Phantom of Barker Mill case was all sewn up. But something about what Mrs Barker was doing felt wrong or off, or... something.

As the England opening batsmen were clapped onto the pitch, I fell asleep still wondering what she was up to.

Breakfast and Brett Barker Friday 15th October 0907hrs

A restless brain had driven me from bed at 0615hrs. I had been awake for a while by then mulling over what I had missed. Jagjit had said that Mrs Barker was meeting with the senior partners at his firm today. She was going to be discussing a big property deal involving waterfront land on the Thames. The Mill was on the Thames riverfront and there was something entirely suspicious about her actions. I did not know what was making my Spidey-sense twitch yet, but I intended to find out.

At some point today, I would visit Mrs Collins again to provide a report on last night's events in person. It would wrap up the case and provide a chance to hand deliver the bill for my services. It was a secondary task that could wait though.

For the last almost three hours, I had been crawling through all the information I had gathered on the mill, the case, the Phantom, and I had not yet determined a new theory. I did have some new unanswered questions though. Why would Mrs Barker be seeing commercial real estate agents? Who was the young man in the Nissan Skyline at her house? These were just two elements that were bothering me.

Today I would find out what was going on. I had seen the Nissan Skyline at the mill so that was where I was going.

Bull and Dozer were snoozing in an early morning sunbeam on the sofa in the lounge. We had taken a decent walk this morning while I spun a few ideas in my head, so I was content that they were fine to be left. Dozer twitched a back leg while I watched and let out a snort. I was not sure they would even notice I had gone. Nevertheless, I gave them each a pat and received a grumbled complaint from Bull as my reward.

My bag and keys were on the kitchen counter. I drained the last of my tea, visited the smallest room and with the determined step of a man seeking righteous justice I set off.

Then I went back and got my phone and set off again.

The roads were clear and free flowing on the short run back to Barker Mill. In the car, I recapped the information I had and questioned it.

Mrs Barker had engaged me to prove that Brett Barker was responsible for her husband's death. I had subsequently discovered that Brett had arranged for a supply of fake drugs which he had switched for his grandfather's heart medication. This was the damning piece of evidence. Amanda and I had found both the original drugs and the remainder of the fake drugs hidden in a compartment in his wardrobe. Brett had *motive* – inherit the mill, and *opportunity* since he lived in the same house and worked in the same building. Brett had also used Owen Larkin to pose as the Phantom. My belief had been that the fake heart meds were taking too long to kill his grandfather off and Brett had sent Owen to the mill late one night to shock the owner and cause a heart attack. The hot glove and the Phantom's cloak had been found in Brett's office. Combine this with the purchase of the fake meds and it all pointed to Brett. If I did nothing now Brett would be found guilty and that would be that. His plan to sell off the mill would be scrapped, and Mrs Barker would get the justice she sought.

So why is Mrs Barker now talking to real estate people? I kept coming back to that question. She might have a completely legitimate and unrelated reason. That felt tenuous though.

This wasn't getting me anywhere. I tried coming at it from a different angle, one where Brett Barker is completely innocent. Staying with this premise, if Brett was innocent someone would have had to have planted the hot glove in his office and the pills in his apartment. They would also have had to pay for the pills to be manufactured using his credit card. Also, Brett wanted the mill broken and devalued. If he was innocent of causing the death of his grandfather, was he also not guilty of sabotaging the mill? I could not make sense of it because whichever way I looked at the case I could not come up with a reason for Brett to cause damage to his own mill. What gain could there possibly be?

Then a further thought surfaced. During the raid on the mill, Big Ben had been adamant that the chap he tackled had been taller than Owen Larkin. Had Owen been standing on something, or had it just not been

Owen? Did he have time to kick Big Ben in the nuts and get to the other end of the mill to then be chased back towards us by Hilary and Basic? If not, then who had been inside the mill to kick Big Ben in his testicles?

Furthermore, what about Jagjit and Poison's claim that they had been following a cloaked figure. They had also claimed it was taller than Owen Larkin. Maybe six feet tall had been their estimate. So... so... there was something key here and I was just not seeing it.

The two chaps at the hospital – Gary and Chris. Chris had claimed the Phantom he had chased and had then been attacked by was a girl.

I drummed the steering wheel with my fingers and tried to force my brain to connect the dots.

OMG! There was no way this thing was that convoluted. Dots were finally joining in my head. Well, more sort of leaping and crashing into one another than joining. The connections they were making would be ridiculous if they did not actually fit the circumstances so well.

I punched the phone button on my console. The in-car system spoke to me. I instructed it to call Amanda.

She picked up on the second ring. 'Tempest? What's up?'

'Can you get to Brett Barker?'

'Can I? Why do... no, forget I asked. Yes, probably.'

'I need you to ask him what his plans for the mill are.' I was thinking as I was talking. 'Find out if he was actually causing damage. I doubt they can charge him with anything regarding sabotaging his own mill, but I need to know why he was doing it.'

'Ok, I'll give it a go. I'm not sure if he will speak to me given that I arrested him.'

'You can tell him that this might get him out. Tell him I think I have solved the case this time. But please stress that I need his help if he is innocent.'

'I thought you were convinced he was guilty.'

'I was. Long before I got anywhere near proving it. I was blind to other possibilities and it seems I was wrong from the start.'

'I'll let you know how I get on.' She disconnected.

I had reached the A2 offramp. I indicated and swept down and under a flyover. I would be at the mill in moments. There were several people that I intended to see, I just hoped I would catch them all here on a Saturday morning.

I turned into the mill entrance. The security guard waved me through the gate. There in front of me and easily visible was the Nissan Skyline. Now that I was looking at it properly I could see just how much love, attention and mostly money had gone into it. It looked like it had just rolled off the assembly line, but from a factory where they add every conceivable non-stock styling and performance extra. This thing was shaved and slammed. It must be worth fifty grand, I estimated. It was not a car a young man could afford unless it was:

A. not his.

B. provided to him by a rich uncle.

C. reward for services rendered to a rich widow.

I hit it with my car.

I already knew that he was not one of the Barkers. Given that there were only two people living at the house and I had seen him leaving there early in the morning it had to mean he was sleeping with one of them. My money was on Mrs Margaret Barker. But Mrs Barker was hot. Very MILF hot. So, why would she bother with a young, spotty, geeky teenager?

The only answer I had was because she wanted him to perform tasks that he otherwise might not and was using sex and very possibly the car to ensure he did them.

The car alarm was blaring. I got out of my car and walked around to inspect the damage. By blind luck and a bit of aiming I had managed to hit it with a bit of my bumper that already had a scuff on it. I had been meaning to get it fixed for months. Now I would have to. The damage to his car was minimal; a slight bruise to the front bumper, but on such a treasured item it was serious enough.

I only had to wait a few seconds before faces appeared at the windows of the offices that overlooked the car park. I had no idea where this chap worked. However, my hunch was it would be a role that brought him into regular contact with Mrs Barker and thus he would most likely be in the offices and not the foundry.

Sure enough, less than a minute after the alarm started the young, spotty fellow exited the main office building and headed my way, his pace hurried.

'Oh my God. What did you do?' He asked disbelievingly as he came breathlessly to a halt.

I let him take it in for a moment. He plipped the alarm off.

'Are you blind?' he asked. 'What have you done to my car? You had better have some good insurance.'

I said his name, 'Martin,' his face froze. I could see him trying to work out how I knew his name (It was on the pass displayed on his dashboard – Martin Wilkins). 'Martin, you are in a surprising amount of trouble.' I was still guessing most of the details, but I either had this dead right or dead wrong and since I had already crashed into his car I might as well carry on assuming I was right.

Martin stood about six feet one inch tall. He had on flat, office shoes and was skinny.

When he said nothing, I continued, 'Where are you hiding the Phantom cloak?' I watched his eyes and breathing looking for facial cues. I knew they would tell me everything and they did. Even before his lips moved I knew he was guilty. I was guilty too. Guilty of not listening. 'My

270

big friend. The one you kicked in the nuts? Let's just say that he is the least of your worries.'

'I don't know what you are talking about,' he stammered.

'Is it in the car, Martin? Or have you stashed it at the Barker house?' He was looking a little sick.

There were still faces at windows watching us but thankfully no one else had come out.

'Martin, we are going to do our insurance paperwork so that people watching do not come over. While we do it you are going to answer my questions.'

'And if I don't?'

I fixed him with a stare. He swallowed. 'Then I will have a police friend here shortly to ask the questions for me. Would you prefer that?'

I got my insurance papers from my glovebox and we began to chat.

How many phantoms can you count? Friday 15th October 1057hrs

My talk with Martin had been most enlightening. I had let him go when I felt confident I had extracted a full and accurate story.

He was not the only person I wanted to speak to this morning though. I strolled around the back of reception without bothering to pass through it. I was done with all that nonsense. Using the age-old policy of look like you belong here, and people will ignore you, I wandered unchallenged into the main office building and up the stairs.

Just down the corridor towards Brett Barker's now vacant office, was the open plan area I had passed several times previously. The desks in it were arranged in neat clusters of four with dividing barriers to give the individual some semblance of privacy or perhaps the purpose of the barriers was to demark one desk from another. I wasn't sure. The barriers were high enough though to hide most of what the person on the other side was doing but not so high that two seated persons could not converse over the top of them. Most had things pinned to them. A postcard here, a note or a photograph of the children there. I could not see who I was looking for and was starting to feel a little exposed just standing in the middle of the office looking around. The lady nearest me was about to ask me a question, probably if she could be of assistance, when my quarry appeared, emerging from an alcove I had not noticed. She was carrying four coffee mugs.

I was guessing that she was my quarry actually. I had never met the lady, so I was using a few clues from the last week as I pieced together how dumb and blind I had been.

The girl, I say girl, but she was possibly twenty or more, saw me watching her and looked at me.

'Kerry?' I mouthed in question.

Her eyebrows raised. It was her. I went to her desk in the corner of the office where she was now handing out the mugs of coffee to the three other ladies seated at her cluster of desks.

'Kerry, good morning. My name is Tempest Michaels.' I handed her my card. 'I have been hired to investigate the Phantom.' I watched as her face turned red. 'Might we have a word in private?'

Kerry looked at me. She had tears in her eyes and was blushing a rather incredible shade of scarlet.

'Perhaps we should find your grandfather.' I suggested. I took her arm gently and led her unresisting form from the room. Her colleagues gave her some questioning looks and I noticed her shaking her head at one or two of them, answering some silent questions about whether they should intervene or not I guess. No one did anything to impede our exit.

I gave Kerry's arm a squeeze. I wanted to impart a sense of calm authority. Nothing bad was going to happen to her. Well, probably not, but I had truths to uncover.

Brett's Truth Friday 15th October 1303hrs

I left the mill a while later having extracted everything that I could from Kerry, her grandfather Old Sam, and Ronald. Most of what I learned was surprising. I was heading now to Jagjit's place of work, although I did not know where that was beyond that it was in Canary Wharf in South London. Mrs Barker had been altogether naughty, and I was off to burst her bubble. My phone helpfully located the building that Jagjit worked in and provided a tube station that I needed to get off at all without me needing to stop walking. I arrived back at the mill carpark, slid into my car and aimed its nose at the exit.

I had been played like a fiddle right from the start. Margaret Barker, I now refused to even think of her as Mrs Barker, had lied to me. She murdered her own husband and planted a trail of breadcrumbs for me to follow to her stepson Brett. I had obeyed her wishes better than a trained dog. Now I was mad and about to get even.

I called Amanda.

'Tempest,' she answered with excitement. 'Have I got news for you?'

'Brett is totally innocent and has been working in the best interests of the mill all along,' I said.

'Yes,' she paused. 'How do you know that already?

'I also know that Margaret Barker killed her husband. That Brett is innocent is the only explanation left that makes sense.'

'Do you want the details?' Amanda asked.

'Yes, please.' I listened as Amanda explained what Brett had told her. Most of it was just as surprising as the information I had dragged out of Kerry and her grandfather. I was feeling generally surprised today. Not only at the truths I was now discovering but also from what I was learning about my childish, fragile ego and how gullible I could be.

At the end of her report I told her where I was going and what I needed her to do. She promised to get it done and that I would see her shortly.

Benover Commercial Property. Friday, 15th October 1357hrs

I arrived at the Benover Commercial Property Developers and Architects Agency in Canary Wharf by tube. It simply wasn't practical to drive there, so I had ditched the car at Dartford train station and taken my second train that week.

Google Maps on my phone took me to the building, otherwise, I might never have found it in the bustling concrete jungle. Towers stretched into the sky as if trying to escape the earth like rockets, only to find their feet still attached. Stood outside a building that my phone assured me was the right one, I could not see the name of the business. Only when I went inside and studied the information boards displaying business names did I find it located on the seventeenth floor. The lobby corralled people through a security process which included bag search and x-ray body scanner but started with a check of identification and appointment. People with passes were going in, but without an appointment, I was directed to the security desk where I met security guard Carl.

'Good afternoon,' I began, only to have him lift a hand to silence me.

'Do you have an appointment, sir?'

'No. I,'

'Next,' he called, turning his attention away from me. He was impressively rude.

I swallowed my anger. It was unlikely to get me inside the building any quicker. Instead of wasting my breath attempting to speak to security guard Carl, I learned from him and didn't bother. I called Jagjit and when he didn't answer I looked up the landline number for the business and called that instead.

'Benover. How may I direct your call?' was how the lady answered the phone. Her accent was Toronto, not unusual in London to find people from somewhere else in the world.

276

'Good afternoon. My name is Tempest Michaels. Can I speak with Jagjit Singh please?'

'I'm afraid he is in a meeting, sir,' she replied without hesitation. From Jagjit's brief description, the deal with Mrs. Barker was a big one. Jagjit was a rising junior at the firm and might very well be in the meeting with her.

'The meeting with Mrs. Barker?' I enquired.

'Yes. That's right,' she replied brightly.

'I have information pertinent to Mrs. Barker. I need to deliver it by hand. Can you please have security at the front desk allow me through?' It was an outright lie, but I calculated that knowing Mrs. Barker was there and why and saying I had come to mess the deal up would be less likely to get me through the gate.

'Just one moment, sir,' she replied, and I could hear her typing. 'You should be able to pass through security now. Just speak with one of the guards on the front desk.'

I strolled confidently back to the desk and security guard Carl.

'Hello again,' I addressed him engagingly.

He just stared at me.

'I think if you check my name you will find I am cleared to enter.'

He just stared at me.

'Thank you,' I said and took my turn at being ignorant by turning my back and leaning against the counter while I checked my phone.

He gave up after a few seconds and clicked a few keys, reading my name from the driver's license I had placed on the desk. He buzzed open the security gate for me to start the process of being x-rayed and searched. He did it without a word and refused to make eye contact when I picked up my I.D. from right in front of him. He did make a point of nodding to the chap doing the body scan though, so I wasted a further five minutes taking off my shoes and belt and emptying my pockets as the *randomly selected* person.

The elevator was waiting for me as I pulled my belt back through the loops on my trousers as I crossed the atrium. Up seventeen floors, I exited into a wide corridor. A brass looking sign on the wall directed me left to find the Benover offices.

Through glass panelled doors, I found a young woman sitting behind a glass and chrome counter. Behind her head was a large and ornate sign telling me I had found the right place. I went in.

'Good afternoon,' I said, looking around. 'Tempest Michaels. I called from the lobby.'

'Yes. Would you like me to show you to the meeting room?' she asked.

'Yes. I would.' Super.

She led me down a short corridor. I could hear voices ahead of me muffled by the walls. We reached a door marked on the outside as the Board Room and she politely knocked on the door. The conversation inside paused, at which point she turned the handle and let me into the room.

A dozen faces turned to look at me, including Jagjit's. He looked horrified and like he was going to say something. I winked as we made very brief eye contact. I dismissed him before he could speak though and ignored the other occupants as I scanned the room. Margaret Barker was sitting near the head of the table next to an elderly man in a well fitted three-piece suit. To her other side was Owen Larkin who looked shocked and angry. Another big piece of the puzzle fell into place.

She looked nervous as I said, 'You did not cover your tracks well enough, Margaret.'

'Who the devil are you, young man?' asked the elderly gentleman rising from his seat. The owner perhaps.

'My apologies, sir,' I said, addressing him directly. 'Mrs. Barker is guilty of murder, among other crimes and her accomplice Mr. Larkin is involved also. The land she is attempting to sell you for redevelopment is not hers.'

Mrs. Barker spoke. 'You overstep your bounds, Mr. Michaels. Besides, the shares will be mine long before the deal goes through.' I watched as she placed a hand on Owen's forearm to keep him in place or from speaking.

'Oh, Yes. The majority shares pass from heir to heir do they not? Unless the heir is found guilty of criminal behaviour and given a custodial sentence.' Her eyes widened. 'I have been doing some digging this morning. You see, Brett is innocent. I found the breadcrumb trail. It wasn't easy to get the firm's lawyer to talk. I had to get Old Sam and Ronald involved to achieve that.'

Around the table, the suited attendees were keeping quiet and listening. Most were pushed back in their chairs and listening. The elderly gentleman was looking at Mrs. Barker. She said, 'Those two idiots? You waste my time and yours, Mr. Michaels. Go home. Keep your bonus and stop being ridiculous.' Her confidence had returned.

'I think not, Margaret. You found Martin Wilkins, seduced him with sex and money and had him supply you with fake heart medication for your husband. Then, you arranged for him to be employed at your firm in a position that pays more than it should so that he would keep quiet while you waited for your husband to die and for Brett to fall into your neatly crafted trap.' She said nothing. 'You also took Mr. Larkin here as a lover because you needed to keep Brett distracted and to plant evidence in his office. Who better to act as the double agent than his own man.'

I turned to look at Owen. 'What did she promise you? Money? Her eternal love?'

I saw him move but expected that he would just get out of his seat and start shouting. Instead, he leaped onto his seat and then the table so he could dive at me. He is lighter and shorter than I and was fuelled by anger, rather than fighting knowledge. I was caught momentarily off guard, but amid the sea of shocked faces, I was able to react fast enough. I feigned a

279

move towards him as he lunged, then spun away at the last moment, sweeping his hands up and away from me as they tried to grasp my face. He shot by me with his hands now no longer protecting his face and slammed into the skirting board of the wall behind me. He lay still. I calmly bent to check his pulse, then rose again satisfied that he was just knocked out and would most likely come around again quite soon.

His attack had happened so fast that my own pulse had not had the opportunity to react.

'Brett is being released from custody as we speak. When forensic accounting goes through his records, will they find that he made the payment to Palmer Pharmaceuticals from his office? Or will it be that it was made from the office of the Financial Director of the firm as she has access to everyone's company credit cards?'

'Is any of this true?' asked the elderly gentleman, staring at Mrs. Barker.

On the table in front of them was a large architect's drawing of a riverfront paradise. It showed large buildings surrounded by trees and green areas. The buildings might have been offices or residential accommodation, but the piece of land shown was unmistakably the site of the Barker Mill. She had plotted to get rich.

I wondered how long ago she had started planning this moment. Was it years? Had she married George Barker with a plan in mind? Had she unwittingly discovered that with her husband dead and Brett incarcerated she would become the new recipient of the mill and then plotted to make it happen? I would never know.

Jagjit had stayed quiet thus far but caught my eye now. He looked like he wanted to ask me something, but I shook my head and looked away. I doubted it would serve him well at the firm if they learned he was an acquaintance of mine. We would talk later.

Mrs. Barker still had not answered the elderly gentleman but was now getting up and gathering her things. If she planned to leave I would make no attempt to stop her. The police would pick her up soon enough, but as that thought was thinking itself, I heard voices in the corridor outside.

The door opened, and the same young lady showed in two men in shabby suits. Amanda was behind them. Mrs. Barker looked ready to kill; clearly incensed that her plan was unravelling.

I stepped out into the corridor as the two men showed their warrant cards and introduced themselves. Now my task really was done, and the case truly closed. What I would do with my knowledge of the Phantom I had not yet decided. It was quite an intriguing story, but I was keeping it to myself for now.

Amanda had not gone into the room so was left with me in the corridor. Behind me, we could hear Mrs. Barker being read her rights.

'Hey, how's it going?' I asked her.

'Working for you is certainly different,' she replied. I was not sure if this was a good thing or a bad thing. So, I asked her. 'Good mostly,' she answered.

I did not press for more detail.

'I am done here, I think. Case solved, nothing else to do. Mrs. Barker was good enough to pay us already. Shall we get a coffee somewhere?' Mr. Wriggly had already noticed her cleavage was visible and that she looked as sexy as hell in her tight jeans today. I was just trying to be polite and engaging but, as always, he was whispering other thoughts directly into my brain.

'I have to go, but thank you. I am going back to Dartford to see Brett released from custody. He would have been transferred to prison tonight or tomorrow morning rather than held at a station.'

'How is he?' I asked.

'If anything, he is grateful that we exposed his evil stepmother's plans. I will be filling him in on all the details on the way to Paris.'

'Paris?' I asked, already certain I knew the answer.

'He offered to take me for dinner again. Now that I know he is innocent, I could not think of a reason to reject him.' Mr. Wriggly made some seriously displeased noises and comments about the tiny penis Brett would most likely be wielding.

I nodded, just so that I had something for my face to do. 'Well, enjoy your trip, I guess,' I managed, trying to keep the disappointment from my voice. 'I will see you on Monday?'

'No, I have a shift then, but I will call you for a catch up and I am free later that week.'

'Okay. Speak later then.' I turned and left her to whatever tasks she was still to perform with the two plain-clothes officers and headed back out of the office to make my way home.

Walking through Canary Wharf, I called Mrs. Collins. I owed her a full report in person and was quite thankful when she said not to bother and requested a written report instead. I imagined her affairs were most likely in disarray, her husband booted out, business no longer tenable now she could not trust her staff and perhaps a complex divorce to sort out. I silently hoped I would not be called upon to provide statements or act as a witness if a divorce were to go ahead.

Forty minutes later and back at Dartford station I collected my car, thankful that I had prudently paid for a full day's parking as right then the car next to mine was receiving a fixed penalty on its windscreen in a sticky bag.

Rochester High Street Flower Shop. Friday, 15th October 1600hrs

I drove back to the office in Rochester. My working day was very much at an end and as I had nothing more that I needed to do before I went home, I intended to try one more time to catch up with Hayley. It had now been most of a week since we had spent the night together and I had received no response to my earlier text. I was not sure what that meant but it felt unlikely that it was a positive sign. I elected to buy some flowers and drop them off at the coffee shop. If she wasn't there, I felt certain that one of her colleagues would let her know that I had brought them in for her.

There was a florist just a couple of doors along from the coffee shop, so I went in there and asked for a bouquet of pretty, pink flowers. I did not want red roses because they suggested a deeper sense of affection than I wanted to convey. It was supposed to be a token of affection, or gratitude maybe. I waited patiently while the lady pulled the bouquet together and wrapped them up for me.

Outside it was beginning to get dark. I was still buoyant from finishing up the Phantom case and caught myself humming a happy tune as I strolled airily along the street.

The attack came as a surprise.

I reeled from the initial blow to my face, shocked more than hurt but went with the strike to put distance between myself and my attacker. Then the information update arrived in my brain and I realised I had been slapped. Not punched or kicked or hit with a weapon. I had been slapped on my face. And the slapper was Hayley.

She was stood facing me now, her chest heaving from the surge of adrenalin. 'You utter git,' she spat at me. 'Are those for her?' she asked indicating the flowers.

Utterly befuddled, my mouth opened and closed a few times while I struggled for an answer.

'Answer me, you pathetic man whore,' she demanded, screeching. People were stopping to watch the street theatre now.

'Her who?' I had to ask.

'Wha...?' she started to ask. 'You men are all such players. You think you can just shag us and shag everyone else.'

'I bought you flowers,' I managed weakly, still having no idea what was going on. 'I don't know who else you think I have been shagging, but...'

'Shut up!' she screamed, cutting me off. 'I saw you with the cute blond three times this week already.'

What blond. I asked myself. Amanda? When would she have seen me with her?

'Don't bother coming here for your coffee.' She twirled and stormed back inside the coffee shop, leaving me on the street with more than a dozen strangers all staring at me. I looked at them now. They each decided the show was over and drifted away. I looked at the flowers in my hand and walked over to a bin. As I was about to throw them in, I saw a copy of the local paper, The Weald World shoved loosely in. It was the headline on the page that caught my eye:

Klown attack?

I picked the slightly crumpled paper out of the bin, inspected it briefly to ensure there was nothing icky stuck to it and stood in the street reading the article.

Klown attack? Following recent reports of clown activity, this reporter believes there is something sinister going on. Graffiti adorns our walls telling us the Klowns are coming.

Below there was a photograph of a wall with that exact message displayed in crude spray writing.

Fourteen attacks have been recorded in the last week, each with escalating violence. The latest attack occurred in Canterbury where Judith Tennant suffered a stab wound after being chased by a clown on her way home from work. Miss Tennant described her attacker as a traditional circus clown in every way except for the face paint, which was horrific.

I kept reading. The article was written by Sharon Maycroft, a person I knew quite well and had an unfulfilled promise by her to get together for nocturnal activities soon. Given how much my right cheekbone was stinging now after my last bout of nocturnal activity had somehow gone awry, I might steer clear. She was, however, a reliable reporter. Klown reports were becoming popular. It was a case for the police really, not for me. But I did have a plea for help already so I could envisage myself being drawn into the Klown silliness yet. Sharon outlined how many attacks had taken place and where. They were all in different towns across Kent and the description of the attacker in each case was similar, but also dissimilar enough to make it sound like there might be more than one person. Sharon was hinting at this, but it seemed more likely to me that it was the same guy dressing differently each time.

I put the paper back in the bin. Decided to keep the flowers and headed back to my car. Despite my stinging face and marked downturn in the likelihood of Mr. Wriggly getting any action this weekend, it was, nevertheless Friday night and that meant the pub beckoned. I had a steak in my fridge waiting to hit the pan and life was good enough to be savoured.

The Dirty Habit Public House. Friday, 15th October 1917 hrs

The dogs had been glad to see me as usual. I sat on the tile in my kitchen and fussed them for a while. Then, because it was almost dinner time, I cracked a can of dog food and sat on the floor once more, stroking their fur while they ate. With bellies full, they lost interest in me and headed for the back door. I would be taking them for a long walk to the pub shortly, so sent them to relieve themselves in the garden while I made a cup of tea.

As I walked to the pub an hour later, my own belly full of steak and sweet potato fries I looked back on the case. I had taken Kerry with me to track down her grandfather. We found him in his boiler room with Ronald. They had both greeted Kerry as she went through the door before me, asking her what she was doing down on the shop floor, but stopped talking quickly when I came in behind her. Their immediate silence told me I had guessed right.

I told them that Brett was innocent and that another party was to blame then implored them to tell me the truth. They had looked at each other and said nothing, but when Kerry started talking instead, Old Sam waved her into silence saying that she would only tell it wrong.

Old Sam had seen Mr. Miller wearing the Phantom outfit on a fateful day in his first month at the mill. When Barry had fallen from the rafters and he had followed the shadow, it was distinctly Mr. Miller's face that had appeared from beneath the cowl of the cloak. For days he had wondered if he should say something but had not done so because he could not work out what to say or who to say it to. He spent months searching different areas of the mill for the Phantom outfit, wondering where Mr. Miller had stashed it.

He very quickly found though that he had become Mr. Miller's favourite. He was given the best jobs to perform, those that carried some degree of responsibility and some weeks later, when the owner, Mr. Barker had visited the foundry to view production, he had been introduced to him as one of the rising stars. Bewildered by the praise, he had caught Mr. Miller's eye. Mr. Miller just winked at him and made a shushing motion with one finger to his mouth.

The Phantom attack had been solely to stop Barry from shagging his daughter, Old Sam was certain of that. Whether the Phantom had ever been real he could not say, but no other attacks happened for several years and when the next incident did occur it had happened when Mr. Miller was in plain sight. Old Sam decided that it was just an accident and nothing to do with the Phantom at all, but everyone had automatically blamed the Phantom as if no other explanation was needed. Mr. Miller had joined in the chorus and had used it as a warning that the Phantom protected the Mill and was displeased with output. For a month production had increased by twenty percent with no extra hours being worked. Old Sam had learned something about people that night. He was soon promoted to a supervisory position above many of the older men that had trained him.

To Old Sam's knowledge, Mr. Miller never saw a need to play the role of the phantom again. In 1987 Mr. Miller retired. Old Sam considered going to visit him at home to ask him about the Phantom but before he could do so Mr. Miller suffered a heart attack and died. A week later a black cloak and an articulated steel hand with an asbestos handle had arrived in a parcel addressed to him. There was a handwritten note which Old Sam produced from a locker against the wall behind him. It was crumpled and tattered from age but still perfectly legible.

Dear Samuel,

I came into the possession of the Phantom's hand many years ago when my father retired. I have been sworn to secrecy my entire life, but perhaps in death, I can finally tell the truth. The first Phantom was nothing more than a shadow seen by my Grandfather. He made a comment as a joke but the chap next to him took it seriously and when someone was hurt the next day in an accident the Phantom was blamed, and the legend was born. My Grandfather was a senior Mill supervisor, much like me and saw an opportunity to influence and motivate the workers through the Phantom. He used it to get more from them, to stop them wandering off for a crafty fag and to explain away equipment problems to the owner when he had himself messed up. My father took over from him and I from my father. I confess that I used the Phantom for my own purposes and that I should not have. It was not my intention for the walkway to collapse and cause such terrible injuries. I merely wanted to frighten Barry.

I have no son of my own, so I pass the Phantom's hand and cloak to you to do with as you please. I believe you to be a trustworthy man and hope that you will act in the best interests of the mill.

Yours

Archibald Miller

When Brett Barker began to wield his power and started to speak out against how the mill was run, Old Sam had chosen to bring the Phantom out of retirement. He had never worn the cloak himself and now he was too old to do so. He confided in an old friend at the mill and together he and Ronald had hatched a plot to frame Brett Barker. His granddaughter Kerry was reluctant at first but had relented when they convinced her everyone's job was in danger.

Brett Barker had no intention of shutting the mill. He had a secret deal with Zoom-It, the massive online retailer. He was going to sell them steel at almost cost price to meet their European building plans and had struck a deal that meant any equipment in poor repair would be replaced at Zoom-It's expense. He had a chance to secure the future of the mill and thus everyone's jobs for the next decade and could simultaneously get new foundry equipment. All he had to do was target some of the older machines to accelerate their wear. He had secured his family legacy but fought with his grandfather who could see no reason to change anything about their current operation. Under an iron-clad non-disclosure agreement, he could not even tell his grandfather what he had planned. The only person he had involved in the meetings with Zoom-It was Owen Larkin. That was why Brett Barker had continued to deal with him after his grandfather fired him and why he paid him off.

Owen Larkin was working for Mrs. Barker though. Every decision Brett made Owen relayed directly to her. Every plan, every thought that Brett had was shared. The man Brett trusted above all others was the one betraying him at every turn. It had messed with Owen's plan when the crane lockouts appeared in his car and the old man had fired him. Brett came to the rescue though - the irony was stark. Brett had not been at the other end of the phone call I had overheard outside Owen's house. He had seen me and called Mrs. Barker. Together they played me like a fiddle and nearly got away with it.

Mrs. Barker had full access to all the firm's credit cards so had been able to make the payment to Martin Wilkins using Brett's card. She had seduced poor Martin Wilkins and used money, sex, and gifts like the car to make him play the Phantom. She had him make up the fake heart meds then quit his job at Palmer Pharmaceuticals to then take a job at the Mill where she had promised him a brighter future. She had at least delivered on all her promises, but I had to wonder what her end play was for him. Would she have killed him off too? He had gone to George Barker's office the night of his death on her instruction. In bed, she had told him that she wanted to be with just him and they could be together if he would help her get rid of her husband. George had a weak heart and a fright might end him. Martin had obeyed her instructions willingly. He had knowingly provided fake heart medication and had known what it was for. When he and I had finished our little chat in the car park I had advised him to turn himself in. He had not done so and had been arrested trying to board a ferry out of Dover.

Kerry was guilty of burning Chris Partridge. Old Sam and Ronald had convinced her to play the Phantom. She was supposed to sabotage Mill equipment and very carefully endanger members of the workforce – played cleverly by Old Sam and Ronald. When the police became interested they would then leave a trail back to Brett Barker so that he would be blamed for the accidents. It had been Kerry that had taken the crane lockouts and placed them in Owen's car. They were supposed to be in Brett's car, but he never left his keys where she could get to them she said. She had been going into the mill at night and loosening bolts or cutting wires. It was damaging the mill's output, but they agreed it was a necessary step to get rid of Brett Barker. Chris Partridge had gone to school with Kerry and had teased her about her weight for years. When he followed her into the boiler room that night she remembered how much she disliked him and grabbed his arm with the hot glove. She seemed genuinely regretful though and I felt that he had probably earned his injury. I told her that I would not be sharing her secret. Owen Larkin, Martin Wilkins, and Margaret Barker would be charged with conspiracy to murder George Barker and the attack on Chris Partridge could get swept up into the investigation.

There had never been a Phantom. It had always just been a man in a costume, or it had been nothing at all and superstition had allowed people to blame their mistakes on a mysterious figure. Now that I knew the truth of it I could reveal what I had learned. I could hold a press conference if I chose to and expose the Phantom as a sham, but I had no current intention of doing so. My focus was already moving to the next case, whatever that might be.

Crossing the pub car park, I could see Jagjit, Hilary, Big Ben and Basic all sitting around our usual table. The warm light from inside was inviting. I went inside to a warm greeting from my friends. I gave them my usual salutations and left the dogs with them to get my round of drinks in.

The simple task of retrieving a round of cold drinks proved to be fraught with complication though as stood staring at me from behind the bar was Natasha. Her expression was probably best described as frosty, but I fear that term fails to capture adequately the ice spilling from her face. There was no one else waiting at the bar and we had already locked eyes. I had nowhere to go but straight towards her to meet my fate.

Natasha and I had enjoyed a lunch date a couple of weeks back during which Natasha had kissed me, poured out her heart and left the ball firmly in my court. Since then life had gotten away from me, I had lost her number and despite attempts to find a way to make contact, I had not done so. Natasha was lovely to look at, delightful to speak to and was probably excellent girlfriend material. However, because I am stupid I have been fawning over Amanda and neglecting the perfectly obvious choice right in front of me. That I had found time to message Hayley, arrange a date and spend a night rolling around naked with her proved that there had been time for Natasha had I been thinking straight.

'So, what can I get you, Mr plays-it-cool?' Natasha asked.

Bugger. I had not intended to play it cool with Natasha. Indeed, I could not remember ever purposefully playing it cool with a lady. What could I say at this point though?

'Sorry, Natasha,' I tried. 'I had every intention of calling you. I lost your number.' As I said the words I realised just how weak they sounded. 'I planned to call you.' Her expression and stance had not changed one bit.

'Well, you didn't call me, Tempest. It is what it is.'

At least she was talking. Maybe I wasn't sunk after all and this was salvageable with a rueful smile and a heartfelt request for a second chance.

'Just don't bother trying to call me now.'

Or maybe not.

'What can I get you?' she asked again.

'Two pints of lager, please,' I replied glumly.

Natasha poured the drinks, took my money and deposited my change in the charity jar on the bar without asking my opinion on the matter or even looking my way. Suddenly the pub felt like a much less enticing place to visit.

I took the drinks back to the table where the chaps were all engaged in conversation.

'What are we talking about, chaps?' I asked, sitting down.

'Embarrassing sexual escapades,' answered Jagjit. 'Hilary was just regaling us with a story. Do you want to back up and start again mate?'

Hilary took a swig of his drink and started talking. 'So, I was seventeen and getting my first ever blow job. The girl's name was Tracy Hunt. Well, I had a bit of a dodgy tummy and I desperately needed to fart, but I figured I could hold it and there was no way I wanted her to stop. I'm sure you can all see where this is going, but there I was lying on the bed with her head bobbing up and down. It went on for ages and my need to fart got worse and worse and then I hit climax and my ability to hold it in left me. I let out a total felt-ripper of a fart that must have gone on for five seconds. By the time all the gas inside me had vented itself to atmosphere, she had already left my bedroom and the door was slamming shut.'

We were all laughing at his expense, which was the point of the story of course. Big Ben seemed to find it funnier than the rest of us though.

'I never saw her again,' Hilary said. Big Ben snorted his drink, 'and when I looked between my legs there was a single piece of sweetcorn that I had ejected from my bum.' Big Ben now had tears rolling down his cheeks. 'It was like life was giving me the finger.'

'Now that was a great story,' acknowledged Jagjit.

At that point three ladies walked into the pub, the cool air spilling in around our feet. The conversation stopped though and we all took a draught from our glasses as they passed.

They got to the bar and were out of earshot. Big Ben leaned forward conspiratorially so that he could speak to us in a hushed tone. 'I have always wondered how couples keep sex interesting when they have been together for years. I have always found that I can never see a girl for more than a week because the sex gets better for a few days and then starts to tail off after you have done all the experimenting stuff.' Thankfully he did not feel the need to graphically regale us with exactly what experimenting meant to him.

'Anyway,' Big Ben continued, 'I have read that there is a simple way to ensure you make the lady scream during sex even when the relationship has been going on for years.'

'Oh, yes?' said Hilary, now looking interested to hear what Big Ben had to say.

'Yes, chaps. The trick is that you phone her up and tell her what you are doing.'

All the Women Gone. Friday, 15th October 2306hrs

As I walked home, being led by my two little dogs, a thought occurred to me. I still hadn't checked my phone to see the message I had sent to Hayley. What had I sent her that had made her so angry? I read it now and saw my error immediately. I had addressed the text to Jane and not to Hayley. Jane had walked in right when I was writing it and I guess my brain misfired when I was trying to work out how to start the message. From Hayley's perspective, it must have been like saying the wrong name in bed. If read from the perspective that it was genuinely addressed to a girl called Jane, then I had been bonking her as well as Hayley. Is this why words like darling exist? To avoid such pitfalls? In just a few short days I had managed to lose every woman I had been interested in or who had shown interest in me.

Hayley had seen me with Jane, put two and two together and come up with the completely wrong answer. I had already learned that she was a passionate woman, so I was telling myself that reaction was in character. Natasha's brief interest had quickly waned when I failed to call her. I had spurned Poison's advances because I felt that I should. Going home to an empty bed that could have her nakedness writhing around in it instead made me consider that it might not have been the best decision though. Sharon Maycroft had suggested she was in my debt and would be paying me with sex but that had been weeks ago, and I had not heard from her since. And Amanda, the jewel in the crown, the brightest berry on the bush, was currently in Paris have the knickers romanced off her by a multi-millionaire playboy. Mr. Wriggly was so disappointed he was refusing to talk to me.

The sky was clear tonight which brought a chill to the air. The rain and clouds of the week had been keeping the temperature up. It felt like frost might come and it matched my cold mood.

Epilogue: The baby Shower. Saturday, 16th October 0900hrs

Saturday morning rolled around, and it was baby shower day. It was usual for me to have a decent lie in on a Saturday morning. My life in the army had been filled with early morning physical training sessions which would often start at 0600hrs and thus had me out of bed a good while before that. This led to the practice of having a few pints on a Friday night and a lie in on a Saturday. Today was no different and I had stayed in bed until almost 0900hrs. The dogs had held their bladders for long enough by then, so I had rolled out of bed and let them into the garden.

While the dogs ran around outside, I went to the bathroom. I inspected my face, convinced I must have a black eye or at least some bruising from the slap Hayley gave me. There was no visible trace though, just a tugging sensation in my face as I moved my jaw.

I could hear the dogs barking to be let back in. They had completed whatever tasks they reserved for the garden and wanted their breakfast. I dealt with them, put the kettle on to make some tea and pulled out the toaster for crumpets. I love crumpets. They are not on the list of anyone's nutritious diet, but they were too good to never eat. I made my cup of tea while the toaster worked its magic and through timing born of the benefit of experience, the crumpets leapt into the air just as I was placing my cup of tea on the breakfast bar. I ate four of them smothered in melting butter and then ate a pink grapefruit so that my breakfast was not just stodgy white carbs.

The baby shower would dominate my day, but my caseload was empty again, at least until Monday when I would begin looking for a new case. For now, I had nothing better to do and was glad for it. I had organised virtually every element of the baby shower and had paid for most of it from my own pocket. Had I not done so, the party would most likely have been arranged at my parent's house or the church hall and my mother would have invited dozens of little old ladies from the church who somehow knew my sister and me, but like off-screen characters in a movie, we had heard their names, but could not actually remember ever seeing them before. Instead of that, the party was at a very pleasant tea room in Rochester High Street. Rachael would have an afternoon with her friends, most of whom were still childless and several of whom were single, which was of some interest to me since I would at least be there to meet them at the start.

I bumbled around the house for a while and took the dogs for a nice walk but at 1120hrs it was time to go. I intended to make sure the venue was to my liking and would stay to greet my sister and her friends and of course my mother and her friends. The venue had a function room and would serve a thoroughly British afternoon tea with platters of freshly made sandwiches and trays of unctuous cakes and warm scones with accompanying jam and clotted cream. The place was called Fleur-de-tea, I had eaten there before, an experience which had provided the confidence that my sister would be well looked after, well fed and entirely separate from other customers. I also knew that they were not licensed, so my mother would be cut off from her usual supply of wine and would stay sober and thus more manageable for the event.

In my car on the way there, I ran through the event in my head. There were thirty guests coming, all women. I would settle my sister in as the centre of attention and make sure my mother was given pride of place next to her as the grandmother of the imminent offspring. I was balancing the sensibilities of one with the demands of the other. I introduced myself to the proprietor and exchanged a fifty pounds note for his assurance that the ladies would, in fact, be well looked after. There was a further fifty on offer if I heard a good report from the ladies later. He seemed only too pleased to take the money and do exactly as I had asked.

He asked if he could get me anything and supplied a cup of tea upon my request. I watched him make it to be sure that he used fresh water, not already boiled and thus deionised water. He knew his business though and could make a good cup of tea. He did not charge me for it, which was sensible. I would have hit him with a raised eyebrow if he had.

I relaxed with my beverage in one of the window seats just watching the world go by outside. Before my thoughts could drift, a face appeared right next to mine on the other side of the glass, and then another face right next to it. The faces belonged to Karen Archer and Sophie Sheard, two girls I had gone to school with. Only they were not girls now. I had emailed them this week to organise the party but had not communicated with either of them since we left school almost twenty years ago.

I smiled at them. They waved, went to the door and came inside. Unsure of the correct protocol, I elected to get up and offer my hand to shake but Sophie got to me first and wrapped me up in a hug. Then kissed my cheek and made way for Karen to do the same. We started chatting and generally catching up, but within minutes others joined us and then my sister arrived, bereft of children for once.

Mother would be here soon, so I escorted Rachael and her friends to the private function room and left them there.

'Where are you going?' asked Rachael.

'Outside to receive mother and confiscate her wine.'

'Will you be back?' asked Sophie.

'No. I think this is an event for ladies. My part in the proceedings is largely complete.'

Sophie followed me to the door. 'See you around, Tempest. I have your contact details now.' She gave me a smile, which I returned and then I was out of the function room and heading outside. Sophie had been flirting with me. It was pleasing.

I did not have to wait long for my mother. She had walked to the venue flanked by a dozen of her pensionable aged friends. I recognised a couple of them.

'Hi, Tempest,' she said as she approached.

'Hello, mother.'

'Why don't you all go inside?' I asked of the ladies with mother. 'I just need a quick chat with my mum.' They filed in offering greetings as they passed. Once the last one was inside, I turned back to my mother. 'Hand it over,' I instructed. 'You can have it back later?'

'Hand what over, Tempest,' she replied knowing full well what I meant.

I played along though. 'The cold bottle of wine you have hidden in your handbag.'

Mother allowed her shoulders to slump. 'Alright, Tempest. You win,' she said and pulled a nice-looking bottle of crisp Italian Pinot Grigio from the depths of her bag. 'Anything else?' she asked, handing it over grumpily.

'Yes, mother. Enjoy your afternoon,' I said kissing her cheek. 'And remember that this afternoon is all about Rachael.'

'Yes, Tempest,' she replied, her tone changing to one of contentedness. She was happy to be a grandmother.

I watched as my mother went inside, then left the delightful tea room behind me and headed back to my car. I stopped though as a thought occurred to me: Mother had handed over the wine far too easily.

I backtracked the few paces I had taken and peered through the window. Across the room, I could see Rachael surrounded by her friends and mother's little old ladies, all of them fussing around her and making her feel special. Exactly as it was supposed to be. Off to one side, my mother was fiddling around in her undergarments and laughing conspiratorially with a lady I knew to be one of her closest friends. As I watched, she pulled a hip flask from its hiding place. It was undoubtedly filled with gin and was why she had given up the wine with so little fight.

I chuckled to myself, congratulated her on a game well played and left her to it.

Postscript: The Klown. Saturday, 16th October 1217hrs

Across the road, he stood in plain sight. His intended quarry had not seen him though, too wrapped up in his own life, his pathetic hopes and pointless dreams. He watched as the man walked away from the tea shop.

He called himself Deadface. He was a Klown. He wore oversized shoes, though not so oversized that he could not run in them. Colourful trousers held up with braces rather than a belt. A garish, multi-coloured jumper of horizontal stripes and he had a large plastic flower pinned just above his left nipple. In his right hand, he held a solitary balloon on a string. It fluttered forlornly in the light breeze, pulling against the string and being held in check only to reach for the sky again immediately as if the only thing it wanted was to escape the creature holding it.

His face was painted. Mostly it was white, except around the eyes which were a very dark blue and the mouth which was a bright red. The manner in which these areas had been decorated betrayed his true nature. The paint to his eyes might have just been thrown at his face. The lines between dark blue and white were not crisp or defined. It gave his eyes the appearance of two holes that might go straight through his head, or worse, go in and then descend to hell. The mouth looked more like a chainsaw wound.

He reached up with his left hand to scratch his face. In it, he held a long, razor-sharp blade, the hilt of which had finger loops that resembled a knuckle duster. From each knuckle protruded a half inch long spike.

The awful wound beneath his nose opened. 'Not yet, Tempest Michaels. Not yet. But soon.'

He turned and walked away.

The End

299

Don't miss the extract from the next book on the following pages though

Note from the Author:

Hello Reader,

It's a warm day in June 2020 as I write this note some two and a half years after I first published this book. It was when this book came out that I started to believe I might be on to something with my fun little hobby. I had written my whole life, winning my first award when I was just ten years old.

It was never viewed as a viable career though, not be me or my parents, into the army I went, somehow surviving twenty-five years of service and many different conflicts.

Anyway, publishing this book opened a floodgate, which just shy of two years later resulted in me quitting my well-paid but soul-destroying corporate day job to do this full time. Last night, a little before midnight as I sipped a gin and tonic, I finished my thirty-seventh novel. Writing has given me a lifestyle I could only imagine with any other form of employment. I spend my days in a log cabin at the bottom of my garden with a dachshund or two on my lap or curled at my feet while I craft adventure and mystery. It's what I want to do, but should I decide I feel like mowing the lawn at ten in the morning on a Tuesday, who's going to stop me?

I followed my dream and maybe you can too. It took a lot of work, getting up early and going to bed late for almost two years as I created enough of a library to support myself when I went full-time, but it has been worth the effort.

I hope you enjoyed this book and Tempest's developing story. There is so much to come but if you want some for FREE, there a link below to get you three FREE books. The FREE collection includes the origin story and how he came to be a paranormal investigator. All I need is an email to send them to. It will cost you nothing now or ever.

Take care

Steve Higgs

June 2020

Extract from The Klowns of Kent

Fennucci's Italian Family Restaurant, Faversham. Monday
October 24th 1900hrs

Having called the proprietor earlier he knew to expect me and had set
out a table at a point that intersected where he claimed the footsteps
usual tracked. The restaurant was completely empty, I was the only
patron. Okay it was 1900hrs on a Monday evening but even so, a
successful place would have people in it. The owner's name was Georgio
Fenucci which sounded very Italian, unlike the man himself who sounded
like he hailed from Essex. I wondered if the name was fake but refrained
from asking.

He had opened the restaurant five years ago and had enjoyed a steady
stream of clients ever since. That was until three weeks ago when the
footsteps started to occur. On the first night that they had manifested he
had been in the kitchen when he heard a rush of people coming down the
stairs from the upper dining room. Worried there might be a fire or some
other disaster unfolding he had rushed out into the restaurant still
clutching a spatula in one hand, then watched in horror as almost all his
customers disappeared out of the door. His staff had gone also, all except
his wife and the slightly deaf bar man.

He found his wait staff outside in the street and slowly convinced most
of them to come back inside. Maria, one of the girls that had been
working upstairs explained what she had heard. They went back upstairs
and of course there was no ghostly noises to listen to. Maria and the
others had been adamant that they had not imagined it and corroborated
each other's stories.

Georgio described being angry at the time because he suddenly had an
empty restaurant and he had to throw food away. He did nothing about it
though and since so many of his staff were telling him the same thing he
felt that he could not hold them to account or call them liars. Then the
same thing happened the next night, after which some of his staff quit
and then the night after that. It was on the third night that he witnessed
the phenomenon himself. By then he had become convinced that this was

an elaborate hoax and so had seated himself in the upper dining room to see if they dared to perpetrate it with him there.

Instead he got the fright of his life as, clear as anything, an invisible person walked across the room, their footsteps audibly striking the floorboards. A few seconds later he was alone in the room still rooted to the spot when the *ghost* ambled back again.

I listened to all this with my notebook out, taking notes while we were still downstairs in the bar area. He had regaled Amanda with the same story on Saturday morning, but her shift pattern had not permitted her to stay for the evening to witness the event. There was one detail missing though.

'My colleague made a note that you heard music.'

'Yes.' he replied. 'The ghost walks across the room several times most nights. Some nights not at all, but more often than not now the haunting occurs. It is usually accompanied by the sound of someone playing the cello. It is much fainter than the footsteps and I dismissed it the first time I heard it. After three weeks though I believe the two noises are linked and I have the ghost of a musician haunting my restaurant.'

Georgio went on to complain about how his business was suffering and how he could not sustain the current level of income for very long. The phenomenon only occurred in the evenings, so he was able to conduct lunch trade, but the word was getting out and several customers that he had considered regulars because they came in most weeks had already stopped visiting.

I thanked him for his detailed explanation and went upstairs to find a seat. There was a lot of choice as I was the only person in the restaurant. Presently a waitress appeared and took my order, returning a few moments later with a glass of ice and a bottle of sparkling mineral water. I had ordered carpaccio to start and a seafood pizza as my main course. I was hungry and looked forward to the food. While I waited, I pulled out a few items I felt I might need: A piece of chalk, a tape measure, a stopwatch and a tuning fork. I placed each on the table at the seat adjacent and to the left of mine so that they were within easy reach when I needed them, and so that I could grab them with my uninjured side.

Idly wondering how long I would have to wait for my food, I realised there was something niggling at me. I had forgotten to do something or was supposed to do something. It was the same feeling I had been wondering about earlier, but the memory still refused to coalesce. It was hiding in the corner of my mind, showing me glimpses but not revealing itself. I told myself that if I concentrated the answer would come to me. Just then I heard the door open downstairs. That I could hear the entrance door moving was a clear demonstration of just how quiet the restaurant was. I had instructed Georgio to not play any music tonight – I wanted as little background noise as possible but the silence in the building was striking. Then I realised that I recognised Frank's voice coming from downstairs. He was talking with Georgio and there was a third man's voice in the conversation.

Clomping footsteps on the wooden stairs preceded the appearance of Georgio, then Frank and then Dr Lyndon Parrish.

'Good evening, gentlemen.' I said to attract their attention. Frank and Lyndon both looked surprised to see me, so they were not deliberately gate crashing. 'What a pleasant surprise. Won't you please join me?'

'Tempest.' Beamed Frank. 'Lyndon plans to catch the ghost.'

I nodded, unsure what I could say to that announcement. I had my own theory about what was causing the phenomenon and it was a little less than paranormal.

'Mr Michaels, I must apologise. I had no idea you would be here.'

'Did Mr Fenucci hire you?'

'Goodness no, this is pro bono work. I am new to the game unlike you, Mr Michaels. I need to build up my reputation. This will do me no harm at all. Of course, had I known you were here I might have come along anyway to watch the master at work.' Lyndon strode across the room to shake my hand. Both he and Frank were carrying bags.

'Do you mind if Frank and I remain and attempt to catch the spirit?'

'No, please.' I indicated that they should carry on. I wanted to see what he planned to do.

Lyndon spoke briefly with Georgio who then departed and laid his bag on the floor. From it he extracted a piece of equipment I recognised – it was a PKE meter. Mr Reginald Parker had tried to sell it to me recently. I had all but laughed at him, but it seemed that he had found himself a customer after all.

Next out was a piece of clunky steel with a lid and a long electrical lead. Frank was emptying his bag at the same time. Onto the floor his spilled several items of recording equipment, what looked like motion sensors and accessories like tripods to mount it on.

I looked at the few items I had on the table and smiled to myself. 'How is it that you plan to catch the ghost, Lyndon?' I asked.

Lyndon stopped what he was doing and stood up. 'First we have to establish that there is a ghost. Not every report of supernatural activity has a genuine entity at the end of it.'

Or none at all. Ever.

'Then I shall trap it inside a circle and using this,' he showed me a fancy leather pouch with a drawstring at the top, 'I will anchor it to a new object and remove it from the premises.'

Frank saw me looking at the little pouch and answered my question just as I was opening my mouth to ask it. 'It's ghost dust, Tempest.' When he saw my continued curiosity, he spoke again. 'It is created from ectoplasmic slime by a process of desiccation, but it can only be performed by a single shaman in South America. The secret is passed down to only one member of the tribe on his death bed. It is incredibly rare.'

'No doubt.' I was continuously amazed at the odd stuff that Frank came out with and the vast variety of weird things he knew.

The waitress reappeared with drinks for Frank and Lyndon and my carpaccio. Frank and Lyndon showed no interest in food, but I tucked into my starter hungrily. It was as delicious as the dish always is and a generous portion as well.

Just a few bites in though I heard the noise that had had brought me to the restaurant. A very distinctive set of footsteps walked across the room towards me. The waitress screamed and fled, running down the stairs and very possibly out of the restaurant and into the street. Frank and Lyndon both jumped up and I had to go around them with my piece of chalk. Lyndon was shouting hasty instructions to get the recording equipment ready and fiddling with the little bag of super expensive ghost dust. Wincing at my ribs because I was trying to move fast, I got to where I believe the noise has started and made a mark on the floor then drew a line following the footsteps that were still travelling across the room.

They went right through the table I had been sitting at but terminated just a few feet beyond. I caught up with them and crouched down. Reaching up with one hand and without looking I found and grabbed the tuning fork. I marked another spot on the floor with the chalk, ignoring the ruckus behind me. Frank and Lyndon were doing something complicated.

The footsteps started up again but this time I was ready for them. My hands were on the floorboards feeling the vibrations the footsteps were making.

'It's a classic non-forming, type three entity.' yelled Frank to Lyndon, excitement in his voice. 'This is huge!'

I had a different theory. Namely that they were both full of crap.

'Can you trap its energy?' Frank asked Lyndon.

'Yes, I think so. I just need to...' Lyndon scrambled across the floor ahead of where the steps were going. He was scribbling odd symbols with a silver marker pen. I stood up and followed the direction the floorboards went rather than follow the footsteps. The boards went to the wall but looking down it did not look like they stopped there.

307

Using the tuning fork, I tapped on a board then held the butt end of it against the board as it vibrated. Then I did the same again on the board next to it and the one next to that. Then I walked across the room to beyond where the footsteps had started and tried again. I got a very different result.

'Dammit.' Swore Lyndon. 'It didn't work.' Whatever hokum he had been trying to do had failed apparently. He looked quite despondent.

I went back to the table and picked up the tape measure. I measured to the wall. Then I went to the point where the footsteps had started again and measured to the front on the building. The sound of someone playing a cello started. It was faint and sounded like it was coming through the floorboards. I smiled to myself, pocketed my tools and went down stairs.

I looked around for Georgio, but he was outside in the street. I could see him through the window with his arm around a lady in chef's clothing. I exited the restaurant and joined them in the street.

'Mr Fenucci. Shall we put an end to your ghost problem?' My question was met with quizzical expressions. I ignored him for the moment and turned around to look back at the building. The restaurant was positioned in a long row of very old looking buildings all joined together like terraced houses. I would guess that they were easily four hundred years old and possible even older than that. The front façade was constructed using solid looking wooden beams – Tudor design I believed the correct term to be. The plaster between the black beams was bright white but that was not what I was looking at. I was looking at the windows of the upper dining room and what was adjacent to them on either side.

To the left as I looked at it was a shop that sold antique clocks and watches. The shutters were down covering the large windows and protecting the goods inside. On the upper floor there were lights on. The shop looked new.

'How long has the business been there, Mr Fenucci?' I asked.

Early Shift

Don't Challenge the Werewolf

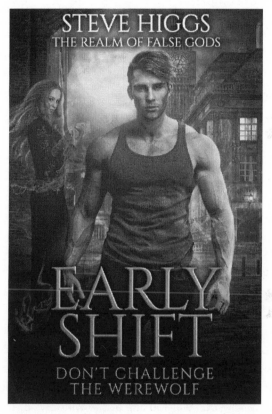

Don't pick a fight with him. You won't lose. You'll die

Zachary has a secret he tries to keep under wraps ...

... if only people would let him.

When he drifts into a remote farming community looking for work, the trouble starts before he orders breakfast. Normally he would just avoid the trouble and move on, but there's a girl. Not a woman. A little girl, and the men that want to dominate the village threaten her livelihood.

And that just won't do.

There's something very rotten in this community but digging into it brings him face to face with something more powerful even than him. Something ancient and unstoppable.

He has no choice other than to fight, but who will walk away?

As the false gods find their way into the realm of mortals, how many mortals will rise to defend the Earth?

Be ready for war.

NIGHT WORK

BLUE MOON INVESTIGATIONS BOOK TWELVE

STEVE HIGGS

To do list: 1. Solve big case while boss is away. 2. Have serious relationship dramas. 3. Jump a river with a car.

What the heck did I get myself into?

My name's Jane Butterworth. For me, the paranormal is just a day job. I work at the Blue Moon Investigation Agency, a firm that specialises in cases that no one else will take, cases that start at strange and unexplainable and tier rapidly south from there.

My boss, Tempest Michaels, is away dealing with a Yeti in France, but the enquiries keep coming so when Chief Inspector Quinn of the local police wants to hire the firm as special consultants, I sign us up and take it on myself.

But a swamp monster? Really?

Bodies of dead cops have been showing up in nearby Biddenden Lake, the site of an unexplained death three years ago. Is there a link between that death and these? The whole area is steeped in ancient history, ghost stories are two-a-penny here but am I really cut out to be a detective?

Time to put my big girl pants on.

Crossdressing isn't always glamourous.

More Books by Steve Higgs

Blue Moon Investigations

Paranormal Nonsense

The Phantom of Barker Mill

Amanda Harper Paranormal Detective

The Klowns of Kent

Dead Pirates of Cawsand

In the Doodoo With Voodoo

The Witches of East Malling

Crop Circles, Cows and Crazy Aliens

Whispers in the Rigging

Bloodlust Blonde – a short story

Paws of the Yeti

Under a Blue Moon – A Paranormal Detective Origin Story

Night Work

Lord Hale's Monster

The Herne Bay Howlers

The Realm of False Gods

Untethered magic

Free Books and More

Get sneak peaks, exclusive giveaways, behind the scenes content, and more. Plus, you'll be notified of Fan Pricing events when they occur and get exclusive offers from other authors because all UF writers are automatically friends.

Not only that, but you'll receive an exclusive FREE story staring Otto and Zachary and two free stories from the author's Blue Moon Investigations series.

Yes, please! Sign me up for lots of FREE stuff and bargains!

Want to follow me and keep up with what I am doing?

Facebook